The
STORY
SHE LEFT
BEHIND

ALSO BY PATTI CALLAHAN HENRY

The Secret Book of Flora Lea

Once Upon a Wardrobe

Surviving Savannah

The Favorite Daughter

Becoming Mrs. Lewis

The Bookshop at Water's End

The Idea of Love

The Stories We Tell

And Then I Found You

Coming Up for Air

The Perfect Love Song

Driftwood Summer

The Art of Keeping Secrets

Between the Tides

When Light Breaks

Where the River Runs

Losing the Moon

The

STORY
SHE LEFT
BEHIND

A Novel

PATTI CALLAHAN
HENRY

ATRIA BOOKS

NEW YORK   AMSTERDAM/ANTWERP   LONDON
TORONTO   SYDNEY   NEW DELHI

ATRIA
BOOKS

An Imprint of Simon & Schuster, LLC
1230 Avenue of the Americas
New York, NY 10020

First Atria Books hardcover edition March 2025

ATRIA B O O K S and colophon are trademarks of Simon & Schuster, LLC

For information about special discounts for bulk purchases, please contact Simon & Schuster Special Sales at 1-866-506-1949 or business@simonandschuster.com.

The Simon & Schuster Speakers Bureau can bring authors to your live event. For more information or to book an event, contact the Simon & Schuster Speakers Bureau at 1-866-248-3049 or visit our website at www.simonspeakers.com.

Interior design by Kyoko Watanabe

Manufactured in the United States of America

1 3 5 7 9 10 8 6 4 2

Library of Congress Cataloging-in-Publication Data has been applied for.

ISBN 978-1-6680-1187-4
ISBN 978-1-6680-1189-8 (ebook)

For Meg Ruley

My literary agent
Who loves all the very best things in words and stories
and champions them with her whole heart

Language is how ghosts enter the world.

—ANNE MICHAELS, "WHAT THE LIGHT TEACHES US"

I was a while away from your beauty.

—"SWEET COMERAGH," IRISH FOLK SONG

CHAPTER 1

BRONWYN NEWCASTLE FORDHAM

Bluffton, South Carolina
1927

It is two o'clock in the morning when she leaves everyone she loves. At the edge of the May River, she unties the ropes of the Chris-Craft from the cleats of the weathered dock and steps into the boat. In the velvet quiet, a new moon cowers behind its dark cloak; the stars flare as bright as the fire that is sending her away.

She will be long gone before the tide returns in six hours to fill the marsh and secret waterways. She knows the tides of this estuary without having to look at a nautical chart or check the battered barometer that has always hung on the screened porch of their shingled house. She has planned this escape to the minute, and she does not hesitate.

The boat rides on the outgoing tide, and the wind-puckered river pushes it gently toward the sea, catching the current more quickly than she'd anticipated. Flickering lights of Bluffton dot the coastline like fireflies. Any minute, she'll start the engine and navigate the boat toward Tybee Island and then into Savannah.

She stares at the ink-dark sky, at Orion and the Big Dipper. She doesn't want to witness the familiar and loved landscape disappear.

Her mind begins to form a list, a habit she's turned to since she was a child.

First, she lists what she's brought with her: a coat, a change of clothes, a hundred dollars in cash that she took from the envelope they kept for emergencies, a notebook and a pen, as well as a leather satchel that contains the words she's spent her life finding and creating.

The boat bobs and sways and she stares out to the horizon, waiting to start the engine. Her thoughts tick past what she's brought and move to all she is leaving behind: the quiet crash of the incoming tide onto the oyster shells outside their window; the gray-shingled house that has protected her for ten years now; the room where she writes and reads in a chintz chair with the stuffing blooming out of the seams; the dimming of the day when longing rises and she dives into the warm waters of the river; the midsummer's ivory bloom of the gardenia bush that she planted with her daughter; the soft caress of a breeze when she sits on the porch; her husband reaching for her in their bed and winding his fingers through hers while the crickets seem to cry.

And: Clara.

She holds the gunwale to steady herself as she walks to the cockpit. She presses the button to drop the single engine into the water while a surge of primal need for her daughter flows through her, causing her to sway with dizziness. She draws on her strength and on the knowledge that if she returns to her house, the world will do to her in full what it's done only until now in part.

She thinks of the beauty of this place that she will carry with her: a place where fireflies decorate the nights and pine needles gather in soft beds, where sunrise tosses diamonds onto the water, where minnows flicker silver on the river's surface.

The losses mount and she thinks nothing of what others might say, thinks nothing of her own well-being—Bronwyn needs to move forward and away from all that will come to pass if she stays. There are things that cannot be undone.

The unseen world has always called to her. She knows what she must do—she will *become* unseen. This is the answer for the character that she created, and this is *her* answer. Their destinies were always tangled together, she knows that now.

She finds the boat's starter and presses it; the motor purrs, the water churns behind, and she pushes the throttle forward. She places her hands on the wheel. These are her waters, and she does not have to see to know the way.

CHAPTER 2

CLARA HARRINGTON

Bluffton, South Carolina
November 1952

She disappeared twenty-five years ago when I was eight years old, and still my mother appeared to me every day. It might be in a turn of phrase I used, or in the song of the rising tide behind our house, in my daughter's creative energy as she gathered moss for a fairy house, or in the clues and messages my mother taught me to look for in the natural world. She seemed to be everywhere and nowhere all at once. She was absence, she was presence, and she was mystery.

Because of that pervasive energy, I created something in my life that was mine alone. My art was just that—my private place, my passion, my refuge from the larger world that no one else could touch.

Or so I believed.

In our blue cedar shake house on the spartina-edged waters of the May River, I disappeared into the world of a hedgehog named Harriet. I was painting her for a children's book. I held my sable-hair brush over the canvas, readying for the whiskers' fine lines. The lush and immersive landscape in the story made me look forward to entering the author's imaginary world every day, despite never having met her. I was her illustrator.

I loved this little hedgehog with one ear who struggled to find her place in a land of lakes and mountains, of magical talking animals and wide spaces overflowing with wildflowers and willow trees. For me, Harriet's spirit was an echo of my eight-year-old daughter, Wynnie, an allegory of Wynnie's own struggle to fit in with her third-grade class, with her thick glasses and her fragile lungs.

Now, in the sunroom I used as an art studio, Harriet's whiskers quivered under my brush when the broken ring of the doorbell's song startled me. I dropped the paintbrush onto the tarp cloth and nearly knocked a watercolor palette from the side table.

There often was a charge of change when I moved from one world to the next, from the imaginary to the real. I always needed a moment to return. The clock on the far wall told me that four hours had passed while I worked. I'd missed lunch completely, and now Margo was here for the newspaper interview we'd arranged.

I'd planned to clean up first, to present as the professional artist who had just won a major award, but that time was gone, and Margo knew me better than that anyway. I rushed to the front door, wiping my hands along Nat's old button-down I used as an art apron, a mosaic of paint blotches and bleach.

On my front steps, beneath the shade of a live oak spreading its gnarled arms in every direction as if searching for something it hadn't found for the past two hundred years, Margo stood in a flowered cotton-print dress, her hair styled in the newest curly bob. I couldn't help smiling at her obvious attempt to be polished, at how she needed me to see her as a real reporter, just as I wanted her to see me as a professional artist, even though we'd survived braces together and all those bad haircuts and the dateless high school homecoming dances in smelly gyms.

I hugged her. "Come in, come in. I'm sorry I lost time. I do that sometimes." *Always*, I didn't say.

She followed me into the house I'd grown up in and now lived in with my dad, where she'd been more times than could be counted, her high heels clicking on the hardwood floors.

"Thanks for doing this," she said. "Mr. Farnam is so impressed that I nabbed this interview." In her nervousness, her laugh erupted in a snort that made us both burst out as if we were thirteen again.

"It's just me, Margo."

"I know, but this is such a big deal, Clara. Winning a Caldecott is huge."

"Thank you. I'm really excited." Afternoon sunlight sifted through the east window, leaving daffodil-yellow stripes on the counters and hardwood floors, the oak kitchen table, and the far wall painted spring green. I motioned for Margo to follow me. "Let's sit out on the back porch; it's so warm for November. Do you want some lemonade?"

"Have anything stronger?"

"Seriously? It's two in the afternoon."

"Kidding. I'm kidding." She seemed embarrassed. "Lemonade is great."

Our house was perched on an oyster-shell outcropping at the end of a rutted road in Bluffton, South Carolina, a small coastal village curled around an estuary, a moody body of water. When the waters rippled over the shoreline, the oyster shells sang what my mother always called "their tidal song." Margo and I sat down at the old iron table with the rusted edges with the garden stretched before us, its autumn colors bright before the silver-gray river. The pink and white camellia bushes were in late bloom; goldenrod scattered about the yard was bright against autumn's heather-colored grasses.

I'd spent all morning in Harriet's world, but this was mine, complete with creaky floors and old hinges, the tilted decks and briny aromas, the peeling white trim and cracked porcelain sink beneath the kitchen window. It was all perfect. It was my home.

Margo used her napkin to wipe a damp spot off the table, opened her blue notebook, and set it down.

"Looks like you're ready," I told her.

She smiled at me, took in a deep breath, and exhaled her first question. "Clara, did you start illustrating books because your mother wrote a famous children's book?"

I shook my head because although I'd felt this question waiting for me from the moment she rang me requesting an interview, I'd hoped, for friendship's sake, that she would try to protect me. "Margo," I said, "come on. You know I don't like to talk about her." I took a sip of my lemonade and wished for the something stronger that she'd joked about.

She fiddled with her blue spiral notebook, bit the end of her well-chewed pencil eraser, and tried again. "I'm just asking what people will want to know. That's not an unreasonable question. It's my job."

I looked away from her to the marsh grasses fading from green to brown now. It wasn't Margo's fault she had to steer us into uncomfortable waters. Even the Caldecott committee had summed me up this way in their recent press release: my famously lost mother and her book, my job teaching art in elementary school, and my daughter. These were the things that defined me. At least they hadn't mentioned my divorce.

Here in Bluffton, there were very few secrets. That's the deal you make with yourself when you marry, live, and work in the same town where you grew up. Assumptions are made that become difficult to shift. As claustrophobic as a town this size could be, there was also great comfort in the deep familiarity of place and friends like Margo.

"It's the Caldecott," Margo said, trying to get me to focus again. "Clara, this is a really big deal. You're going to be famous. No one in our town has ever been famous unless they're a war hero."

I leaned toward Margo. "Who here even knows what a Caldecott Award is? I'm not going to be famous. I'm an elementary school art teacher. I am mostly a working stiff splattered in paint and globs of paste."

"When the awards ceremony happens in Chicago, don't think they won't ask you these same questions."

"Listen," I said, "even in my best dreams, I didn't dream this. When they called me last week to tell me I'd won, I couldn't absorb the words. I don't know what my illustrations are about—there isn't some psychological underpinning, near as I can tell. I have just always needed to capture what I see around me. Been obsessed with art and drawing since I can remember."

"How did the author, Eliza Walker, find you?" she asked, scribbling. "She's such a well-known author, and you're just getting started as an illustrator—respectively, I mean. And doesn't she live in Maine?"

"She saw my work in some Little Golden Books I did and asked her publisher to contact me. I sent my illustrations to New York, and that was that."

"Have you met her?"

I shook my head. "I've never even spoken to her. We've corresponded. She's complimentary and kind, and very formal. I love bringing her Maine landscape to life as beautifully as possible," I added, trying my best to give Margo quotes for the article. "And yet this award?

I am floored. Over the moon. Honestly, I can't really believe it. But famous? No."

She laughed, and with that, her voice returned to normal, to the woman I knew. "Famous in this town, though, right? I'll bet your dad is so proud. Does he still work at the same hospital in Beaufort?"

"He does, and he's so proud of me." He'd cried when the call came and hugged me so hard it hurt. "Wynnie, too," I said. "She thinks I'm going to bring home a trophy. I had to explain that the prize is a coin."

"How about . . . ?" Margo bit her lower lip.

"Nat," I said. "It's okay. I'm fine talking about him. He's very happy for me."

This was true. He was. My ex-husband wasn't an evil man, just one who loved gambling more than he loved us. And even that notion had some falsity built into it, because honestly, I did believe he loved us more. But his compulsions or addictions led him to other places. And that led to losing our house, and that led me to the divorce attorney who really didn't have much work in a conservative small town like this, and then that path took me back to my childhood home.

One thing always leads to another, as they say.

Margo clicked her nails together in a nervous habit that chipped her pink polish. "I remember you drawing little pictures in the margins of all your notebooks. You were always so talented, and you deserve this award." On the river, a shrimp boat was passing, its nets hanging like curtains on either side, while laughing gulls and terns followed in dancing loops, hoping for scraps. Suddenly her mood changed. "Clara, do you think there are things we are meant to do? That there's such a thing as fate?"

"Fate. It's such a big word, isn't it?"

"Yes." She met my gaze.

"Fate. Destiny," I said. "They're ours to make." A briny breeze floated off the bay and lifted my hair, and I had the strangest sensation that this was something my mother had once said. That this voice was her voice speaking through me, an idea that both warmed and chilled me. "I believe there are many things we're put here to do. Don't ask me by whom, because I don't have that answer. But I think we come with many fates built into us and we can't fulfill all of them. We choose."

"Many fates," she said. "We choose. I like that."

"And yes, maybe my art is one of mine."

She scribbled on while I read her notebook upside down, making out the words: *many fates.*

"Do you need anything else? Wynnie will be home any second." My ears were already attuned for the rumble of the school bus, for the clatter of my daughter running through the house, calling, "Mama."

Margo closed her notebook and relaxed, leaning back in her chair. "I am so proud of you, Clara. Really."

"Thank you. That means a lot to me. You know where to find me if you need anything else."

"Thank you. And congratulations."

After she left, I stayed outside waiting for Wynnie. I'd already made her a peanut butter and honey sandwich and cut off the crusts, a snack that we'd take out on Dad's old trawler. It was part of our routine, whenever the weather held. Before Dad came home, we'd cast the net for tiny silver fish and watch the sun move lower in the sky.

Still, just below my thoughts of Wynnie, Margo's question itched. *Did you start illustrating books because your mother wrote a famous children's book?*

I hated that idea. Hated it. And yet, had I?

CHAPTER 3

CHARLIE JAMESON

St. James's Square, London

It was a bitterly cold and damp November evening, but as Charlie stood in his father's library, in his world of books, he felt warm. The room overflowed with everything his father once was to the world and to Charlie.

Three weeks had passed since burying his father. This day marked the first time Charlie had ever entered his father's library without knocking and hearing the gruff but friendly *Join me, Son*.

The London house was dark at seven p.m., and Charlie was alone. Outside the windows, lanterns flickered on St. James's Square, and the second-floor library was as still as the crypt they'd lowered Callum Jameson into.

Charlie had put this off long enough.

He'd canceled the Lads' gig that night, the first time in eight years. But his Celtic band members understood. They could do without him for one night, they told him with a slap on the back.

Charlie flicked on every lamp in the library and inhaled the room's faint aroma of charred wood. In the brick fireplace where granite quarried from his mother's family's land in the Lake District surrounded the grate, ash, dusty and gray, settled beneath charred logs. The Jamesons were among the fortunate few who could still use natural wood, while most of London suffered with the cheap, nutty coal that put out more smoke than heat. The spent remains of the fire had settled under the grate for three weeks now, an artifact of the moment when

Charlie's father had placed his hand over his heart, looked up at his son, and said, "Well, isn't this odd? I do believe I'm having a heart attack. Come, Charlie."

Those were his last words, one hand on his chest, one reaching out. *Come, Charlie.*

Callum Jameson had celebrated his fifty-sixth birthday with a grand party in this very house only four months ago. He'd left his twins, Archie and Charlie, and their mother, Pippa, far too soon.

Directions were clear: The family's finance company was to be inherited by the two brothers. Archie was to take over the investment firm, founded in 1690, built from scratch by Mother's Burrough family and grown into a megalith of success by her Irish husband. Charlie was to remain at Burrough's Holdings under his brother's leadership, continue in his music career, and manage the house in the countryside.

In addition, Father had instructed Charlie to preserve and catalog his extensive library here in London.

Charlie understood the direct imperative to continue his music career: the Celtic drum he played was the last remnant of Callum's Irish descent. His father played the round calf-skinned drum and attempted to teach both of his sons as well. Only Charlie took to it.

There was no other direct family but a second cousin surviving Callum's passing. His mother, father, and brother had been killed in a 1916 IRA uprising in Dublin when Callum was twenty years old and off in America studying mathematics.

Archie, Charlie, and Pippa were his family. And this library—well, it was most definitely beloved, as well.

Charlie sat behind his father's mahogany desk in the library while his mother grieved at their country home and Archie waded through paperwork at the company's London office.

When Charlie was a young child, he sat on his father's lap at this desk while his father pored over history books and maps. Father read wild tales of the Nordic and Celtic myths, and together they listened to Verdi's operas and Celtic folk music. Callum knew how to speak the old Irish-Gaelic language but rarely did so, though he taught his sons a few Gaelic songs, as if the pain of all Callum lost could be imparted *only* through music.

This room was his father's domain, his geography, always in perfect order. No one walked through the door without Father's permission, but when they did enter, they gained passage to another world—or so Charlie had once thought.

Where should he begin in this room of floor-to-ceiling pine bookshelves, where oil paintings of their lands and the wildlife it contained hung? The oak walls glowed with the honey hues of aged wood; the evergreen damask curtains shielded the evening light from entering the lamp-lit room. Leather-bound volumes filled the shelves, and a tall rolling ladder stood in the middle of it all. This library was his father's doing, his lifelong creation. Antique maps, leather volumes, and rare editions filled every crevice.

Callum Montcrest Jameson III seemed to have been a man of contrasting interests: money management and mythology. With his booming voice, his tall, imposing presence, Callum embodied both archetypes confidently. Friends and family said that Callum's twin sons split his personality into two parts. Archie inherited the logic, and Charlie the mythos. Charlie earned a master of studies in history from Oxford, while his brother's degree was in finance from Cambridge.

It was easy to categorize the twins this way, but they were one family, both with their own interests, both caring deeply about the family's investment company.

On the desk, Callum's walnut pipe bowl spilled tobacco onto a leather blotter the color of soil, exactly where he'd dropped it that evening when he'd collapsed. A silver-framed photo of Philippa and Callum on their wedding day in the country. One of Archie and Charlie sat to the right: the twins at five years old in a blue rowboat on their beloved lake, Esthwaite Water. The twins posed with a trout they'd caught and would cook for dinner, so small it would only provide a single bite for the four of them. You'd think they were whale hunters by their prideful grins.

A neat pile of papers sat stacked in the center of the blotter: a report from the bank that Charlie would need to pass along to Archie. And then, as always, there was a book of history, this one about the Vikings who invaded Ireland and brought with them the Celtic culture that endlessly fascinated Callum.

What happened to all that knowledge that Callum collected and carried in his soul? What happened to all that wit and wisdom? Where was it all now? Charlie sagged with grief.

With a deep breath, Charlie stood and walked to the phonograph. The record playing the day Father died still sat on the turntable. Charlie clicked the on button and dropped the needle onto the vinyl. *La Bohème.* Charlie wondered if he would ever be able to hear the opening strains of the opera without thinking of his father—without mourning his father, to be more exact. No one had read more than his father, from the prophets to the poets, from the classics to modern literature. The loss of Charlie's father made the world feel deeply empty and unsteady, wobbling beneath his feet.

Music fueled his melancholy, and he paced the rectangular room, his eyes scanning each section: Mathematics, Fiction, Art, Antiquities, History, Maps. On the lectern that displayed whatever book, map, or illustrations Father was studying sat a 1745 map of the family's six acres of land in the Lake District.

Halfway around the room, Charlie stopped pacing when his gaze snagged on something new. On the bottom shelf, atop a pile of leather boxes that held ancient maps, sat a brown leather satchel, worn and scratched, its brass buckles tarnished.

He crouched and slid out the heavy case. The thrill of the old hunt with his father returned. How many times he and Father had browsed through antique shops and attended auctions to find just one more map, one more book, one more . . .

Charlie set the satchel down on the desk. He was certain the leather bag hadn't been in the library before. It would have caught his eye among the many piles of books and carefully boxed and labeled papers. The tarnished latch was designed as an eagle, the beak clutching the hook.

Charlie folded back the flap to glance inside, seeing nothing but papers. On top sat an envelope, and he pulled it out to read the words on it: *For Clara Harrington only. Further instructions inside.*

He grabbed the stack of papers, at least three inches thick, and slid them out. Reaching inside, he felt only the disintegrating silk lining. He thought about the legendary story of Hemingway's suitcase, how early in his career his first wife, Hadley, had lost a bag carrying years of the famous author's work on a train. It was never recovered.

These were the kinds of stories that sent Callum and Charlie on joyous hunts. Once, as they traipsed down Cecil Court, Charlie asked his father, "What if we found Hemingway's suitcase?"

His father laughed and jostled Charlie. "What if we find the lost papers of Shakespeare?"

Point taken. Maybe it was all a dream, but it was nevertheless a dream they'd happily pursue. The joy was in the journey, not the execution— or so Father always said. Charlie wasn't so sure.

Charlie lifted his reading glasses from the desk and slid them on. He bent over and spied a note, carefully handwritten in a near-perfect script on the top sheet. *The contents of this satchel are to be given only to Clara Harrington of Bluffton, South Carolina.* Then a phone number and address. *She must retrieve these papers in person. They must never be mailed. The sealed letter inside is to be read only by her. Le draíocht.*

The author scribbled one more note on the bottom left side: *Please tell Clara that I've saved this language for her, Bronwyn Newcastle Fordham.*

Charlie knew that name, but how?

Lifting the note from the pile, he saw foreign words with pages and pages of what appeared to be a dictionary of terms. Even as curious as he was, he would not show these papers to anyone: they were meant for one Clara Harrington in America.

Charlie's father had soaked him in old Irish folklore as a child, and he knew enough Gaelic to know that there were *mallachtai*—Celtic curses and spells when breaking a *draíocht*, a charm or enchantment. He wouldn't dare bring either onto his head. Charlie would heed Bronwyn's request.

CHAPTER 4

CLARA

Bluffton, South Carolina

The second-grade students buzzed with end-of-the-day energy as they returned their crayons to their wooden boxes and folded their drawings. Billy Markman ate another glob of paste and didn't think I noticed. I headed toward his side to gently remove the jar from his hands when the overhead speaker buzzed with static.

"Mrs. Harrington, please come to Principal Alexander's office."

"Ohhh," Gina, with the pigtails and lacy dress, said. "You're in trouble."

I smiled at the little girl and shivered in fake fear. "Oh no!"

The class laughed and started a chant. "Mrs. Harrington is in trouble."

I motioned to my classroom assistant—a shy student teacher finishing her elementary school internship—to take over the class for the last few minutes.

After my daily admonition to "bring your inside feelings to the outside in your art," I left the room.

I took my time walking to the principal's office, enjoying the hush of empty hallways, the aroma of the spaghetti and meatball lunch wafting out of the cafeteria, and the framed pictures of the hundred-year history of the Bluffton Bobcats students lining the walls.

A photo of freckled me from third grade hung askew on the wall of fame, with the caption *Illustrator* on a shiny brass plaque. That little eight-year-old girl knew so little, with so much pain ahead of her. I was happy to be the me of now, no matter the circumstances: divorce, living in my childhood home, confronting an unknown future.

Sure, I wasn't the traditional 1952 housewife, the epitome of a *Woman's Day* magazine cover model. I didn't own pearls or do housework in heels. I didn't join the PTA or the Supper Club. I didn't wear cute headbands and dresses with cinched waists. But this was my home, and I was loved. If a few moms looked at me sideways when I picked up Wynnie from school, or if I wasn't invited to the newly minted Tupperware parties, I was fine with that.

There weren't a lot of options for my skill set, teaching and illustrating, and I was lucky enough to be doing both.

I opened Jim's office door without knocking.

I stopped short.

Wynnie stood in Jim's office, which always reeked like an ashtray.

Her face was downcast and her chin nearly rested on the neckline of her blue dress with the smocked sailboats around the collar. The front of her dress was bunched into her knotted hands.

"Wynnie?"

She looked up at my voice. Her little pink glasses were crooked on her face, her wandering left eye trying to focus on me. Then she tossed her body into mine and buried her face in my art apron, her glasses falling to the ground. "I'm sorry, Mama."

I picked up her glasses and asked Jim, "What happened?"

"She was hiding in a broom closet so she wouldn't have to go home with her father."

"But she comes home with me today," I said, placing my finger under Wynnie's chin to lift her face to mine and slide her glasses over her tear-filled blue eyes. "Wynnie?"

"Sorry, Mama. I got confused. I thought today was Friday."

"I teach on Tuesday and Thursday," I said. "You know that."

"She scared her teacher to death." Jim reiterated his stance. "Miss Perkins thought she lost Wynnie." He paused. "Listen, we need to know if something is happening at home with her father."

"Nothing like that," I said, standing tall to face him with conviction. "Wynnie just likes being at home with me. Nat is a good man."

"I hate the carnival, and Daddy said that's where we're going."

Jim shook his head, his mouth like a puckered fish. "Well, little miss, you can't hide from adults." He looked at me and spoke. "They will assume that you ran away."

Like your grandmother hung unspoken in the room. Bluffton was still reeling, twenty-five years later, from my mother's disappearance. Decades of time passing didn't mean much in a place like this.

"I'll talk to her," I said as the school bell clanged in the same dull tones it had when I was a child.

"I'm happy it's Thursday, and I'm sorry if I scared anyone." Wynnie wiped at her tears and lifted her chin to Jim Alexander.

He opened the door in dismissal.

We drove home in quiet camaraderie, Wynnie next to me on the bench seat of the station wagon reading *The Borrowers*, her face close to the page.

Inside the house, Wynnie dropped her daisy-covered lunch box on the front bench and ran outside to play in the back garden. I made my way to the den and saw the *Bluffton Gazette* lying open on the oak coffee table, folded to the center, where the headline read: *Local Illustrator Wins Caldecott Award*. Ah, Margo's interview had been published that fast, in one day.

The story was printed in a column next to ads for Harvey's Cafe and the new Electrolux washing machine, guaranteed to make a wife's job easier. In the photo I smiled tensely, sporting a bob I had grown out long ago when I gave up the idea of a stylish hairstyle.

I skimmed the story, reluctant to read about myself. I was jittery to see what threads Margo had pulled from my life and our conversation. The last lines read: "Fate and destiny, they are ours to make. We choose from many fates."

I sounded ridiculous! I crumpled the paper in my hands. Did I even believe the things I said?

Had I chosen my motherless fate? If I had, I'd been too young to know I was sending her away, that my choices would upend our world.

That morning when everything changed, that morning in 1927, I was eight years old when Mother ran to her writing room to capture a line that suddenly came to her. *I want the sky to split open*—that was it. She said it out loud, kissed me with the elation she felt when the right words found her, and then dashed off. "Be right back."

This happened. Sometimes she'd return a minute after she'd written it down or an hour later, after she'd poured out what needed pouring. Her sudden disappearances were disorienting as a clap of thunder on a sunny day.

While I waited for her to return, I flopped from the couch to lie flat on the carpet, moving my tiny wooden dolls around the dollhouse Dad had made for me, the furniture exact replicas of our own.

A cigarette, Mom's cigarette, teetered on the edge of a pale blue ashtray, the one Dad had given her for her birthday last year. A little glass-blown bird sat on the tray's edge near two curved dents in its bowl.

Absorbed in the miniature version of our life, I didn't see what was happening in the larger and realer version until I smelled the burning carpet. I must have accidentally toppled the cigarette from its ashtray when I'd moved to the floor.

The fire was alive. Otherworldly.

Flames were already racing from the base of the coffee table across the brown shag carpet and toward my dollhouse.

A spark leaped onto my fingers holding the small wooden doll, shocking me like the sting of a hornet. I dropped the doll onto the carpet, where the flames were hungry for the fiber.

I screamed for Mama, my voice ripping from fear.

A thousand new flames appeared, catching the ends of the curtains, gobbling the dangling pom-poms I'd sewn on with my mother, one by one, during a rainy afternoon. The flames inhaled the sleeve of my shirt with the tiny mouse ballerinas dancing on the fabric.

Her absence was as terrifying as the flames. Her ability to be there in full and then gone completely was something I had come to know, but now panic consumed me. Pain ripped through my hand and arm, the flames leaping from my sleeve as I froze, motionless and screaming.

She appeared at last, running to me, reaching for me. Her long dark hair flew free from the pins she usually wore; her red-and-white house-dress with the cherries on it swayed.

She smothered the flames with a blanket, and then took me in her arms. She ran outside, carrying me and uttering *Adorium* over and over, as if this word, the one she created, would remedy the terror and pain.

———

A crow called from outside, and I shook myself from the memory, like shedding a heavy coat. I returned to my life, with twilight softening the contours of the den that had been restored over the years, the fire flaming only in my memory.

Knotty pine plank walls and a drafty sliding door to the back deck that overlooked the bay stood as always. The carpet had changed a few times through the years but somehow remained the dusty brown of a chestnut. This room held my worst nightmare, and yet there was nothing left to recall the flames and that singular day.

Outside, Wynnie knelt on the ground in the white-fenced-in garden. She squinted into the setting sun and placed another twig on the fairy house she was building. A white camellia was tucked in her hair. Her pink glasses reflected the light, her coppery curly hair springing loose from the braids I'd plaited it in that morning.

I slid open the door and called out: "Nearly time for dinner!"

She looked up and smiled. "Can Emjie come?"

"Yes! You two finish what you're doing. It's nearly dark."

I folded the newspaper and tossed it into the brass bin next to the fireplace for kindling.

The last words Mother had written in this house echoed now: an incantation, a wish, and a curse.

I want the sky to split open.

CHAPTER 5

CLARA

Bluffton, South Carolina

Wynnie ran into the kitchen, bringing with her the aroma of garden soil and briny air, something elemental. She bolted into my arms, and I hugged her close. "Tell me a story from your day while I make us dinner."

"I have a good one," Wynnie said.

"Well, do tell."

"Sammy Fletcher called me *four eyes*, and guess what I said this time? Just guess."

"Tell me, darling," I said, and tried to hide the hurt. Wynnie could read my expressions as surely as she could read a book. Kids teased her about how small she was or how she couldn't run with them because of her asthma, and then made fun of her glasses, always teasing about the glasses.

Wynnie had all these things, funny eyes and weak lungs, because she arrived in the world too early. The whole point wasn't that she came early, but that she came at all; her life was miracle enough for me. I told her this all the time—she was my *miraculum*.

She climbed up the step stool I kept next to the counter, so she could be face-to-face with me. "I told Sammy I have better sight than he does, even if my eyes don't work. I see things he can't see, and I'd rather be me."

"Brilliant," I said. "Who taught you to say that?"

"Emjie."

Emjie, the main character from my mother's novel. Emjie, the character who made Mother famous. Emjie, my daughter's imaginary friend.

"Oh?" I said, and thought of how she'd described Emjie. I tried to imagine Emjie here, with her long dark hair in a crown of braids, with her dainty nose and her eyes that Wynnie described as being as green as the emerald in her crayon box. Sometimes Emjie wore a dress made of ferns, and other times one made of kelp and oyster shells. But Wynnie had moved on.

"Mama?"

"Yes?"

"What is *Howdy Doody*?"

"A television show, sweetie."

"The kids are talking about it. Will we get a TV?"

I wanted to reply yes, but the cost was a waste. We had the radio, records, and endless outdoor activities. We had art and each other and a little boat that ferried us into the bay. We had friends and Dad. "Probably not any time soon. Trust me, you aren't really missing anything." I thought about many ways we weren't the same as the other families. It wasn't just the TV. It was the way I didn't doll up for car drop-off, the way I was left out of the Tupperware parties, the bridge club, and the twittering gossip at the playground. I wanted to fit in—who didn't? I gave up after I left Nat, the invisible brand of *D* on my forehead.

Wynnie was quiet for a moment and then said, "I'm probably not missing anything. What's for dinner?"

"Macaroni and cheese with ham," I told her. "And broccoli. You must eat all of it, not just the macaroni, or I won't make it anymore." I kissed her cheek and lightly tugged her braid.

She jumped down, all energy and joy, and sat at the kitchen table, on which her sailboat puzzle spilled out in a disorganized jumble. She separated the edge pieces into a little pile while I stirred the pot on the stove and asked her, "Is Emjie eating with us tonight?"

She didn't look up but instead sorted the puzzle pieces, focusing with intent, and that was when the phone rang.

The radio hummed a staticky version of "Tell Me Why," and I picked up the wall phone receiver.

"Hello?"

"May I speak with Clara Harrington?" asked a man with a British accent.

"Speaking," I said, stirring absently, thinking of the man who had called me about the award and how this was the second man to call in a week's time, when a man hadn't called me in years.

"I need to talk to you about some papers belonging to someone named Bronwyn Newcastle Fordham," he said.

The wooden spoon fell from my hand to the hardwood floor, flecking the stove with yellow dots. I turned down the radio and walked to the other side of the kitchen, as far as the coiled cord would allow, to move away from Wynnie.

"Okay, Mr.—"

"Oh, how rude of me. I'm sorry. I'm nervous, and I've lost my manners. Charles Jameson. Charlie," he said. "I'm calling from London. The papers I found," he continued, "appear to be some kind of dictionary of words, but words I've never seen."

I laughed. The key to Mother's lost words? A prank, a ploy to get me to talk and give away what I knew about her sequel. I'd been here before. I exhaled in relief. This was most assuredly a man who wanted information I didn't have. Dad and I often received letters and calls, though not as many lately. Most were journalists who thought they might have a new angle to the mystery; others were students writing papers about my mother or crime writers seeking inside information we didn't have. *I can't tell you what I don't know,* Dad told them again and again.

He continued. "It's all in an old leather satchel. I'm calling to tell you about it, to try and describe what is here."

"Mr. Jameson, that's impossible."

"No, long-distance phone calls are quite possible." He laughed.

"No, I meant—"

"I know. A poor joke, should have kept it to myself. But it's not impossible. I'm looking at everything right now." I felt Wynnie's eyes light on me, and I turned away as he said, "Let me describe what's here. Dark brown leather bag. Very scratched. A brass latch shaped like an eagle. Green silk lining. A pile of handwritten papers with words of a language I don't know."

"You have my mother's language?"

"Oh, Bronwyn Fordham is your mother?" His voice lifted in surprise.

"Yes. *Was* my mother."

"Grandma?" Wynnie piped up from the table.

I put my finger to my lips to shush Wynnie.

In the background was the rise and fall of music, something baroque and haunting. "I know this sounds barmy, but hear me out. I don't want anything from you, but it appears that Bronwyn . . . your mother had some requests."

Bird wings slammed inside my chest. *Had.* Past tense. Dizzy, I leaned against the counter. "What do you mean?"

"Along with all these papers, there's also a letter addressed to you."

"If you're after the sequel, I promise you we don't have it here," I said. I wasn't lying. It was hidden in a lockbox across the Savannah River.

"The sequel?" he asked.

"Her book. We don't have it."

"I don't know anything about a book." His statement felt honest.

Wynnie followed me around the room, right on my heels. *Stop,* I mouthed to her.

"What is he saying?" Wynnie asked in a loud whisper. "I want to hear."

I shook my head at her.

"You found this in your father's library. Who is your father?" I held my hand against my chest as if I could slow my heart from racing to his answer.

"Callum Jameson. He passed away three weeks ago. I'm just doing what the note requested, so now you can decide what to do." His voice went a little cold.

"Mr. Jameson, I am so sorry you lost your father. So very sorry, but if you have what you think or say you have, can you please send it to me?"

"If this belongs to your mother, I know this must come as a shock, but for now, there are things you probably should know."

"And what would those be?"

"The note states that you are to be given these papers in person. They are not to be sent by post or transit."

"Please tell me exactly what the note says?" I didn't want to flirt with the desperate hopes that flickered around me, but I was begging for information.

Mr. Jameson read aloud in his charming accent: "'The contents of this satchel are to be given only to Clara Harrington of Bluffton, South Carolina. She must retrieve these papers in person. They must never be mailed. The sealed letter inside is to be read only by her. Le draíocht.'"

"Draíocht?"

"Ah yes, it's Gaelic. It means charming—roughly translates as a spell for enchantment."

"Well now," I said, "that would be something my mother would write."

"I won't get in the way of any enchantment or curse." He attempted a laugh and then cleared his throat. "There is another note at the bottom that states: 'Please tell Clara that I've saved this language for her, Bronwyn Newcastle Fordham.'"

For me.

My body tingled; electricity raced through my veins. Something for me from my mother. "Is she alive?" I asked in an exhale.

"I'm sorry; I have no idea, really. This is just as confusing for me."

"Mama!" Wynnie was pulling at my sleeve. "What. Is. He. Saying?"

I covered the mouthpiece. "He's just a man looking for information about Grandma."

"I hear you," he said with laughter.

"I'm . . . confused." I pressed my fingers against my forehead.

"I am as well."

"It's all too extraordinary," I said. "You should know that this satchel and those papers have been assumed to be in the deepest part of the sea by now, along with her. I need a moment to think about this. May I call you back?"

He gave me his phone number, and I wrote it down. My voice sounded young and vulnerable when I said, "Please keep everything safe. Please."

"I will, yes."

"Thank you so very much." I placed the phone in its cradle and sank to the stool.

"Mama?"

I looked at Wynnie. "It can't be true."

"What can't be true?" My dad's voice filled the room as he walked through the back door from the garage. His wrinkled suit and iodine-stained lab coat hung loose on his thin frame, and he carried the haggard look of a day that hadn't gone well. He walked straight to the bar between the kitchen and the den and poured himself a bourbon in a cut-glass tumbler.

Wynnie and I watched silently as he downed it, then turned to us both. "What can't be true?" He repeated his question softly.

Wynnie ran to his side and looked up at him, adoringly as always. "Some man just called Mama and said he found"—Wynnie drew out the tension and grinned at her papa—"the lost words you and Mama talk about, the ones Grandma took with her."

Dad set down his glass and smiled sadly. "Again. Someone else? What's their story this time?"

"A man from London called. His name is Charles Jameson, and he says he found her papers in his father's library," I said.

Dad froze a moment as if he'd seen something dangerous over my shoulder, but then his smile reappeared. "Sure. Did he also find a unicorn and elf?"

Wynnie laughed and ran back to the kitchen table and her puzzle. The fun was over for her.

I lowered my voice and stepped closer to him, resting my hand on his arm. "Dad, he said there was a sealed letter for me."

"You aren't falling for it, are you, ladybug?"

My dear dad, a surgeon, was a kind soul who never remarried after his wife disappeared. When Nat and I divorced, when I discovered our bank account was depleted and we had lost the house, I moved back to our family home. Nat's family in Georgia refused to help, and four years later I still hadn't found a new place to live for many reasons, but mostly because I loved Dad, and I loved Wynnie growing up around her papa on the edge of the tidal bay.

The loss of the money, including the royalties from Mother's famous novel that Dad gave me, wasn't just awful for our marriage, but also the loss of a grand dream. I wanted, desired, and needed to use that royalty money for good and not material gain, to open a school of art for young children with wild imaginations, where I would teach them that it was okay to be different.

Nat robbed me, literally, of that dream.

I told Dad, "No. I'm not falling for it."

"Good girl." I watched his face. Some days when he returned from the hospital, he looked many years older. Today was one of those days. His blue eyes, so like mine that people commented when they met us—*same shape, same color; you're the spitting image*—were rheumy and lid-draped with fatigue.

"You all right, Dad?"

"I lost one today, ladybug. A ten-year-old boy to a car accident. These are the tough days when I doubt my decision to become a doctor. I'm going to leave you and Wynnie to your dinner. I ate at the hospital, and now I'm going to bed early." He poured another inch of bourbon, took his glass, and walked away, and then stopped, turned to look at me. "I'm not happy you went through that god-awful divorce. I know it was tough as hell. But it means so much to me that you're here. You and Wynnie—my girls. Even though there is enough paint and paper to hold an art festival in here."

I laughed. "Living with me is a mess, isn't it?"

"It's beautiful."

"I love you, Dad."

"You too, always."

How we came to Bluffton was because my father met and fell in love with Mother in Boston. At the time he was in medical school at Harvard, while she worked for the *Boston Herald*. After they married in 1917, he brought his bride home. In Boston, Bronwyn's fame followed her like fog. He wanted to have a simpler life and a family with the woman he loved, not the famously enigmatic author who was forever being scrutinized.

But no one wanted to hear that story.

Her writing earned her phenomenal success and accolades. But her disappearance instantly transformed her into a mystery, an enigma, a literary cold case to be solved. Hers was the legend of the lost, mad artist.

But the world didn't know everything.

No one did.

CHAPTER 6

CLARA

Bluffton, South Carolina

My mother's love was as overwhelming as her abandonment, both with me even now.

When I was a child, we played a game of disappear and reappear. There was no simple hide-and-seek for my mother. No, ma'am, she was more fun than all the other mommies.

One afternoon, at seven years old, I hid in the closet of her writing studio behind an old fur coat, from the days when she lived up north, somewhere I'd never been. It smelled of must and wet animal. I slid down the back wall, landing upon a pile of books. I scooted to the side, and with a sliver of light falling in around the door, I spied a pile of papers bound with a rubber band.

I'd never seen these papers before.

I knew this old house's every nook and cranny, its every creak and corner. I could walk its halls with my eyes shut. I'd hidden in all its secret places—from the eaves behind the stairwell to the crawl space under the house, a damp hutch of dark soil and scuttering animals.

How could something possibly exist in our house that I'd never seen? I heard Mama calling my name in her singsong voice, looking for the invisible me.

Clara, Clara, Clara.

She'd always find me, though sometimes it took a bit longer because I was very good at disappearing. Or so she said.

In the closet, I brought my knees to my chest and listened. Even if

I stayed hidden here for a long time, her voice calling my name would keep me feeling safe and expectant, a giggle trying to burst through, a deep desire to be found, to be seen by someone who truly loved me.

Waiting, I slipped out the top pages and saw her slanted penmanship. I squinted for a familiar word, but these were words I'd never seen. Pages upon pages of them. French or German, maybe Spanish, I didn't know. I knew one word, a name—*Emjie*. My mother's imaginary character from her first novel, one she wrote when she was twelve years old, a novel so famous people still sent her letters that she asked Daddy to toss in the trash.

The door opened, and I pulled my feet toward me and put the papers down. Then Mother stood in the doorway, filling the entry as completely as she filled my life, backlit in her tall and willowy beauty, like a tree reaching over a river. Her dress was green cotton, and her long dark hair was tied up in a loose ponytail.

She pretended not to see me, then she uttered the word *miraculum*.

When she said that word, I appeared to her. The mysterious-sounding word's meaning, she'd told me some time before, was "an object of wonder."

She repeated it—*miraculum*—and her eyes widened as if I'd just materialized before her.

"There you are!" she called out.

There you are.

"I thought you'd never find me!" I said. These were the same words we always said, the incantations we spoke in the same order each and every time.

"I will always find you."

I will always find you.

Mom pushed aside the coats and reached down to tickle me before gently pulling me from the closet. Next she bent down to hug me—my favorite part, so I allowed her to hold me for a moment.

After we stood, I reached into the closet and presented her with the pages in my hand. She took them, a look of sadness falling over her face.

"What's that?" I asked.

Tears filled her eyes, and she opened her mouth, but not a word came out. I tugged at her dress. "What is it?"

"A book." She held it to her chest with both hands as if it were a kitten who might escape. This was the first time I realized there was a part of her I didn't know, something secret and hidden.

"What book?" I asked, not yet desperate, just curious. Desperation came later.

"Another Emjie book, what is called a sequel."

"There's another Emjie book?" My heart raced toward her answer. Her first book, *The Middle Place*, ended with her character stuck between worlds. Now Emjie might be saved.

"Yes. One where she tries to come home."

"Tries?"

"That's what it is all about—the attempt to return home."

"But I don't know these words," I said.

She sat on the edge of the bed and patted it, indicating that I should sit next to her on the blue quilt.

When I did, she put her arm around me and pulled me so close I felt her ribs beneath her dress. "Not all the words we know can describe how I feel about everything. Sometimes I must write new words, and they help me understand, say, how I feel."

"So you make them up?"

"It doesn't feel that way. It feels like I find them—like they're words that have been lost by the people who decided what words we would use."

"Who else knows them?"

"No one."

"Please teach me. I want to know."

"Someday I will," she said.

"Why not right now?"

"Okay, one word." The playful mother returned, a sly smile and a nudge. "*Adorium*."

"*Adorium*?" I asked, tasting the word on my tongue and liking it already. I could speak an entirely new language with my mother. Make it ours. All ours. There were other tongues to speak and other worlds to explore.

"*Adorium* means 'great love,'" she said. "The kind of love I feel for you. The kind of love that obliterates all sense and logic and makes the world appear just as it is—completely and utterly magical. *Adorium* is knowing that all things are one and we are all things—the love that made you and the love we came from and the love we return to." She stopped, as if she knew I could not keep up, drowning in the waterfall of her definition.

"That's so much for one word," I said.

"Yes, that's the very point of it all. Sometimes the words we have aren't big enough."

"One more?"

"Later," she said. "When the time is right, I will teach you each and every one of them."

CHAPTER 7

CHARLIE

London, England

I was a while away from your beauty.

Charlie sang the lyrics from his father's favorite song about his Irish hometown in Waterford, a haunting melody. The women stilled and the men took slow, deep breaths so they wouldn't betray their emotions.

Even if they didn't know the Irish words he sang, the soul understood the longing and exile.

So, I came back to you . . . Sweet Comeragh.

He sang the song first in Irish and then in English, and throughout his singing, the crowd sat still.

When he finished, everyone leapt to their feet, clapping and whooping, ready for frenetic fun—a reel, a rocking song, anything but dwelling in their own unfulfilled longings.

The Sheep and Lion was full to the walls. It was the last song of the Lads' set, and the crowd hollered for more. The golden glow of the dim lighting, the open wood beams of the low-slung ceiling, and the heat of the fire in a stone hearth made the room seem separate from the world outside, a nest of comfort. No one wanted the night to end.

Charlie bowed out and handed the microphone to Fergus, who would launch into a bawdy ballad to close the night. Charlie made his way through the crowd, feeling slaps on his back and shoulders. *Your father would be proud. Sorry about your loss. Well done.*

He found a spot to stand at the sticky bar and leaned across to order a shot of whiskey. Benny the bartender slammed one down in front of

Charlie, a golden glow inside the cut glass with the crest of the pub. "On the house, mate. When are you going to put your songs on a record and be too famous to come here anymore?"

Charlie lifted his shot, drank it down, and felt the warm burn. "Never." He smiled and turned around to watch Fergus close the night.

He never played his drum to become famous. That wasn't his goal. He barely liked being on the stage, but he did it for the love of music.

His father, yes, he was proud that Charlie played that drum and sang the old songs.

Chelsea, his ex-fiancée, had also been enamored of his playing. The night he met her was at a pub just like this one, and even as he chased away her memory with another shot of whiskey, it turned around and found him. He recalled the way she sat in the front row in her tight sweater dress, tapping her toes and tossing her auburn hair. The way she found him at the bar after the set and told him about how the music made her feel, the way she sat next to him and leaned in so very close.

How had he not seen the falseness of her? The hard core of her insincerity?

It was possible that he noticed it, or that's what Fergus told him when it ended. "Mate, by the time you saw the rot, you were already long gone."

"I don't think I was ever fully aware."

"Deep down, in that murky subconscious of yours, you knew."

And maybe Fergus was right. When Chelsea tried to explain to Charlie that she was in love with his best mate and that Charlie had never truly given himself over to her, he saw it was true: he'd held back. The things that mattered—the *anam cara* of it all—were never between them.

The breakup was placed at his feet. The tears. The handwritten calligraphy invitations that were destroyed. The phone calls his mum made to friends and family to cancel the wedding. And he never tried to right it; he never told anyone the truth about seeing Chelsea and his university mate Graham kissing in the garden.

Everyone believed that Charlie was heartbroken because his fiancée left him for his friend. But *heartbroken* was the wrong word.

Disgusted and relieved seemed more relevant.

Later, he'd heard the murmurs—*Didn't go to his best mate's wedding. Couldn't get over it. A fight in a London pub.*

From the gossip, people believed he'd been hurt. He had been, but only by Graham, who hid their secret love story. Chelsea—well, he might have lost her, but his mate was the larger blow, and he was still unaccustomed to their distance.

He was startled from his malignant memories.

"Charlie." He heard a soft voice and turned.

Millie Barker. The sweet and fragilely beautiful girl he'd known since childhood. "Hallo, Millie." She stood next to him and turned to watch the band. She held an empty glass in her hand, and he bought her another gin and tonic.

They leaned against the bar, and her arm was against his, and then her hip. He felt the heat of their bodies finding each other. "That was beautiful tonight," she said. "You . . . I mean your singing. Especially that last one."

"Thank you. Father's favorite."

"I'm sorry for your loss," she said, and turned to face him, placing her hand on his arm. "I loved him. He was so . . . sweet and yet so—"

"Much a man."

"Yes." She smiled sadly. "That would have been batty for me to say."

"How's your family?" he asked.

"Batty."

"Then all is well," he said, and they laughed, clinking their glasses together.

Logan, the flute player, walked by and slapped Charlie's back. "Always the one wooing the girls," he said. "Good to be you."

Charlie scoffed and looked to Millie with a blush. "He's drunk."

"But he's right," she said.

He nudged her and knew she meant no harm. How lovely to know someone enough that one didn't have to explain his past to them. Now the band packed up. In the commotion, and as the night ended, the bartenders hollering out for last call, Charlie tossed his drum case over his shoulder and walked into the night.

Unseasonably warm, the sky clear, a single cloud moving slowly across the star-streaked sky.

Lonely as a cloud.

The Wordsworth line from the poem about his beloved Lake District ran through Charlie's mind and he almost laughed. It was as if his father walked alongside him tonight, his mind whispering things his father might utter.

Father had warned him about Chelsea, but not in direct words. He never said anything directly, as if the Irish in him allowed him only to go around things, around and then back again. Father might tell a story about a changeling turning a princess into a witch or the flight of an owl that warned of deceit. Charlie heard his father's warnings but paid him little mind, for Charlie thought, or he believed, he was in love.

Such a farce. He coughed out a laugh and lifted his face to the new mystery in his life. "So who was Bronwyn Fordham, Father?" he said to the night sky. But there was no answer.

The sky wheeled and the stars blended; he'd drunk one shot too many. He needed to remember that whiskey was never the answer to grief; it was the gateway to grief, and to the softest and most beautiful memories.

Like this one: the morning when he sat in a rowboat on Esthwaite Water with his father and his brother, Archie. The twins could not have been more than twelve years old. The boathouse across the lake was smudged with a woolly mist that hovered thick over blue waters. The lake rippled where a fish jumped. Geese squawked their secret language. Father uttered a sentence in Irish.

"What did you say?" Archie asked.

Father looked to the sky. "I didn't realize I'd spoken aloud."

"You did," Charlie said. "What was it?"

"Ah, lines from the Irish poem 'Cill Aodáin.' We memorized it as children." He closed his eyes. "It means 'The Land Where Everything Grows.'"

Charlie and Archie sat still, their father the center of the morning and of their world. "Why did you stop?" Charlie asked. "Stop speaking Irish? Let it go? It was *your* language."

"I didn't let it go, Son. It let go of me. It was as much a part of me as my skin and bones, as the very beat of my heart. But when something breaks the heart, things fall out of the cracks and fissures, and Gaelic was one of those very things."

Charlie and Archie didn't fully understand what Father meant or how to remedy something that made him so sad. Instead of responding, they sat quietly.

Finally Charlie asked, "What's the word for *lake*?"

"An easy one, Son. *Loch*."

Charlie and Archie repeated the word and held their fishing poles above the water, glancing at each other in their silent brotherhood.

Now in London, far off, a siren howled, and Charlie found himself not on the edge of the lake but the edge of High Holborn. He would know what to say to his father now. "If it hurts, if the words bring back the pain, use them all the more until they heal you."

How could Charlie have known the truth of that so long ago? The more he sang the old songs, the more he understood his connection to his father wasn't just in life.

Charlie made his way toward his flat, which was only a ten-minute stroll. His place with the wide, tall windows looking out over the River Thames, the concrete floors that he'd covered in old rugs he'd found in his parents' attic, a mishmash of furniture, and a bed covered in quilts from his childhood.

He'd wanted something of his own when he'd bought the flat. But now he wanted something he could hardly name. Something of his father and of family, of roots and lake edges. "Charlie?"

Charlie spun around to see her coming toward him on the pavement, picking her way slowly through the darkness, the careful walk of some-one who was deep in the drink.

"Millie!" He held out his hand to her as she stumbled toward him. "What are you doing out here?"

"Trying to catch up with you."

"Oh?"

She stood on her tiptoes and pressed her lips to his, a searching kiss that he returned. She pulled back and held her hands to either side of his face. "I have wanted to do that since the third year of primary school."

"Oh, Millie, you don't want this or me." He spoke gently, placed his hands on top of hers, and took them from his face. Her pink lipstick was smeared, and he wiped it clear for her.

"What if I do?" She wobbled. "What if I do want it and you just don't know everything?"

She swayed in the internal wind of whiskey, and he slipped his arm through hers. He would not leave her alone on the street. He walked her to his flat, guided her back to his bedroom. She reached for him, and he gently laid her down and placed his quilt over her.

"What are you doing?" she asked.

"Saving you from regret." He kissed her forehead and walked out.

Another thing that didn't heal grief—bringing a drunk and beautiful girl to his flat. He'd learned that lesson by trial and error.

He grabbed a piqued blue wool blanket from the closet and slumped onto the couch. He was asleep within minutes, dreaming of Esthwaite Water and his father teaching him *amhrán*, the word for *song*.

CHAPTER 8

CLARA

Bluffton, South Carolina

I suspected I wouldn't fall into sleep with the news from Charlie's phone call buzzing inside me like a plucked guitar string. With the first hint in twenty-five years that my mother might be alive or that she wasn't at the bottom of the sea with her created language, I was animated with a desire I thought long quieted.

We learned to live with certain things we never thought we could, and these two mysteries—what happened to Mother and what her sequel told me about her and her fictional character Emjie—would never be solved. I'd accepted this with resolute calm.

If I truly didn't care anymore, as I'd told everyone for years, then why was my heart rolling over, my skin prickling, my throat clogging with tears? Why did hope rise like some disquieted bird from its nest?

I picked up the phone receiver from my bedside table and dialed Lilia with the same phone I once called her from when we were kids, tiny hearts painted on the receiver with Magic Marker, a remnant of high school years.

This was not the proper order of things: me in my childhood bedroom with my eight-year-old daughter sleeping in the spare room that was once Mother's studio, sharing the two-sink Jack and Jill bathroom.

I leaned back on the pillows of my bed while I waited for Lilia to answer.

"Hello?"

"Lilia," I whispered.

She knew me so well that with a single utterance of her name, she asked, "What's wrong? What happened? Is Wynnie okay?"

"Yes. Yes." I covered the phone with my hand in an imitation of the days when we'd talked into the night, when I was trying to hide from my dad that I was up late. This time I was trying to keep from waking my daughter. "Wynnie is completely fine. A phone call came today."

"Oh?"

"From a man in England." I swung my legs off the bed and sat up, wound the coiled cord between my fingers, and stared at the bulletin board across the room, on which my high school graduation photo still hung crooked.

"Well, that's very mysterious."

"He says he has Mother's papers."

"Old stories of hers?" she asked.

"No." I took a breath. "Her lost papers. Her words. Her language."

"*Clara!*" I pulled the phone away from my ear. "Tell me everything."

I did. I told her everything about Charlie's call, just as I had told her everything about my life since second grade, when we first met on the playground. "I thought I was past this, Lilia. I thought I'd accepted it all, and now here I am ready to dash to England on the word of a stranger."

"Listen to me," Lilia said. "I've watched you suffer about your mom, and I've wanted to fix this for you for the past twenty-five years. Now you have a real chance to find something out, maybe even learn what happened."

"But do I really want to know?"

"Yes, of course you do." In the background a deep voice called Lilia's name. "Hold on, I'm talking to Clara." Then back to me. "Yes, you want to know. You've always wanted to know, even when you proclaim that you do not."

"Yes."

"Do you think she's . . . alive?" Lilia asked so quietly it was only because I knew the cadence of her voice so well that I understood what she asked.

"Do I dare hope?"

"Yes, you always hope. Clara, this is what you've been waiting for."

With *I love you*, with *goodbye*, we hung up. Lilia, as always, was right.

Without my own mother and lacking aunts and female cousins, I relied on Lilia and her mom as the women in my life. Who was I supposed to go to when my monthly started, when I felt the stirrings of adolescence, when I needed my first bra? Lilia and her mom, Lynn, were there, just as they'd always been, with open arms and open door. No questions asked, even as I heard the whispered phone calls between Dad and Lynn, an odd dual parenting with my best friend's family.

I slid off the bed, knelt on the braided rug, and pulled a faded blue suitcase out from beneath my bed. Once full of things that belonged *to* my mother, it was now a repository for all things *about* her. Before I opened it, my fingers absently ran over the burn scars on my arm, a habit when I was nervous or lost in thoughts about Mother.

I clicked the scratched metal latches, and the top popped open. The aroma of paper and dust rose from the interior—a sensory memory that vaulted me to childhood.

Years had passed since I last sifted through these things looking for my mother. I fanned out the photos. She was called *handsome* and *elegant, stunning* and *striking.* As an adult, I looked more like my dad, but if I stared hard enough, I found pieces of her in my cheekbones, chin, and wavy hair.

My memories of her were hazy at best. But that night, I remembered something new—a simple moment unadulterated by photos, articles, or analysis.

I was seven years old and rounding the corner to eight. It was the year I ran home from school every day, not to play with my friends, but to be with my mother.

This was the year she taught me to plant a garden in the square plot of dark soil, elaborating on how the wild violets would show up every year, a capsule unto themselves, and that they were Shakespeare's favorite flower. She taught me how to float under the bay's waters while grasping the dock's pillar, holding our breath and listening for the scratch and snuffle of sea life. The year we ran through a neighbor's fields under every full moon to create a fairy circle of cotton pods and make wishes that never came true: to fly with eagles' wings, to see an elf, to breathe underwater. It was the year she taught me how to boil indigo and make paint for my little drawings, how to plait my own hair, and how to dig into the dark mud for oysters and slurp them from the shell while they were still warm with life.

That seventh year of my life I lost two teeth, and I knew the tooth fairy was my mother when she left pressed flowers instead of coins.

She would spring to life with "I have an idea."

The ideas ranged from rowing the canoe to the far side of the river to search for sand dollars on the sandbar, to painting shells for a wind chime, to sewing pom-poms on the bottom of the curtains to brighten the house, to pressing flowers between thin pieces of paper to salvage their fading beauty.

That brightest year ended abruptly just before my eighth birthday, when she'd taken to bed with something Dad called *melancholy*, something I didn't understand and hoped would be cured.

After weeks of coming home from school and standing at her bedside, bereft, believing that possibly my real mother had died and another had replaced her, I needed to lure her out of bed.

"Mama." I danced around her bed in a fairy costume she'd made for me with scraps of filmy silk. I'd hoped to draw her to me, to the garden, to life.

She held out her hand, the simple gesture that made me fall madly in love with her every time she did it. I knit my fingers in hers, and she rose from the bed in her white cotton nightgown. "Take me somewhere, sweet fairy," she said.

I pulled her along until we were outside and lifting our faces to the river's breeze with its comforting aroma. At the end of that spring, she'd left the garden unattended, the flowers and vines tangling together with a wildness that had us both pretending we'd found a secret hideaway.

She plucked ferns from the earth until she carried a pile of them in her arms. "You choose the flowers, ladybug, and we'll make a dress of ferns and flowers."

I have no memory of making the dress, but somehow the day was spent, and evening light transformed the sky.

We wore those dresses over our nightgowns. If Dad was angry about the infestation of baby spiders or the small red ant bites all over my arms that he treated with a thick pink paste, I don't remember.

Mom hung our dresses on hooks outside the house, where towels and bathing suits were left to air-dry. The next morning, and this I'd never forgotten, those fern dresses were gone as surely as if they never existed. Sometimes I wondered if we just dreamed the same dream.

This was how the memories were for me: a piece here, a tear there, a shadow across the room, and I reconstructed a mother who loved me, a mother who made fern dresses and told stories of sleeping in sea caves.

Inside the suitcase rested books, articles, papers, and the six pages I'd xeroxed of her sequel when I'd visited the lockbox in Savannah years ago. The contents were a hodgepodge: one hardcover of *The Middle Place* illustrated in the margins with my childhood scribbling, an unauthorized biography by Brian Davis, psychiatric studies of her published in medical journals, newspaper articles, and magazine pieces.

There was also the scrapbook I'd made with every picture I'd found of her, and a manila folder stuffed with papers with the name *Bronwyn* written on the cover in my handwriting. I'd drawn vines, flowers, and butterflies around each letter of her name, fairies and nymphs at the edges. I'd illustrated her name with the only kind of love I'd known how to give an absent mother.

Then, finally, there was one other scrapbook.

I leaned against the bed frame and pulled out the book with the dark green cloth cover faded to a misty emerald, splotches of mossy color seeping through, and a tear on the top left where the fabric peeled away from the cardboard.

I paused before I opened it. It had been years since I'd touched this, and now one phone call from across the sea and my obsession returned.

Inside this album weren't photos of my mother, but of every kind of mother I could find: the ones in the ads for Electrolux and in picture books, ones I drew from the wicked stepmother in "Cinderella" to Marmee in *Little Women*. Inside were clips of mothers from illustrated fairy tales and photos of my friends' mothers that they never knew I took from their houses. This green cloth scrapbook held all the possibilities of what could have been instead of what was.

"What do you want from this?" my dad had asked when he found it. "She isn't in here," he'd said with a choked voice.

"But what if she is?" I'd told him. "I just have to keep looking."

I didn't need this scrapbook anymore, and before I opened it and spiraled down the abyss of wishing and wanting, I dropped it to the carpet and instead lifted the manila folder with the illustrated name *Bronwyn* on the front.

The articles written about her were clipped together: pieces from newspapers, police reports, the syllabus for classes on her fantasy work and what it might be trying to say. All these documents were an amalgam of who and what the world deemed Bronwyn Newcastle Fordham to be: a missing genius, a literary mystery, or a cocktail party anecdote.

But for me, she was one thing only: my mother.

What the world knew about her were facts lined up in articles.

These facts were repeated: Bronwyn Newcastle Fordham's first (and only) book, *The Middle Place*, was published in 1909, when Bronwyn was twelve years old, a child prodigy author, and for that anomaly, she was still studied by fans and scholars. At the end of her famous novel, she'd left her character, Emjie, in limbo, caught in another world and unable to reach home.

Days after a house fire, in the middle of the night in 1927, Bronwyn fled her half-burned house in the family boat. She took with her a hundred dollars and a change of clothes (tweed trousers and a cream-colored fisherman's sweater).

To add to the allure of the literary mystery, for those who cared and followed the story, the most intriguing part was how she took the dictionary of her created words with her, stashed inside a leather satchel, leaving her sequel unable to be translated.

The day after she left us, our Chris-Craft was found floating in the ocean and out of gas off Tybee Island. Mother and her leather satchel were never found.

I dumped out the file of these inane articles looking for only one with a photo of the missing satchel she took with her, the case stuffed full of her created language.

The article was from the *Bluffton Gazette*, 1927—"Death in Local House Fire"—slumped yellowed and crumbling on the top of the pile.

Twenty-five-year-old Alex Prescott, a Bluffton firefighter, has lost his battle for life after a week in the Savannah hospital. During a local fire in the Harrington home in Bluffton, he plummeted through the floor to a sub-basement below and became trapped, the crawl-space doors locked from the outside.

Bronwyn Newcastle Fordham disappeared from her family home. Bronwyn's daughter, eight-year-old Clara Harrington, suffered from burns on her arms and chest, and she recuperates at home.

After police discovered the family boat off Tybee Island, the search has been called off, and Bronwyn's disappearance leaves another family in mourning.

I turned back to the remaining papers to search for a specific photo. The aroma of musty disintegrated paper sifted through the air. And there it was—a photo of the satchel that held my mother's language. A close-up of the eagle latch, just as Charlie Jameson had described.

CHAPTER 9

CLARA

Bluffton, South Carolina

"Mama!" Wynnie's voice floated above dreams of a garden, a fern-covered dress, waves crashing into a sea cave. Then my neck burned with a twisted ache from sleeping on my bedroom floor, my face squashed on a newspaper. All around me lay the detritus of my mother's life.

I sat up and rubbed my face.

"I'll be late for school," Wynnie said. She looked down at me, dressed in striped-orange pants and a polka-dotted red top. Her hair was wild about her face, and there was a patch of maple syrup on her cheek.

"Oh, ladybug." I stood up. "I was so tired I fell asleep on the floor."

"Papa made me breakfast and said to let you sleep." She was grinning with this rare treat.

"Would you actually call it breakfast?" I asked, and ruffled her hair. "Or dessert?"

"I would call it breakfast, yes." Her smile lifted. "I have to take my bag to school today because it's my weekend with Daddy."

"I know, baby. I know. I called him about the carnival and told him you didn't want to go."

She nodded and then asked, her eyes narrowed at me, "Did he listen?"

"Yes, he did. Now let's get you ready to go."

Wynnie looked around me. "What's all this?"

"Old papers about Grandma. I was looking for . . . something."

"For what?" She picked up the biography and read out loud, "*Child Genius: The Wild and Tragic Life of Bronwyn Newcastle Fordham.*"

I kissed her and took the book from her hands. She did *not* need to read about her grandmother's adolescent escapades before she met my dad. "This book isn't for you or for now."

"Why not?"

Oh, the everlasting temptation to say *Because I said so.* I told her, "Another time. Now run and get your bag and let me get ready. We'll make sure you have everything you need for the weekend."

"Daddy says he's bringing his girlfriend, Nicole, and she's bringing her son, stupid Sam, who wants to go to the carnival."

"No name-calling," I said.

"That's not name-calling," she said. "That's just a true fact."

"Versus a false fact?"

"Exactly."

She ran off, and in a flash of knowing what to do next, a seizure of understanding, I slipped into Dad's private study and opened his top desk drawer. In the back right corner, taped down and hidden under a pile of forgotten tax documents, I ran my fingers over the iron key that had been hiding there for the last twenty-five years, the key to a lockbox in Savannah where Mother's sequel rested in the dark.

I ripped off the yellowed tape and the key slipped out. I folded my fingers around it, as if hiding this act from myself.

"Mama?" Wynnie called for me and I slipped the key into my purse, its weight barely noticeable compared to its import and meaning.

"Coming, love!"

I dreaded my weekends without Wynnie, not only because I missed her, but also because I worried about her with Nat. Even if he'd been gambling-free for a year, there was always a chance for relapse, and I knew too much about it.

When people cluck clucked about my divorce, when they offered sympathy with a false look of pity, I'd nod and say thanks instead of what I really wanted to say: "It's a relief." But that relief didn't mean I liked sharing my girl or didn't worry every single minute she was out of my sight.

⁓

Wynnie arrived in the middle of a full moon April night over eight years ago. When the low pains woke me at two a.m., I let out a strangled noise that roused Nat. "What is it?" he asked, reaching across the warm sheets for me.

"The baby," I said. "Something is wrong." Then a warm sensation flooded between my legs and the sheets dampened. I jumped out of bed, tripped in the tangled sheets, and grabbed the bedside table to balance.

The milk glass lamp shattered on the floor; I stepped on a sliver of its shards.

It wasn't time. Wynnie wasn't meant to arrive for another two months. Her due date, June 15, was circled in both blue- and pink-colored pencils on the calendar in the kitchen. This was April. Nat hadn't assembled the crib. I hadn't bought diapers or finished the Winnie the Pooh mural in her nursery.

These were my inane thoughts as the pain grabbed me again, twisting the center of my body.

I gasped, stumbling, leaning against the wall, bent over as I made my way to the bathroom. Had my water broken?

I'd combed through all of Dad's obstetrics books and knew about the first sharp pain and the damp run between your legs: "breaking your water." *Now labor will begin.*

This was too early—I was doing motherhood all wrong.

I clicked on the bathroom light and looked down. It wasn't water. Blood soaked the front of my white cotton nightgown, creating crimson dots on my feet and on the pink fluffy bathroom carpet.

Nat was at my side before I could call his name. He wrapped me in towels, picked me up, and carried me down the stairs, murmuring words of comfort. *It's okay. It's okay. We'll be okay.* He bundled me in the passenger seat of our black Dodge.

He pulled away from the house and I cried out, "I want my mom!" My voice rent the air.

Nat sped through the dark neighborhood streets, flickers of shrimp-boat lights in the bay, a quiet, sleeping world. I was still awake when he screeched up to the blinking emergency sign at the hospital. I was still awake when they put me on a stretcher, and then barely awake as I was wheeled into an operating room. Darkness crept around the edges of my sight.

A quick sting of a needle and the anesthesia flooded my veins. I fought against the oblivion. I would not disappear on my child. I would not leave.

I would not.

When I awoke, the nurse with the swan hat and the crisp uniform was at my side, and the doctor in a white coat leaned over me with the stench of ammonia. I fought through the fog. "Tell me," I said, my voice broken with fear.

"It's a girl," the doctor said in a solemn voice, avoiding eye contact. He adjusted a machine that was tethered to me by a plastic tube that entered a vein in my left arm. "And she is safe in the special baby care unit."

I sat up and vomited on him, on the blankets, and all over myself. I didn't pay it any mind. "Take me to my baby."

The doctor nodded at the nurse and the darkness again encroached, closing in. I scrambled for the needle, scratched to pull it out, and didn't wake until the next day.

When I awoke, I understood that my mother was right about this: there is an unseen world, a place where phantasmagoric images rise and fall, where light beckons and darkness looms at the boundary of sight. It isn't so much terrifying as wondrous, or that was my experience.

Which drugs coursed through my veins and created such images? In what everyone believed was sleep, I saw my mother, soft and hazy, alive in this world, not in another. She walked through a woodland and beckoned me forward. She sat in a library and looked up from a stack of books. Her face wasn't the one I saw in all the photos, black-and-white and young, but that of a woman aged, but not old.

I spent those sleeping hours visiting the places and spaces of dreams. There were estuaries where I played with my childhood friends, nearly all who'd moved away but Lilia. There was my honeymoon with Nat— one we never actually took, but promised ourselves we would one day—a trip to England. There were snakes, a lot of snakes, and in the dreams, I wasn't fearful.

Before I woke, Mother stood in the woodlands holding out her hand to me. My God, how I'd wanted to take her hand for so long, and there she was reaching for me instead of me reaching for her. Her hand was soft, warm, and alive. Her smile lifted her cheeks, and her brown eyes were deeply warm. She pulled hard, my body jerked, and I awoke in the hospital room.

Mother had often called our existence an earthbound life, and as I fought my way back to the world and to my daughter, I believed Mother was calling me forward to this life.

I'd never told anyone that story, and I never planned on doing so.

It was mine to treasure.

When I opened my eyes, the hospital room was empty but for the beeping machines and the blazing light of the overhead fixtures. My eyes hurt when I focused. Stainless steel and bland beige walls, a Pepto Bismol–colored plastic pitcher, brown-freckled creamy Formica, and a long metal pole that held liquid dripping into my vein. Two plastic prongs in my nose and a tube I could feel between my legs.

My daughter.

I tried to call out, but my voice was trapped.

I must have faded away again because when I opened my eyes, Nat stood next to me, stroking my hair with his eyes closed.

"Nat," I said.

He jolted, cried out, "Clara! Oh my God, you scared me to death."

"Our daughter?"

"She's in the special baby care unit. She's the tiniest and most beautiful thing you've ever seen."

"Is she . . . all right?"

"They aren't sure," he said. "They just aren't sure. But I believe she will be. She's strong like you, I can already tell."

"Tell me everything. And don't leave a thing out. I need to know."

And he told me the story of Wynnie's birth: They'd wheeled me into the ER and performed an emergency C-section, trying to save me and save her at the same time. She'd been blue, and my heart rate was falling. Placental previa. My placenta had ripped from the lining of my uterus, and we were both dying.

"I'm sorry," I said to Nat. "I couldn't hold on to her. My God, I am so sorry."

"No!" he said, and covered my face with chapped-lip kisses. "It is not your fault. The doctor told me over and over that it's not your fault."

The way he spoke made me believe that at one moment, or maybe half a moment, he'd believed it was my fault and they'd reassured him it was not.

"There's something else," I said. "I can see it in your eyes. What is it?"

"Not now," he said.

"Now."

He took both my hands in his, squeezed them. "She is beautiful, and she is ours, and she is going to be okay."

I closed my eyes and saw my mother's face, her hand pulling me forward to life. "We'll name her Bronwyn."

Nat coughed a laugh. "We are going to name our daughter after your mother?"

"I would like that, yes." My voice was fading, but my resolve was not.

"We agreed on Marjory, didn't we? We'd call her Margie after my mother?"

I stayed silent. He wiped the tears from my face. "We don't have to decide right now," he said.

I didn't tell him that I thought Mother brought me back here to this room, to this life with him and with my daughter. I said only one word. "Please."

Behind Nat, a flash of white and silver. The doctor stood with his lab coat and stethoscope, and I shifted my gaze from Nat to the doctor. His hands slid into the pockets of his lab coat, and his face took on a mask of what I believed was concern. "You have a strong girl there," he said. "She's going to be all right, I believe."

And she was.

⸻

I later learned what Nat kept from me that day in the hospital room. Wynnie would be my first and last child. I was also taught about the aftereffects of premature birth. It all paled compared to her life.

She stayed a month at the hospital in an incubator with bright lights to warm her. I held her hand through a hole in the container that resembled a spaceship, and I pumped my breast milk that they then dripped slowly into a tube down her nose until her suck reflex emerged. The first time I held her, I wept so violently they nearly took her from my arms. Her left eye wandered, and her eyesight would always need help.

Dad explained to me that the lungs were the last and most important things in development, and that she might always have asthma or respiratory infections, but it was manageable. Now, eight years later, we had adrenaline shots I carried everywhere, and we had aminophylline pills that melted under her tongue. As for her brain, they said we'd have to wait and see.

Well, wait we did, and what a beautiful brain she had. My girl was whip-smart and curious and quirky. Small for her age, but who cared so much about that? Not me.

Now she sat next to me in the car, wearing her mismatched clothes that she picked out that morning, her pink glasses specially designed in Charleston at the eye clinic, and her feet propped on her weekend bag.

"Mama?" She rested the back of her head on the window and turned to face me.

"Yes?"

"Are you going to call that man back?"

"What man?" I feigned innocence.

"The one who says he has Grandma's things."

"Yes, I am."

"Good." She glanced out the window. "I bet it's real this time."

"Why do you say that?"

She was silent for a few beats and then said, "Emjie thinks so."

"Well," I told her as I pulled in front of the school, "I hope she's right." I parked the car, and we both climbed out and stood in front of the orange-hued brick building. I looked up at the entryway, at the double doors, at the memory of Dad dropping me off for school instead of my mother.

Wynnie opened the school door and didn't even look back as she ran off, braids flapping in the wind, her duffel bag bouncing against her shoulder blades. I reached into my purse and felt the heavy weight of the iron key that I'd slipped from Dad's desk drawer without telling him.

It was time to retrieve the sequel, to set my hands and eyes on the story that haunted our lives with its unreadable words, its secret messages, and its untold story.

CHAPTER 10

CLARA

Bluffton, South Carolina

The lace of iron pilings sent spiderweb shadows across the bridge's road-way. Low, flat warehouses squatted on the far side of the crinkled surface of the blue-gray river. Overhead, a cloudless sky touched down on a city growing into its own. I dared not look left or right, a plummeting fall to a river that flowed to the sea, a riverboat making its way beneath the arches.

I followed the road snaking its way to the Savannah Federal Bank, where the key would open a metal box in a back room behind thick locked doors, containing a novel that many thought gone forever. False sequels had come to light, and other authors had offered to write the follow-up to Emjie's life, desperate to release her from the limbo where Mother had left her.

Dad refused them all. He knew where the authentic one rested in peace, with no way to translate it.

The day after he entombed the sequel's pages at the bank, long be-fore a bridge arched over the river, I asked him, "Dad! What if I want to try and read it one day?"

"Then you can go retrieve it." He took my hand and led me to his study, showed me the key's hiding place. "Ladybug, I see no reason for such a thing, but if you'd like to go, here is the key."

"We could get it translated," I told him. "There are people who spe-cialize in these things."

"We will never translate that novel, Clara. Never. If she wanted it to be read, she would have left her language for us."

I was fifteen years old, angry, and completely soaked in self-righteousness as words I regretted poured out in desperation. "You don't want to translate it because you think it will prove she was insane. You're scared of what it might say. You're a coward."

"All of that is very possible," he said, and kissed my forehead, tears in his eyes.

"Why?" I asked when the tears were spent, and he took me outside to sit on the edge of the dock. "Why did she need her own words? Weren't we and our language enough?"

"She wanted a word for everything. She believed . . ." His voice changed, as if the middle held something soft inside. He cleared his throat. "She believed that the words we use were made for the people who didn't notice the world. She wondered about the existence of words for things that people like her, and you, notice."

"Like what?" I asked.

"The shade of blue when a rainstorm whips across the river and pebbles the surface. The feeling of missing something you never had. The shiver of recognition when something that is meant for you crosses your path."

"Yes," I said with a feeling I wanted to name. "Like a word for the feeling when something is so big that it puddles in your chest, sits like a lake."

"Yes." He let out a sound that was half sob, half sigh.

We sat on the edge of the dock, our feet dangling over the outgoing tide. Spring green, the brightest of all the greens, flickered on the marsh grasses. A dolphin's sleek gray body rose from the waters, a baby at its side, swimming with a synchronicity that made my chest ache with loss. I let out a cry and Dad pulled me close.

"How could she have done it?" I asked.

"A long time ago," he told me as if starting a bedtime story, "when she was only a bit older than you are now, before I met her, when she was seventeen." He shuddered with the story he was about to tell. "Your mother's mother, Martha, decided that her daughter's genius had grown into flights of fancy that were dangerous. She decided that your mother must be treated."

"Treated?"

"A psychiatric institute."

"What?" A blow to my chest that took my breath. Dad was pulling aside the curtain and showing me the inner workings, the cogs and gears of my mother's leaving.

"Yes. It was the most horrific time of her life."

"Worse than when her father left her?"

"Yes. As she described it—they tried to fix her in windowless rooms with sedatives and hypnotics. It was a living hell, she told me. With forced bedrest and words like *schizophrenia*, all because she could not do as her mother wanted."

"Which was?"

"After seventeen years of nurturing her creativity, of allowing her to never go to traditional school, of using her writing for family gain, Martha decided it was time for Bronwyn to buckle down with a job that left your mother listless and depressed."

Images of horror flooded my mind. I remembered an afternoon when Lilia and I had sneaked into the back door of the theater to watch *The Snake Pit* with Olivia de Havilland, a movie in which she was locked up and treated with ghastly remedies. We left the movie in the middle, agreeing that our parents were right to forbid it, unable to stomach the terror. This could *not* be what happened to my mother. She was . . . normal and kind and smart. "Dad, her mother sent her away? To a psychiatric ward?"

"Yes. For a month."

"You think this is why she left us? Because her mother did that to her? So she left *me*?"

"I don't know, my ladybug. I am just telling you the story, so you know more of her than you did before."

I wept in my dad's embrace, and the gentle-eyed dolphin dove deeper into the waters and disappeared.

This memory of Dad's story, of the truth that had been hidden from me, returned now. For years, and sometimes still, I fell asleep wondering what it must have been like to be locked up this way, to have your thoughts altered and your creativity stifled. It was one more scrap of her life I would keep, for I had so little.

I came to myself at a red light in Savannah's downtown, under the shadow of Spanish moss dripping from live oak trees. I found a parking spot a block from the white marble edifice with the fluted columns—a stately place to hide Mother's madness, some might say.

The presiding assumption—the one published in that dreadful biography, in articles and opinion pieces—was that in great despair Mother swallowed sleeping pills and carried her life, language, and secrets to the bottom of the sea.

She was unstable, they said. A touch of madness, you know. One merely needed to look at her youthful escapades to understand that Bronwyn was ill-suited for motherhood. She was a rare genius; that was proven.

Everyone knew that being a genius rarely made for a happy life.

When I was a child, there were times when she would disappear for a few days and then return regretful, sad, and promising to try anything Dad suggested. She'd swallow the white pills I never knew the name of and keep regular hours, her face placid. The mommy who ran through the garden, built forts, and stayed up all night writing would disappear. But then inevitably she would return to herself one bright afternoon, and we'd run to the horseshoe-shaped beach behind our house and swim in the briny waters.

Dad told me later that Mother hadn't been afraid of anything in the world except the psychiatric hospital, with its pale, lifeless walls and windowless rooms, with the white coats on doctors and the silver trays of medicines.

My mother's lack of maternal watchfulness was roundly condemned in the book *Child Genius*. To biographer Brian Davis, Bronwyn Newcastle Fordham was formed and fashioned of bits and pieces of myth, a few photos, stories, Jungian analysis, and imagination.

But to me, Mother had been everything from the love of my life to an evil character in a morbid fairy tale. I'd looked for her in every face and friendship of my life. Therefore, it made sense that I hoped Mr. Charlie Jameson was telling me the truth and there was something of my mother waiting for me in England.

I opened the heavy wooden door to the Savannah National Bank and walked toward the teller's desk, key in hand.

In the kitchen, I rested my hand on top of Mother's Emjie sequel sitting on the counter and counted ahead to England's time zone: five p.m. I picked up the phone's receiver and dialed 0, instructed the operator to connect me to the London number, and tried not to think of what this overseas call would cost.

I wondered if all of this was just another vain attempt to answer the questions that could never be answered: Why did she leave me? Where was she if she was at all? And the most important of all—why hadn't she loved me enough to stay, no matter the cost?

Out the window over the sink, a blue heron stood regal on the edge of the oyster shell outcropping. Still and quiet, ethereal. Mother once told me that the Greeks knew the heron was a messenger from the gods, and if one visited me, I better pay some mind.

Staring at it now, the blue-gray wisps of feather under its chin, the arc of its neck in a soft C, I believed her.

What? I asked it.

The heron didn't answer, but after clicks and static, Charlie picked up. "Hallo!"

"Hello, it's Clara," I said. "Clara Harrington."

"I was hoping it might be you ringing me." His voice held laughter below that lovely accent. "I kept recalculating what time it was there and was nearly set to ring you."

"No need. Here I am."

"I know this is quite unsettling," he said.

"I have questions," I told him as I paced the kitchen holding the blue pottery mug I'd made for my father in fifth grade. Dad kept every gift, from the potholder I created at summer camp to a picture I painted of him in third grade. He always felt as if he could make up for a lost mother by being double the dad. The fact that it didn't work that way didn't mean he ever stopped trying.

"All right," Charlie said. "If I know the answers, I'll tell you. Go on, then."

"Did you look at the sealed letter?"

"No, it's sealed." Exasperation flowed across the lines.

I wondered about Charlie's age, what he looked like, the library, too. I wanted an image of the situation. "Does anyone else know about this?"

"No."

"You haven't called Boston University or any of the places that store her papers?"

"No. Mrs. Harrington, you can either come retrieve these papers or not. You are not obliged to me or this case of papers in any way. I can donate it or destroy it, and we can pretend this never happened. I would understand. I might do the same."

I didn't correct him about my marital status, for Mother must have written this note before my marriage or she would have added my married name, Carter, which I didn't use professionally.

"I can't let you donate or destroy it," I said, leaning against the counter and closing my eyes. "But I'm not even sure how I'd get there."

"There's an ocean liner. The new SS *United States*, fast as can be. It takes four days from New York to the Southampton docks, which is a few hours by train to London. My brother has traveled this way many times for business visits to New York."

"Mr. Jameson, I'm an art teacher and illustrator. To buy passage to England might not be possible for me."

What didn't I tell him? My husband lost all our money; there was nothing left. I couldn't leave my daughter alone for the ten days or two weeks this journey would take. This was an impossible situation.

"I understand," he said. "But we must find a way to make this right."

"I want to know something," I said in my most professional voice. "Will you please share one of the words with me?"

Papers rustled and a door opened and closed; there was a muffled conversation with someone, and then he was back. "*Wondalea*: explore the sky, to fly across a starlit path and shadow the moon."

My head floated above, as if I were watching a woman, a woman who was me, in a kitchen holding a phone.

A starlit path. Shadow the moon.

It was really her.

The impossibilities of my life faded. I would rise to this moment.

"Thank you," I said. "I will get back to you very soon." I hung up without waiting for his goodbye. I bent over, my hands on my knees, and took long, deep breaths.

Wondalea.

This was no prank. This man across the ocean, in a library in London, held my mother's lost words.

Finally, here was the key to translating her sequel, and possibly, if I allowed myself the luxury of imagining it, the answers to her vanishing and whereabouts.

For all my wondering, for all my wishing, for all my imaginary scenarios, now I stood in my childhood kitchen where she once made chicken potpies and angel food cake. If the sky were now splitting open, I was suddenly terrified for what these lost and secret words of hers might show me of her troubled mind and decision to leave.

I made my way outside, staring across the bay. The heron had vanished with whatever message he carried. The day turned drowsy under a low woolly sky that hinted of a coming storm.

The lawn sloped down to the horseshoe-shaped beach, where oyster shells crackled and settled along with the tides, where our rowboat sat upside down for the season, its oars hiding beneath.

When I lifted my eyes farther to the horizon, there was the expansive view that sometimes, when I was a child, made me both dizzy and thrilled. What a large world there was out there; but mine was here, on the edge of earth and sea, safe.

Wondalea—the word coursed through my body. I wanted to paint, to illustrate the word that my mother formed in her imagination.

All plans for the day fell away. From the market to Christmas shopping, my to-do list became irrelevant, and I found myself in the sunroom with my easel and watercolors.

Time was lost when I found myself here; minutes and hours were no longer real in the way I understood them in daily life. Time collapsed in on itself and images rose. Instead of finding something, I was letting it find me. The images came for me instead of my pursuing them.

When the phone rang again, I thought maybe an hour had passed, but it was three p.m. I dropped the paintbrush on the palette and hustled to the kitchen.

"Hello?"

"Clara? It's Charlie again. Nighttime here, but what does it matter? Please don't think me rude or intrusive, but I've decided to buy you a ticket to England by ship."

"Thank you so much for your kindness, but no," I said. "I can't let you. I will figure out a way myself."

"Listen to me," he said. "And hold on, because I've practiced for a bit, and I don't want to muddle my words."

"Did you actually write down what you want to say?"

A long moment of silence and then a laugh. "Yes, I wrote it down, so please allow me to read."

Laughter bubbled up from me as if a cork had popped. I liked this man, Charlie Jameson. Whether he was old or young, I had no real idea. If his dad had just died, he was probably older, maybe in his fifties at the youngest? The image of Alec Guinness in the movie *Great Expectations* popped into my mind: a swoop of blond hair and the lifted eyebrows of the curious.

"Mrs. Harrington," he said, "I don't know who your mother is. Can you tell me?"

"Please call me Clara."

"Clara," he said, and I liked the roll of his *r* and the rise and fall of my name in his voice, as if I were suddenly someone else. "And please, I'm Charlie."

"Charlie," I said. "My mother. Well, she was a famous author who disappeared over twenty-five years ago. She wrote a book called *The Middle Place*, a children's novel about a little girl named Emjie. She simply vanished in 1927, and it is widely assumed that she drowned with those papers you have."

"Ah!" A sudden outburst, and I imagined him popping himself in the forehead. "Yes. Yes. I know about this. The author who vanished. Boston, am I right?"

"Not entirely wrong. That's where she's from, but she disappeared from here, from South Carolina."

"Well, for some reason unbeknownst to me, my father had her papers. They are in his library, and I am responsible for them. I cannot keep them, and I cannot mail them. I know you need to come retrieve them. So, for that, I will purchase you a ticket on the SS *United States* to sail here. It is a four-day journey." He paused and I allowed the silence to fall between us. "Okay, your turn to say something. I've completed my speech."

"Well, Mr. Jameson, I'm glad you told me you wrote that down because I would have thought I was speaking with the prime minister. Thank you for the kind offer, but I can't let you do that," I said. "Even with your lovely speech and generous offer. I'd have to bring my daughter, and this is the holiday season and I teach and . . ."

"There will always be something."

"Excuse me?"

"Do you know how many things I meant to do with my father, believing there was loads of time to do it? Trips and excursions and just an ordinary day fishing? There wasn't time. But you must make time. I will purchase your daughter a ticket as well. It's only one cabin, still. I would like to get these papers in your hands. It feels as if I'm going to be haunted by your mother at any moment."

"Well, I am haunted by her every day," I said.

"I'm sorry for that," he said. "I truly am."

I placed my hands on the sequel still sitting on the counter, as if it might give me the answer of what to do. "If I am to come to England, it will be under my own steam," I said firmly. And a plan budded in my mind.

With the lost words of my mother, I would translate and sell this sequel to the highest bidder. I could buy my own ticket to England and then open the art school I'd dreamed of opening. First, I needed to dig into my meager savings.

"I'll get back to you with my plans," I told him. "I'm coming to England."

We hung up, and I thought of Nat picking Wynnie up from school at that moment, of being without her for the weekend, of sailing on an ocean liner to England, of taking a two-week leave of teaching, of my father alone, and of course, always, of my mother.

As a child, I had visions of her walking through the front door, dropping to her knees, and holding out her arms for me. "There you are," she said in this imaginary scenario. "I'm so sorry, darling. I was lost, but not to worry, now I am home."

CHAPTER 11

CLARA

Bluffton, South Carolina

"I have to tell Nat today."

Lilia and I walked along the sidewalk of downtown Bluffton, ambling slowly under the shadows of swaying palmettos. It was the warmest November on record, so we carried our light coats over our arms. She'd met me after church with her family. We'd just finished Sunday lunch at Café Harvey and were walking to prolong our afternoon. We were rarely alone anymore—I had Wynnie and she had her five-year-old, Bella.

The air was thick with unshed rain, and a breeze flapped the shop awnings like sails. Live oak trees arched over us, and lampposts stood as sentinels along the sidewalk. The cry of a seagull overhead. Everything was closed on a Sunday, and we paused in front of the bookshop where there was always a copy of *The Middle Place* for the curious who made a sojourn to Bluffton to see where Bronwyn once lived. Purple and yellow pansies spilled from the window box below the book displays.

"Nat is not going to be happy," she said before she bent over and picked up a white ibis feather caught in a sweetgrass bush. She handed it to me. "Signs everywhere."

"It's a sign, but for what?" I asked. "Don't go? Go?" I took the feather from her and smiled, feeling loved.

"It means you're meant to go, silly. A feather. Fly away!"

Lilia and I could, and often did, make signs out of anything. We knew how to confirm whatever we wanted just by saying, "It's a sign."

I stared at her and thought again how chic she was, how she'd become a mother and wife with such ease, wearing the cotton dress with a Peter Pan collar, pantyhose, and the pin curls I could never seem to perfect. "Did you sew that dress?" I pulled at her sleeve. "This is something. I really have no idea how you do everything with such ease. You're my best friend and I can't even begin to understand your endless abilities."

She laughed. "I couldn't draw a potato if I tried, so nothing out of you." Her face grew serious. "You're going."

"Yes. In three weeks. It's decided. Wynnie's been with Nat all weekend, so Dad and I worked it out. I'll use my savings and on November thirtieth we'll board the ship Charlie suggested. I've had our passports rushed and Dad wanted to help, so he booked us a place to stay in Covent Garden. But I'm telling you, Nat will lose his mind. I'm bracing for it."

We paused as Mr. and Mrs. Hightower walked past us arm in arm, singing out a greeting in unison. She'd been my piano teacher as a child, and he'd been my lawyer in the divorce. This was small-town life. We greeted them, and then Lilia turned back to me.

"So what if he loses his mind?" She wiped her hands in a motion as if dusting them off. "Swish-swish, be done with what he has to say or think or do."

"I can't, though. He's still her father. Wishing him ill feels like wishing it on her, too."

She placed her hands on my shoulders. "Because of him, you've lost everything. I don't care what he thinks about the first real chance you have to find out about your mother."

"I didn't lose everything. I lost money, a house, and a marriage. But I have everything, literally everything in the world that matters."

She hugged me. "Yes, you do." She bit her lip. "Must I always be the one to say the crass thing?"

"I guess you must—what is it?" I smiled at her, for she had always been the truth teller in our friendship.

"If you translate this novel, you will finally be financially free. I know, I know—you don't like to think of it that way, but, Clara, it's still true. I know you admire that sequel for the art of it or to find out what happened to Emjie, or, more important, what happened to your mother, but it will also save you."

"I've thought the same thing," I said. "I drove to Savannah on Friday and took it out of the lockbox. I have it at home."

"Wow. This is happening. All these years . . ." She hugged me and held on a bit longer than usual. What a thing to be loved the way she loved me, from beginning to now, even with all I'd lost.

"I love you," I said.

She pulled back and smiled before she snuck a peek at her watch. "I have to go, but you're coming tonight, aren't you?"

"Tonight?"

"My Sunday-night dinner party. And you *are* coming."

"Not if you're trying to set me up with Bill's business partner. Nope. No. Nope."

"Setting up. Seating you next to him. It's all semantics."

I'd told her before but kept it to myself now. Desire burrowed underground the day I discovered Nat's betrayal. It was now interred beneath layers of time and heartbreak. Sitting next to a good-looking man at a dinner party was not going to dig up what might be buried for good.

I shook my head. "I just can't, Lilia. Wynnie comes home tonight, and I must tell Nat."

"You can't use her forever as an excuse not to fall in love again."

"Go on, you," I said. "Get on with your day and tell Bill hello and hug little Bella for her aunt Clara."

"Good luck," she said before she turned and made her way to the far parking lot. Another hour before I faced the music, and I wanted to walk down to the town dock and sit at the water's edge with the London guidebook I'd borrowed from the library.

My legs dangled over the edge of the dock. A young boy wearing a baseball cap too big for his head and his father in overalls stood at the far end with their fishing poles bowed over the dimpled water. A weathered shrimp boat with its nets dangling off the sides and seagulls following in hopes of scraps eased by me.

I opened the guidebook, three years out-of-date, titled *London A to Z*. The first page displayed a map of the city with the blue snake of the River Thames slicing through its middle. A spark, something born of desire and adventure, lit the tender dried wood of my life.

On the back porch of our home that evening, Nat, Wynnie, Dad, and I sat in the wooden chairs. Nat had finished regaling us with their weekend activities when I told him what I'd decided over the weekend—Wynnie and I would sail to England. We'd be gone for two weeks total—nine days on train and sea, and five days in London. We'd pick up Mother's papers, see some educational and historical sites, and then sail straight home.

When I finished telling him, a nervous flutter nestled in my chest. I knew what would come next, and I was right.

"No you aren't," Nat said. "Hell no."

Wynnie ignored him and danced around the back deck. "We're going to museums and art galleries. We're visiting libraries and Westminster, where the queen will be coronated. We're going to the Tower of London and Big Ben!"

I laughed, and Nat slammed his hand on his leg and stood up. "Stop! This is irresponsible. You're in over your head."

"Nat," I said calmly, my voice even, "it's all set. I have a sub for my class. I'll call Wynnie's teacher and tell Jim Alexander that it's an educational trip, which it is. We have tickets on the *Silver Meteor* train to New York City, I have two second-class tickets on the SS *United States*, and Dad has rented us a flat in Covent Garden. It's happening fast, but it's happening in three weeks." I know I sounded high-minded, but I needed the false bravado to get through it.

"No," he said. "How can you afford this?"

Here it was—the part I'd hoped he wouldn't ask about. But I would not lie. "I took the money from my savings. I'll be able to pay it back when I have the sequel translated."

"That's risky, and you know it," he said.

I tried not to laugh at him but failed. "Are you serious, Nat?"

He ignored the obvious gibe and went straight for the heart of it all. "The damage your mother has done to you and to most of the people in her life is enough for me to know that the last thing I want is for you and Wynnie to go running into danger to find her. And to spend what you've spent years saving."

"Into danger? The war has been over for nearly six years. London is full of the most beautiful sights and galleries in the world. You and I wanted to go together. Remember? We made plans, so now suddenly it's not safe?" I kept my voice soft, modulated with effort.

"You and me going is a hell of a lot different than my Wynnie going."

"*Your* Wynnie?"

"Yes, mine too. And none of her doctors are there. What if something happens? What if she needs something and she has an attack?"

"Stop," I said as I watched Wynnie deflate, fall into a chair.

"I forbid it."

"Forbid it?" I coughed out the response.

"I think we all need to calm down," Dad said softly. He took Wynnie's hand to lead her inside.

When the door shut, Nat's face formed itself into a mask of anger, which I knew was nothing more than fear. I had so little sympathy for him left in me, and that broke my heart.

What if Mother knew where so many of her royalties had disappeared to? It made me sick even as I reminded myself to see the man I once loved, the man who existed beneath the addiction and compulsions.

When I was sure Wynnie was out of hearing distance, I used words I'd swallowed for so long. "You're the one who has wanted to translate this sequel for all our marriage. You're the one who said it might help us, and now that we aren't married and you can't spend the money, *now* you don't think it's a good idea?"

"Low blow, Clara. Low and cruel."

"Maybe, but true. Since when have you been able to forbid me? That is as absurd as it gets, Nat. If you ever had any right, you gave it up when your choices broke us apart."

He closed his eyes, and beneath that mask of calm, rage brewed, a river that flooded into our life and marriage when his gambling took hold of him.

He took in a slow breath. "What if she needs an injection?"

"I'll take the medicine with me, just like I always do, anywhere we go."

He glanced out to the bay as if he could see England. "And what day exactly are you planning to leave?"

"The *Silver Meteor* train leaves November thirtieth from Savannah, a twenty-four-hour ride to New York. I have our passports. Then the steamship departs on December first and docks on December fifth. We'll stay for a few days and then turn around and come back."

"I'm serious, Clara. I have a terrible feeling about this."

"I'm serious, too, Nat. This man in London has my mother's papers. All my life I've believed they were at the bottom of the ocean, and I just cannot leave them there in a stranger's library. There is a letter for me in there, and I feel like I've waited my whole life to read it."

He shook his head, and with his lips drawn together, he created a disapproving look that always set me on edge. "I know you have, Clara. You were always so desperate for your mother. I just didn't think you'd do something foolish like take our daughter across the ocean, all for these crumbs of her."

I flinched with the sting of those words.

Desperate.

It was such an ugly word, so thick with the truth.

CHAPTER 12

CHARLIE

London, England

Light glowed from the library windows, beacons in the foggy morning. The gray and creamy Portland stone of 14 St. James's Square, the London Library, overlooked the iron-fenced park.

In Charlie's quest to learn more about the author whose papers were in his father's collection, he stood outside the library around the corner from his parents' home, fifteen minutes before opening time, waiting in line for the door to swing open. That chilly November morning, the men in line chatted about Agatha Christie's new play set to open at the New Ambassadors Theatre, about the Harrow and Wealdstone rail crash, about their support or objections to Churchill. Charlie waved at a neighbor who was walking his beagle across the park.

Clara Harrington from America and her eight-year-old daughter would sail here in two weeks' time. They rejected his tickets and bought their own. Charlie Jameson's logical plan was this: hand over these papers, remove their declarations of charms and secret words from the library, and move on with all the other matters surrounding his father's estate.

As his mother often told him, Charlie's logical plans rarely went as expected, curiosity yanking him as surely as the tides changed the course of unmoored ships. And she was right. He'd been unable to pluck the splinter of this missing author's story from his mind. For a week he'd been researching and reading, trying to find the story of the author's life and understand why she wrote new words, only to abandon them all in Callum Jameson's office.

The heavy wooden door opened, and Charlie climbed the marble steps of the sixteenth-century building and made a beeline for his favorite desk under the eaves in the philosophy section. The back of the library had been bombed only eight years ago, destroying over sixteen thousand books, and still the building stood proud, draped with the scaffolding and dust of repairs. Every room was a solace of reading, with the floor-to-ceiling bookstacks, the plush chairs, the labyrinth of rooms and stairs to hidden corners.

Grief was a strange and oppressive burden, tossing him from fatigue to manic organization, from one all-night bender to a week of solitude, during which he wanted only the sound of birds and the sights of nature, of something alive, growing, and thriving. Now, it seems, he was diving into the world of a stranger, and it was a relief to walk into the familiar lamplit room, where long oak tables glowed with brass desk lamps.

How he loved this building! If it was possible to love a building, and he didn't see why not. People loved food or music, but he was enthralled with the stories inside the stone dwelling. Virginia Woolf, Bram Stoker, and Agatha Christie—all were inspired or wrote in the Victorian building that seemed built of books. This mysterious place with thirty-seven staircases and over seventeen miles of books enchanted him. He thought of all the precious things it stood to protect and hold.

He passed the mythology section when the pang, the ache of missing his father, hit him like a blow to his chest.

"Mr. Jameson!" a voice bellowed, and Charlie turned to see T. S. Eliot, the newly appointed president of the London Library, making his way toward Charlie. He hadn't seen Thomas since Callum's funeral, and Charlie hoped condolences weren't forthcoming. Charlie was right tired of making other people feel better about the passing of his beloved father.

"Hello, Thomas." Charlie held out his hand. "Good day."

"Good day, chap. Here for research?" Thomas's accent was more Boston than British, as he hadn't come to England until he was twenty-five. But dressed in a tweedy three-piece suit, a white collar, and a dark tie, he was thoroughly English in his mannerisms.

"I'm researching an American author named Bronwyn Newcastle Fordham."

Thomas stared at Charlie and frowned, smoothed his oiled hair, and said, "Name sounds familiar."

"She was a famous American author who disappeared in 1927. Wrote a bestselling children's book in 1909. That's about as much as I know."

"Ah! Yes, yes, she was also a Bostonian. I remember now. Wrote that book as a child. What's your interest there?"

"Curious, that's all. Doing a recent investigation into literary mysteries, and her name came up. I assume the library will have something interesting."

"I am sure we will." He threw his arms wide as if to encompass the Victorian temple to literature. "Some believe we should dismantle this place." He stroked his clean-shaven cheek. "An atrocity. Civilization would be damaged by such an idea." He shook his head as if waking from a dream. "You go on now. Do your work." Then he paused. "I miss your father something fierce."

"As do I," Charlie said. "Thank you."

Thomas walked off and Charlie made his way toward his favorite desk—up two flights, to the left, and back down a small side stairwell—only to find someone had beaten him to it.

Choosing instead to sit in the maroon-and-cream reading room, he set down his briefcase and made his way to the reference desk to ask about books by or about Fordham.

Hours later, he'd skimmed *Child Genius: The Wild and Tragic Life of Bronwyn Newcastle Fordham*. Her children's book, *The Middle Place*, sat at his side unopened. The biography contained police notes, scraps of information, and the history of her life. There was only one photo of the tall, willowy woman in the book; she stood in a forest, looking over her shoulder.

Charlie scribbled notes on a paper pad and fell into the lost life of the author. Clara Harrington in South Carolina, who had her own eight-year-old daughter, had herself been abandoned at eight by a mother who sounded both charming and tragic.

From what he gathered, Bronwyn had been wounded by her genius and then scarred by a family who believed they protected her by never sending her to school and then slowly abandoned her in stages.

Excerpt from *The Wild and Tragic Life of Bronwyn Newcastle Fordham*
BRIAN DAVIS

Bronwyn Newcastle Fordham was destined to become a writer. Born in the forested lands of New Hampshire in 1897, no one knew how early that prophecy would come to pass. Her parents, Martha and Wendall, understood they had been gifted with a special child by the time Bronwyn was speaking in full sentences at ten months old. At two years old she insisted on knowing every letter and its sound and then formed those letters with crayon on coloring paper, trying to string them together into words.

The label *genius* was first whispered in hopefulness and then uttered out loud with hubris. Out of the genetic threads of their ancestry and a wise choice in partner, Martha and Wendall unwittingly but proudly produced a verifiable child prodigy. Martha and Wendall rearranged their life, for there would be no common school for Bronwyn, no children as playmates or the silliness of small games. They would treat her as the extraordinary creature she was born to be. She was reading books by three years old and making up her own stories by three and a half. She played the violin and piano and memorized long passages of poetry before she turned four years old.

This family of three lived in a rambling, brown-shingled house with acres of forest out the back door, piles of books in every room, and warm fires during the coldest months. Bronwyn had wild brown hair and large brown eyes that absorbed everything around her. Like the stories she would one day write, Bronwyn saw the animation and light in every living thing in the natural world. She was stifled when inside the house unless she was reading or writing.

Bronwyn reveled in the natural world behind their home, digging for seeds, roots, and answers to the questions that kept her buzzing: Was there a reason for it all? Was there a force that made things grow? What and who was she to this world? She was most preoccupied by what she could *not* see, what lay just beyond the edges of her sight and knowledge, the unseen world, the invisible world, the one she believed was just as real and that she could find if she just tried hard enough.

She built forts in the forest and then insisted her mother and father spend the night outside with her, for she was afraid to miss anything the natural world might tell her. She collected flowers, bug carcasses, and rocks. She kept these things on windowsills and shelves all over the house. She dragged her father's typewriter into her room and began to write stories of fairies and imaginary creatures.

Her mother told her of the Tír na nÓg and the magical world beneath the earth in Ireland, where time passed differently, one year there equaling one minute in our world. Bronwyn believed in this land, and she wanted to create one just like it. Martha taught Bronwyn Latin and Greek, and both seemed as casually easy for Bronwyn as English.

Bronwyn was shunned by children her own age, something she never understood. Teased about her references to astronomy, nature, and literature, she never found a way to connect with the children around her. Sitting on the hill outside her house, she watched other children play tag and felt excluded in a way that left her angry and deeply hurt at the same time. By the time she was near to eight years old, she understood that the only friends she might find were the ones she created, so she began to build her fantasy and imaginary worlds, as well as her own language.

The adults who visited her parents and gathered in the living room to talk about academic theory bored Bronwyn. "Find more interesting friends," Bronwyn once told her parents after sitting at the top of the staircase and listening to the party below.

Martha and Wendall didn't dare have any more children, for who could match Bronwyn's precocious spirit? No one. This creature of such intelligence and imagination made them believe that they'd been given more than they could ever ask for in a child. Anyone else would be a disappointment.

On Bronwyn's eighth birthday, she wore a dress of pink taffeta and a headband of yellow silk. After she blew out the candles in the buttery icing of an angel food cake, she announced that she'd made a gift for her parents. All those hours at the typewriter were for a purpose, she told them. She'd written a book called *The Middle Place*, a magical story about a young girl named Emjie who could move between her world and the world of faeries.

"Just you wait," she told them. "There is a shocking ending that will keep you guessing."

She understood suspense and drama, having already read enough Shakespeare and Kipling, enough Dickens and Melville, to know that a story must have conflict and mystery, love and hate, romance and evil.

There were others there that night for the party—her three older cousins and two sets of grandparents, an aunt and uncle— but only her parents understood that she was serious, that their eight-year-old daughter had actually penned a novel.

But no one ever read that version of *The Middle Place* because that same night flat, black clouds moved quickly across a stormy New Hampshire sky. The pages sat on the kitchen table, with a blue ribbon wrapped tightly around the pile of story. A twister touched down in the small, quiet neighborhood, ripping the roof from the Fordham home and flooding the first floor. Bronwyn's story was scattered across the neighborhood and forests of Willingham. The pages were lost for good.

For months, locals would find a page here or there and not know what it was, a remnant of something larger to be sure, but of what they had no clue, and they'd toss a page into the trash or leave it in the gutter where they found it.

While a tarp covered the Fordham house and workmen dried the water from the floors and carpets, Bronwyn spent weeks searching the forest for her story. She wept to her parents that it was possible that Emjie sent the storm to keep the story from being told, that Emjie didn't want her existence to be exposed.

This was the first time Bronwyn's parents feared that Bronwyn's imagination might be a bit *too* much, that their isolation of her hadn't done her any favors. It was the first time they tried to get her some help, some professional help from a specialist in child prodigies.

Under the psychiatrist's direction, Bronwyn's schedule grew stricter, her schooling more focused, and tutors were brought in. With these new structures around her, a seed of sadness found its way into the soil of Bronwyn's heart, and with each day it seemed to grow. Her freedom was curtailed, and panic blossomed from melancholy. The cure for feelings she'd never felt and had a hard time labeling could be found only in writing—Bronwyn would not let Emjie be scattered to the winds. She set out to write the story again, this time using the carbon copies she'd seen her mother use when she wrote stories for the newspaper.

She had to begin again, to start over, and by the time she had rewritten the novel at eleven years old, her parents understood that what they had once been proud of was creating a fracture in their child's psyche that might be far too deep to mend. Bronwyn's imagination was too bright and too clear, and it terrified her family. She believed in make-believe. She told them of her own world as she babbled in a language she'd created, saying that the words they'd taught her weren't enough for the beauty of the unseen world.

This wasn't the kind of intelligence they'd expected or wanted. This kind of wild intelligence needed to be curtailed and bound.

The strain on the marriage pulled a worn rope to its breaking point. When Wendall announced his great love for his secretary and moved to New York for a new job with a publishing house, Martha and Bronwyn were left stunned and bereft. Wendall unequivocally completed the triumvirate of their world.

Wendall had decided that quite possibly genius wasn't so wonderful. He wanted an ordinary life—a wife and a child who didn't read by three and sing songs created of her own language and rattle the house with her questions, worrying them with her disappearance into the wilds of New Hampshire.

"She's yours now," he told his wife. "You fought me at every turn to do it your way, and now you can."

And he was gone.

From that moment on, Bronwyn was reckless and irresponsible, a behavior born of confusion and heartbreak.

One afternoon in November of 1908, when Bronwyn was eleven years old, she rode the train from New Hampshire to New York and begged her father to return. Meanwhile, Mother wrote letters and enlisted friends in their campaign. Nothing worked. He stayed in New York with the petite secretary, and then he married her, and they had their own children. His penance? He helped publish his daughter's book.

Twelve-year-old Bronwyn's novel, *The Middle Place*, was released in 1909 to great acclaim.

The success didn't sate her broken heart, and at only fourteen years old, bereft, Bronwyn somehow talked her way onto a steamship as a cabin boy, taking up with a captain twenty years her senior. She then convinced her mother to sail the world with her so they could write about their adventures together. Eventually her mother became disenchanted with a life at sea and with a daughter she did not understand, and dropped Bronwyn off with family friends in San Francisco.

Abandoned to strangers, this wounded girl turned sixteen while living with a family she didn't know. Miserable, she ran away to eventually be discovered in a slum hotel in downtown San Francisco. She was promptly sent to a juvenile detention facility, which caused such despair she tried to jump out a window.

Finally, Martha came to retrieve Bronwyn, and they lived together in Boston, where Bronwyn took a job as a copy editor, a daily chore that she described as moths eating her soul.

Then came along Timothy Harrington. *True love.* And together they moved to Bluffton, South Carolina, where they settled down and raised their daughter, Clara Harrington.

Charlie looked up from his reading. This might have been where Charlie could say, "And thus her happy ending." But alas, it wasn't.

Afternoon light fell lazily through the windows when Charlie read:

These are believed to be the last words Bronwyn Newcastle Fordham ever wrote:

> I want the sky to split open.
> I want the sky to split open and reveal the secrets of the
> Universe.
> I want the sky to split open, to rend down the middle and
> rain down its stars and its secrets. If destruction is the result,
> so be it, for I want—no, I need—to know if there is anything
> that truly matters beyond what I can see.
> I want the sky to split open . . .

To no avail, scholars, students, and journalists have been searching for her lost sequel and the dictionary of her language ever since.

Charlie had read enough, and his mind was full with facts of a woman's life that somehow intersected with his father's. He roused himself
to leave the library. He'd promised Archie he'd stop by the bank to sign
some papers, before heading on to a gig at the Penny Pub with the Lads.

After gathering his books he waved goodbye to a few friendly faces
before entering the sunlight of a crisp afternoon in St. James's Square. It
was always a shock to leave the hushed rooms and dusty light.

He flung his briefcase strap over his shoulder and headed toward the
bank, his thoughts circling around a secret language that a woman from
America had created and hidden from the world.

He thought about the daughter, Clara, and the granddaughter, and
tried to imagine them. He thought about his father and whether he had
anything to do with the author's disappearance. He thought about the
curse of Bronwyn's genius and wondered how a father could desert a
daughter after turning her into the prodigy that she became.

He was astute enough to realize that he was avoiding his own life by
dwelling on another's. He sought a respite from grief in the mystery of
a woman whose papers were hidden in his father's library, a connection
he didn't understand but one that lured him irresistibly into her secret
world.

CHAPTER 13

CLARA

The Atlantic Ocean

"Hallo!"

I startled and sat up, embarrassed to be found asleep. Wynnie was dozing on my shoulder, and we were slumped into the couch of the ship's library. I blinked and closed my mouth. What a sight I must be, draped in my yellow slicker, my hair damp with rain, my head back and my mouth wide open in sleep.

On day three aboard the SS *United States*, the ocean liner had plunged and risen with a storm, and Wynnie and I found shelter from our seasickness in the library.

A man with a ruddy complexion under white hair and with a beard like Santa Claus stood in the library. His voice interrupted a dream in which I was falling, falling, falling through a wide-open sky, until I remembered I could fly. I was just about to lift my wings.

"Hello." I blinked to clear my eyes. "So sorry. We must have dozed off."

"I'd say so." He laughed and adjusted his tartan vest. The aroma of pipe smoke and something woodsy surrounded him, and it was surprisingly comforting.

"The ship," I said. "It's . . . still."

"Yes, the storm has passed. Or we sailed right through it to the other side."

"Oh, thank goodness. I wasn't doing so well, as you can see."

"No one but the hardiest of us do well in seas like that." His British accent was now obvious, and I wondered if this was the type of man Charlie Jameson might be—an older man with a beard and rimless glasses, an air of sophisticated kindness, and a quick laugh. I hadn't asked Charlie anything about himself. How old was he? What was his job? I knew only his address near St. James's Square.

Wynnie woke up and rubbed at her eyes. "I am so happy we're off that roller coaster," she said.

She caught the gaze of the man who stood in front of us and went quiet.

He nodded at her with a smile, and she relaxed. He pointed to my lap—a copy of *The Middle Place*, which Wynnie had found on the shelves. "Good book, isn't it? It was one of my children's favorites," he said. "I always found it a bit whimsical, to be frank—a little child flitting between worlds?" He laughed good-naturedly. "Probably a deficit of imagination on my part."

"The author is my grandma," Wynnie said with a smile, and slipped out of her rain jacket.

"Your grandma, you say?" The man lifted one eyebrow and sat in the green velvet armchair across from us.

"Wynnie." I squeezed her leg.

He smiled, one that was both curious and ready for conversation. It had been this way for most of the journey: people eager for chatting, seeming to grow weary of their traveling companion and ready for new company. Our dinner table was composed of two couples, one on their honeymoon and the other an older couple on their way for a tour of England. They spoke to Wynnie and me more than to each other.

"Are you from England, I assume?" I asked him, desperate for a change of subject from my mother and her novel.

"Cumbria, the Lake District," he said. "I'm on my return journey home after a visit with my son in New York City. Why he wants to live there is beyond me." He shook his head and exhaled through pursed lips. "After the war, he'd had just about enough of England. I believe he'll come home eventually, but for now he seems quite happy with the hustle and bustle of a city that would drive me to distraction."

"I think that's why people like it," I said. "It drives them to distraction."

"For some, maybe. My son says it is the people, the interesting humanity. He can't get enough of it—the energy and verve of it all."

"Not for me," I said. "Give me my small town, some paints and canvas, my little girl"—I pulled her close—"and a wide-open view to the water."

"Exactly!" He clapped his hands together and then reached into his breast pocket to retrieve his pipe and a packet of tobacco. "Do you mind?"

"Oh, not at all," I said. "But don't be offended if we leave. Honestly, you are welcome to your pipe, but Wynnie here has sensitive lungs, and sometimes—"

"Oh no, then. No. I'd rather forgo my pipe than have you two lovely angels leave me."

I believed we'd moved on from Wynnie's declaration until he leaned forward, placed his palms on his knees, and spoke to her again: "Your grandmother, you say?"

"Yes, she's my mother's mother." She tapped my cheek in an endearing little motion. "That's a grandmother."

He looked at me and a sparkle filled his green eyes behind rimless spectacles. "Is that so? Or does your sprite here have a wild and wonderful imagination?"

I would not lie in front of Wynnie. "She does have a wild and wonderful imagination, but also, yes, the author is . . . was my mother."

"And this her only novel, if I remember correctly?"

"Yes."

"Why didn't she follow a book this famous?"

"She disappeared twenty-five years ago."

"And we're going to find out what happened to her," Wynnie said.

I should have been stricter with Wynnie about what to tell strangers, but she hadn't said a word at our dinners or social hours. Not a peep at the shuffleboard or the movie theater. Nothing to anyone until now, in this library.

"Are you journeying to see her play?" he asked.

I was fully awake now. "Her play?"

"Yes, indeed. Well, I don't rightly know if it is *her* play, but it is a play in Cumbria based on that book you have there on your lap. It started maybe five years ago or so at the local playhouse. It's called *A World Apart.* I always hope it will end differently, but it never does." He laughed. "I'm assuming that is why any of us see something over and over—either we hope this time it will end differently or we love the magic of a particular story."

"Yes, I don't think you're the only one. I still wish it would have ended another way."

The man settled back in his seat. "I'm Finneas Andrews, by the way. I'm sorry for not offering a proper introduction when I burst in here."

"Clara Harrington." I held out my hand. "And this is my daughter, Wynnie." We shook hands. "And it would have been hard to offer a proper introduction when I was asleep," I said.

His laugh echoed in the room, a wonderful one that could ease any tension. "Well now, how interesting that the author is your mother."

"I must be honest—I don't know anything about this play you're talking about. Can you tell me more?" I was confused, because surely I would have heard about this. Dad needed to give permission for every production, reprint, or version of *The Middle Place*. But he'd never told me about a play in England.

Wynnie picked up the book from my lap. "In the play, does Emjie wear a skirt of ferns?"

"Oh yes she does," he said.

"Mama!" Wynnie placed the book on the coffee table. "We must go. We are going to . . ." She looked at the man.

"Cumbria: the most beautiful part of England and quite possibly the planet. But I am decidedly biased about my view of the world."

I patted Wynnie's leg. "We're visiting London. Not the Lake District."

"It's an easy train ride," he said. "But I'm sure whatever you must do in London will fill your days with great pleasure." He glanced between us. "Are you truly going to look for her?"

"No," I answered quickly. "We are not. She left when I was eight years old; she's a mystery to us, just as she is to the rest of the world. But . . ." I shrugged and tilted my head toward Wynnie. "A child's heart never gives up hoping."

"You're right," he said. "And I'd wager that a daughter's heart never gives up, either."

"You're right," I told him, feeling a swell of tears. "But dreams are dreams."

"Oh no, no," he said, and smiled at me. "Dreams are so much more than that. They are visions of the future, they are whispers of our desires, they are hope. We cannot and we must not live without dreams, Clara."

I laughed. "Mr. Andrews, if I may ask, exactly what is it that you do in Cumbria?"

"I had a psychoanalysis practice in London but longed for the land of home and returned to the family farm and our Herdwick sheep years ago."

"Then for you, dreams indeed are more than just dreams."

Finneas nodded and smiled before glancing at Wynnie, with the book in her lap. "You like to read adventure stories?"

"I do!" Her smile widened, her eyes bright behind her glasses.

He walked to the shelves, ran his hand along the books until he made a noise. "Aha!" He pulled one out and brought it to Wynnie. "*Swallows and Amazons*. It's set in the Lake District. I believe you'll love it."

Wynnie immediately opened the illustrated book with the mirrored lakes, rounded mountains, and pebbled shorelines. "Look, Mama!" she said. "These look like your paintings."

"The author painted them himself," Finneas said.

I remembered Mother had once read this book to me. What happened to the book, I had no idea, but I was happy to see it again, like an old friend.

CHAPTER 14

CLARA

England

The docks of Southampton appeared as an industrial-style Monet painting, blurry and clouded by fog. Iron pilings and stumps of moorings reached above the concrete wharf. Ships and sailboats, tugboats, and the long needle of steamships filled the waterways. Feathered smoke rose from striped stacks. This was not how I'd imagined England, this workaday port shrouded and hidden beneath the gray.

"Mama?" Wynnie snuggled close as we stood at the railing. "This isn't . . . very pretty?"

"No," I said. "I'd have to say you're right, but this is only the port. The city of London itself is a jewel. We'll get there."

We'd adjusted to the languid time spent at sea, where there was no rush to be anywhere because we were carried along in the womb of the ship's steel hull, in the simplicity of days I hadn't experienced since summers with Mother as a very young child, when it felt like the world was waiting for me.

Wynnie and I read books from the immense library. We ate in a dining room swathed in chintz and made small talk with the other passengers, who seemed to loll about in a happy stupor. We learned to play table tennis and shuffleboard, laughing at our ineptitude. We listened rapt to the orchestra at dinner and slept more than we ever did at home, the lullaby of the sea a sedative. Often we'd stand at the edge of the promenade while Wynnie stared at the churning waters, willing a whale to appear. We didn't talk about what we might or might not find when we arrived in England, or the possibility of my mother being in London—it was as if we'd made a silent pact between us to each wonder alone about her.

The ship glided toward the dock, and Finneas stood by Wynnie's side. If we had sailed a few more days at sea, I'd call him a friend.

A blue-and-white tugboat guided us to the docks. The ocean liner serenely eased its way in, and I wondered how a hulk of iron this large could glide like a ballerina into such a small space. Men hustled on the dock, grabbing ropes; sailors scuttled to and fro on the starboard deck where we stood, and then all went still.

We'd arrived.

"It's a sure pea-souper," Finneas said.

"A what?" I shivered in the cold and brittle air. My scarf and gloves didn't seem a match for the wind. I had not expected this weather.

He ran his hands through the air. "It's a combination of fog and smoke."

"Why pea soup?" Wynnie asked, placing her mittened hands in her coat pockets, ducking her chin into her woolen scarf.

"You'll see," he said. "The air turns a bit green."

"Green air?" Wynnie asked. "Yuck."

"Yes, sometimes it is."

The horn blared our arrival, and Finneas bid us goodbye with our promises to visit him if we made it to Cumbria. I knew we wouldn't go, but it was lovely to think so.

After disembarking, finding our way to a taxi, and bundling our valises and cases into the trunk of the vehicle, we were soon on a train for the two-hour journey to London.

After the train ride, we caught another taxi and wound our ways through streets shrouded in fog—lanterns flickering, people bustling past buildings and towering pinnacles, a ribbon of a river to our left—and then we stopped in front of a row of townhomes. "You're here, ma'am. Would you like me to help you with your bags?"

"That would be lovely," I told him.

Dad had arranged for this rental flat, and now here we were, dragging our cases down a long hallway painted a dreary industrial brown. At least we were on the ground floor: number seventeen. I opened the door, and was I expecting something different from what I saw? I must have been, because I smiled with relief. It wasn't my favorite trait, to be sure, but the way a space and place felt and looked, the welcoming feeling of it all or not, affected me in a way that could set me on edge if it was too dreary.

We stood in an open space with floor-to-ceiling windows that looked over a city so veiled that the streetlights pricked the fog like stars at midday. Car headlights and gas lanterns struggled.

"It's like we're inside a milk bottle," Wynnie said, and ran in a circle around the room. "It's perfect."

It *was* perfect. A large, high-ceilinged room surrounded by light-oak paneled walls and worn hardwood floors. A crystal chandelier hung from the center, and cream-colored furniture filled the room—a couch and two chairs. A rectangular wooden coffee table and a console with a battered TV, antennae pointing east and west. I took my valise from our cabbie. "Your city looks like an impressionist painting right now."

He laughed. "You know, it is rumored Monet came here to practice painting the light in fog."

"I believe it."

I dug into my purse and pulled out some shillings. "Thank you for helping us."

He bowed out and the door clicked shut. Wynnie walked to the window. "Let's unpack," I said to her back. "And then away straight to Mr. Jameson's place in St. James's Square. I mapped it out and we'll grab a taxi."

"Are you nervous, Mama?" Wynnie asked without turning around.

"I am." I went to stand beside her.

"Sometimes we don't really want what we wish for."

"Wynnie, where did you hear something like that?"

"*The Middle Place,*" she said.

"Ah." I exhaled. "Yes."

CHAPTER 15

CHARLIE

London, England

Charlie paced his childhood home waiting on the woman and child who were meant to arrive in the next hour.

Moira, the Jamesons' housemaid of many years, bustled upstairs. Mum was away in the country. Since his father died, it'd been said numerous times that Charlie might as well move into this St. James's Square house. But this was the place of his youth, not of his adulthood. The oak floors creaked, and he knew where to stop to avoid the house's song under his feet. His nursery was on the third level, his playroom on the second, and both were remnants of another time.

Now, he sat for a quick lunch of grilled sausages and tomatoes that Moira had prepared. The Fordham biography lay next to him on the mahogany table with the family crest in the center. He'd been reading the book in slow bits over the past week, noting how the writer's life was completely unorthodox until she met Timothy Harrington, settled down, and moved to South Carolina.

He skimmed an article once published in *Vanity Fair*, in which Bronwyn and Timothy spoke of their first meeting.

Bronwyn Newcastle Fordham: We met on a snow-white day in January. I sat in the library, not a student, but young enough to be one. I was meant to be working on an essay for *Harper's Bazaar* about my travels to Tahiti on a sailing schooner. But instead, I worked on creating a dictionary of my invented language. I lifted my pen to see Timothy standing under the domed light as if life had spotlit him for me. I stared; he felt familiar and deeply intimate, as if I'd known him before—a long time before—and then forgotten him. And there he stood, waiting for me in the Harvard Library.

Timothy Harrington: I was there looking for an edition of *Great Expectations* for my literature class. I felt her eyes on me, a pleasant sensation, a tingling, and warmth. I turned to see who had found me, and I saw Bronwyn sitting at a desk beneath an east-facing window. Snow fell outside and gathered on the sill in small drifts. Her right cheek rested in her palm as she propped herself on her elbow and looked at me with a playful smile. Her thick glasses created mirrors in the light, and I saw my own face in her eyes, something I will never forget. I saw myself in her eyes.

BNF: He walked over to say hello and spied my work on the desk. The first thing he said to me was . . .

TH: What is that?

(Laughter)

BNF: Not even a hello.

TH: And she told me, "It's my language."

BNF: Mine, I told him. And I'd never told anyone before. Well, except for my god-awful father and distant mother. They had once cared . . . but now . . .

TH: But now I cared.

BNF: We haven't stopped talking since.

This account was so delightful. Until now, reading about Bronwyn, Charlie found a bitter brew of a short life with so much tragedy. So why, after such a happy marriage, did she run?

The author, Brian Davis, believed it was the 1927 fire that sent Bronwyn away. He surmised that the fireman's death and the police coming to question her caused her to panic and run.

Charlie now understood that Fordham's *The Middle Place* sequel was the mystery that kept her alive in certain literary circles. A lost novel written in a secret language was bait for anyone who loved a good mystery. If Charlie hadn't read her biography, he would have thought she had disappeared on purpose to gain notoriety and interest. But she eschewed notoriety; she avoided being known.

As Charlie folded his napkin and rose from the table, nervous energy ran through him while he waited for Bronwyn's daughter. He found himself again in the library.

Charlie ran through the numerous options of how this language had found its way into his father's library, just as he'd been doing for three weeks.

The first assumption was that his father had found it in an old antique shop or at an auction. But the personal letter to Clara led Charlie to believe it was much closer to the bone than a simple find. Or it could have been dropped off by a friend or given to him by someone else to hold for safety. Charlie's mind rattled from morning to night with unfounded guesses.

The front doorbell jangled through the house.

Charlie walked toward the foyer, imagining the woman and child who stood on the other side on the flagstone entryway. He prepared himself for Clara Harrington with the lyrical southern accent. He imagined her as a tall and handsome woman, someone with the aquiline nose and almond-shaped eyes of her lost mother, whom he'd seen in the one photo in the biography.

Charlie walked down the hallway, past the gold-framed stern faces of his ancestors, and around the center table, where winterberry and myrtle flowers spilled from an iron urn.

He opened the door.

The woman on the threshold was startlingly different from the one he'd expected. She was tall, about that he'd been correct, but she was a wisp of a thing, nearly fragile, bundled in her coat and hat and gloves, her chin tucked into her scarf. Chestnut curls framing her face, a shy smile on red lips, and round blue eyes beneath thick eyelashes. She emanated a sense of still beauty, a *caílin álainn*.

"Hallo," he said. "You must be Clara and Wynnie."

CHAPTER 16

CLARA

London, England

"Yes, hello," I said, and held out my free right hand while Wynnie clung to my left. The man held my gloved hand for a moment, our gazes locking. With his curly dark hair and thick eyebrows low over the deepest brown eyes, he appeared accessible and friendly, someone you'd trust. He was clean-shaven, with a slight furrow between his eyes as if perpetually curious.

So no, he did not look like Finneas Andrews, not one bit; he looked more like Clark Gable cast as a British library owner. "And you must be Mr. Jameson," I said.

As if he had just remembered he still held my hand, he dropped it quickly. "Yes, yes, call me Charlie, and come in, then!" He opened the door wider.

Behind him gaped a foyer with a creamy marble floor and golden-oak paneled walls, a space larger than my entire kitchen and living room combined. In the center, an urn of flowers spilled pink and cream petals onto a circular mahogany table, and on the walls hung gilt frames around oil portraits of men and women I assumed were relations. So many portraits. A curved stairway wound upward against the wall with a gleaming wooden banister, a lion carved into its main balustrade. The only time I'd ever seen anything like this was in movies.

This was quiet grandeur.

Was it possible Mother left us for wealth and surety, for gilt frames and winding staircases and handsome men with titles like *Lord*?

Wynnie and I entered and shed our coats, which Charlie took in his arms. "Come," he said. "Let's get you a cuppa. It's a pea-souper out there."

Wynnie's eyes went wide, chandelier light glinting on the lens of her glasses. "I thought people weren't allowed to live in museums."

Charlie's laughter boomed through the foyer. "It's not a museum. This is a home."

Wynnie set her shoulders back. "Your home?"

"My parents'. Yes."

"Oh, wow." Then she placed her hand over her mouth as if she'd already said or done the wrong thing.

"Come see the museum's artifacts," he said with a teasing lilt to his voice, making Wynnie giggle as we followed him through a curved entryway that led to a drawing room on the right of the hallway. Tall windows allowed light between the blue damask curtains, the fog beyond creating a sense of time and place unmoored. In a brick fireplace big enough for Wynnie to walk into, a fire crackled and spit sparks up the chimney. Flames charred the brick, and a pile of ash lay gray and high like dirty snow beneath the logs. The mantel was carved of oak, and above it hung a portrait of an older man sitting regal in a large chair.

A tripping feeling from my heart pressed against the pale-blue cashmere sweater I'd bought just for this trip. It would be like me to come this far and then pass out in front of the handsome British man with my mother's papers.

"Make yourselves comfortable," Charlie said. "I'll hang your coats and have Moira bring tea."

"Thank you so much," I said. "We"—I touched Wynnie's shoulder— "are so grateful." I paused, for although I was itching to get my hands on the satchel, to see the object I'd been wondering about for twenty-five years, I also wanted to pause in this warm home. "What a respite this home feels like after the travel."

"I'm glad that you could both come. You must need warming up, as I'm sure it's been a long journey."

He walked out, presumably for our tea, and Wynnie and I sat on the emerald-green velvet couch. She snuggled next to me. Outside, the bustling St. James's Park was shrouded in fog, the bare trees soft-edged and the iron benches more like ideas than objects.

Wynnie and I looked at each other and raised our eyebrows in an unspoken *Can you believe this?* just as a woman bustled in carrying a silver tray with dainty porcelain teacups edged in gold, a teapot hidden beneath a quilted green cozy, and a plate of creamy scones. Little silver bowls with clotted cream and raspberry jam edged the tray. And then finally a pitcher with milk so frothy I wondered if she'd whipped it.

"Hallo!" she said with such eagerness I thought of a puppy romping around the room. She set the tray down and grinned. "How was your journey? Are you tired? Do you need anything else? Do you like cream and sugar with your tea or just plain? You are both so darling."

She did not take a breath between questions. "Our journey was long and beautiful. We aren't so tired ... yet. And we both love cream," I told her with a gentle smile.

"And sugar," Wynnie said.

Moira moved to pour the tea and I held up my hand. "We can do it. Please don't bother."

She lifted her face to mine. Her cheeks ruddy and her eyes a dark brown, the same color as her hair, which was pulled back into a lace cap. A young woman, maybe in her late twenties. Her uniform was ironed so precisely that I imagined her each morning pressing it in her room, wanting to impress her employer. She smiled and hustled out.

I poured my tea, added cream and sugar, and handed Wynnie a scone on a fragile china plate. "Be careful," I said.

She took a bite and groaned in exaggerated style. "Oh, Mama, this is the best cookie I've ever eaten."

"It's called a scone," I said. "And you'll love it even more with that clotted cream on it."

She scooped a large dollop onto the scone and then with a full mouth said, "Can't I have tea?"

"I'm afraid the caffeine might make you feel funny. You've never had it."

She was content with her snack and leaned against me before pointing up. "I think that's the other Mr. Jameson, the one who died," she whispered.

I looked to the portrait of a man who could be Charlie if he were older, sitting in an ornate wooden chair. A brown-and-white-speckled spaniel sat next to him, and the man's hand rested on the dog's head. A small smile played on his lips, and if I wanted, I could imagine the man saying "Hallo" in a booming voice.

"How many people do you think live here?" Wynnie asked me.

"Just one now," Charlie said as he returned to the room. "My mum. And not very often at that."

The satchel dangled from his right hand, and he set it on the coffee-colored lacquer table, shoving aside large books of maps and art.

Here was the thing with an object that had held a mythical quality for all your life: it was just an object when it all came down to it. A beat-up leather case with an eagle-shaped brass buckle. It didn't shimmer, nor did a golden light rise from its center whispering, *Here are all the answers you've been seeking.*

Wynnie stood up and walked to the coffee table. She placed her hand on the satchel and then knelt before it. "It's real," she said.

"Yes," Charlie said, breaking the reverie. "It's very real."

Wynnie looked at me over her shoulder. "Mama, may I open it?"

I nodded.

Wynnie undid the buckle and then took a breath and lifted the flap, let it drop back. There was the green silk lining and there was the pile of papers inside. No doubt—this was the satchel that Mother had carried out the back door of our home twenty-five years ago. The satchel she'd taken into the boat in the middle of the night. This was the case that literary enthusiasts were seeking.

"Mama," she said, "I'm afraid to touch the papers."

I patted the couch next to me. "Sit. I'll get them."

I lifted the satchel carefully, bringing it to my lap and peeking inside to see the sealed envelope Charlie had described to me on the phone. My breath caught just seeing my name in the cursive script I'd know anywhere.

I took the envelope and slid it into my purse, separating it from the rest of the papers. I mustered all my willpower not to rip it open, but I needed to read my mother's letter in private.

I slipped out the papers and put the case aside to set the pile on my lap. It was three inches thick, with various sorts of paper, as if collected over time and with imagination. On the top sat a piece of paper with one sentence handwritten in cursive, a sentence that would need to be translated once I made my way through the makeshift dictionary.

My fingers tingled with the memory of my mother's oak writing desk with the dark-green blotter, a black Remington typewriter, and scattered papers with words I could not read. Cigarette butts in a glass tray, a bird's nest and assorted feathers, seashells, and cracked pods spilling their seedy contents.

I shivered.

"Are you cold?" Charlie asked.

"I'm fine," I told him, shaking off the image of this language on a different desk in another room.

"She always says that," Wynnie said, and then imitated my voice nearly perfectly: "'I'm fine.'"

Charlie laughed and walked to the fireplace, dropped in another log, and stoked it with an iron poker. "Sounds like your mum might be British. We are always all right, thank you very much for asking."

The tense atmosphere in the room broke, and I told Charlie: "Southerners and Brits aren't so different in that way." I placed the papers back inside the bag and snapped the buckle shut. "May I see where you found this? I have so many questions."

"So do I," he said. "And sadly, I don't think I have very many answers. This is as mysterious to me as it is to you, I am quite sure."

"You've never seen this?" I patted the satchel. "Before you called me?"

"No, never."

We rose and followed Charlie down the oak-paneled hallway, the aroma of damp wool and lemon polish around us.

As soon as Charlie opened the thick wooden door with the egg-shaped brass knob, the library encircled us with books. The lights of a glowing wooden chandelier sent long shadows across the desk, the shelves, and the gold-framed maps hanging on the edges of the bookshelves. I'd assumed, wrongly, that libraries like this existed only in castles or universities.

"Wow," Wynnie said, and ran into the middle of the room. "Look at this! I could live in here."

"My father fairly well did," Charlie told her.

I stood, silent, and tried to imagine my mother in here. Had she once stood in this library, handed over her papers to the man whose oil portrait hung above a fireplace in the drawing room?

"Where did you find it?" I asked.

Charlie walked to the left bank of shelves and then squatted down to rest his hand on top of a set of large wooden boxes. "Here, above the map storage."

"How did you even notice?" I swept my hand around the room. "There are thousands of books in here. Boxes and leather and—"

"Nothing was *ever* out of place in my father's library, and this was." He walked to the lectern. "Whatever is placed here is something he is studying or reading. Nothing haphazard, nothing without thought."

Wynnie walked to join him and stood on her tiptoes to gaze at the map. "It's of Cumbria." She squinted through her glasses. "Year fourteen twenty-three." Wynnie looked at me, and I read her mind as if she'd said it out loud—Finneas on the ship told us, *There's a play in Cumbria based on that book.*

I shook my head no. The room now hummed with hints. This family was tied to my mother, that much was obvious, and if Charlie Jameson was hiding anything, I didn't want to push him away. *Careful, slow,* I thought.

Wynnie made her way around the room. I could see that there was nothing out of sorts in this room. Yes, a satchel on a bottom shelf would be noticed.

Wynnie pointed at an oil painting over the fireplace. "Who is that beautiful lady?"

"My mum. Philippa."

"She is beautiful," I said.

"Yes. That's her wedding portrait," he told us.

I stepped closer. The portrait displayed a young woman standing in a garden surrounded by roses, an arbor of climbing jasmine arched over where she sat. Her blond hair was high in a chignon and a multistrand pearl necklace adorned her neck. The dress shimmered bright green, cinched at the waist with skirts that blended into the garden. "She likes gardens, I assume?"

He laughed. "Very good deduction. Yes, she *is* a garden in many ways.

That's where she is now—at our country house, where she spends her days in the gardens, or, now in December, in the greenhouse."

"Country house?" Wynnie asked. "It sounds so fancy."

"It is," I said to her.

I swear Charlie blushed. "Not as fancy as you imagine. It's been in her family for over a hundred years."

I nodded. "Does she know about this? About my mother's satchel?"

"No. The letter said to tell only you."

"But maybe she'll know something," I said, feeling a surge of hope. "Maybe she knows where your father got this, where—"

"She won't know."

"Would you mind asking her?" Frustration bubbled, and I assumed he heard it in my voice.

"Listen," Charlie said with a gentle tone, "she just lost her husband of many years. She's in mourning. This library was my father's. No one else came in here unless invited, so my mum would have no idea why the papers of a woman who disappeared twenty-five years ago would be here."

Wynnie came to my side then, sensing the change in his tone. She took my hand.

"I understand," I said.

"Anything I know about your mother is something I've learned in the last weeks by reading articles and her biography. I don't know why her papers are here. I wish I could help; I really do." He paused. "Where are you staying?"

"In Covent," I said, and told him the address.

"But we're going to the Victoria and Albert Museum today!" Wynnie told him. "Twelve and a half acres and forty-five galleries." She paused dramatically. "And a library even bigger than this one. Over seven hundred thousand books. Can you believe it? Seven hundred thousand."

Charlie laughed, his face again relaxing. "How do you know such things?"

Wynnie tilted her head. "I read."

"Of course you do."

I squeezed Wynnie's hand and told Charlie: "She notices everything. Every. Thing. And then remembers it."

"Oh, to have that skill."

"I think we should be going. We don't want to be a bother, and we have plans for the museum."

He smiled and motioned for us to leave the library, and we walked out together. He retrieved our coats and hats from hooks in a small room to the right of the front door. We were buttoned and zipped when Charlie said, "You know how to find me if you need me."

He opened the door, and we were met with a bank of fog, seeing only about ten feet in front of us. "Find you?" I asked. "How do you find anyone or anything in this?"

He held out his hand and wiped his fingers through the misty air. "It's a thick one, but it will pass. Always does."

Wynnie coughed and placed her hand on her throat. "Does it always burn?"

I bent down and buttoned her jacket to the top, bundled her scarf tighter. "It burns?"

"In my throat," she said.

"It's the sulfur," he said. "Sometimes people are sensitive to it. It's normal."

"It's not normal for Wynnie," I said.

"It's asthma," Wynnie said. "I have asthma."

"It's probably best you stay inside as much as possible during the next day or so," he said. He moved to close the front door and then paused. "Let me know what you think when you read everything? Will you?"

"I will. And please let me know if you learn anything else."

"Yes. You know where I am if you need anything, anything at all." His look seemed to convey an understanding that somehow our parents were connected and yet neither of us knew how.

He shut the door gently. He'd done all that my mother's letter had requested—but I wanted more.

CHAPTER 17

CLARA

London, England

The fog rolled in feathered wisps. Above us, chimneys chugged out more smoke, joining the haze in a dance that might have been beautiful if it weren't green, thick, and pungent with poison. The pavement ran like a river next to the Thames as Wynnie and I followed the flickering lampposts.

We'd planned to take the walk back from Charlie's house to our flat so we could stroll along the river, pass Victoria's Gardens, and see the sights along the way, but Wynnie's eyesight was even cloudier as the fog settled on her glasses. She wiped at her lenses with her mittens, and we walked slowly as I guided her away from obstacles.

It hadn't been this dense on the taxi ride to Charlie's. Now the fog was gathering forces near the river, thickening so we could see only five to ten feet in front of us as it rolled off the Thames. I held tight to Wynnie's hand, but still she bumped into a lamppost. I pulled her closer so we could walk hip to hip, hand in hand, quiet.

I wondered what she was thinking as my mind circled around the letter in my purse instead of the danger. If the air hadn't been so dense, I would have sat us on the first bench and read my mother's letter. God, I wanted to read it now. How long had this satchel been in Mr. Jameson's library? Had his father known he was dying and put it in there for Charlie to find? Questions bumped into one another.

Puzzle pieces felt scattered across a miles-long landscape, and a shiver of foreboding gave me a chill along my neck.

Wynnie coughed, and I stopped, jolted from my thoughts. "Are you all right?"

She smiled wanly and pointed ahead of us at the tower of Big Ben and the pinnacles of Parliament rising into the thick air, clouded but visible in their iconic shapes. Big Ben chimed the quarter hour with four notes from Handel's *Messiah*, and we stopped to listen, gazing at the well-known landmark, where wisps of smoke curled around its face in a ballet of wind and moist air. Slowly closing in on the tower, the fog transformed into a dark veil, as if Big Ben were entering a period of mourning.

A bump from behind, and Wynnie and I found ourselves sprawled on the ground, my purse and the satchel flying from my hands as I reached to break my fall.

"Mama!"

A man's voice emerged from the fog. "I'm sorry. I'm so sorry." A hand reached down to help me. But I didn't want help; I was scrambling for the satchel, running my hands along the pavement, crawling to the place where it threatened to tip over the concrete edge into the roiling waters. I grabbed the leather handle and pulled it toward me.

"Mama!" Wynnie's voice again twisted into the memory of my own voice as I cried out for *my* mommy while fire licked at my sleeve. Past and present blended, folded themselves into a fabric of confusion.

"Mama!"

The fog rising from the river clouded my sight; panic turned me around. I didn't see her. I didn't feel her. I crawled on my knees at the edge of the river, one hand clinging to the satchel. I screamed her name and scrambled to my feet. "Wynnie!"

I spun around and she was at my side, holding my purse in both hands. Her glasses fogged, her face streaked with soot, and a tear in her wool stockings where her knee had hit the pavement, a dab of blood soaking through. I pulled her close and bent over so my chin rested on her head. "Sweetie, are you all right?"

"I am."

"Again, I'm sorry." The man's voice once more. Wynnie and I separated to see him standing there with his hands in the air as if surrendering. "This bloody fog—it will be the death of us. You mustn't stop in the middle of the pavement. Keep moving or else you'll be tipped into the river. Be mindful."

I clung to the satchel as if it were alive and might run off. My hands were tightly bound: one clinging to Wynnie and the other to Mother's language. The image of Wynnie falling into the river made me shudder. I moved us away from the edge.

"You could have knocked us into the water," I said with a voice choked by the very image of it, the certain death of it.

"Then one might want to stay away from its edge." The apology vanished, replaced with defensive anger. Then he hustled off, bundled beneath a dark trench coat, his hat low on his forehead.

"Are we lost?" Wynnie asked me, and a slight wheeze in her voice whistled in the air.

My heart rolled over and a spear of clarity pierced my confusion. Danger was with us now: we might not have fallen into the Thames, but now Wynnie's lungs were clamping down. I took a breath and tried to sound calm. "We aren't lost," I told her. "We are facing Big Ben." I pointed. "The top of Westminster is ahead and to the right, and the Victoria Gardens are right beside us on the other side of the road, even if we can't see them."

Wynnie moved closer, and I put my arm around her. "Yes," she said.

Reviewing the *London A to Z* guidebook over the past three weeks, we'd memorized the map around our flat. We'd traced our routes and made our plans. In my mind's eye, I saw it all and told her, "Only two blocks up and then we'll turn right and into Covent, and soon we'll be at our place with the big windows," I said. "We'll eat a snack. How does that sound?"

"Okay." Her voice was tight, and then a coughing fit took hold of her. She fell against me to catch her breath. The wheezy whistle told me the truth: the tiny alveoli in her lungs were shrinking against the moist and damp air, clamping down in rebellion.

My chest tightened in fear; sweat prickled my neck. I took my purse from her and dug into its depths for what she needed.

A shot of panic—I gasped when I came up empty.

The adrenaline shots. The aminophylline pills. I needed them both, but I'd left them in the large tote in the bedroom at the flat. My God,

I'd been careless. I'd been more worried about finding my mother's lost satchel than I was cautious about my daughter's health.

Guilt flooded my mouth with a metallic fear. No matter how I'd like to prove that I was not my mother's daughter, here I was making mistakes that proved I cared more about other things than Wynnie.

"Let's get across the street," I said.

We made our way across the zebra crossway. "It burns." Her voice tight and high.

On the other side of the street, I bent down and faced her. "We are only a few blocks away." I picked her up and carried her on my hip, although she was too big for such things anymore.

She nodded but didn't speak. She was conserving her air. If she was headed for a true attack, I didn't have long. I stumbled the next blocks in a nearly blind panic.

Regret and fear burdened every step. I climbed the hill along the Savoy Theatre and across the street to Covent Garden. Away from the river, the fog was less dense, enough to find our way home.

Pouring sweat beneath the layers of wool sweaters and coats, we reached the front of the flat, where I set Wynnie down and she slumped to the ground, taking small sips of breath. Her face was pale, her lips colorless. For God's sake, I didn't even know where to find a doctor in this city.

I dug out the key and shoved open the door. "Just a few more steps, love. We are here."

I half dragged her down the hallway and then shoved the key in the door of number seventeen, dropping my purse and the satchel at the entryway. I sat Wynnie on the couch and bolted into the bedroom. I dumped my tote on the bed and scattered its contents across the pale yellow quilt. Pens and lipstick, a book on London's museums, and a packet of tissues. There was the brown wooden box Dad had packed for me. I opened it and grabbed the syringe from the silk lining, slipped the needle into the rubber stopper at the top of the bottle of adrenaline, and withdrew two milliliters. I slipped the pill bottle into my other hand and ran back to the couch where Wynnie still sat, her head leaning back, her lips bluish, and her eyes shut.

I lifted her skirt, and through her thick woolen tights, I stabbed her thigh with the needle and pushed in the medicine, all the while cooing over and over, "It's okay; it's okay; it's okay. Breathe slowly, baby. Breathe all the way down. Now open your mouth."

She did just as I said, because she knew the little pill that I would slide under her tongue would return her breath. Aminophylline, a bronchodilator, would work with the shot and her lungs would open.

I knew the dangers of her asthma; we all did, but still, here I was.

What a fool I'd been, leaving her meds at the flat.

Nat was right.

I was in over my head.

"Breathe," I said, "breathe deep, my love. Breathe."

CHAPTER 18

CLARA

London, England

Wynnie's breath returned.

I slumped to the floor. This was the closest call Wynnie'd had since she was six months old and I'd found myself in a car wreck on the way to the ER. By the time the ambulance arrived, they'd needed to use a bag and oxygen. I nearly lost her, and that horror never left me. I often woke from a dream, frantic and sweating, trying to run with her through the hospital doors, but my feet were leaden, and no one could hear me scream.

Wynnie slid off the couch and into my lap, snuggled up next to my chest, breathing in and out, in and out, slowly, surely. "It's okay, Mama."

"No, it most assuredly is not. I should have never left without your medicines. I was too eager to get the papers, to find the letter."

"So was I."

"Wynnie, you're eight. You can be eager whenever you please. I should have known better."

"It's all right now, Mama. Emjie told me it would be. I wasn't scared."

"Well, I was."

Wynnie snuggled closer. "I want to tell you something," she said.

"Yes?"

She lifted her soot-stained face, inky black rubbed across her cheeks and now smudged on my sweater. "I was going to tell you when we got here, but then I sort of forgot until right now."

"What is it?"

"The last night on the ship, I dreamed about Grandma."

"Oh, you did?" I ran my fingers through her tangled hair, pulling at the strands to separate them. Her face was still cold to the touch and her eyes were dilated so wide that I was sure she saw the world askew.

"She was in a garden."

Just as she was the night I floated above my own body, the night I nearly lost myself. Had I ever told Wynnie about my dream of Mother when I gave birth to her? Had I ever told anyone, and Wynnie overheard it?

No, I *knew* I had not.

It made sense that this was how my daughter would see my mother, because the most famous photo of her was in a forest, looking over her shoulder with a smile of satisfaction. In the photo in the woodlands of New Hampshire, right before she met my dad.

"I know you think it's because of her photo," Wynnie said as if my thoughts had bubbled up and out of my lips.

I let out a nervous laugh. "Maybe so."

"But that's not it. It wasn't *that* photo. She was old, and it was a garden."

"Did she say anything?"

"No. She didn't see me."

I hugged Wynnie close and listened to her even breathing, holding her and thinking I should just turn around and go home, get back on that ship right now with our things, Mother's papers, and our safety. I would call the cruise line in the morning and inquire about an immediate departure.

"Let's stay in this evening," I said, "and skip the museum. The air is obviously unhealthy."

Wynnie stood up now. "Let's look at the papers?" she asked with a grin.

"First food," I told her. "I don't want all those medicines in your empty stomach." I wanted to move slowly now—my need to rush into things had nearly cost my daughter an attack I couldn't fix. *Slow. Easy now*, I told myself.

She sighed in resignation, an audible exhale that was clear of wheeze.

"They've been gone for twenty-five years, so another few minutes won't matter so much," I told her, and ruffled her hair.

The rental company had left us canned soups, eggs, milk, and a few things in the small yellow refrigerator. We ate a cup of potato soup and snuggled down on the couch. Wynnie turned her upbeat self again, as if the episode had never happened. Her lips and cheeks shone pink, and she was jazzed up, as she often was after the adrenaline flooded her body. She jumped up and paced around the coffee table and then pointed at the satchel.

"Mama, are you going to open it or not?"

"Right now, I am going to make sure you're all right."

"I'm fine. You know that." She plopped down next to me. "Now open it. I want to read it, too."

"Sweetie, I think the air here is bad for you. I think we need to leave London."

"Go to that place Mr. Finneas told us about? The place with all the lakes and where Grandma's play is?"

"No. We need to go home."

Wynnie pushed away from me and slid to the other end of the couch. "Mr. Jameson said it's going to pass. That the fog rolls in and the fog rolls out."

"This feels worse than a little fog," I told her. "I could barely see. It burned your lungs."

"I know. But next time we'll bring my medicine. I want to see the museums and Buckingham and inside Westminster, where the queen will get her crown, and you promised we'd climb to the very top of St. Paul's. Do not make us leave, Mama." Her voice choked with tears. "There are so many things I want to see, and maybe we can go to Cumbria and see that country house and the play."

"Not at the expense of your health."

"My health," she said. "Always my health. I'm so tired."

"Lie down, sweetie," I suggested, squeezing her toes inside her tights.

"No, I am tired of it being the reason we can't do things."

"We will do all the things we can. I promise." I looked to the windows and pointed. "It looks like it is ten at night outside, and it's only four thirty."

"It's kind of pretty in its own way." She lifted a biscuit from the plate I'd brought out and took a bite. "Now open the bag?"

I retrieved my purse from the entryway where I'd dropped it and reached inside for the letter. Nothing. My heart plummeted. The letter. Mother's letter. I flipped the purse over and dumped it onto the coffee table. Nothing. I would never know what she wanted to say to me. I felt a sob bloom below my breast.

"It's not here," I said.

"What isn't?"

"The letter." I imagined it floating down the river, sinking and sinking just as once I'd imagined the pages of her language. "No, please," I said. "Not again."

And then I shoved my hand into the side pocket.

There it was. I exhaled and slipped it out.

I then pulled the papers out of the satchel. Wynnie and I both stared at the top, where a sentence was written in Mother's language. Wynnie set her hand on the pile and then blurted out in a way that meant she'd been holding it tight, "I saw something in Mr. Jameson's library."

"What did you see?" I gripped the letter.

"Grandma's biography. The one Papa hates." She wiggled her toes and scooted closer. "I saw it on the desk. The *Wild and Tragic Life* book."

"It was there?"

"Yes, and I have to tell you something else, Mama."

"What is that?"

"I've read it."

I leaned closer to her, squinted at her with a lift of my chin. "What? When?"

"I found it in the town library last year, and I read it little by little when you let me stay in the afternoons."

"And you didn't tell me?"

"I'm sorry. I knew you didn't want me to, but once I saw it, I couldn't stop. And I'm almost nine years old, Mama. I'm not a baby anymore." She sat up straighter and exhaled.

"I know you're not a baby, but I didn't want you reading some hogwash that some stranger wrote about *our* family."

"One part of it made it sound like Papa might have hurt her or made her disappear."

"That might be why he doesn't like the book." I tried to make light, but my laugh was off, nearly a cough. "He had nothing to do with her leaving, honey. She just walked out one night and never returned. When we can't explain big things about people we don't know, we make up stories."

She nodded. "I just wanted to know her. Know about her. She is my grandmother."

"I know, baby. I want to know about her, too. Let's read the letter first?" She wiggled closer and nestled under my arm.

My name was written on the front of the envelope in Mother's slanted handwriting with the long drop of the leg in the letter g. *Clara May Harrington.*

No married name.

The envelope was sealed shut, which meant that no one, including Charlie, had read it.

I slipped my finger under the lip of the envelope and carefully ripped it open. I pulled out the letter, my heartbeat racing toward its unknown words.

CHAPTER 19

CHARLIE

London, England

Charlie Jameson packed up his rosewood bodhrán drum and grabbed his thickest wool coat from the closet in the back of the house. The aroma of mothballs and dust wafted out as he buttoned up.

Tonight he would play the instrument his father had custom-designed for him, the eighteen-inch drum along with the bulbous beater that was hand-carved from the same rosewood from Ireland. The flat custard top reminded him of crepes his mother made. The beater was worn smooth by his hands. The sound from this instrument was deeper and more resonant than Charlie's other bodhráns, and he played this one only with the full band, the Lads, with their Irish flute, mandolin, fiddle, and guitar.

"Moira," he called out toward the kitchen.

"Yes, Mr. Jameson." She appeared in the doorway, an eager smile always on her face, her round cheeks flushed with the heat of the kitchen.

"I'm headed out. I'll spend the night at my own flat. If you need anything, just let me know."

"Would you like me to stay, sir?"

"Yes, if you don't mind."

She nodded with a shy smile. He was quite sure she loved being alone in this six-bedroom house in London. She'd been with the Jameson family for over ten years and probably knew a lot more about Callum than she let on. Maybe Charlie should ask *her* about the mysterious pile of

Bronwyn Newcastle Fordham's language, but Moira was already lost to the back of the house.

Loss. A simple four-letter word that carried so much more than it could hold within its tall start and curved end.

Between grief and nothing, I will take grief.

These were the words of William Faulkner, spoken by his father to Charlie when he was eighteen years old one afternoon at the edge of Esthwaite Water. The sentence returned to Charlie now. Father's bits and bobs of wisdom, usually borrowed from books, often rose in Charlie when he needed them most. At least those things hadn't died with him, or wouldn't unless Charlie let them.

Charlie always wanted to be like his father, but now he was left with only himself as he hoisted his canvas case with the drum tucked safely inside, an emblem of his father, of old music, and of the days he wished he could retrieve and live again.

People left. People died. People changed. Love arrived hot and fast and then found its way into the arms of another.

This was the way of the world, and always had been.

You have a word for any of that, Bronwyn Newcastle Fordham?

He found himself asking this out loud as he opened the front door and stepped onto the front stoop. He shivered. The temperature had dropped at least ten degrees, as near as he could tell. He thought of Clara and Wynnie when they'd left him only a few hours before, shivering in the cold, headed back to a flat in Covent Garden, walking through an unfamiliar city in this thick fog.

If Father hadn't told him about Bronwyn, who was Charlie to nose into their private business? He did what he'd been instructed in the note: *Give this to Clara Harrington.* He wasn't required to do any more than that.

Clara of the long, dark eyelashes with something ethereal about her, as if she had alighted from the fog and floated into his house. Clara, it was clear, was desperate to know where the papers came from and why they found their way into Father's library. There was something familiar and tender about her, something he couldn't place, even as he stared at her.

But Charlie had other things to worry about. There was the cataloging of the library, oil paintings, and antiquities Father had collected. Concerts with the Lads. Visiting and checking on Mum and the land in Cumbria. Company meetings.

Tonight Charlie would put all that aside, for only in playing with his band, only in losing himself in the music, did the demands of the mad world quiet. The beater moving back and forth in his hand to the rhythm of a folk song sung in Gaelic took him somewhere peaceful. Sure, this world always waited for him, but to step out of it for a bit was a gift.

He pulled back the wool sleeve of his jacket and checked the Bulova watch that his father had left him: four fifty p.m. There was enough time to check on Clara and Wynnie, if that was what he felt like he should do.

Was that what he felt like he *should* do?

Charlie slammed shut the front door more forcefully than was necessary by half.

He walked down the marble front steps and into the fog. Flakes of soot floated through the air as dark snow. The cheap coal that Londoners were forced to use in these lean days was filling the air with its debris, clogging lungs, eyes, and mouths. He looked up; smoke rose from nearly every chimney on this bitter evening, adding to the soup of sulfur.

He thought of the little girl, Wynnie, whose blue eyes saw everything in the room, her gaze alert behind those thick pink glasses. *It burns*, she said. *It burns.*

He wondered if they'd gone to the museum or if they'd found their way back to their flat in this mess.

Charlie hustled toward Covent Garden.

He'd be quick, just check in on the way to the pub. It was the least he could do after summoning them across the ocean.

CHAPTER 20

CLARA

London, England

I unfolded the letter. If there had been any doubt where this had come from, now it was clear: this was not a forgery; it was undoubtedly Mother's handwriting. Wynnie sat by my side, the click and whir of the two-bar electric heater the only sound. Then, outside, a siren blared.

"Please! Read it," Wynnie said.

I nudged her and looked down.

Dearest Clara.

No date. No place.

My darling daughter. Doesn't it seem so dramatic to start with "If you are reading this . . ."? So I won't.

Instead, I will start with an expression of my great love for you. If you have ever doubted it, and I am sure that you have, please do not. Leaving can be a greater kindness than staying, and this is true for me.

I should not have left you alone by a burning cigarette, not for even a minute. For that lapse in judgment, I will live for as many days as I have left in fathomless regret. But I cannot return to you in anything but this letter, for to do so would ruin both your and my beloved Timothy's lives.

It is here in this pile of papers that you will find my dictionary. I began to create these words when I was five years old. I have always

*and desperately needed to find a way to describe a world in which I
felt so alone. The many languages I was taught were never enough
for me.*

We create words to define our life, and then they begin to define us.

*People who cannot choose their destinies often need to create
words all their own. For all my life—however long it is or was;
I don't know as I write this, of course—I have added words and
phrases to this list. You may do with this as you please, for it is
yours—keep it, publish it, or use it to translate Emjie's sequel. These
are now your choices, as I have saved this for you.*

*Clara, I have sewed myself into my secrets and there is nothing to
do but live in here, stitched into this world of exile.*

Only for you.

Adorium,
Mom

Wynnie sighed when I finished reading it out loud. "'I have sewed
myself into my secrets,'" she said quietly. "That's so pretty and so sad."

"She was both," I said. "Pretty and sad."

"What is that last word?" She ran her finger over *Adorium*.

I was thrust back in the closet during that day of "disappear and reappear," back to the slanted-light afternoon when I'd found the sequel's
manuscript, to the moment Mother told me the definition of this one
word. Through the years I'd memorized its definition, once hearing it
in her voice but now in my own as I told Wynnie: "It means the kind of
love that obliterates all sense and logic and has the world appearing just
as it is—completely and utterly magical. This word is the knowing that
all things are one and that we are connected to all things—the love that
created you and the love from which we came and the love to which we
will one day return. The greatest love."

Wynnie's eyes filled with tears that ran down her right cheek, creating a path through the smudged soot. "That is so beautiful, I feel like I
could float," she said, and sat back on the saggy couch as the light outside dimmed and dampened.

Still holding the letter, I walked to the window. Outside, the lanterns flickered inside the suffocating fog, strangled by the air. "We need to stay in this evening," I told Wynnie. "I'll cook up that sausage and we'll have a nice, quiet night. Tomorrow the fog will be gone, and you and I will visit that museum."

"Okay." She paused. "Mama, I bet Papa is wondering what you found."

"I'm sure he is, and I'll tell him everything once I look through *all* of it." I turned to her. "Wynnie, sometimes I feel as if you are too young for all of this, for what I have shown you here. There must be no fear that I will leave you. Ever."

"Mama, I'm not scared of that. I've never been afraid of that."

I nodded and felt the swampy feeling of my mother's abandonment, along with the surge of anger that I usually pressed down. I wanted to scream, to holler out that no good mother would leave, and yet this letter seemed to shimmer with love, and I felt as Wynnie said—I might float.

I was standing at the window, wondering if I'd made a terrible mistake coming here, when Wynnie jumped up, a blanket wrapped around her shoulders, and came to my side. "Let's make up people stories," she said, and tapped on the window.

This was a game I'd played with my mother and then taught to Wynnie—a pastime as we waited in the car or a queue at the market.

"All right," I said. "Look down there. See that man walking slowly in the fog right outside. Who is he, and where is he going?"

"He's a doctor and he's headed to the hospital, where a lady is having a baby who will one day find a cure for asthma," she said.

I laughed and hugged her.

"That woman?" I asked, and pointed at a short woman in high heels and a red coat. She carried a market bag and swiped the air in front of her as if she could move the mist like windshield wipers.

"She's late for a date and she has the food. She is very worried. Her roommate told her to leave earlier, but she didn't. Her last boyfriend left her for a very tall woman and she's worried because she's not tall."

"Your imagination!" I said. "It's a wonder. And the man?" I pointed to a tall man moving quickly, with a large case bouncing against his hip.

"That's Charlie Jameson on his way to visit us," she said.

I laughed again, but then stopped, because Charlie Jameson indeed stood outside, squinting at the numbers on the building. Moments later a staticky buzz filled the room and we both turned to each other. "Are you going to let him in?" Wynnie asked.

"I am," I said, and tussled her fog-tangled hair.

"What is he carrying?"

"Hard to tell."

I pushed the button that opened the front entryway and then opened the door to watch him walk down the hallway. He wore a long gray wool coat, and his shoulders were covered in black flakes, as if he'd walked through a snowstorm from a dark fairy tale. A round case hung off his shoulder, a Celtic knot design emblazoned on its cover. He smiled as he neared us, and he removed his wool cap. "Sorry to bother. I wanted to make sure you were both all right. This is a bloody wicked night, and Wynnie . . ." His gaze wandered to her.

"Come in," I said. "Warm up for a moment."

He entered and placed his case on the chair by the front door.

"What's that?" Wynnie asked him.

"A drum. I play in a band."

"Oh!" She clapped her hands together. "Can we come hear you?"

"Tonight's in a pub," he said with a grin. "Your mum might not be up for taking you to a pub in London at the moment." He looked to me. "Am I right?"

"You are right." I smiled at him for saving me from explanations.

Silence fell over us; the heater clicked and buzzed. He ran his left hand through his hair. "I thought you might have gone to the museum," he said.

"The air worries me with Wynnie's asthma, so we are waiting until tomorrow," I said. "She had an attack on the way home."

He took a step toward Wynnie. "Are you okay? We have a family physician. I can call him, and he will come straightaway."

"We have medicines," I told him. "And she's fine for the moment, but could you possibly leave us his name and number in case we need it later? It would be nice to have it."

"Yes, absolutely." He paused. "I was worried about you—people get lost in this fog. They can't find their way. They—"

"Mama never gets lost," Wynnie said. "We know our routes and we know our way. Don't you worry about us."

He laughed, and it was such a booming sound, filling the room. I wondered what his father had been like, if he'd been as jovial.

"Will you play the drum for me?" Wynnie pointed at the round case.

"Wynnie!" I said. "He's running late for a performance. He doesn't have time for such things."

"Yes I do," Charlie said, and reached for his case. "For this sprite, I have all kinds of time."

I motioned. "Please sit. I'm being rude. Between the travel, seeing Mother's letter, the fog, and the weird, dreamy way the world seems to be closing in on us, all of it has me a bit on edge. Forgive me."

Wynnie sidled up next to him. "Mama is really nice. And fun. Just give her a chance."

I rolled my eyes at him to say *kids these days*. "Please let me get you something. At least a cup of tea or coffee?"

"Thank you so much, but I don't need anything. There'll be fish and chips waiting for me at the pub."

"Mama, please, can we go? Just for a little bit? I want fish and chips, whatever they are, and I want to hear Mr. Jameson play."

Charlie saved me when he shook his head. "Not on a night like this. Tomorrow it should clear, and you can visit all the places you've planned in that busy head of yours." He sat on a large, cracked leather chair and unzipped the canvas bag. He pulled out an eighteen-inch drum, a circle bound by dark wood and a black metal band, all covered in a creamy skin or leather I couldn't identify. It was stained with unidentifiable marks, telling of a well-worn life.

He held a twelve-inch wooden stick with two bulbous ends and then glanced at the coffee table, where the letter sat open. "Did it give you what you needed?" he asked.

"What I needed?" I stared at those dark eyes and shook my head. "No."

He nodded, and with the polished stick, he began to beat the skin of the drum, back and forth, a slow rhythm and then faster, while he stared at me as if he saw through me, or maybe into me.

What I needed?

Nothing would ever give me that, because what I needed walked out the door twenty-five years ago. I wanted to tell him this. I wanted the man playing the drum to know that nothing could fill the void left by a mother who walked out.

Instead, I told him, "It was an 'If you are reading this' letter."

"So, she's . . . gone," he said, without missing a beat.

"I assume so, but the question is—then—how does your father have her papers?" I tapped the pile while he played.

Hypnotized by the soothing beat of the custard-colored drum, I felt a low vibration echo in my chest. Each beat or roll sounded like its own language, one of melancholy and hope blended in a low, warm hum. Tones rising and falling depending on where the beater landed.

The sound seemed to guide Charlie's hand more than his hand guiding the sound. There were clicks as he hit the edge of the wooden rim, and the room thrummed with the sound, the air shifting around him. Wynnie cuddled into me, and then Charlie sang. His voice rose deep and resonant, as if someone else had entered the room. He closed his eyes, and I did the same.

He sang in another language, one I didn't know but felt the strength of at the very center of my body, up into my throat as if I were trying to release something that was stuck.

I wondered if this was how my mother once felt when she could not express herself, the reason she made up words because the ones inside her weren't enough. It was a feeling much like melancholy, but also like hunger.

I wanted to reach out and hug Charlie, but he seemed unapproachable, a man unto himself. Who was I to think that he'd want me to hold him? I sensed some old hurt in him, the same that was in me, but that was most likely fancy thinking. He was a stranger, and I knew better than to put my own rising feelings onto someone else. I'd learned my lessons about attractions—I couldn't be trusted with them.

When Charlie finished singing, tears ran down my cheeks. I didn't understand the language, but somehow I knew what it evoked—the singular ache of losing something so dear that you cannot recover.

There was a part of me that didn't want the song translated, because whatever Charlie Jameson sang allowed me to finally, for the first time since the phone call, cry for all that was waiting in these papers, and also irrevocably gone.

CHAPTER 21

CLARA

London, England

At six p.m., it was so dark outside that the flicker of the gas flame was barely visible. The evening carried weight, pressing in on us. It was hard to believe that only this morning the ocean liner had glided into Southampton, and we'd boarded a train to London.

Charlie was gone, off to his gig, and his song echoed through the small flat as if he'd left us a gift. When Wynnie asked him about the lyrics, he'd smiled and said, "Do they matter?"

"Maybe not," I told him.

"I'll bring them to you tomorrow," he said. "It's an ancient Celtic song, and it won't do any good at all if I just ramble off the exact translation. It will lose its power."

I thought about that sentiment all evening, about how discovering the exact meaning of a word might remove the energy of it, of how this might apply to my mother's sequel.

By six thirty, Wynnie and I had used the dictionary of Mother's words to decode the handwritten note on the first page. The dictionary wasn't in alphabetical order, so we sifted through the mismatched papers, trying to find each word used in the sentence.

The papers were stained in some places, crumpled in others. There were no numbers, no way to know which order Mother once wrote them. These "lost words" were not created all at once. I was sure no language ever had been. Some pages were notebook-lined, like they'd been ripped from a child's composition book. Others were smaller, made of fine cotton stationery, and still others were blank pages of linen paper, the ripples of torn dots at the top revealing an art notebook as the source.

Eventually I would have to put the words in alphabetical order in order to read the sequel.

Each of Mother's words had more than one meaning: some defined images, others a feeling, so the translation of her opening sentence could say many things. Most of her words were visual; I imagined many of them as illustrations.

Then Wynnie called out: "Look what I found!"

She points:

Enchantia: wild world, experienced as bright birdsong on a windswept morning.

She'd found one of the words we needed, but she was asleep by the time I finally untangled the sentence on the cover page of Mother's dictionary.

This wild world holds more than you can see; believe in make-believe.

I wrote this on a large piece of white notebook paper and left it on the coffee table before I carried Wynnie to bed. I tucked her in and then returned to the small living room and lit a candle.

Hours slipped out from under me as I read and reread her lost words, with definitions like:

Loneliness at the heart of things. Believing you will find what will quench the longing, but there is nothing, not of this world.

I attempted to find a rhythm and order to the words. With the heater hissing now and again, I created a list of categories:

1. The natural and unseen world.
2. Escape and fear; fairies and demons.

3. Longing and loss.
4. Love and people/family.
5. Forgiveness and regret, and a loneliness that sang of melancholy.

This progression from number one to number five happened over many changes in pen and paper.

My eyes stinging with fatigue, I finally found my way to bed. I didn't think I'd sleep, what with Mother's language rattling around in my mind, her words that described the world in such dreamy, eerie language. I finally fell into a dreamless sleep, only to awake in what I believed to be the middle of the night.

When I looked at the black clock on the bedside table, it read 7:45 a.m. The urine-colored fog was worse now, pressing against the window, threatening to enter the bedroom. It was dense and eerie, a glowing specter. Disgusting.

Wynnie slept next to me, breathing quietly and evenly, a sound that made me feel a hot rush of gratitude. I kissed her cheek softly and snuck out of bed. I laid one more blanket over her.

The frigid kitchen slept under a hazy light; I buttoned the sweater that I'd slipped over my flannel pajamas and lit the gas burner, clicking on the heater beneath the kettle. The water boiled and I brewed myself a cup of tea, wishing for Dad's strong coffee. I clicked on the radio.

"Good morning. It's eight a.m., and this is your news. The fog has enveloped London today."

I listened to the broadcaster go on in a thick accent about the new queen's stamp, about Churchill's opposition, and then about the fog:

"Prepare for train delays and clogged traffic. The Richmond bridge is closed."

Charlie had suggested this was normal, but there was no one around to check this with. All the photos I'd seen of London were bright and cheery—Big Ben glowing against the blue sky; red double-decker buses traveling along lantern-dotted streets; London Tower looming, with a British flag waving in the breeze.

I would not allow this weather to keep me from taking Wynnie to the museum. She was counting on it. I carried my tea to the living room and spied Mother's language where I'd left it on the coffee table. I read the sentence again, the one I'd deciphered as best I could.

This wild world holds more than you can see; believe in make-believe.

It summed up her life, of how often the unseen world seemed more real to her than the seen world. It was possible that this idea was what took her from us.

I reached for her letter to me and read it again, the fourth time now, as if I might find hints between the lines, discover the one word that told me where she was or if she was alive. Her sentiment—"I have sewed myself into my secrets"—vibrated in my chest. Tears filled my eyes, and I set the letter aside.

Today would be about Wynnie, not Mother and her puzzles and mysteries and pages and pages of created words.

I would be a mother instead of searching for one.

"Mama?" Wynnie's sweet voice interrupted my reverie.

"In here," I called.

Wynnie appeared in her flannel pajamas decorated with tiny bunnies. "Is it night still?"

"No." I patted the couch. "Come sit. It's just the fog that makes it look that way. It's already after eight."

"Is it like this all the time?"

A tendril of fog seeped under the windowsill and slithered toward the ceiling.

"I don't know, baby. But it's not gonna hold us down. After breakfast, off to the museum we go."

⌣

As soon as we stepped outside my eyes stung, the air seeming to be made of fire sparks. The smudged shapes of buildings appeared, no lines or edges to delineate form, as if someone had erased the surety of the structures.

Wynnie's face was burrowed into her scarf. "Are you okay, little love?" I asked.

"I am!" She lifted her face and smiled. "I am."

"We'll walk through Covent Garden," I told her, "and cut up to Orange Street. The map says it's only point-three miles to the National Gallery at Trafalgar Square." I patted my purse. "I have everything we need in case this fog bothers you again."

We moved slowly; it was the only way. The smog wasn't better today, it was worse—thicker, coarser, and I could see only a few feet ahead. The Christmas lights on houses and trees floated like fallen stars. Women adorned in fancier frocks wore chiffon scarfs over their mouths, and men in suits pressed white handkerchiefs over theirs. They were accustomed to this air, I assumed. They soldiered on, and so would we.

Covent Garden's courtyard melted into the earth, and it reminded me of the horizon behind our house in South Carolina, the way the line between earth and sky folded into each other during a storm. People-shaped forms wandered through the maze of vendors. Inside the stores, lights flickered on one by one. The wooden carts sold baby spruce trees for Christmas, while flower and bakery vendors dotted the courtyard.

We made our way to a pastry cart, and I paid a few shillings for almond croissants, flaky and warm. We nibbled them while we walked toward the museum. From a side alley, a man moving too fast ran into us, knocking Wynnie to the ground. "Careful!" I yelled at him.

"So sorry, excuse me," he mumbled, and reached down to help her up, but I swatted his hand away.

Then he was gone, and Wynnie stood to brush off her coat. "I'm fine, Mama."

"I think we should go back. I don't like this."

"We're almost there. We can't turn around! You promised we'd see a real Monet painting." She stamped her foot in a feigned tantrum, and I shook my head. What child cared to see Monet? Wynnie.

Fog slithered up the lamplight poles, and a policeman holding a fire-lit torch ran past us toward the sound of breaking glass. Wynnie moved closer to me.

A symphony of coughing surrounded us.

This could not be normal no matter how many people were out and about.

We rounded a corner, and I pulled Wynnie along. "I see the Trafalgar lions," I said. "Almost there." But doubt surrounded me as slowly as the fog, winding up and around me, squeezing my heart. We skirted a bombed-out hole with a shaky bridge of wooden slats over it.

"Look out for those," I said. "They're dangerous—caverns exist below. They're left over from the war's bombings."

"Like the sea caves in Grandma's book?"

"No, nothing like that. Nothing at all like that."

We reached the edge of the square, where the massive Barbary lions crouched on a marble platform, staring across London. Pigeons squatted on their blurry heads.

"Mama, I read all about these lions in that tourist book."

"And?" We stopped at the bottom of the column, looking up at one of the four.

"They are made with the bronze of French and Spanish ships defeated in the Battle of Trafalgar."

"Whoa," I said. "I didn't read that part."

"Mama, you have to read all of it!"

I laughed at my daughter, at her awareness of small details, at this miracle of who she was becoming. "And," she added, "only the manes are different."

"Fascinating." I took her hand and we made our way across the plaza to the bottom of the museum steps, looking up at a columned building with a domed top. The railing was worn smooth by decades of hands running along its carved way, and we climbed. We reached the top, where another policeman with a flashlight stood at the front door. He waved the light toward us. His tall, cone-shaped hat sat atop his head, and a mask that looked like a dog muzzle covered his nose and mouth. Wynnie slid behind me.

He held the flashlight to light his face and shook his head. "Sorry. It's closed today, ma'am. Most workers couldn't get in."

"Oh no," I said.

"Ma'am, the streets are clogged. Trains wrecked or delayed. Bridges are closed. It is best for both you and"—he looked down at Wynnie—"your daughter to head back to where you came from and stay inside unless you absolutely must leave."

I crouched down next to Wynnie, and she wiped at her glasses. "Oh, Mama, this is so sad."

"I'm sorry, baby. Maybe it will burn off like Mr. Jameson told us."

"It always does," the policeman said as he waved his flashlight toward the fog. "It's just a particular London day."

I checked my watch. What should have been a seven-minute walk had turned into a thirty-minute sojourn.

We turned around and began the trek back to the flat. If we needed to stay in there for four days, we might as well head back to South Carolina. Disappointment flooded me. I had been so resolute, so sure about this trip and what it meant for me and Wynnie.

I held Wynnie's hand at the corner and hesitated in the eerie green light. The man next to us took two steps, inched forward, and then hurriedly rushed across the zebra crossing. We lost sight of him in the fog.

I squinted, feeling helpless, when devastating sounds filled the air—a thump and a whack, the sickening sound of a moving vehicle hitting a body, a shattering of glass. A scream. Headlights desperate against the impenetrable fog.

"Mama? A car just hit someone!"

I couldn't answer. I couldn't move. I needed to help this man. I needed to protect my daughter. I needed to find my way to the flat. These combating needs pushed and shoved inside me, but by instinct I moved toward the sound of screaming, where a crowd was gathering. A man hollered that he'd run and call an ambulance.

There was nothing for me to do.

"We need to get to the flat," I told Wynnie.

I gripped her hand and then bent down to press my forehead to hers. "The traffic is stopped right now. We will make our way across and then down two blocks." My mind was scrambling through landmarks, through corners and parks and by rushing rivers.

"Mama, I think he's—"

"Wynnie. Come."

We inched across the street, past the gathering crowd standing over a body strewn across the pavement. Even in the dank and heavy air, I saw the cherry-red stain grow in the street below the shape of a man. I shielded Wynnie from the sight with my body and reached the other side with relief.

"You're crushing my hand," Wynnie said.

"I'm sorry, baby. I can't let go of you."

She coughed, a tight sound that was a portent to a graver sound that would follow—*the* wheeze.

As we hustled through those streets, I made my deal with God—I would never again care about finding Mother if Wynnie would be okay. I should have allowed the satchel to fall into the River Thames when that man knocked into us yesterday. I should have stayed in Bluffton with Dad. I should have—

A woman, small and slight, appeared near me now. "You best be moving along. This fog is a bandit's pleasure."

One thing at a time, I heard Mother's voice say, the soft inflection of it coming to me in a memory of us building a house of twigs and moss over a month's time.

I reached into my purse and fished out a pill, bent down to Wynnie. "Put it under your tongue just in case. I don't like that cough."

"I hate the way it tastes." She pulled a face and then opened her mouth. I slipped the pill under her tongue, took her hand.

We must do only one thing at a time.

Mother's voice was clearer and closer than it had been in years. Her language was bringing her back to me.

CHAPTER 22

CLARA

London, England

We were lost.

Desperately lost.

By moving quickly past the accident and running down the pavement, we'd become turned around. People rushed by, their faces covered in scarves and masks. Tall woolen hats loomed like towers on top of dark figures. Long black coats billowed like the wings of a crow. The white marble of a building glowed to my left. Wynnie coughed again, and this time the telltale wheeze whistled through the exhale. If I didn't find my way, we would be standing here on a sidewalk in London while Wynnie was having an attack.

"Mama," she said softly, "Emjie says to turn left at this corner."

Street signs were hidden, appearing as creamy unreadable rectangles fastened to the sides of buildings, high enough to be shrouded in the veil of smoky air, the letters blurring together.

"I can't see the street sign on the building," I told her. "I don't know if this is Garrick. We need to turn on Garrick."

"It is," she says.

I usually didn't argue with Emjie, but now, how was I to rely on my daughter's invisible friend? It seemed absurd, but one thing I'd figured out through the years—Emjie was the part of Wynnie that knew things, and Wynnie wanted Emjie to get the credit.

"Why does Emjie think this is the street?"

"There, that." She pointed at a small garden statue of a gargoyle on the stoop of a doorway. "She noticed that when we passed it before."

"Yes," I said. "Good girl."

I felt sick and dizzy as we bowed our heads through the fog toward our flat. Would my daughter need to save her own life, since I could not?

Voices swam through the air, slow and distorted. *Help me. Where am I? Leave. Please let me in. It's an emergency.*

I need to get into number seventeen.

Charlie's voice.

We walked directly into him. He stood at the front of our building, hollering into the intercom speaker.

"Oh!" He grabbed me by the shoulders with his leather-gloved hands and drew me so close that his forehead nearly touched mine. "Clara, it's you. Thank God. Are you all right?"

The sound of breaking glass, the holler of a man: *Come back here, you scoundrel.*

I clung to Wynnie's hand. "I need to get her inside."

The buzz of the door—someone had heard Charlie's plea. We stumbled down the hallway, smoke curling behind us, the cold snapping at us with a bitter bite. We reached number seventeen. "Do you have the key?" he asked.

I fumbled through my purse and looked up in despair. "The key . . ."

"Mama, you put the key in your pocket when we left. Not your purse."

I reached into my pocket and felt the cold weight of the brass.

I shook off the dread and we made it inside. Wynnie's breath whistled in and out, hands splayed on her knees as she leaned forward in that terrifying posture of air hunger. I unbuttoned her coat and removed her scarf.

I ran for the bedroom and the little wooden box with the adrenaline and the syringe. I jabbed the needle through the plastic top and drew up the lifesaving clear liquid with shaking hands. I caught my reflection in the mirror and gasped: my face was streaked with dark soot, and it looked as if I'd crawled inside a chimney, cleaning it with my cheeks and nose. My hair hung in greasy strands. This was what the air was made of.

This was what my darling daughter was breathing into her fragile lungs. I had exposed her to it again. I was a fool.

Back in the living room, I knelt before Wynnie. "Please take a deep breath," I said, and held the syringe, unsure if we'd need it.

Wynnie smiled. "I'm all right, Mama, honestly. Now that I'm inside."

Charlie was pale beneath his soot-covered face. "Are you okay?"

"I am," she said, looking up at him. "I am."

She didn't need the shot, and we all sat in silence as Wynnie breathed quietly and the sounds of horns and sirens blared outside. Charlie watched Wynnie closely; his hair was freckled with flakes of soot, and it covered the shoulders of his woolen coat. His handkerchief was looped around his neck, where he'd pulled it down, and there was a demarcated line where his lips and chin had been protected.

Finally he asked, "What happened?"

"I thought we were fine," I said. "I did. I'm such a fool. I listened to the broadcast, but I didn't know . . ."

"I've never seen it this bad. It's the bloody cheap coal that Churchill allows." Charlie perched on the coffee table and leaned forward to wipe my face with his thumb, rubbing off the soot. "I'm going to call our family doctor, Maycombe; he can help us."

"Charlie, listen to me. This air is poisonous to her." I pulled Wynnie close, and she allowed it. Tears clogged my throat, and anger burned in my chest. I wasn't exactly sure where to direct the anger. Possibly toward Mother? Or Charlie's father, for leaving behind these papers without explanation? Or at myself? The anger flamed in me and at me.

Charlie spoke slow and steady, bringing me back to the room. "The city is clamped down. Railroads aren't running. Bridges are closed. Police and ambulances can't get through—"

I interrupted his litany. "Listen to me," I said. "I must get her out of here. I don't care how."

Wynnie walked over to the window and pressed her forehead against the glass.

Charlie told us, "I would normally suggest we take her to hospital, and they might give her oxygen there, but the wireless says they are overwhelmed and don't have enough staff or oxygen." As if to reinforce his point, a siren squealed, halted, and rose again outside.

Nothing existed alone; it always tangled with something in the past. Here I remembered when I was twelve years old, and Dad and I had visited New York City for an adventure to see the tree at Rockefeller Center and the store windows. We'd been on the long ride up in the elevator to the top of the Empire State Building when halfway there it screeched to a halt. We'd all been crowded in the small space. The lights blacked out. A woman began to cry. I needed to find the bathroom. Dad murmured words of comfort that the elevator would start up again soon. He sang "You Are My Sunshine," and the trapped crowd joined in, alleviating the panic. The elevator lurched and rose again, but the few minutes trapped felt exactly like this moment in our rented flat: desperate helplessness, a sense of impending danger.

"I am going to ring Maycombe." Charlie went into the kitchen, where he used the black phone to dial a number he knew by heart. I followed him and heard the dull ring of it for a long while, ten chimes at the least. I thought Charlie might hang up, but he stood there with a fierce look on his face, as if with his sheer determination he could get the doctor to answer.

"Maycombe," he said. "We have an emergency. I have a friend visiting from America, and her little girl, who is . . ."

"Eight," I said.

"Eight years old, and she has . . ."

"Asthma," I told him.

"She has asthma, and this air is making her sick. Can you help us?" A long pause and I heard only the mumble of the other man's voice. Then Charlie again. "Yes, she has shots and some pills." He looked at me.

"Aminophylline," I said, and he repeated the word.

Charlie nodded as the other man spoke, and then he turned away from me. Panic rose like a tide that washed onto the beach, scooped up the flotsam and shells, and then receded, only to force its way farther onto the shore with the next wave, seizing more of the land and shoreline, bringing in more debris.

Charlie hung up and exhaled. I grabbed his sleeve. "What did he say? Can he help us?"

"He said we must leave. No one can help us, and it won't get better.

The hospitals are full. Doctors can't make calls—many of the streets are shut down. He said to give her Liquifura when we arrive at my house."

"Liquifura?"

"It's a cough medicine."

"That is not what she needs." A pressure built in my chest, a need to exhale in a scream, but I controlled it.

"I'm only telling you what the doctor said. We must leave."

"Okay, what next? What can I do?"

"We're going back to my house now. It's only a few blocks away and I can walk it with my eyes shut tight. Wynnie just took her medicine, so we can make it, am I right?"

I nodded while pressing my fingers into the corners of my eyes. I could cry later. I could cast blame when we were safe.

He continued, "We'll get out of here and go to the countryside, to my mother's house."

I nodded.

"We'll leave now," he said. "Bring only what you can carry."

I ran to the bedroom and packed quickly, thinking of my mother and her midnight escape. I grabbed my tote with the easily accessible meds, and one change of clothes for each of us. Then I took the satchel with Mother's papers and my small purse with cash, tickets, and passports. This gathering took less than five minutes. I took one last glance at our large suitcase, packed with all our clothes and sundries, with the things we thought we'd need.

Wynnie and I were leaving with a stranger to a place I'd never heard of, and yet it was an easy choice.

CHAPTER 23

CHARLIE

London, England

Charlie Jameson held tight to two hands, one on either side: Clara and Wynnie. Wynnie had refused to be carried, saying it would slow them down. The threesome moved slowly toward St. James's Square. Charlie felt a fraud, an actor in a bad movie, trying to portray bravado and knowledge. His heart hammered. He'd promised to get them out of London, but he had no idea if he could do so.

Charlie understood weather systems. Everyone in London had a good chin-wag now and again about the moodiness and dampness of winter. But that day, unbeknownst to Charlie and most of London, the warm, wet air from the Gulf Stream swirled toward and then hovered over London, captured by the many fingers of the city's buildings and homes.

The mist joined the coal smoke in the air in an alchemic brew, creating a green and brown glow. Light seeped through the fog, shafts of it struggling to find a way through. The eerie greenish fog flowed through the streets, fluttered over the River Thames, and then settled in for a good long stay.

"An anticyclone," the BBC declared on the morning wireless between the news of Mr. Churchill being booed by the socialist opposition and Her Majesty giving a dinner party for the ministers at Buckingham.

But no one, including Charlie Jameson, believed the fog would stay for long, or that it would gather forces to create a deadly viscous murk, like they were inside a bottle of spoiled milk. They could see maybe three feet ahead at most. Londoners, including Charlie, believed that this was just another foggy day, another misty, moist December. *Get on with it, chap.* They'd borne up under such times before and they'd bear up under them again, because this was what it meant to be Londoners, a people who'd survived much worse than hazy skies.

The war was only over six years gone, and bombed-out spaces were still scattered about the city, gaping reminders of what was not quite past. *Move past it* was the cry of the government and the people. But the economy still suffered, patrons arriving at the bank begging for one more month's grace before they repaid their loan, aghast at their empty coffers.

What was a bit of fog to them?

Now only the light of the fiery torches penetrated the fog. The headlights of cars, the sirens on ambulances, and flashlights were swallowed and strangled by the sulfur.

Charlie used hedgerows and iron fences to guide them and then cut through alleys he knew by heart. The sun hung listless and useless, defeated. An ambulance blared its siren and strobed its lights while being slowly guided by a torch along Charles II Street.

This catastrophe was his responsibility. He'd brought this woman and child here. He could have taken the papers to her in America, couldn't he have? If he'd known, if he'd only known. He felt a guilty twist in his gut. He wanted to care for her, protect her and her child.

Charlie had told Clara he could find his way home with his eyes shut tight, but ensconced in fog, he wasn't sure he could find his way a single block.

"I can't even see my feet," Clara said, her voice muffled beneath her scarf.

"Are we lost?" Wynnie asked with a cough, and his heart squeezed in panic.

"No," Charlie said. "Another few blocks. That's all."

Running feet, sirens, an oily sensation in the air, grime in his ears and eyes. His beautiful city crippled by smoke and soot. Two American guests now his responsibility.

"Keep going," he said. "Keep moving. Hold on to me."

The world was blotted out. His eyes ached and the fog seemed to be doing nothing but gaining power, rolling in and around itself like a great storm at sea. Hulking forms of cars were abandoned on the side of the road; twice they heard the sickening crunch of metal on metal, the outlines of everything smudged with an eraser.

They moved slowly, quietly, shuffling more than walking until he told them, "We're here."

He fished into his pocket and drew out his key, held its familiar edges through his gloved hand. He inserted the brass and the tumblers fell away. He turned the egg-shaped knob, opened the door, and the three of them stumbled into the house, nearly falling into the entryway, the specter of fog following.

He slammed the door shut and took Clara and Wynnie into his arms. They were so fragile. Clara's head at his shoulder, Wynnie's at his waist, all of them knitted together by fear and then safety.

"We're here. We're okay," he said. "We'll get out of here. I promise. The car . . ."

Wynnie pulled away first, and in the chandelier's sparkling light, he saw her face was smudged with soot and her eyes were wide behind her glasses, which were smeared in a gray grime. He reached down and took off her glasses and tried to wipe them clean with a handkerchief from his pocket, but he only made it worse. She pulled down the scarf she'd been using to cover her mouth and nose.

"I've had bad dreams like that," Wynnie said. "I felt like I'd fallen into one of my bad dreams."

"It was terrible," Charlie agreed. "That's true. But here we are. Safe. I will have Moira make us something warm to eat, and then we'll head to the country."

That was when he looked at Clara, her face resolute with determination, holding back whatever fear must be quivering inside her. She placed her hand on top of Wynnie's head.

They all heard the music: Vivaldi at full volume from a room down the hall.

"Who is here?" Clara asked.

Charlie didn't answer her because he didn't yet know. Were Archie and his wife, Adelaide, in the house?

The three of them walked through the marble foyer under the crystal chandelier, down the wood-paneled hallway of ancestors, and then to the right, where Callum's library door was shut, as it almost always had been.

They raised their eyebrows at each other.

Even if Charlie had left the phonograph playing, which he surely hadn't, it would have run its course by now. The needle would be turning on the inside edge of the record: swish swish swish.

Charlie pushed the door open.

It took him a moment to absorb the scene, so unexpected, his mind couldn't catch up fast enough.

Moira, he realized with an electric shock.

It was Moira, and she was oblivious to the open door. A fire burned and crackled in the hearth. Orchestra music filled the room. And there was Moira in her dark dress without the white apron, and she was dancing with her eyes closed, tears pouring down her face. She appeared serene, gently swaying, twirling, her hands lifted in surrender. Then the music shifted, the crescendo winding down. She stopped and pressed her hands to her heart, swayed.

Charlie walked to the phonograph and lifted the needle, the room suddenly going silent. "Moira?" Charlie said her name softly, and she stopped, hesitated, and then opened her eyes to see the threesome, grimy and cold, wrapped in soot and wool.

"Oh!" She let out a pained cry and covered her face with her hands as if this could make her disappear. "Sir, I am so sorry. I thought . . ." With her eyes covered, she ran, bumping first into the desk, then into the standing brass lamp, and then into Charlie. He steadied her gently.

"Are you all right?"

She dropped her hands, opening first one eye and then the other. She straightened her shoulders and met his gaze. "Sir, I am not all right. I might die of embarrassment right here. I might just wither on the floor and never recover."

He shook her lightly. "Look at me."

The tears in her eyes overflowed, small trails on her cheek that she didn't wipe away. "I thought you were gone for the day. I didn't know you were returning. You said . . ."

She took two steps back and slumped into a leather lounge chair, bent over, and put her elbows on her knees, her head down as if she might be sick.

He leaned forward to listen carefully as she spoke softly. "I am mortified beyond understanding." Then she seemed to pull the threads of herself together, exhaling and sitting up straight, pulling her shoulders back. "Let me explain. I miss your father something grand, sir. He was good to me. Better than my own father ever was. I miss him so much. I thought if I spent some time in the place he loved more than any other, I might be able to say goodbye to him. He loved your mother something wonderful and taught me things. He let me borrow books from this library. He treated me like a real person."

"Yes, that was his way. I miss him, too." Charlie eased the words into the room, hoping to calm her. She seemed to be hiding something, but he wouldn't push the poor girl anymore. She was distraught. "We need to find something warm to eat and then leave quickly for the north. We must get Wynnie out of the city."

Moira jumped up as if electrocuted. "Let me help."

He nodded and then turned back to Clara and Wynnie, who looked as if they'd fallen into a weird dream and didn't know how to wake up. "Upstairs on the top left is a guest room with a bath and fresh towels. Go clean up and I'll quickly pack. We'll leave in thirty minutes' time."

He walked out of his father's library, past the weeping Moira with her mysterious grief, past the woman and her daughter who needed protection.

"Can I ask you something?" Charlie heard Clara's voice and he stopped and turned.

"Of course, what is it?"

He noticed that she wasn't speaking to him; she was standing in front of Moira.

Moira nodded.

"Did you know anything about this leather satchel of papers that Mr. Jameson had in this library? A woman, maybe? Someone who helped him?" Clara asked.

Moira glanced around the room. "No, nothing."

Clara shot him a look and he smiled sadly. This woman so desperately wanted to know about her mother. What a pair he and Clara made—both needing to know about why his father owned these papers. Possibly that was why he felt he needed to pull her into his arms and hold her there until this was solved.

Clara took her daughter's hand. "Come now, let's go clean up."

Moira led Clara and Wynnie to the guest room, and Charlie stood alone in the library, his head dizzy with the unexpected sight of Moira dancing alone in his father's library.

He shut the door and rushed up the stairs to pack his own bag with the little he kept here. Leaving was imperative; the mysteries must wait.

CHAPTER 24

CLARA

London, England

Wynnie stood quiet and still next to me, her cheeks glowing where I'd scrubbed her face with a washcloth in the small bathroom. We'd bathed as best we could, leaving the cloth and towels stained dark and smeared with soot. I piled them in the bathtub, and we dressed. I wore the only pair of slacks I'd brought with a pale blue sweater, and Wynnie had on a wool dress and tights.

"We are headed to the country," I'd soothed her. "It's going to be an adventure, and everything is going to be fine."

My voice held false cheer, and she heard it. We made our way downstairs to find Charlie and Moira in the kitchen.

The lamp on the sideboard sent spears of light through the murky air. It was midday, no later than noon, and yet it appeared to be twilight outside, headed quickly toward night. Moira bustled about the warm, oak-cloaked kitchen, wrapping sandwiches and cheese in parchment paper. In her black uniform and white apron, she looked like she'd stepped out of a Jane Austen novel.

Charlie was dressed now in tweed pants and a thick gray sweater, his face clean-shaven, his hair sending droplets of water onto the pine floors. Wynnie and I didn't wash our hair—I was afraid that heading into the chill with wet hair would clamp her lungs down.

The wireless radio droned from the corner of the kitchen.

"Scotland Yard has instructed not to leave your house unless necessary . . .

*Traffic delayed . . . Cars abandoned on the road due to fog and ice . . . Birds
falling from the sky . . ."*

"Turn that off," Charlie said to Moira. "Please."

Moira hustled to the wireless, and in her feverous rush, she turned
the sound up instead of down, the news blaring into the kitchen.

"Train crash . . ."

We startled. Wynnie put her hands over her ears and Moira twisted
the knob the opposite way, and we plunged into a quiet that was as eerie
as the damning news. Then she handed him a basket. "I've packed food
for you and the ladies."

"It is also for you. You'll come with us." Charlie turned to me. "I've
already put my bags in the car and told Mum that we are coming," he
told me. "Is everyone ready?"

"Yes." I pointed to our bag.

He lifted a brown bottle and silver spoon from the side table. "Okay,
let's give Wynnie a dose of Liquifura, and that might hold her. Dr. Maycombe said it would help as we leave the city." He poured the viscous
liquid into the spoon and held it out to Wynnie.

She looked to me, and I nodded. Wynnie closed her eyes and swallowed and then shuddered. "Disgusting."

A noxious smell permeated the air, something of garlic and rotten
socks left in the rain.

Charlie lifted our valise. "I'll sort this for you." Then he leaned down
and picked up the satchel, handed it to me. "Now you carry this."

I slipped the bottle of Liquifura into the valise. We bowed our heads
and lifted our scarves over our noses and mouths to make our way to the
detached garage that Charlie told us was once a horse stable. We entered
the space through a side door and Charlie slammed it behind him.

A pale blue Beetleback Vanguard sat in the middle of the garage, its
pointed nose and wide-set headlights straddling a silver grille. Inside,
crimson leather glowed from the two rows of seats. Charlie opened the
trunk and tossed in my small valise with the meds and our clothes. I held
tight to the satchel and my purse.

He shuffled around to a shelf and retrieved a lantern and matches.
"We'll need this when we get to the streets. Clara, hold on to them?"

I threw the satchel and my purse onto the back-seat floorboards and took the lantern and matches from his hands. Then Wynnie and I slid onto the long bench seat in the back, the plush leather cool beneath us.

Charlie opened the driver's-side door and nodded to the other side of the car. "Climb in, Moira."

Moira ran to the passenger side.

Charlie slid open the garage door and the fog seeped in, tobacco-stained and thick. Charlie moved to the driver's side, climbed in, and slammed the door shut, so the car shook. He set his hands on the leather-wrapped steering wheel and exhaled in one long breath before starting the car. He seemed to be talking to himself when he said, "It's usually a five-hour drive, and I have a full tank of petrol."

Wynnie smelled of garlic and soot and soap. I took deep breaths all the way to the bottom of my lungs as if I could breathe for her.

Charlie eased the car out of the garage and onto the side street. "It's worse than I thought," he said. He stopped the car, although we'd only traveled a few feet. "Someone needs to walk in front of the car with the lantern. Even the headlights aren't enough."

"I'll do it," Moira said. "Please let me help."

"No!" I sat straight up, knowing that this was mine to do. The knot of determination inside me, the place that the important parts of me formed around, spoke for me now. I was going to help us find our way out of this.

Over the seat I handed Charlie the lantern; he flicked a match and lit the wick. I climbed out of the back seat and pulled my scarf over my nose and mouth.

"Mama?" Wynnie reached for my hand, and I kissed her forehead before I stepped out. I held out the lantern and walked slowly ahead as Charlie followed. Cars in front slowed us down, and horns honked to little use.

I drew on the pool of strength that I'd been filling with a resolute ability to do what was needed since the day Wynnie was born. I would walk to the ends of England to save her, to keep us safe. I emptied my mind of all doubt, of all fatigue, and the low buzz of fear eased as I walked step-by-step at the edge of a road to guide us.

All around me were abandoned cars and trucks, shattered bikes, dead birds, and the crumpled detritus of an automobile wreck: a shattered side mirror, a bent bumper, and broken glass. Still, I walked and lit the road for Charlie. My arm ached and my hand cramped and I didn't waver. The flame licked at the edge of the glass and fought with the green fog for dominance.

After how long I didn't know, Charlie stopped the car and climbed out. He came to me and took the lantern. I dropped my arm and shook out my hand to return blood flow to it.

"Clara, you can let Moira do this now."

"No. It's mine to do." I slid the scarf from my nose and mouth, tasted the damp wool on my lips.

He rubbed soot from my cheek with his thumb and I held my hand over his for a moment. "It's going to be okay," I said.

He nodded and cleared his throat. "Yes. But we can't stay on the main road anymore. There are too many wrecked and abandoned cars," he said. "Up ahead you will see a sign for Kilburn. Follow it and guide us to the left and we'll go into the back roads."

"That's the *very* long way," Moira called out from the front seat, her head hanging out of the window.

Charlie turned. "Close the window!" Then he looked to me. "It will be longer, but I know it will be clearer than this. Are you okay, Clara? You can have Moira do this."

Wynnie was burrowed into the back seat, watching me. I walked to the rear of the car and pressed my hand to the window, waiting for her to get her hand on mine.

"No, I'm good," I told Charlie. "You get in, let's go."

CHAPTER 25

CLARA

Leaving London

I had no idea if a minute or ten or thirty went by. We passed a stranded ambulance and a crushed bike, abandoned cars. The red-circled speed limit signs were turning clearer. The black roadside directions with the large white arrows pointed us around the curves. Twice we drove on the grassy edges of the road to avoid a clogged roadway, and we'd barely made any progress. My legs were nearly numb with cold, and my breath rattled. I tasted the damp threads of the scarf covering my nose and mouth.

The disembodied lantern was a floating, glowing balloon. The light issuing from Charlie's car was so weak that the headlights might as well have been turned off, just two glazed and useless eyes.

Charlie and I worked out a system. If I floated the lantern in toward the windshield, Charlie must stop for something in the road—a pedestrian, another car, an abandoned bike.

Now a blob filled the middle of the road, and I swayed the lantern for him to stop. Charlie braked, parked, and joined me. "A cow," he said. "There's a dead cow in the middle of the road." He shook his head.

"A dead cow," I said, disbelieving it even as I saw it. "Death is in the air."

"Clara, I'd like you to get in the car with your daughter and let Moira do this."

"No," I said as firmly as I knew how behind the scarf covering my mouth. Then from behind, a crushing mechanical sound as another car hit the rear of Charlie's Vanguard.

Charlie walked to the back of the car and other figures joined him. Sound was as warped as sight, and words overlapped in low voices: *cow; dead; field; together.*

Figures huddled over the road, pulling and heaving the cow out of the way toward the frost-crusted hedgerows.

I turned away and peeked into the car, where I saw Wynnie rousing from sleep, sitting up in confusion, rearranging her glasses to assess the situation. Charlie came to me and gently placed his hand over mine on the lantern. "I can see better now. You can get in the car with your daughter."

"I will walk from here to the country if need be."

He uncurled my fingers from the top ring, releasing my hand from the tight knot, and took the lantern from me. "You've brought us this far."

I returned to the car and slid into the back seat, where Wynnie looked at me. "Mama?"

"It's okay, love."

Charlie again placed his hands firmly on the wheel, gripping it as if it might run away, and then the car began to move again. Moira sat in the front, looking straight ahead. "I would have carried the lantern."

"I know," I told her, and set my hand in Wynnie's, knitting my hands to hers.

Moira turned to look at me. "You are such a good mum."

I would have thanked her, but tears clogged my throat. Charlie drove along the back roads and the dirt roads, avoiding the traffic on the main thoroughfare.

The fog continued to thin until the trees weren't shrouded in a Cézanne painting, and leafless arms scraped the low and cloudy sky. The dark ribbon of the road emerged, and the fields on either side revealed themselves, with dark wooden fences and rock walls as a boundary between us and the fields. We were, as near I could tell, the only ones on a bumpy and rutted lane.

Wynnie dozed again, and we were all quiet until Charlie slowed down and then pulled onto a gravel road that led into a low-cut field. Safely off the road, he parked among the russet-colored mounds of cut hay.

We'd been traveling for hours, and I needed to find a bathroom and food. I'd eaten nothing since breakfast but the bitter coffee in the thermos. I gently laid Wynnie on the leather back seat, and she stirred, opened her eyes, and sat up. "Mama?"

"I'm here." I pushed open the passenger door and put my feet on the soft earth. Bronze and dried leaves were scattered beneath our feet. The air, although clearer by bits, was still bitter cold, frigid at its center and inescapable.

"The fog . . . it's gone?" Wynnie asked as she slid across the seat to join me outside.

"Not entirely, sweetie, but at least Mr. Jameson can now see to drive."

"What time is it?" She removed her glasses and rubbed at her eyes.

I checked my watch. "Five in the evening," I told her. "Now if you're coming out, wrap your scarf around your neck and mouth and bundle into that jacket."

She nodded and did as I asked.

"Let's take a break," Charlie said, and climbed out of the driver's side, squinting into the fields and then up and down the empty road. "Let's eat what Moira packed, and then I need to figure out exactly where I am, how far we are from Cumbria and on what road exactly."

"Cumbria." I repeated the word as Wynnie climbed out of the car and lifted her face to a gray-veiled setting sun. She took a breath, and although the whistle remained, she stood firm.

"That's where the play is," Wynnie said.

"The play?" Charlie leaned back on the fencing and stretched his neck left and right.

"One we heard about on the ship," I said, and squeezed Wynnie's hand. She looked at me quizzically, but I shook my head. "You don't know what road you're on?"

"I don't," he said with stark honesty, not pretending to have any control over the situation. "All that mattered was getting us out of the city. I turned when there was a block in the road, and I kept pointing north." He pointed to a compass on the dashboard in the car, its needle the only thing that wasn't confused about its place in the world.

Moira dragged out the picnic basket and set it onto the hood of the car. I'd buried the feeling of hunger, but at the sight of food, I was famished. "I need to . . ."

Charlie smiled. "So do I." He nodded to a bale of hay to the left of us. "Looks like the best we can do."

I nodded. "I think so. Come with me, Wynnie, let's make our way to the very fancy loo."

Moira handed us some napkins from the picnic basket, and we laughed. The sound released the tension that coiled between us. Now we shared a camaraderie that we didn't turn into words but knew was genuine. We'd escaped the fog. How long it would take us to get where we were going was to be seen, but we were safe, and we were together in that escape.

When we'd finished behind the hay, Charlie did the same, and then Moira.

We ate slowly, savoring every bite of biscuit and ham, of cheese and sliced oranges. The landscape undulated away from us, and far off I heard the rush of a river. A cluster of alders stood to our left side, the gnarled trunks twisting, the ground beneath carpeted with dead branches and dried russet leaves. The sweet treats that Wynnie pulled up from the bottom of the basket were beautiful—tiny meringue cookies with little raspberry centers. It was all hilarious, eating this dainty, civilized lunch while we looked like we'd just climbed out of a sewer pipe.

"What's it like where you live in America?" Moira asked us as she took another cookie and gobbled it quickly as if someone might snatch it from her.

"It's home," Wynnie said, and paused while she found more cookies. "A home of rivers and big oak trees, with docks and the best shrimp you'll ever eat in all your life. Cute homes and dirt roads and a town that cuddles up to the water."

"Sounds so beautiful," Moira said.

"It is," I told her. "It's a coastal village on what is often called a river but is a bay. It's a tight-knit community built around fishing, oysters, and the tides. The American South is at best complicated; at its worst, it is coming out of a terrible period of slavery and war. But its surface, its natural world, is breathtaking and haunted."

"Just now out of it?" she asked.

"No, it's been a hundred years, but the echoes last. My dad is a doctor. Our town, Bluffton, is all I've ever known. Born there, raised there, married there, and Wynnie, too. It is simply beautiful, and the people are for the most part kind. I guess like most small towns."

"Married?" Moira tilted her head, and I saw her gaze slip to my empty ring finger.

"Once, yes. Not anymore."

"But he's my father," Wynnie piped up.

"Yes, he's an amazing father." I wiped crumbs from Wynnie's face and then kissed her cheek.

"He had a money problem," Wynnie said to Moira, and shook her head in an imitation of my own dad that was so precise I suppressed a laugh. "So Mama and Daddy just could not stay married under those circumstances." She parroted words I'd spoken so many times.

"Wynnie!" I told her. "They don't need to know all of that."

"They are our friends now," she said. "They're saving us!"

Charlie looked at me with a smile full of warmth. "If I'd known children were this wonderful, I would have had some."

I smiled in return. Between us rested something kind, something made of our parents' secrets and a child's honesty.

"Let's get where we're going," Charlie said, and he began to clean up.

Moira wiped her face with a dirty handkerchief, making the streaks worse. She coughed and turned away from us, spitting onto the ground. "I'm so sorry," she said in a choked voice. "That was vulgar. But I don't want to swallow that amalea."

An electric shock arrowed through my temple. My right arm tingled, and I came near to her, smelled the dank aroma of sweat, dead fire, and dirt. "How do you know that word?"

Amalea.

Darkness in the unseen world.

CHAPTER 26

CLARA

Leaving London

Evening was turning to night, the fields now glowing and the salmon-tinted horizon melting away. The leafless trees turned haunting.

"How do you know that word?" I asked again. I could see the word on the first page of Mother's language collection shimmering in the air.

Moira set her lips straight. "It's a word I saw in those papers. That one word rose off the page and went to my heart straight like an arrow."

"You read the pages? The note said that they were meant only for me."

"What note?"

"The one inside that said the pages were meant only for Clara Harrington? That one."

Moira looked at Charlie, who smiled and told her, "Yes, there was a note."

"I didn't see that. I swear. All I saw was all those words, one after the other, with translations, and I thought it was a secret book of Callum's, that it was . . . his. And after finding it in his safe, I thought that putting it in the library was the right thing to do. I didn't mean to do anything wrong at all. I didn't take anything." Her thoughts words rushed out in a river of words. She stopped, took a breath. "I loved him like a da, like one I never had. I love the family." She paused and then said softly, "Loved him." She rolled back her shoulders. "The papers were important to Mr. Jameson; that much I knew, but not why. I wanted Charlie to find them, so I put them in a place that would be obvious."

I stepped closer to her. My heart raced ahead of her and toward her answers, which were coming too slow.

"The day after he . . . died, I went in to clean his study. The safe was unlocked and open. I am sure he meant to lock it before bed as always. But instead . . ." She took a breath. "I saw it there, that satchel half in and half out. Maybe I should have let it be, but I didn't.

"I opened the bag, and I saw all those words and knew it must be for you, Mr. Jameson." She looked to Charlie. "I have never, in all the years, not once, seen that bag before. He must have *never* taken it out. I took it to the library."

"Why not leave it where it was for Charlie to find there? Or Mrs. Jameson?" I exhaled audibly.

"I wanted to peek at it, I did. I thought they were his words and I wanted to read some of it. I was mighty sad, and I wasn't thinking right. I took it all down to the library. I'm sorry about that. But I never saw a note—just a few words on paper. I thought they were Callum's. I was looking at those words, wondering about them, when Charlie arrived home that evening. I didn't have time to take them and put them back, so I placed it where it might be seen."

My rising rage fizzled quick and sharp, like touching the end of a match with wet fingertips. Moira was desperate to understand a man she loved and seemed to worship. She was looking for some understanding of him in his absence. I was no different. I sacrificed so much, traveling across an ocean, putting my daughter in danger, emptying my savings, all because I was desperate for understanding my own mother and what she loved and created and wrote.

We weren't so different, Moira and me. My self-righteous anger did us no good while we stood on the side of the road with only a picnic basket and a few clothes.

"I understand," I said.

She looked up from beneath grit-coated lashes. "I am terribly sorry, ma'am. I lost my da and I have never understood any of it. He left when I was but two. This life takes so much from us, and I just wanted a little something of my own. My *very* own. And to understand a secret piece of

Mr. Jameson seemed like something of my own, but it was not. I didn't know it wasn't his and his words."

Charlie stood with his hands on the picnic basket as if frozen by the admission, by the image of Moira in his father's personal effects, by a young woman so enchanted with his father. But I knew the deep longing to understand someone you loved who seemed far from you, someone impossible to truly know unless you found an artifact of their life you could turn over and analyze.

"You have something of him," I told her. "You have your relationship with him. That is only between the two of you. What he taught you, what he showed you, and how he respected you, that is your secret piece of him. I have my own secret pieces of my mother, and I don't know what it means yet, but I know you don't need to be sorry anymore."

The sound of tinkling bells made us all turn to see a figure emerge from the side of the misty field, a woman in a long, flowing yellow skirt. Her dark hair was held back by a headband. She called out. "Yoo-hoooo!"

We all stared at her as if she were made of mist and trees, as if she'd risen from the earth.

Charlie spoke low, almost in a whisper. "A rough sleeper," he said.

"A what?" I asked him.

"A vagrant."

The woman made her way to us and stopped with a smile. "You appear to be lost."

Charlie nodded. "Yes, could you possibly tell us *exactly* where we are?"

"I can," she said. She stared at us, her face round and her nose and eyes the same, as if she'd been composed of circles. "If you'll offer me a ride, I can take you where you need to be, as well as getting me nigh on the road a bit farther."

"Where do you live?" Charlie asked, in a voice as cold as the winter air.

"I was separated from my people last night. I am sure they are a bit up the river. If you don't mind taking me, I can guide you." She paused. "Where do you need to be?"

"On the road toward Cumbria."

"Ah, you are so close, now, in Cheddleton, too far east to get to the main road. Now you must navigate past the McWalters' farm and farther west."

Wynnie hid behind me, and Charlie stepped close to the woman. "Can I pay you for your trouble?"

"I'd just like a ride," she said. "Merely a ride. You know, just because I ain't fancy doesn't mean we are the demons you make us to be."

"Only demons are demons," Charlie said. "Now, we're getting back on the road if you can guide us."

"I surely can," she said.

"Sir," Moira said, stepping close to him, murmuring something I could not hear.

Charlie's voice carried, even as he tried to whisper. "We need her help, and we shouldn't leave her alone on the side of the road."

"Yes, we could," Moira said.

"She has dark edges," Wynnie said quietly, and I wasn't sure if anyone but me heard her.

Charlie looked at the woman as she walked toward the car where the door had been left open.

She climbed into the back seat, and we followed, Wynnie and I on the other side so she sat against the left passenger door. With the aroma of something herbal I could not name, of cigarette smoke and a sweet, overripe smell I associated with sickness, the woman leaned forward and guided Charlie through the streets. Finally, we stopped at a field across from a blue-painted farmhouse, lamplight in the windows like small suns too far away to reach. "I can walk from here," she said.

I thought about the life of those living out here in the country, of how close and yet how far away they were from London that they had no real idea of the peril we'd escaped.

The woman tapped Charlie's shoulder. "Now you will take a left up there at the crossroad. Follow Parkland until you reach Sutherland Road near the Newspring Fishery, then bear right. That will take you straight to where you need to go."

"Thank you." Charlie parked the car at the soft edge of the road, and the woman, who had never told us her name, opened the left passenger-side door, and then reached down. I thought for a moment she was tying her shoe or adjusting her skirt. Then in a movement so fast it took too long to register, she jumped from the car and ran.

"Stop!" I hollered at her as Wynnie screamed, "No!" in a yell so loud that Moira gasped while Charlie sat squinting into the fading sunlight, unable to see what had just happened.

But I could see. I could see that as she ran, she held in her left hand my purse, and in her right, a worn leather satchel.

CHAPTER 27

CLARA

Leaving London

"Stop!" I hollered again through the open passenger door.

The leather of the satchel glowed in the evening light, bouncing against the woman's hip as she ran. The blue fabric purse that I'd bought just for this trip, when I'd had great hope, hung from her left hand as she faded into the mist.

I was the first out of the car; Moira hollering, "No!" but frozen in the front seat, Wynnie fumbling with the right passenger door and Charlie looking over his shoulder at me with a question on his face. "She took my things!" I cried out.

The field stretched toward a future I couldn't see, and from left and right, there was nothing but frosted fields.

In one breath I summed up the situation—even though the most important things, Wynnie's meds, were in the trunk of the car, the woman carried my passports, my money, and Mother's papers. Now Moira was out of the car and I hollered over my shoulder, "Stay with Wynnie."

I bolted after my purse and my papers. Pure instinct—the choice to run after her was as instantaneous as the flame of the match that had set our life on fire, the spark that had brought us here to this very moment.

I ran after her fading figure, her daffodil-colored skirt a wing in the air as the only way to track her. She receded into the mist with papers that would do her no good. "There is nothing in there for you," I hollered, pumping my legs, feeling the singe of soot damage in my lungs, sensing the fatigue of the past days and my trek along the foggy roads as I carried the lantern. My body disobeyed the urge to run faster. Now, Charlie behind me, calling out, "Clara!"

The woman was moving from my sight. These papers, the translation I came for, and the desire to protect Wynnie as the woman disappeared with our tickets, money, and passports surged through me with a swell of energy. Within a few steps, I reached her and tossed my body onto hers as Charlie caught up to us.

The ground was wet and spongy. My ears pulsed with the rush of adrenaline and blood, the sound of a river over rocks. All around us, in the dusk, white pages fluttered, rectangles rose and flew across the field of icy-tinged grass. My mother's lost words let loose.

I saw then—the sound of the river was not in my ears but came from a very real surge of water cutting through the field. The woman, Charlie, and I were at the river's edge on the marshy ground. The sharp reeds and the nettles stung my hands and arms.

I jumped off the woman to save the pages that fluttered from the empty satchel, releasing her.

She took that chance and again she ran off, leaving the now-empty satchel and taking my purse, muttering in a language I'd never heard, but still I felt she was cursing at us. Charlie first checked on me: "Are you all right?"

"Get her!" I said, and we both chased after her as she splashed across the river, jumping from rock to rock in a manner that suggested she'd done this many times before. She knew her way.

Charlie jumped into the river, his shoes being sucked into the dark mud.

From the other side, now free, the woman turned to us and held up my purse, uttering a curse I didn't understand, or maybe it was a victory call.

Then other voices joined hers, along with the backfiring of what I assumed was her getaway car beyond the river.

Charlie yanked his feet from the sucking black mud, leaving his shoes behind. In his gray wool socks, he waded through the river, sliding and slipping. "Stop!" I hollered to him from the banks, my own feet sinking.

He turned. "Your purse!"

"You won't catch her. She's gone. Help me with these pages."

He turned back but looked longingly over his shoulder. He wanted to save us from the loss, I knew that, but there was nothing now but to grab what pages we might. The thief was gone.

I slipped off my shoes and, in my stockings, I made my way into the rushing river. The icy water shocked my body, stealing my breath and stabbing my skin with painful needles of cold. My feet slid along the pebbled bottom as the waters reached my knees. I had no time to waste—I grabbed at pages floating by, pages that sank, and then there were those just beyond my reach as I tried to wade toward them, slogging and slow in the moving current.

"Clara!" Charlie's voice reached out to me. "No! Let them go!"

But I was past myself now, above my body and outside of the normal concepts of time and place. The words of my mother were disappearing, and it felt as if I were losing her again and again. The pages fluttered across the water, lit by a setting sun.

Charlie screamed from the banks. "Get out of the water, Clara! It's dangerous. There's a current. Get out."

I couldn't hear his commands as anything to obey; I was not leaving the river until I retrieved every page I could. Some made their way down the river, and others sank beyond my reach. But the ones I could grab, I did. One by one, I nestled them beneath my jacket and sweater, placing their remains against my skin. Even as I knew I was freezing, I barely felt it. It was more of an idea than an actual sense.

"Clara!"

With that call of my name, my stockinged feet lost hold of a mossy rock and slipped out from beneath me. I dropped into the water, finding myself under a frigid, flowing rush that was oblivious to my plight, merely doing what rivers did and flowing to its destination with little regard for what might be in its wake: my mother's words and me.

I held my breath, opened my eyes beneath the water, and tried to find purchase, but could not until I felt a yank on my shoulder and searing pain in my arm.

Then there was air.

"My God, Clara. Stop!"

I gasped. Charlie held fast to me, and he was up to his waist in the water, his coat shed on the riverbank.

My body shivered so violently that my teeth slammed on top of each other uncontrollably. "Wynnie," I cried out, and clambered out of that river, sliding and crawling to solid ground.

Charlie held the empty satchel in his hand, and I forced myself into a run across the field, away from my mother's words, and toward my daughter.

I reached the fence line, and there Wynnie and Moira stood at the side of the car, watching us. Wynnie's arms were crossed, and her head was tilted in that adorable way, her glasses crooked. Her curls were loose from their braids, and in the misty moisture they sprung wild about her face.

I threw my arms around her.

"You're wet!" She pushed me away and shivered. "Mama, what did you *do*?"

"I fell into the river trying to save the pages. I-I was chasing that woman. She took our purse."

"I knew that lady wasn't good," Wynnie said.

"You did?" I bent my forehead to hers, my body shaking as if the earth trembled beneath me.

"I told you I saw her dark edges. She was about to do a bad thing." Wynnie looked past me.

"Yes," Charlie said, now at our sides. He looked at me with such fear, and I wondered what he saw. "Take off your jersey and pants," he said as he shrugged off his coat. "Now."

I shuddered so violently that I couldn't do as he asked. The icy water seeped deeper than my skin; it was moving into my bones. I was freezing from the outside in, and all to gather a few pages. There was something innately and deeply wrong with me, something broken, and I knew it even as I felt the pain.

Sacrificing my body for Mother's words was irrational, and I felt fiery shame even as Moira lifted my soaked sweater over my head and pages fell to the ground. Moira unbuttoned my pants and helped me step out. My hands trembled without control. I stood in my underwear in front of Charlie, unembarrassed and too cold to care about anything but warmth.

He ran to the trunk of the car and pulled out his brown suitcase, unbuckled it, and grabbed a sweater from its depths. He came to me and slipped the itchy wool over my head, guiding my arms through the sleeves; the sweater fell to just above my knees. Finally, he placed his large coat around me like a blanket.

"Clara, we have hours to travel. You must get warm. Now climb into the car, all of you." His words were adamant, but his tone was gentle. I heard a tremble of fear.

Moira took the pages that had fallen from my body when she removed my clothes, and she gathered them into a pile as Wynnie and I climbed into the back seat.

Once I was inside the car, wrapped in his sweater and coat, Wynnie sat next to me, and Moira handed me a kitchen towel from the picnic basket. "Dry some of your hair, Miss Clara."

I was quaking too violently to do much of anything, so Wynnie rubbed the towel on my hair, squeezed the river from the strands as best she could.

"I'm sorry." I let out a sob.

"I should have never given her a ride," Charlie said. "I had a very bad feeling, but I was desperate for directions. Now we need petrol and it's getting dark."

Wynnie set her hand on the back of his arm as he faced forward. "It was still good of you to give her a ride. You can't stop being good because someone else is not."

Then I saw in my mind's eye my purse hanging off her shoulder. "Our passports," I said. "Our tickets and money." My voice was as cold as my body, and it quivered as I spoke.

"We will get you new passports and tickets," Charlie said. "But you should *not* have gone into that river. That was dangerous."

"I know," I said. "I know."

There I was, freezing, my child watching me with shocked eyes, and all because I wanted pages and words to describe a world I'd lost years ago?

There went my hope to translate her sequel and discover if there were secrets and hints waiting for me in its pages. There went the chance to get back the money I'd siphoned from my savings. There went all of it—hope and money—disappeared into a river, across a field, and into the hands of a stranger.

Even as I trembled with the chill and the ice of remorse, I wanted Moira to tell me—*how many pages did we save?*

CHAPTER 28

CLARA

Lake District, England

"We're here," Charlie said.

I didn't so much wake in the back seat of the car as emerge from something so deeply annihilating that no memory of dreams or even of falling asleep remained. The first blow of feeling was the heat behind my eyes, the rage of burning fever.

I sat up with the satisfying weight of Wynnie's head in my lap. Charlie parked on a gravel drive. The house towered above us, glowing in gray and white, as solid as the mountain behind it. Smoke rose from a chimney. A granite roofline sloped over the glow of lights inside the middle windows and the moon's wan glow offered only hints of the landscape.

"What time is it?" I croaked, my voice broken.

"One a.m," Charlie answered.

We'd traveled another four hours while I'd slept. My exhaustion weighed on me like a sack of rocks.

Wynnie stirred and then sat up to stare out the window. "This looks like a storybook." She opened the passenger door and climbed out. I followed and placed my feet on the pebbled drive, my legs shaking and nearly giving way; I grabbed for the open car door. I didn't care what this house looked like or where we'd landed—I needed to lay my head on a pillow.

We stood covered in black soot, damp and shivering, hidden by the night, with only the glow of a gas lantern over the single front door covered by an arched entryway. I wore Charlie's sweater beneath his coat and my skin itched. We took in deep breaths of fresh night air, and Wynnie leaned against me. "It doesn't burn anymore," she said.

The front door opened, and a woman appeared silhouetted by the light from inside. She stood regal, a tall woman with her hair loose around her shoulders. "Charlie!" she called out, and took two steps toward us on the landing. "I have been worried to death. The news on the wireless is awful. Get in the house. There is food waiting for you—come, come."

Charlie carried our belongings inside, and I imagined our other luggage sitting unattended in the flat in London, my purse being rummaged through by thieves, its belongings flung across the river, sinking to the bottom with Mother's pages. I imagined my money trading hands and my passport sold, my tickets for home tossed as trash.

I shivered.

I took Wynnie's hand, and we walked up the stone stairs to the entryway, which had an inner and an outer door. The floor below was parquet, and a flowered globe light hung above me. Once we were inside, the entry foyer gave an overall impression of dark wood, with a stairwell to the left that climbed along the wall, flowers in vases, and stern faces in gold frames. Doorways to the right were closed tight; an arched hallway was dark before us.

Mrs. Jameson clasped her hands in front of her. "I am Philippa Jameson, and you must be Clara and Wynnie." I nodded at her, with little use for language. "Would you like something to eat? A cup of tea? What can I do for you?"

"Mum," Charlie said, dropping our bags on the bottom step, "they need a doctor."

"Follow me," Mrs. Jameson said.

Wynnie pointed up the staircase at a stained glass window with floral patterns looming over the foyer. "Is this a magical house?"

He laughed. "It's been in our family for nearly a hundred years now. A little shabbier in the morning light, but at night like this, I agree. Magic. Now let's get you warm and fed and let Doc Finlay give a good look at both of you. We'll deal with your passports and everything else tomorrow."

"You keep a doctor here?" I asked, unable to decide if I was freezing or burning, the feeling abysmal either way.

"I called before we left." Charlie put his hand to my back and guided us to the first door on the right. "You're burning up."

"I am, yes."

He opened the thick door to a room with tall windows overlooking an unknown landscape hidden in the cloak of night. "Clara," Charlie said in a voice so warm and kind I wanted to fall against him, to feel his solid body, to fall asleep for as long and as deep as I pleased, but Wynnie was next to me, and she was all that mattered. "I'm so sorry I let that woman into the car."

"Don't be sorry. You didn't know—"

"Miss?" I turned to Moira's voice. She held out a pile of papers, wet, mostly destroyed, and far thinner than they'd been hours ago. "I will place these in your room. This is the little we saved."

A rush of sorrow and dread arrived with a realization that everything I came for was mostly gone. Whatever I sacrificed to be here wasn't worth the wet pages she held, the dregs of my hope.

Charlie placed his hand under my elbow and led me farther into the drawing room with dark paneled walls where logs blazed in the fireplace; the furniture was covered with leather cracked with age, all with a patina of brown glaze the color of rich chocolate. He set me in a chair and looked to his mother. "Mum, how about some warm blankets and tea for Clara?"

A bald man sat in the largest chair, slouched over his paunchy stomach. His mouth was open, soft snores emanating in time with the rise and fall of his tweed-covered chest.

"Finlay," Charlie said, and the man opened his eyes.

I held Wynnie close, and although she was alert and fine, the whistle only I could hear rattled in her chest. Through the blur of fever and thirst thick in my mouth, I took in some details. A leather kit sat at the man's feet, and a large silver cylinder stood by his side. I recognized the oxygen tank and wanted to weep with gratitude. Charlie Jameson brought us out of the fog to this house of slate, stone, and grand rooms, where an oxygen tank sat waiting. Lamplight glowed in the room from every dark-wood tabletop.

Dr. Finlay took only a breath or two before he jumped up and came to Wynnie, bent down to look closely at her. "Child, come here." He motioned to a chair under a large standing lamp. "Let's have a look at you."

Wynnie checked with me, and I nodded to her. She sat in the leather chair and looked up at the doctor. He snapped a stethoscope to his ears and set the drum of it on her chest. "Wheezing." It was unclear who he talked to as he examined my girl. "Lips slightly hypoxic. Alert.

"Can you take a deep breath?" he asked. His tobacco-stained teeth and yellowing nails told me of a cigarette habit that ran contrary to a man helping someone's lungs open.

Wynnie nodded and took a deep breath that sent her into a spasm of coughing. The doctor reached for a contraption I'd never seen—a pewter teapot without a spout, but instead a black tube poking out from the middle of it. Dr. Finlay held the tube out to Wynnie and told her to inhale. She nodded and took a deep breath.

She sighed deeply. He rolled the oxygen cylinder over and placed a mask on her face. "You're going to be fine."

"What was that?" I pointed to the contraption.

"A Mudge inhaler," he said, and now directed his attention to me. He was an older man with purple pouches under his eyes, a gobble of loose skin on his neck, lines etched across his forehead and around his mouth. But beneath all of that were blue eyes so clear they looked like mountain lakes.

"What's a Mudge inhaler?" Every word I spoke scraped my throat like sandpaper.

"It has a very small amount of opium to relax her lungs and allow the oxygen to enter. I suggest you both get cleaned up, get some food into her, and take her to bed." Then his thick brows lowered, and he moved closer to me. "What about you?"

I gave a slight shake of my head, indicating that I was fine.

He narrowed his eyes—did he believe my motions or my words?

Charlie was there now, his hand on my shoulder. "She actually is not all right. She went into the river—long story—and now she's burning with fever."

"Oh, dear God," he said. "You need a warm bath and bed, or between the cold and the fog, it will all end up in *your* lungs." He looked up to Charlie. "You didn't tell me."

"It just happened on the way here."

"I'll leave you with some cough expectorant and aspirin. But you must tell me if she's not better in two days." He looked to Wynnie. "I believe you'll be fine by morning. Both of you off to warm clothes and bed. Now."

Wynnie looked up at me, and her eyes behind her smudged glasses took on a hazy glow.

Everything was moving in slow motion, and what he'd said about the Mudge inhaler filtered into my fuzzy brain. "Opium? You gave my daughter opium?"

"Just a titch. Enough to allow her lungs to relax and for her to sleep."

Moira returned to the room with a bowl of water in her hands. She knelt before Wynnie and took a steaming cloth from the water. Carefully she wiped Wynnie's face and hands. "You're going to be all right, little one."

Mrs. Jameson paced the room, asking if we needed food, bringing me a cup of tea that I didn't touch. Wynnie looked at me from under her oxygen mask, her language garbled, but I understood it well enough to know that she said, "I'm tired." And with that she closed her eyes.

I looked to the doctor. "How long does she need the oxygen? I'd like to get her in a bed."

"Just a few more minutes and then off to bed. She will be fine by morning. I am much more worried about you."

"Thank you," I said. "But Wynnie is the one I am worried about. My heart has been bouncing out of my chest and I—" I stopped. "Do you think this fog damaged her lungs even more?"

"It's hard to know," he said. "You got her out of London, out of that sulfuric air, and that's all that matters for now."

Charlie held out his hand. "Please, let's get you both upstairs. Moira," he said. "Please draw a hot bath for Clara and . . ."

From there I remembered little: Moira's hands on me as she undressed and helped me bathe, Wynnie asleep, Mother's language whispered over a field of frost and river.

CHAPTER 29

CHARLIE

Lake District, England

Charlie hadn't slept worth a damn. There was within him a strange desire to look in on Clara, check her fever, rest next to her until she woke up.

Instead, he reached over to the bedside table for the biography of her mother and read where the book opened up.

March 25, 1927

Martha Fordham—Mother of Bronwyn Newcastle Fordham
Benjamin Oster—Interviewer, chief of police, Bluffton, South
Carolina

Martha Fordham: As a child, Bronwyn would instruct me to leave
an empty chair at the table for her imaginary friends.
Benjamin Oster: She had more than one?
Martha Fordham: Oh yes, she had many. There was Beethoven
and Chopin. Then there was Emjie and Dingy.
Benjamin Oster: Beethoven and Chopin are real.
Martha Fordham: Sir, those two are *dead*, so if I am saving a place
at the table for them, they are therefore imaginary.
Benjamin Oster: Yes, I hear you. I understand. Your daughter had
a wild imagination.
Martha Fordham: *Has.* She *has* a wild imagination. She believes
in what we can't see. She believes in her make-believe.

Benjamin Oster: Where do you think she's gone?

[*Long pause on the recording*]

Martha Fordham: I wouldn't know. She hasn't spoken to me in
years. I want her to . . . [*pause*] I want her to come home. But
that is something I have wanted for a very long while.

Charlie slammed shut the book. He'd learned enough from Brian
Davis. He wanted to learn the rest from Clara and Wynnie.

He left his room and walked into the hallway. The sound of workmen who'd arrived from Windermere with a truckload of greenery were
filling the house with garland and ribbons, with wreaths and swag and
flowers, echoed below. Charlie greeted them as he walked downstairs
and entered the drawing room to find Wynnie standing at the window,
staring out at the wide expanse of the back gardens that flowed into
pastures bordering the lake.

"Good morning," he said, and she turned to him with a dreamy look
on her face.

"Mama is asleep. She's still sick."

"Yes, I know. Dr. Finlay says she needs rest and she'll be okay. He's
coming back this morning to check on both of you."

Wynnie wore a wool dress that must have been in the small bag Clara
had brought with them. Her hair stuck up and out in a thousand directions, and it made him smile. She was such a lively but polite child, as
if the opposing forces didn't battle within her but partnered into something so charming she seemed to vibrate with sweet mischief.

She was—he disliked this term but could think of no other—an old
soul. She was so fully recovered it was as if the girl who had almost died
in that poisonous air had never existed except for the soot Charlie spied
in the whirl of her ear, the one spot the washcloth didn't reach.

Her glasses were clean now, and she lifted her finger to move them
higher on her nose. "Outside. It looks like the places Mama paints," she
said, and rested that same finger on the window.

He thought of Clara in front of an easel and wondered about her
work. He should have asked her about her art, and he would as soon as
she awoke.

He came to Wynnie's side, and together they silently watched the sheep next door move toward the low hills and a flock of blackbirds unsettling from a low hawthorn tree. Sometimes, busy with his life and concerns, he forgot to stop and notice the sheer beauty of this place. Through Wynnie's eyes he again noticed the mosaic of crags, fells, and lake, a dramatic beauty that changed with every cloud cover and blue sky.

Wynnie sighed. "Can I go out there? Please?"

"First let's sort you some breakfast, shall we?"

She turned and smiled. "Yes, please."

"I'll send up a tray for your mum."

"She cried out a lot in her sleep," Wynnie said, brushing back her hair, her lips now trembling. "Her cheeks were so hot, and . . ."

"I know you must be frightened. But she's just got a chill, that's all," Charlie said, hoping his words were comforting to an eight-year-old. "Dr. Finlay says her lungs sound fine and that she'll be all right. She just needs some sleep."

"It's because of me," Wynnie said. "She worries so much about me."

"No!" Charlie set his hand on her shoulder and bent down to look at her round blue eyes, so like her mother's. "It is the weather and your grandmother's papers and a mean woman who wanted to steal money. None of this is *your* fault."

"That's what Mama would say, too." Wynnie took off her glasses and wiped her eyes with the backs of her palms. "Then she'd tell me I am the best part of everything."

"Well, I believe she's right."

She smiled, and it seemed real now. "She will say we shouldn't have come here, but don't let her think that, okay?"

He nearly laughed. "And why is that?"

"Because she wanted to see those papers and that letter so badly, and she would have always, always wondered. And because I got to eat clotted cream and scones."

He shook his head. "Great point there. Now let's introduce you to eggs and soldiers." He reached out his hand for hers and led her down the hallway.

Charlie and his mother watched Wynnie polish off her eggs with soldiers. They sat around the circular glass breakfast table in the garden room. His mum chatted incessantly with Wynnie, asking about her life in South Carolina, about her favorite books and games, about her journey on the ocean liner. Wynnie was gregarious and open, glancing at Charlie every few sentences as if checking that she wasn't doing anything wrong.

Charlie was reminded of his mum's lovely ease with children. The three of them around the table was a comfort after the escape from London, and he found himself wishing Clara would rouse to join them.

"Why are so many people here?" Wynnie asked quietly, the crumbs of her second scone on her chin and jumper. Charlie reached over and brushed her cheek, and she smiled at him.

"Christmas," he told her.

"Yes," Mrs. Jameson said. "Tradition. Our family always decorates on the same day every year. The eighth of December."

"Why the eighth?" Wynnie asked with a curious tilt of her head.

"It is the Feast of the Immaculate Conception in the Catholic Church."

"Immaculate what?" Wynnie asked.

Charlie laughed and squeezed her shoulder. "It is part of Christmas," he said. "Mum can explain later."

Wynnie grew serious and nodded. "Well, I love traditions. We have some, too. We always guess the gift before we open it, and we always decorate Easter eggs on the back porch."

"That's so lovely," his mum said. "And wouldn't it be lovely if you could see all of this at Christmas?"

Wynnie sat straighter. "That would be wonderful!"

"Only three weeks away," she said.

"I think Mama will want to go home. We haven't had very good luck in England."

Charlie's mum let out a beautiful laugh, a sound he hadn't heard since Father passed, and it warmed him. She'd nearly canceled the yearly Christmas decorations, but Charlie had convinced her otherwise: *Father would not want you to cancel the thing that brought both of you so much joy.*

"My first Christmas without your father. I don't quite know if I can do it," she'd said.

"I will be here. We'll do it together," he'd told her.

Now Mum stood and smiled down at Wynnie. "Why don't you two have a walk around Esthwaite?"

Charlie looked to Wynnie. "Can you do that?"

"Yes, it's good for me, or that's what Mama is always telling me when I want to just read on the couch. 'Let's get some air,' she always says." Wynnie imitated her mama's voice, and again Pippa laughed, and Charlie felt hope, like a small crocus bursting through the frost. "What's Esthwaite?" Wynnie stumbled over the word, lisping at the sounds.

"That's the name of the lake," Charlie said. He looked to his mum. "Don't I need to help you?"

"No, there are plenty of people to bring down boxes and hang ribbons. Now go on, the two of you."

Charlie held out his hand for Wynnie and she took it. If his mum wanted to ask about *why* Wynnie and Clara were in her house, she held those questions inside. When they'd arrived last night and made sure Clara and Wynnie were safely in bed, he hadn't lied to her, but he hadn't told her *everything*.

"Explain it all to me," she'd said.

And he'd told her. "Dad stored some papers in his library that belonged to Clara's mother, something he'd possibly bought at an auction. I don't actually know. I contacted Clara, and she planned a trip to England to come retrieve them. That's when the fog descended."

"Some papers?"

"Her mother was an author."

"Oh," she'd said, "one of your father's collections."

That information was enough for Mum, as other things were on her mind. He'd felt a twinge of guilt.

That was the thing with half-truths—they were usually meant to protect someone. Charlie just wasn't clear yet about exactly who he was protecting, or, for that matter, who his father was keeping safe by holding this satchel from the beginning. But one thing was clear—none of them knew the full story, and he was just as much in the dark as anyone.

Once they were out the back door, he led Wynnie across the flagstone porch, through the silent garden, and down the soft wet grass toward the lake. Wynnie was bundled in a coat and hat and mittens Mum had found in the upstairs closet. She was chattering away.

"Did you live here? It's as pretty as Papa's place on the bay, but not the same. Different but same," Wynnie said.

"It is pretty. I forget that sometimes," he told her. "Thank you for reminding me." He smiled down at her.

"Emjie brought me here before," she said, and stopped. "Those stone walls and that little island in the middle of the lake and the geese everywhere."

"Emjie?"

"You can't see her, but she's right here." Wynnie held out her hand and then laughed. "She threw a little pinecone at you."

"Oh, you have an imaginary friend," he said, relieved that he could now follow her logic. He led her across the lane to the sloping pasture leading to the lake's edge.

"Invisible, not imaginary," Wynnie stated with stern surety.

"Ah," he said. "Would she mind if I told you both all about where we are right now?"

"That's what she wants, too," Wynnie said. "We want to know the name of every tree and plant and bird we see."

He laughed, and the sound echoed across the valley and settled in the lake where he'd spent much of his childhood. He sometimes felt he could see the reflection of his boyhood in Esthwaite Water, a time when he was as close to his brother as the tree's roots to the land.

He tried to fulfill Wynnie's wish. "This lake is called Esthwaite Water. There's another over there." He swept his hand behind them. "It's called Windermere and is much bigger; we can't see it from here, but we can walk there. Both are glacial lakes, carved by ice."

"Ice-carved lakes," Wynnie said. "Wow."

"And the forest there"—He lifted his face to the mountains that looked down at them—"is called Grizedale."

"You are making that up!" she said.

"Indeed, I am not."

She started to run, her arms wheeling in front of her as she made her way to the shoreline. He ran after her. It had been years, too many, since he'd run through this pasture, and the feeling was freeing, making him feel young as he caught up to her at the ice-skimmed edge. A mirror to the sky above, the waters held white and silver clouds, the naked branches of winter, and the body of the fells that rose above them.

He wondered how his family was tangled up with this little girl, how only his father knew the answer.

Boulders were scattered along the edge of the lake, and Wynnie clambered to the top of one. "It's the most beautiful lake I've ever seen," Wynnie exclaimed as she held out her arms as if to hug the body of water. "Bigger than any lake I've ever seen. It's like the place in *Swallows and Amazons*."

"The place in that book is just one lake over," he told her with a grin. "But much bigger."

"I knew it! I can see the little sailboat and the—"

"It is something," he said. "And do you know about the Tizzie-Whizies?"

"Tizzie-Whizie?"

He made his voice low and singsong, a storytelling voice. "At the lake's edge, there are creatures who live along these waters. They have a hedgehog's body and the tail of a squirrel and wings like a bee." He spread his arms, flapping them like a fool.

She laughed and poked him. "You're making that up!"

"Ah, if I am, I'm not the only one."

"Have you ever seen one?" She glanced around.

"I thought I did once, but it disappeared when I drew closer."

"I believe you!" she said with a grin. "My mama illustrates books about a hedgehog. Her name is Harriet, and she only has one ear."

"Does she have the tail of a squirrel or wings of a bee?"

"No! But Harriet is the cutest hedgehog you've ever seen, even if she is different from her friends." Wynnie then mused, "But there must also be fairies here."

"Yes, there are fairy hills near that people say are gateways to a secret world."

"A secret world." Wynnie's face clouded over. "That's where Emjie was stuck for a long while in Grandma's book."

"Tell me about Emjie."

"She's my best friend and the main character in Grandma's book. She got stuck in the dark place, and that's why Grandma wrote a sequel—to get her out. Which she must have done because she visits me. Emjie is the one who taught me to see the smudgy edges of people who are also in the dark place."

"Dark place?"

"Yes, like lies or meanness."

"Do you see any smudges on me?" He meant to ask this as a jolly question, but it came out serious and worried.

"No!" she said.

"Ah, good." He felt a turn in subject was needed and asked, "Have you read the sequel that gets her out?"

"No, it's written in . . . well, you know."

"I do," he said.

"I don't know what she went through to get to the other side, which is what I *want* to know. Because the ending is no fun without the middle parts."

He laughed and wanted to lift her up in a grand hug. "Indeed," he said, "the middle parts make the ending worth it."

They stood silent at the edge of the lake for a while, watching a kestrel swoop overhead and listening to the rustling of something unseen behind them and the long low of a cow from the farm nearby. Finally he told her, "I think we should head back in case your mama is awake."

She nodded, and he extended his hand to help her down from the boulder. Along the way he pointed at the red squirrel who ran across their path. He explained that the sheep they saw dotting the fields with their silver-and-white coats and their wise, tender faces were called Herdwick sheep, and nearly every specimen of that breed lived in the Lake District. A peregrine falcon flew overhead, screeching, and he pointed it out to her, telling her it was the fastest bird in the world. He named the field elm and the bilberry, the English oak and the sycamore.

She tilted her head and her wool hat tipped as they looked up at the back end of three stone cottages. "Are those yours, too?"

"They are part of our land, yes."

"Who lives there?" She squinted into the distance.

"An aunt and a second cousin—one from either side of the family—and the groundskeeper," he told her.

They reached the crest of the hill behind the cottages, and Charlie led her toward an unfinished stone wall encircling a small garden. He meant to cut around to the far side and cross the lane back to the house, but Wynnie stopped and placed her hand on the stones. Green and yellow lichen softened the edges; ferns sprouted from the cracks. "It's not finished," Wynnie said, and then smiled at what Charlie assumed was her imaginary friend, "but it will be soon."

"Yes, Cousin Isolde adds to it all the time," Charlie told her, and then he pointed at the cottage a hundred yards away.

Wynnie lifted her hand to her mouth, bit the edge of her mitten, and pulled it away so she might set her bare hand on top of the stones. "Mama is going to love this. She loves anything that's like *The Secret Garden* or anything that has flowers that grow inside."

"You have a good mama," Charlie said. "You're lucky."

"You do too."

"Yes, I do."

"You know . . ." Wynnie removed her hand and turned earnestly to Charlie, "you're lucky you have a brother. I'm the only one, and because of me, Mama can't have any more kids, and I almost didn't live. Isn't that strange? To think about just not being here at all when I am right here!"

"Strange and wonderful."

"She would never leave me," Wynnie said.

He wondered why there, suddenly, Wynnie needed to say such a thing.

"No, she would not."

As they made their way back to the house, Charlie looked up to the window of the room where Clara slept. He felt relief when he spied her there, a silhouette. He waved and she lifted her hand, palm up as if showing them something they needed to see, something set free.

"Mama!" Wynnie said, and skipped toward the house.

CHAPTER 30

CLARA

Lake District, England

I was in the water again with the satchel, floating through the country-side to join the Thames in London and then toward the sea on a storm-tossed river. I cried out for help, but there was no one nearby. I floated in the sea and held my hands over the moving waters, my legs pulsing beneath me to keep me afloat until I was too tired to kick. I closed my eyes to sink, but a great force rose beneath me and brought me to the surface, where I gasped for breath and woke thrashing in the tangled sheets.

I awoke in a strange canopied bed, my voice crying out for Mommy, a name I hadn't used in twenty-five years. Image fragments appeared in the delirium of a half-sleep fever: rushing rivers and frosted fields, words floating on paper in torn fragments, unreadable and untranslatable, and Wynnie turning blue.

When the fevered dreams broke, I had no real idea of the day or time. *Wynnie.*

I reached my hand across the sheets for her and found only empty space and dented pillows. My heart stuttered and I sat up and brushed back my hair, oily with soot.

I took stock—I wore a white cotton nightgown, now damp and crumpled. I rested under the soft sheets of a bed in a room of creamy vanilla plaster walls, a canopy of lace over the four-poster bed.

Sawrey. Cumbria.

The past days rushed back to me with a full blow of memory.

The travel from London with a lantern.

Poisonous air, burning lungs, cows dead on the road, birds dropping from the sky, and wandering strangers who tried to rob us. No, who *did* rob us. Wynnie wheezing. A doctor.

I shuddered with the memories and slipped from the bed, wondering where Wynnie might be and how long I'd been asleep.

A black-armed brass clock on the bedside table pointed to nine a.m. What day? My body ached with a combination of the worst too-many-beers night and a stomach virus. My head floated and conversely felt heavy. My tongue was thick with raging thirst.

I stood slowly, my legs shaking. A glass of water sat on the bedside table, and I downed it. Black smudges had ruined the white cotton pillowcase. The sheets, too, were gray and streaked with the leftover soot of London.

I walked to the window and gasped.

Outside stretched a breathtaking landscape with a heartbeat both familiar and wholly new. This bedroom was on the second floor at the back of the house, overlooking a sloping, heather-colored field that flowed down to a pewter lake skimmed in the glitter of ice. Stone walls, flinty and gray and white, snaked around the fields. To the right, three cottages squatted below my sight; their slate roofs with orange rounded chimney pots was all I could see of them. A dirt path set with flagstones wound its way down a sloped lawn toward a pasture that ran to the lake's edge.

Even in winter, the landscape was sublime, bare of its finery and revealing its perfect bones. The mountains undulated, flecked by evergreens and naked hardwoods. I wanted to know the name of every one of these trees. The valley was nestled in the upturned bowl of these mountains, dotted with silver-gray sheep on a patchwork of pasture. Patches of green fern and copse, a forest enchanted at the edges of everything.

I wanted a canvas, a palette of paints.

The whole of it made me feel a certain at-homeness, as if I'd been there before, as if my illustrations were looking for this. The lake of light glittered and winked beneath a sky shrouded by lead-colored clouds.

This was a forgotten lake, one I once knew.

I nearly laughed at the unbidden thought. The fever must have been giving me absurd notions while the mist rolled off the mountains and across the silver waters. All was a symphony of colors and textures, and my eyes couldn't find one place to rest.

Inside me, something opened. I'd seen this land before, hadn't I? But that was impossible.

Frost surrounded the window frames, and I breathed on the pane and fogged the glass. I set my hand against it, creating a handprint, as if proving I was real in a geography so far removed from the dailyness of my life that I felt free-floating, separate from myself, as if I stood outside the window looking in at myself. There she is, some other part of me said, a woman wearing a stranger's too-long white cotton nightgown, her hair hanging in sooty fever-drenched tangles.

A soft knock at the door, and I turned to see Moira standing there with a tray of food and a pot of tea hidden under a red quilt cozy.

She beamed. "You are up! Oh, Miss Clara, I am so happy to see you awake. I've brought you breakfast." She set the tray on the pine dresser.

"Where is Wynnie?" I asked.

"With Charlie. She's well!"

"What day is it?"

She went through the motions of pouring tea and adding milk and sugar, of preparing a cup even as she spoke without seeming to take a breath. "You've been sleeping on and off for more than a day. I found you twice at the window and I helped you to the loo, but for all that, you've had nothing to eat. You *must* eat. Mr. Jameson wants to make sure you have some decent breakfast. We've all been so worried. Dr. Finlay told us you'd be fine, seeing as your lungs are clear and all that. Just exhaustion and cold, he said." She covered her mouth. "I'm babbling on when you must be so tired and weary, so confused." She handed me the teacup with violets around its edges.

I smiled at Moira and remembered her dancing in the London library, a look of sheer ecstasy as Vivaldi played on a phonograph. She had been oblivious to the world around her as tears rolled down her face. She'd given herself over completely in the library of a man she admired and grieved.

I took a long swallow and felt the warmth, the sweet and bitter taste that was such a comfort I understood the British infatuation with tea and all its accoutrements. "Tell her to please come here?"

Moira smiled. "She was having breakfast with Mrs. Jameson, but I believe she's already gone out walking with Mr. Jameson. Might you want to eat and bathe before you see them?"

I almost laughed and felt the weakness in even that, my body awake but not fully. "I must look a fright."

"Not nearly as frightful as you were when you were red with fever and delirious with hallucinations." She opened her mouth to speak and then closed it again.

"What is it?"

"Nothing that matters."

"The papers?"

"They are over there." She pointed to the desk, and I looked closer. Yes, there they were—the crumpled, smudged, and ruined papers in a much smaller pile than the original.

"I promise I didn't read them. Most of them are too waterlogged to read as it is. I put them there straightaway so you can look at them when you're ready."

"That's all that remains." This wasn't a question.

"Yes."

"Thank you, Moira."

She smiled with such eagerness that her eyes crinkled with it. "Come down whenever you please. Mr. Jameson said to tell you that there are clothes in the wardrobe that should fit you. Miss Adelaide and you are the same size, but I will say she's a bit taller." Moira nodded toward a large wooden wardrobe at the side of the room, its doors shut tight and a cracked mirror on its surface where Moira and I were reflected in zigzag shapes.

"Adelaide?" I asked.

"Charlie's sister-in-law. Archie's wife."

"Ah," I said.

"Dr. Finlay will be here again soon." Moira closed the door, but the aroma of the sausage and eggs, along with the bitter bite of the tea, had me ravenous. I took a wool blanket from the back of an ivory silk settee and wrapped it around my shoulders.

I set the tray on the oak desk, moved Mother's tattered and mostly unreadable papers to the side, and ate slowly while staring out the window. Every bite of biscuit was rich and saturated with flavor and warmth. The landscape shifted with the rising sun, and the shadows morphed and receded. The naked branches stretched toward a sky they'd never reach.

I looked for Wynnie and Charlie but didn't see them. Smoke rose from cottage chimneys just below my window to the right. A huge, fluffy white dog ran toward a house on the left, and a tall woman bent down to rub its ears.

I avoided looking at the papers, the proof of loss, and the remnants of Mother's language, not nearly enough for me to be able to translate her sequel.

It was clear now: all hope for understanding her—for pulling back the veil that covered her life in language, and for finding reasons and meaning in what she'd done—had vanished, spread across a frosted field, snatched by a thief in the middle of the country.

I covered the finished food plate with a linen napkin to take to the kitchen. It was peculiar to think that I'd been attended to by both Moira and Dr. Finlay, and yet I remembered nothing but my own fevered dreams.

After a long, hot bath with rose-scented soap, wrapped in a soft bathrobe that hung on the back hook of the door, I approached the papers. On top rested a sheet with one word, an ink-bleeding word, *talith*, with the definition:

When the sky breaks open; transformation that changes you into who you are meant to be; into your very essence.

When the sky breaks open.

This was what Mother had been writing about when the fire started. She'd wanted her sky to break open and reveal to her all she wanted to know, to show her all that was hidden from us.

It was possible that this was the word that had sent her from us to transform herself like Emjie, who found another world in *The Middle Place.*

I'd never loved Emjie's ending, no reader really did—how Emjie left this earthbound world for another and became stuck, unable to find her way back to those she loved. This ending hinted that Mother had done the same.

Most of my life I'd believed that if I could translate the sequel and discover that Emjie made her way home, Mother would do the same.

It was a foolish childhood dream.

Here was the thing: I saw it now as if the fever had cleared the fog not only of London but also of my thoughts. I'd believed—and it might be true—that the pages of her sequel held her true self, that there was another mother, and she was hidden in the story. I wanted to know *that* mother so badly.

I wanted not Mother as she was, but Mother as she was hidden from me.

This desire had been germinating in me for so long that my life warped around the idea. Knowing that I would never fully translate her sequel or find meaning in her or her leaving, I sensed peace as it settled over me like the sky settled over this landscape of mountains, valleys, and lake.

In hopelessness, there was a great and wild letting-go.

I stood and walked to the window again and found my hands palm open and facing upward as if something had flown away from my once-clenched fists. Whatever I'd held in desperation floated away, and with an exhale I saw Charlie and Wynnie walking the flagstone pathway toward the house. The mountains ascended behind them and the lake flashed an azure blue, the poplar, the oak, the elm, and the sycamore forming the woodlands around them like an embrace.

CHAPTER 31

CLARA

Lake District, England

The doctor arrived in the bedroom to check on me and declared me well: "A chill and a fever, but lucky none of it settled in your lungs." I was to take the day slowly and rest.

In the wardrobe, I found a simple wool day dress of pale green and an evergreen cardigan with pearl buttons. Adelaide owned very nice clothes—this matched set was about as casual as I could find. Not a pair of trousers in the drawer.

I pulled my wet hair back tightly in a knot. A quick glance in the mirror showed a wan and exhausted woman. I felt ridiculously over-dressed.

Carrying my breakfast tray, I emerged from the room, my face scrubbed and my hair smelling like roses. Voices called out and over-lapped as if there was a gathering. I made my way down the hallway. On the landing I stopped to glance down and saw men in khaki uniforms wrestling a massive spruce tree to stand upright. It must have been twelve feet or more. They hollered directions at one another: *Get it straight! Fasten it at the bottom! Lean it to the left, for bloody sake!*

That was right, Christmas was only three weeks away.

I imagined my own holiday decorations, homemade and so special to me, boxed up in the attic of our home. Dad wouldn't think to bring them down without us.

Dad.

I needed to call him.

I made my way to the bottom of the stairs without anyone noticing me. I found more men hanging garland across the entryways of each room. Along the foyer, large red ribbons were being fastened at the corners of doorways. The whole house smelled like a forest, damp and piney.

Charlie had said that the house would look a bit shabbier in the daylight, but I would use a different word: *cozier*. It wasn't as grand as the night had hinted, but instead it seemed snug, created of soft corners and many rooms. The wooden banister was smoothed and faded by many hands running along its surfaces, the flowered carpet worn thin in the places where feet trampled up and down the stairs. Signs of sweet life.

I had no real idea of how big the house was, how many bedrooms and rooms, how large the acreage. It seemed awaiting exploration.

I heard a woman's voice, and I followed it to a square garden room in the back of the house. The room was surrounded in floor-to-ceiling windows, bright in the morning sunshine.

There sat Mrs. Jameson, holding up a plate to Moira.

I took that moment to stare at her, Charlie's mother, Mrs. Philippa Jameson. She could have been posing for a portrait in the way she sat so still, her shoulders back and her chin up, her blond hair in a lovely pile at the back of her neck, held in place with a golden clasp. She wore a subdued-blue dress with a round neckline and a strand of pearls at breakfast.

On the table sat a newspaper, and the headlines read: *Third Day of a London Particular. Busy Time for Thieves.*

I felt a rush of relief to be here, in this safe and warm home.

Moira spied me and smiled. "You're up. Oh, Miss Clara, you look wonderful. Please give me that tray. You could have left it in your room."

I handed it to her, and Mrs. Jameson looked at me now and smiled. "Well, hallo again! I have been so worried about you!" She stood to greet me, and it seemed that in her silk house shoes she floated toward me. "How did you sleep?" She held out her hands for mine and I allowed this, feeling the warmth of her kindness as she squeezed my fingers in compassion.

"Hello, ma'am. I am so sorry that my daughter and I have intruded on you in this way."

"Intrude? I was desperate for company. Join me! How are you feeling?"

"A little weak, but the food and tea helped. Dr. Finlay is wonderful. Thank you so much for everything. I have no idea where we'd be without Charlie. And Moira."

"Well, you look no worse for the wear, do you?" Mrs. Jameson smiled. "Sit, sit. What can I have Moira get for you?"

I sat in the thickly padded green velvet chair around a glass round table. "More of that lovely tea?"

Moira left the room and Mrs. Jameson said, "Charlie will be so happy you are up and all right. I just spoke with your charming daughter. What a little sprite she is."

"I saw them from the window. They're walking back from the lake."

"They should be here soon, and now, since you are up and all right, my son might smile."

"Mrs. Jameson, I have to truly tell you that this is the most beautiful place I have ever seen."

Mrs. Jameson laughed cheerfully. "I am so glad you could see it. It's my favorite place on earth." She leaned forward. "It is a land created by fire and carved by ice."

"That's so . . . elemental and lovely," I said.

"Yes, a volcano created this land, but glacial ice carved its seventeen lakes. Ours, out the window, is my favorite, and the most beautiful, I do believe." She waved her hand. "See? Esthwaite Water, it sits in the palm of the earth's hand."

I was aiming to tell her she sounded like a poet when I heard the most beautiful sound. "Mama!"

Wynnie ran into the room and was at my side. I drew her close; she smelled of cold and earth and rain. "Where have you been, my darling?"

"In an enchanted land, Mama. Just you wait. There are gardens and a lake and a forest and mysterious stone walls, and there is a hedgehog, Mama. A Tizzie-Whizie."

"Tizzie-Whizie? Is that a candy?"

Mrs. Jameson laughed and looked to her son. "You've been telling this child stories."

Wynnie held up her arms for dramatic effect. "They are these little creatures who live near the lake, part hedgehog, part squirrel, part bee."

"Well," I said, "this sounds like just my kind of place."

Charlie looked at me, his brows drawn together. It was such a warm expression, I could have been fooled into thinking that we'd decided together to come to his mother's country house, that this was a holiday and not an emergency, that we hadn't thrust ourselves into his life.

Wynnie clung to my hand, and I squeezed it. "I feel quite odd wearing your daughter-in-law's clothes, but I have nothing else. I can clean our clothes today, and we will leave as soon as the fog clears in London. I promise we'll get out of your hair as soon as possible," I told her.

"Oh, I am very happy to have you here. Guests always bring this place alive."

Charlie sat on the chair next to me and placed the back of his palm to my forehead, checking for fever. It was a tender gesture, and my chest filled with something very near to longing; it'd been so long since I felt it that I almost gasped. "You're better," he said.

"I am."

"How do you . . . feel?"

"Embarrassed," I told him. "And sorry."

"Don't feel either. Please. I am just so glad that you and Wynnie are all right."

"I feel so . . . untethered; I need to see where I am in the world. A map. It's as if I traveled here blindfolded."

"Well, we'll pull out a map and I'll show you everything."

"My mama loves maps," Wynnie told them, bouncing on her toes. "Loves them!"

I looked to Wynnie. "I do; it's true."

Mrs. Jameson asked, "What do you like about them?"

"The art of them. The way they can shift and change. How they express what they meant to someone in that time, in that world. The overview as if I am a bird." I stopped.

"Sometimes Mama paints on them," Wynnie told them. "She finds old maps at the flea market or in the trash and she paints things on them like birds and trees and—"

"Wynnie, love, the Jamesons don't need to know any of this."

"Oh yes we do," Mrs. Jameson said. "It's fascinating."

I changed the subject. "From the bedroom window I saw the lake and the mountains. What is it all called?"

Mrs. Jameson answered, her voice light and happy to talk about her land. "You're looking at Esthwaite Water, and each fell has its own name."

"Fell?" I asked.

"Mountain. We have Scafell and Helvellyn and Skiddaw and many more. Two doors down is Beatrix Potter's house, called Hill Top. The farm next door is a working farm—you'll hear the cows."

Wynnie snapped her head to me. "Mama, I want to see where Peter Rabbit lives!"

"It is quite something, isn't it?" Mrs. Jameson asked. Then she leaned forward with the fullest smile, her face aglow. "You remind me of Charlie when he was young."

Wynnie lifted her head. "He looked like me?"

Mrs. Jameson burst into laughter. "No, dear. He was just as curious and precocious."

Wynnie straightened her glasses, and I answered her unspoken question. "Yes, that's a good thing." I turned to Charlie. "Have you heard any news from London?"

Mrs. Jameson answered. "The wireless announced this morning that it is still terrible there. Churchill is under such pressure. He's to make an announcement today. It must have been horrible finding your way here."

"Yes, but Moira and your son were quite the heroes."

"I'm so grateful they were there for you." Mrs. Jameson stood. "Now, I'll be off; I have an arts council meeting about the refurbishing of the Broughton Theatre, which is much needed, but will put a pause on all the productions."

"Productions?" Wynnie asked.

"Plays. Right now, we have two of them," she said, and patted her lips with a linen napkin, then set it on the glass table in a motion so practiced I wondered if she knew she'd done it.

"Can I see one?" Wynnie asked. "I love plays."

"Wynnie!" I admonished.

"What?" Wynnie looked at me. "We love plays."

Mrs. Jameson laughed. She was so elegant, with the pearls at her neck, the tinkling laugh, the high cheekbones. I felt like a sack of coal by comparison. She bent a bit to look at Wynnie. "Right now, we have Dickens' *A Christmas Carol* and *A World Apart*, a new favorite around here. We have tickets for tomorrow night," she said. "Front row if you are up for it? It's a falling-down theater, but it's a beautiful tradition."

A warm flame rushed up my spine, but I kept my voice level. "How lovely." *A World Apart.* Finneas had told us that this was the name of the adaptation, the name of the play based on Mother's book. I placed my hand on Wynnie's shoulder and squeezed, praying that she could read my signal to be quiet, not to say anything about her grandmother, not yet.

Something was revealing itself here—a truth or a hint. I wondered if Mother had created a word for this, a word for something emerging and not knowing what it might become.

Mrs. Jameson quietly left the room, and I turned to Charlie. "You didn't tell her why we are here." This was not a question.

"I did, just not everything."

"What did you tell her about us?"

"I didn't lie. But no, I haven't told her about the language. I told her that when I was cleaning out Father's library, as he'd asked, I found some old papers that belonged to an American woman's family and that the woman—you—wanted them back. I told her you'd come on holiday and were meant to retrieve your family papers."

"She didn't ask what those papers were?"

"No. Dad collected all kinds of things. It isn't that she doesn't care about his collection; they have just always had their own interests. She trusts me to get it all in order. You must remember, she is still grieving."

"The play," I said.

"Dickens?"

"No, *A World Apart.*"

"Yes?" He looked at me and then at Wynnie, and back again.

Wynnie answered quietly. "That's my grandmother's story."

"What?"

"It's the theatrical production name for *The Middle Place.*"

He sank back in his seat. "I had no idea."

"Have you ever seen it?" I asked, my hands shaking as I clasped them together.

"Honestly, no, I've never even heard of it. It must be one of their newer productions." I wanted to shake him for the truth.

"Don't you think your mother knows something about mine?"

He looked out to the doorway where his mother had just walked out. "I didn't think so, Clara. But now I'm not so sure."

CHAPTER 32

CLARA

Lake District, England

I left Wynnie in the drawing room with Moira, who was showing her all about the TV with a show called *Muffin the Mule*. Wynnie was infatuated with the screen that flickered with stories, wiggling the ears of the antennae and switching the channels to static.

In a pine-paneled study, Charlie and I stood alone for the first time while examining the remaining and damaged pages of Mother's language, which were spread across a large table in a room at the rear of the hallway. I'd brought them down from my room.

This house sprouted rooms whenever I turned my back, each place with its own personality and secrets, each view more charming than the next.

But this rugged edifice hidden in the bowl of mountains and pastures was *not* meant for me. The study was modest compared to the grand library in London. One bookshelf lined the back wall, and a hulking table dominated the middle. "How big is this house exactly?" I asked. "I can't quite get a sense of things yet."

He leaned back against the table, his palms planted. "Not as large as some others nearly, but it is in many ways the quintessential English country house. It was built for a vicar in 1742. There are six bedrooms, and you're in the one with a view to the lake and Grizedale."

"And there are so many rooms downstairs, too, like there's one for each purpose in life. When I look out the window, I see such beauty."

"We have six acres with three one-bedroom cottages that you can see the rooflines of from your room. There's an empty stable where once horses were kept. Mum is terrified of them, so it's empty and now stores plants and garden tools. She built a greenhouse about twenty years ago. You'll see when you are able to be up and around. There are much fancier homes around here to explore. Castles and monasteries and manors."

"And next door—sheep and cows."

"It's a working farm, and you'll hear them sometimes. I find it a perfect reminder of this land and why we are here."

"And why is that? Why are we here?"

"Me and you? That I don't have an answer for." He grinned, and I nearly thought he'd wink. "But this area exists in all its beauty because of the shepherds and farmers and conservationists who have loved, tended, and cared for the land." He clicked on the brass lamp, and we both turned to stare at the remaining pages. "Now back to the thing at hand." He smiled at me. "Look at this. An entire language. I wonder why she did it."

"Dad told me that she felt there were words the world lost as we moved into houses and into cities. Mother felt like she wasn't so much making up words as finding them. She would never call it *her* language— she would just say that she found words that needed finding."

"My father would agree. I can see why they might have been friends or known each other."

"Why won't you just tell your mother about us?" I asked. "Just tell her about me and about Mother and the words, and we'll see if she knows anything." I tapped the warped pages.

"I might, Clara. But now, no. I don't want to ask why he hid papers from another woman. Let me see if I can figure it out first."

Out the window, Mrs. Jameson was walking toward the lake, her gray coat flapping in the morning breeze, her blue hat a splash of color against a low woolly sky. She walked with purpose in her green rain boots, and her head was held high. Watching her, I longed to be out there, too, to walk across this rugged landscape with its dramatic beauty, touching the stone walls and rough bark of the trees, immersing myself in the glacial waters.

Charlie noticed, too. "This is her life, here in this village with her dearest friends, her gardens, her family, and her theater. I'm afraid of shattering the peace she's trying to find without Father."

"Why would these pages shatter her peace?"

He looked back to me with a sad smile. "Have they brought you peace?"

"Anything but," I said.

"Exactly. She will want to know where they came from and why. Why did my father hide this from her?"

"Maybe he didn't."

"He did."

The way he said it, so firmly, I softly asked, "Do you think my mother was his mistress?" A tingle at the tips of my fingers, a metallic taste on my tongue—signals of danger.

"I don't think so, no."

"But you have thought about it."

"That's one of many things I've thought and dismissed."

"Why think it at all if you dismissed it?"

"Because I have no answers, and in the absence of answers, I find myself creating some. Tell me you don't do the same?"

"I do. I've been creating answers for twenty-five years."

He smiled; we were in this together—creating answers for unanswerable questions. He pointed back at the pages. "Is it okay if I look at them?"

"Of course," I said. "There's not much left to see."

He lifted each page and read the words out loud.

After a long while, time enough for me to glance around the room and take note of the beautiful paintings and the leather-bound books from Tolstoy to Austen to Graham and Lewis, he straightened and took off his reading glasses. "She uses the familiar and makes it unfamiliar. Makes ancient something new, just as most languages do. It's intricate. I'm surprised she's never shared this—it would be interesting to study."

"And now it's gone." The sense of loss brought a sinking feeling, a quagmire of hopelessness. I'd lost what was entrusted to me—Mother's words.

"Maybe someone will find some pages and—"

"Stop," I said, and held up my hand. "I've been hoping for this since I was eight years old, and she promised me that someday she would teach me her language. It's time to give up hope."

Charlie massaged his forehead with his thumb and forefinger. "I should have never given that woman a ride."

"No! This is Mother's fault. Not yours. Or your father's or mine or anyone else's. It is just something that happened."

He tapped the pages. "She must have been educated in Latin and Gaelic, because many of these words have roots in both, but she twists them or adds to them."

"Latin. Yes, she knew Latin. But I don't think she knew Gaelic. She was never sent to proper school."

"Yes. I must admit I read much of her biography before you arrived; she was a genius, they say."

"That desperately awful biography," I said.

"It's not accurate?"

"Some parts were. Yes, her parents recognized her genius when she started reading at three years old and they kept her home, educated her with tutors. So she didn't have friends her age. Maybe that's why she created Emjie. She was always older than her years, which might be why my dad is ten years her senior. But yes, her parents made sure she knew Latin and Greek."

"A very classical education, to be sure."

"Maybe," I said. "Her mother, Martha, didn't like that *The Middle Place* was published when she was twelve years old. Her dad, Wendall, was the one who made sure it happened. Martha said that the publication brought a twelve-year-old too much attention and that my mother never found herself to rights again. At least until she met Dad and moved away."

"What did they have to say about her disappearance? Her parents, I mean."

"They are both gone now. Her father left when she was eleven and started a new family. He passed years ago. She never spoke about him, but I know that his leaving shattered her when she was young—his abandonment is what sent her on those wild adventures around the world once she turned eighteen and was in charge of her own destiny. Those were self-destructive adventures, if you're to believe the biography. You think she'd know the effects of abandonment, but I can only guess that didn't matter to her. That *I* didn't matter to her." I paused on the truth I rarely stated out loud, one that could be found in her leaving, and I barely admitted to myself. I cleared my throat. "And her mother died five years after she disappeared."

"I am so sorry she did that to you and to your dad."

"Thank you, but, please, no pity. I don't want or need it."

"No pity," he said. "Not for someone like you."

I nudged him and heat rose in me. It had been so long since I'd felt a rush like that, I'd nearly forgotten what it was—desire. No, not here, not him. This was the wrong place and person. I took a breath. I pointed to the pages again. "So maybe she learned Gaelic on her travels, but if she did, I never knew or heard her speak it. I will ask Dad."

"I can guess at maybe four of these words, but not their full meaning." He pointed at *Arbormore*. "*Arbor* is the Latin root for tree."

I read Mother's definition out loud. "'*Arbormore:* A tree that has a proper name but feels as if it is otherworldly and should not be categorized. A tree that is a portal to another world. A magical tree.'"

"Beautiful," he said.

"And you know Latin?" I asked.

"Yes, the basics."

"Mother created her first word when she was five years old. This has been gathering for years and years—depending on when she stopped, which isn't clear at all."

He straightened and stretched, his hand on his lower back. "No wonder you want to have all of it—it's her life's work."

"*Wanted.* Past tense."

"Something being gone doesn't remove the want of it," he said. "Now let's head back. After you gave me the contact, I rang the landlord, and he is allowing Archie and Adelaide to retrieve your bags and bring them today. We can figure out the rest of it after I show you around."

I ran my hand down the side of Adelaide's beautiful wool dress. "That's kind of them. I can wear my own clothes and meet your brother."

"You'll adore him. Everyone does."

I began to gather the papers and Charlie set his hand on top of mine, stopping me. "Leave them. Maybe we'll see something later. No one uses this room."

He kept his hand still and it covered mine completely. Our gazes were down at our hands when a soft woman's voice brought us back to rights.

"Well, hallo!" Such a chipper greeting, like a bird had entered the room.

Before we turned, Charlie wrapped his hand around mine, rubbed his thumb on the inside of my palm. A rush of warmth and a need to kiss him. God, was I so desperate that a single touch turned me inside out?

I looked up to see a woman standing in the entryway, her hands on her very slim hips, her hat tipped jauntily to one side, and her red lipstick in a wide smile. Her dark hair was falling over a royal-blue wool jacket. She seemed a cutout of a woman in a fashion magazine. I suddenly felt like a country bumpkin even while wearing her gorgeous clothes.

"Hello, Adelaide," said Charlie. "Come, meet Clara."

Her look wandered to our hands, to Charlie's holding mine, which I immediately dropped.

"Hello," I said. "Thank you so much for allowing me to borrow your clothes and room."

"Oh! I am so pleased I can help. Poor you, trying to navigate your way through all that fog with a child. It was awful for us, so I can't imagine." So proper and charming, I thought. Everything I would never be.

"Well, thank you so much for rescuing me from my soot-covered clothes."

She smiled and her face transformed with it. Something in me wanted to please her, to make her like me. "Your suitcase is here now," she told me. "Aren't you so very pleased to be here instead of that dingy flat?"

"Yes! How is the fog now?"

"Much more manageable, but still thick. It was horrid holing up like that. I am very pleased to make it to the country. How ever did the two of you get out?"

"Clara is the one who led us here with the lantern and her courage." I laughed. "It was Charlie. He drove us here—saved us, to be sure."

"Charlie's very good at such things," she said. "Helping others, just like his father always was." She smiled at him, and he looked away from her, sadness entering the room.

I took a few steps to leave the room and then turned to her. "Lovely to meet you. I need to go find my daughter." I walked out and wondered how could I have even begun to feel like Charlie would pay someone like me any mind when such women were in his life?

I made it back to the drawing room. "Wynnie?"

She looked up and smiled. "Mama! Look at this! There is a television show with men in flowerpots. It's called *Flower Pot Men*. Isn't that the funniest thing you ever heard? Little Weed visits and . . . Bill and Ben live in the garden."

"They live in flowerpots?"

"Yep! I bet Grandma's story would be so fun on television. Everyone would want to see it."

"Love, I need to go back upstairs to rest for a bit." I addressed Moira. "Will you bring her to me when you are done with the men in pots?"

"Of course," she said.

Quickly up the stairs, past the workmen and decorations, and I made my way to the bedroom. I sank to the lounge chair, embarrassed that I was longing for a man I'd just met. This was not my land or my people. I would not be stuck here in a life that wasn't mine and miss out on the life that belonged to me. If I stayed much longer, we'd miss our ship home, but I refused to miss the Caldecott Awards.

My hand was still warm from Charlie's, and a thrill I couldn't yet name. What I'd give for a sketch pad and charcoals, for an easel and watercolors, even for a pencil and notebook.

I'd need to find other ways to soothe the anxiety and unknowing, to pass the days until I could go home.

CHAPTER 33

CLARA

Lake District, England

I sat at the desk overlooking the lake and continued copying over Mother's remaining words and definitions in alphabetical order. A light rain arrived, and it pattered on the window. Outside, on the land that Charlie had told me was a working farm, a herd of sheep nestled against a stone wall, keeping the slanting rain from hitting them, clever little things. I thought of how we protected ourselves, whether from rain or pain, of how these words had been with Mother since she was five years old and how they might be the only thing that never abandoned her and that she never abandoned.

I was alphabetizing them with a need to keep my mind and hands busy, a desire to make order of disorder. This action, simple and consuming, prevented me from thinking about what might be going on downstairs with the Jameson family, about secrets Callum Jameson took to his grave, and about Charlie.

I thought of the woman Brian Davis thought he knew, one who was different from the wife and mother Dad and I knew. Maybe the woman Brian Davis described—the one with the mad affairs and self-destructive drinking and running—was who Mom *really* was. Would she truly be another man's mistress and leave behind everything that appeared to matter the most to her? I needed someone to talk to—to untangle this whole mess along with the feelings that were flooding me every time Charlie came near.

Only Lilia knew me well enough to hear all of this.

Abandoning the task at hand, I pulled out a piece of stationery with the Jameson family crest on it and started a letter to Lilia.

My Dearest Lilia,
I wish you were here with me. I'd love for you to see this land that looks oddly like the one I paint in my pictures. It seems a land carved of streams and filled with lakes, a land of light and shadow. This family has something to do with Mother, and I can't see how just yet. I miss you terribly and I wish you were here to help me unravel the mystery.

I sat back and remembered playing Nancy Drew with Lilia, creating mysteries while we left each other notes around the house and garden. How lovely it would have been to bring her here.

I was putting pen back to paper when the door flew open.

"Mama!" I held out my arms and Wynnie rushed into them. Moira stood in the doorway.

"I have such a good game to teach you," Wynnie told me.

"I can't wait."

I looked to Moira. "Thank you so much for helping with Wynnie. I'm sure I'll be back to full steam by tomorrow."

"It is my pleasure. She is a delight." Moira smiled. "May I bring you both up some tea or would you like to join us downstairs?"

"I think we'll stay right here," I told her. "I think some tea and a nap are in order, right, Wynnie?"

Wynnie eyed me because tea and a nap were not for her, but she knew my looks and she nodded in agreement. Moira bowed out and shut the door.

"What a family," I said to Wynnie.

"Mama, they are so nice! Can we please stay a long while?"

"Most assuredly not," I said in a very bad British accent.

The afternoon passed lazily as Wynnie and I stayed in our room and devoured the tea and biscuits, the scones and clotted cream and raspberry jam. She read *Swallows and Amazons* as I continued to copy over Mother's words and definitions in alphabetical order until my head was woozy with sleep. Wynnie then regaled me with tales of the beautiful land outside, the mythical hedgehog, and the names of trees and birds that Charlie had taught her. I told her she must show me everything, all of it, tomorrow.

"Mum?" a deep voice called out just as Charlie, Mrs. Jameson, Wynnie, and I sat at the gleaming mahogany table in the dining room for dinner. Bone china plates edged in pink roses were set at each place, along with sterling silver flatware with the same crest I'd seen on the doorway the night we'd arrived, and milky-colored linen napkins pressed flat and crisp.

In the doorway stood a man who looked a bit like Charlie, but taller, a shaved face and hair tamed by hair gel and comb instead of Charlie's curly mop of hair. He entered the room in his three-piece suit and tartan ascot, Adelaide next to him, her long hair falling over her sweater sewn with tiny rosebuds.

Archie approached me and held out his hand. "Well, you must be the mystery woman whose luggage needed retrieving."

Charlie stood and greeted his brother with a warm hug. "Hello, Archie. Please meet Clara and her daughter, Wynnie."

I stood to face Archie. "Hello. Nice to meet you. I'm very grateful for your kindness in bringing our belongings here."

"And this is my wife, Adelaide," he said.

"We've already had the pleasure," I told him, and smiled at Adelaide and then asked Archie, "Is the fog clearing?"

"Slowly," he said. "But everyone has a terrible story to tell. I am so pleased to be here with clean air and soft beds not covered in soot. That horrible Churchill and his bloody cheap coal."

"Oh, darling," Mrs. Jameson said. "Forgive Churchill. He brought us through the war, and he'll bring us through this."

We all sat, and Wynnie looked to Adelaide. "I think we are in your bedroom."

"Yes, that's just fine," she said with a smile. "I hope you find some rest here. I do know you've been through quite an ordeal."

The dinner was pleasant, with lively conversation and loads of questions from Adelaide about what it was like to live in America.

Mrs. Jameson lit up in the presence of both of her sons and regaled them with gossip from the village while they chuckled about people that they'd known all their lives.

I didn't feel an outsider; the Jamesons included us effortlessly and encouraged Wynnie and me to give them a picture of our life in South Carolina.

Somehow my mother had brought me here, even if this was not what she'd meant to do, and in every note of the conversation I looked for hints and clues of how we all might be connected: no matter how different we all seemed, I felt my mother hiding in the crevices of this family.

CHAPTER 34

CLARA

Lake District, England

By Tuesday morning, the only hints of my river plunge and the fever, of the soot and the grime, were the dark streaks left on a towel hanging off the bathroom door's hook. Morning sunlight fell on Mother's pages, swords of light hitting the pile as if pointing to it.

A fierce desire for my own bed and the sound of the tide tinkling the oyster bed shoreline washed over me. I took a deep breath and closed my eyes. I wanted my creaking house and my cracked linoleum countertops, my splintered dock, and the tick of the kitchen clock as I silently made coffee in the morning. I wanted to smell the briny aroma as I drove over the bridge and feel the salty air on my lips as I took Wynnie out in the boat.

I missed South Carolina, the simplicity of it in stark relief against the opulence of this house. They might seem to have everything—the house and money and name—but they didn't have the shoreline of the May River. I felt the aching pull of home and knew that today I needed to send a telegram to Nat and tell him what happened and how we weren't coming home on our planned train from New York.

Wynnie and I had slept deeply, and now she stirred, sitting up and smiling at me. "We're still here."

"Where else would we be?" I ruffled her hair and swung my legs from the bed to stand.

She laughed. "I'm happy." She jumped off the bed, her bare feet hitting the carpet as she walked to the window and pushed aside the curtains. "Mama! Snow! We've never had snow."

I realized now that the brightness of the morning sun was the reflection from a soft snow covering the landscape in a mantle of white. "Oh, Wynnie!"

"It's like a . . ." She paused and pressed her forehead to the windowpane. "Like the places Emjie shows me. Like the places you paint in your books about Harriet."

Charlie waited by the back door under the kitchen's low, wood-beamed ceiling with a coat, a scarf, a hat, and thick wool mittens in his arms. "For you," he said, and held them out. "You'll need them today."

I'd agreed to join him on a walk while Wynnie and Mrs. Jameson played the piano in the gallery. Mrs. Jameson was teaching Wynnie chords, and the notes echoed through the house. I was anxious to get outside in the landscape I'd seen only from my window.

I zipped, buttoned, fastened, and tightened all the wool attire Charlie gave me. Then I stood in that weathered kitchen and said, "I will now need to be rolled out of the house and across the lawn."

He laughed and then said, "And you're not done yet." He reached behind and pulled out a pair of green wellies, knee-high rain boots with splatters of mud dried on the toes. "You'll need these. With all the rain and snow, it'll be muddy out there."

I sat on the bench and pulled on the boots, which were a bit too big but snug enough, while Charlie continued talking. "I called a friend at the embassy today about your passport. He said as soon as they open, the process will be expedited. We'll get you out of here, but most likely not in time for your original ship's booking. I'll call the steam line and tell them the problem—we can rebook the tickets as soon as you are ready."

"I can call the steam line, but thank you so much. For a moment, I forgot about all of that. Being here feels as if everything else stops."

He opened the door. A blast of icy air hit my face and I smiled. "I swear I can smell the sea."

"You can," he said. "It's about an hour away, but the wind brings it here. We're not that far."

"Can I ask you a question?" I asked as he shut the door and we headed across the grounds.

"Anything." He set his arm to my elbow to guide me through the winter grass to the stone walkway.

"Why do you know so much about the Gaelic language?"

We walked across a pebbled path, the ground shifting beneath the boots.

"My dad." Charlie opened a low wooden gate, and we had walked out onto the wide sweeping lawn I'd seen from my window when he stopped and looked at me, right at me. "You are a beautiful woman, Clara. Even hidden under all these layers I've bundled you in."

The heat again, the charge of it up my body and neck. In his words, the way he said them, I believed him. I was, right then, beautiful.

"Thank you," I said. "But I do believe you've seen me at my worst."

"If that's your worst, lucky you." He smiled and began to walk again; I followed.

To our left, on the other side of a low wooden fence, the sheep that had appeared as freckles of white from my window moved along the snowy ground, lifting their friendly faces to us in curiosity and then returning to their grazing. A cow lowed from inside the wooden barn. In front of me, a lane wound its way through the land like a silver river. We crossed the road to the soft ground of pasture; to our right were the three stone cottages. The sky sat as a low ceiling of wool and fluff, holding the snow.

Charlie's pace quickened now, and I walked next to him as he shifted subjects. "As for Gaelic, the little I do know is from the songs. My father is Irish, although he moved to England when he was twenty-one, after the Easter Rising. He carried all the old stories with him and passed them on to us. But it destroyed his family and broke his heart."

"What happened?"

Charlie stared off as if he might see it with his father's eyes; he swallowed. "They were caught in the crossfire of 1916. His mum had passed on years before, but his father and brother were in the wrong place at the wrong time, which is all I really know. He promised that one day he'd tell us the whole story, but I guess that won't happen now."

"I'm sorry. These stories our parents took with them should have been told." I took a step and my boot sank deep into the mud, making a squishing sound as I pulled it out. This land was so soft, a welcoming and tender gentleness in the ground.

"Well, he loved the land and its people; one of his great cousins lives with us in that cottage, and she knows some Gaelic also." He waved toward the lake's edge. "Dad told us the stories of the wee folk who live underground, the importance of language to define the world, the hidden secrets of an unseen world."

"Sounds like the way my mother spoke. She always talked of such things. And often it terrified me."

Charlie stopped on the path before the expanse of his world, the cottages and home, the sweeping lawn and wicker-caged gardens, the woodlands surrounding it all. Mounds of moss-covered stone walls and boulders leading us down to the lake on green swells of earth. "Your father loved it here?"

"My father was a man who loved everything. His curiosity and absolute wonder about the world made him that way."

"That's why his library was so important to him."

"Yes."

We continued toward the lake, sloping downhill. "If he was curious about language, maybe he bought Mother's papers from someone else? From a dealer?" I was grasping for answers even as I was marveling at the sights around us, at the jagged edges of the mountains glowing nearly blue under the cloud cover, and the softer swells beneath.

"He could have, yes. When I first found the satchel, I called his dealer at Sotheby's, and he knew nothing of it. Which leaves the mystery of why it was in his safe."

We reached the edge of the frost-crusted lake. A flock of geese startled and honked, scattering across the still waters and creating ripples. I stood quietly and held my hand to my chest and allowed the wild beauty of this place to wash over me. A wind picked up, dancing in the top of the trees, producing a song of wind and branches, a whisper of nature's ease.

"I'd never leave if this were mine," I said. "Tell me about your home."

"Our house was once built for a vicar but has been in my mother's family for almost a hundred years now." He turned to the house behind us. "Built from the slate of these mountains. Like everything around here, it was many things before it was ours. There are much grander homes along this lake and just to the east of us at Windermere Lake, manors built by Lancashire and Yorkshire mill owners, by flax and wool and cotton money. But Mum's family was always in finance, and this was their summer home." He pointed to the left. "And just beyond there, where you can't see, is Beatrix Potter's Hill Top."

"Did your mother know her?"

"Very well, yes. They cared about the same things."

"She was my idol growing up, Charlie. I imagined her as my mother when my real one left. A woman who could create an entire world of bunnies and kittens, of mischief and beauty." I blushed with the heat of realizing I'd said too much, exposed the tender hunger for a mother in the emptiness of not having one.

"That's so sweet," he said. "Ask Mum about her, she'll tell you funny stories. We'll walk up to her favorite tarn when you feel up to it."

"Tarn?"

"A small mountain lake, from the Old Norse word *Tjorn*, meaning 'teardrop.'"

"Teardrop," I said. "That's so . . . sublime."

He pointed toward the woodlands and then the mountains. "That is Grizedale Forest and those are the Coniston Fells."

"Oh, I want to paint this."

He smiled at me. "Your art. I want to know more about all of it."

"I want to know everything about this place." I meant it; I had an overwhelming need to know how this land had formed and came to be, because if it had something to do with my mother, which it was becoming clearer and clearer that it did, the answers were hidden in this landscape.

"That will take some time," he said, and jostled me with an elbow, smiling.

I looked to him. "There was a word in Mother's language she describes as 'the loneliness at the heart of things; believing you will find what will quench the longing but there is nothing, not of this world.'" I closed my eyes as I tried to see the definition on the page, the one I'd written out when I'd copied the words alphabetically. "And that is how *this* feels."

"It feels lonely?"

"No, it feels as if it might expose the loneliness, as if it hints at something you long for but can't possess as your own."

"Yes." He stared across the lake where the geese settled on the other side, where the mountains cast long-armed shadows toward us. "I'm so sorry about everything for you, Clara."

"Please don't feel sorry for me."

"I don't feel sorry *for* you. I am just sorry it happened. Leaving is an awful thing to do to a child."

"It is. Yes. The not knowing is terrible. And now there's a new layer— where has she been all these years, and is she gone now?"

"And why my father—"

"Yes. Our families are—"

"Entwined, yes. I believe they are."

"Is there a way to ask your brother?"

"I will." He leaned down to pick a white feather from the earth, twirled it in his hand. "I was waiting to see what we could discover first."

We. The way he said it felt solid, as if *we* existed.

"Your brother seems so lovely," I said, needing a change of subject.

"Yes, he's very protective of me, as is Adelaide."

"Why?"

"He always has been, just as I have been with him. Because I'm his brother, and his twin, and because they've seen me heartbroken in the last year. My fiancée left me for a mate who she'd been seeing on the side for over a year. For our whole life it's been Archie and me against the world. Side by side."

This was the hurt I saw in him the first time he sang to us the song in the London flat. "I know what it's like to have life unravel in that way," I told him. "Sometimes people are awful to each other."

He nodded, and the muscles in his face twitched.

"Come now." I imitated his speech. "Let's walk before I turn into an icicle at the side of your lake."

He pointed to the left. "We'll take the path around the south side and then come back this way."

"Do you know a lot of people here?"

"Not like Mum. I keep myself to myself most times."

Yes, I thought, that self-possession I noticed the first day.

We passed an upside-down rowboat and walked out on the protrusion of land that thrust itself into the lake. Boulders as big as cars dotted the edges of the lake, mounds of moss on the edges. The snow turned the world into shapes more than images. "Your heartbreak," I said. "I didn't mean to make light. Sometimes I just don't know what else to say. I've always been awkward that way."

"No, it was okay. I'm tired of the *I'm sorry*. I get plenty of that."

We walked in the sounds of the land, the creak of branches rubbing against one another, the soft crack and rustle of the ground beneath our feet. "You said you know that kind of pain?" he asked.

"Yes. My ex-husband, Nat, battled with a different lover—gambling."

"That's quite possibly worse," he said. "Hard to hate an addiction."

"Oh, but I do. And it's so sad that my daughter must have divorced parents when I did so want to give her what I didn't have—two parents at home."

We'd turned back and headed toward the cottages, the ones I had seen from my window, the rooflines and chimneys. He stopped on the path when we neared one of them. Smoke billowed from its single chimney, and inside, a pale light flickered. "I wish that hadn't happened to you," he said.

"Makes two of us." I pointed at the cottage of gray stone, yellow and green lichen growing in its curves and edges. "Is this Snow White's house?"

He laughed. "Looks like it. But no, that's my aunt Nelle's cottage. She's my mom's sister and was born with a disability they've never truly labeled. She's like a child, but a quirky child. The questions she will ask you will startle."

"Like?"

"Today has a bird flown over your head? Are you worried about the fractures under the earth? Can you tell me the name of three gods?" He laughed. "A caregiver lives with her, and we often must find new ones. As sweet as she is, she exhausts them. But my mum, and Father also, always refused to let her be cared for by others."

"They sound so kind. Your parents, I mean."

"They are. Father took in all kinds of strangers and family." He waved to the other two cottages. "And the two others are full also. One is my grandcousin Isolde from Ireland, and the other is the groundskeeper, who is on holiday in Australia now—smart one to leave during the winter to a place where it's summer."

"How is it to have this many people around all the time?"

He pulled a face. "Do I sound like a prig when I describe our life? Forgive me if I do."

"No, not one bit. It's just . . ."

"Unlike yours."

"Yes. It makes my life seem so small."

"There is nothing wrong with small and chosen, Clara."

We made our way around the back edge of the cottages, and my nose felt frozen. I touched it with my mitten and rubbed.

"You're cold," he said.

"It's okay. This is . . ." I pointed back at his house. "I can't find the word."

"But you have a whole list of words in your room."

I laughed. "Indeed, I do."

Nearby, a wooden bench sat under a naked oak tree, and I walked to it, sat down. I shivered with the cold held in its seat. Charlie sat near me, and I told him, "There's another word of Mother's that is closer to what I feel, but it's part of the missing pages, and I only remember its definition."

"Tell me?"

"'A desire with despair at its core and with hope at its edges.' The rhythm and dance of that sentence has stuck with me, but not the word itself."

"Say it again." He took my hand, and I allowed it.

"'A desire with despair at its core and with hope at its edges.'"

"Yes." He held my mittened hand in his and there we sat, and it was this way: ice crackled at the edge of a silver lake; geese flew in a V overhead, squawking their joy at the world; a naked hawthorn tree spread its gnarled arms above the land; and a wet flake of snow landed on my face.

Charlie whispered, "Here it comes."

The cotton whorl of clouds let loose what it held in its cold fists. Fat wet flakes fell around us, dotting us with the opposite of the sooty flakes of London. Something in this—in the sweet release from the sky of something beautiful and not poisonous—touched my heart and I felt tears slide down my face, warm against my cold skin. I wiped them off quickly before Charlie noticed.

I shivered, Charlie stood, and I joined him silently. We walked back the way we'd come, and he told me all that would arrive in spring: the cheerful yellow of the daffodils the first arrival, and then the purple faces of the eyebright, followed by tall, colorful flowers like the wood cranesbill, water avens, and roseroot. He told of how white-felted leaves hung from the rare downy willow. With his every description, the impossible desire to see his world come to life in spring washed over me.

"And the lakes," I said. "So many."

"Sixteen major ones, but ninety-nine if you count all the tarns and ponds and meres."

"You could spend a lifetime exploring."

"Yes," he said. "And I have, and I will. Just like Father. "

"I bet you have a million stories like the Tizzie-Whizie."

"I do, but may I tell you an Irish story instead?" he asked.

"Tell me."

We stood facing each other and he told me, "There was once a great Irish warrior who was sent far across the land to retrieve the gold and treasure of a conquest. He took his most reliable and trustworthy fellows. After carrying the heavy treasure for miles and days, the great warrior sat on a rock and would not move. The fellows with him begged him to move and to carry faster, for the king was waiting for his gold."

He paused and I nudged him.

"The warrior didn't answer anyone. He sat and sat and sat. Days passed until he opened his eyes, and he told them it was time to go. 'What were you waiting for?' they all cried."

"What was he waiting for?" I asked, feeling a truth draw near, a tingle in my chest.

"The warrior told the others: 'We traveled too far too fast, and I waited for my soul to catch up.'"

"Oh," I said, and placed my hand on my heart. "Incredible."

"I hope you can sit still here just enough to let that happen to you."

"Thank you, Charlie. Thank you." I put out my arms to hug him and he held me close, and even through the wool and the scarves and the coats, I felt his solid body. He let go first, and I knew I would have stayed just like that until my soul caught up with me.

I nearly moved to kiss him, but we began to walk again. Rounding the path back to cross the lane, we came upon a wooden sign planted deep in the ground, a hand-carved sign with a word etched on it and an arrow that pointed down the pathway: *Parthanium.*

I stopped, feeling a warm sense of familiarity along my ribs, an opening in my heart. "*Parthanium,*" I said. "'A walled garden; paradise; to find what you are looking for; a place of one's own.'"

I recited as best I could from memory the word and definition I'd read that very morning in Mother's handwriting, in the last of her pages.

Charlie touched the sign. "This is new. I haven't noticed it before."

"Charlie, that is one of Mother's words."

CHAPTER 35

CLARA

Lake District, England

Now we knew: we were tied together.

"I want to help you find out what happened to your mother," Charlie said. "Wherever she is. I want to help you find out why that leather bag was in my father's library and her word is on a garden sign."

"It might mean talking to your mother, and I know you didn't want to bring her into all this. I didn't mean to make my family problems yours." I didn't wipe away my tears; I let them fall because they were warm, and I'd needed them for days now. Wynnie was safe in that solid house across a frost-encrusted lawn. "I thought you simply wanted to hand the papers over and did not want to get involved." I tried to imitate his accent but it came out rough and uneven.

I did make him laugh. "That was true. Then I met you. And now here we are."

"Yes, here we are."

I wiped at my tears.

"What is it?" He lifted my hands from my face. "What did I say?"

I shook my head. "It's not you. Not one bit. It's all of it. All the holding back. For days, I've been terrified for Wynnie, and here we are, safe. I think I am just terribly relieved. All of this is my fault."

"All of what?"

"All of everything. Mother leaving. Wynnie being sick."

"Clara, I am very happy you are here." The warmth of his words flowed through me. "I'm glad to meet the wonder of your daughter. And

I'm pleased to know that mothers like you exist in the world, for you are a glorious one; I can see this is true."

I was silent, absorbing his kindness and the soft sounds around Esthwaite Water: the crunch of icy grass, the lapping of water on the shore. "What a lovely life your mum has built here."

"She is beloved, and she loves. You can see why I might be loath to bring up another woman's satchel."

"Whose daughter and granddaughter are in your house. Yes, I can."

He stopped and then turned when we reached a low stone wall, holding inside its boundary a garden of wicker cages. "Oh!" I said, and walked toward it. "This is like finding a secret garden."

"I showed it to Wynnie, and she said you'd say that."

I set my hand on top of the stones and felt the hum of earth and longing and something primal and ancient. It wasn't a large garden, but it was set apart. "It feels like it holds some kind of magic."

"You should see it when the garden blooms in spring. It's probably one of the most beautiful on the property, but don't tell Mum. She is very proud of her own." He smiled, and for one breath I thought he might kiss me. How lovely that kiss would be near a lake in the countryside of England. He stepped closer.

"Charlie, darling!" A woman's voice called out, and we turned to see two women walking toward us arm in arm.

Charlie waved at them and whispered to me, "Aunt Nelle and her caregiver, Deirdre."

I stared with the slow realization that I was trying to find Mother's face.

The older woman wrapped in a bright red scarf, hat, and coat threw her arms around Charlie, while a younger woman stood by her side and smiled at me. "Hallo," she said.

The older woman, Aunt Nelle, released Charlie and stared at me, cocking her head as if in confusion. This short, stout woman was most assuredly not my mother, and I felt a fool for wondering.

"Aunt Nelle, this is my friend from America. She is called Clara."

"Clara!" Nelle said. "What a beautiful name for a beautiful child."

"Thank you," I said, and I could see now that her face was off a bit, as if her nose and her forehead beneath her hat had been misplaced.

Her wide and round eyes gave her the look of a child. "Pleased to meet you," I told her.

"Do snakes come into your house? Do they find their way under the doors and windowsills?"

"Not usually," I said, having been prepared for her odd questions. "But I will keep an eye out."

Deirdre laughed and placed her hand on Nelle's shoulder. "Come now, let's find those mushroom caps you're looking for." And off they went.

"Mama!" We both turned to see Wynnie running toward us, her red scarf flapping in the wind and her cheeks flushed with cold and excitement.

"Wynnie!" I held out my arms and she ran into them. "I thought you were with Moira." I looked behind her.

"No! I wanted to find Peter Rabbit, and everyone was gone, so I just came out."

"You can't come out here alone. You'll get lost!" I held her tight and looked her in the eyes, gripped her shoulders too tightly.

She broke free of me and clambered to the top of the low wall and held out her arms. "Emjie showed me the way."

"Wynnie." Charlie's voice was low with a roughness I hadn't heard before. "It is dangerous out there alone. You mustn't go out alone. There are paths that lead up into the mountains, where you might get lost by yourself."

"But I'm never by myself," Wynnie said. "Emjie is always with me. She always finds me."

These words caused a shiver to run up my arms and across my scalp; I heard Mother's voice clear and ringing in the air.

I will always find you.

"Wynnie, you may not go into these woodlands alone. I have very few hard rules with you, but this is one."

"I wanted to see the lake again. And I found so many things, Mama! Look!" She dug into her pocket and brought out a broken branch with a mossy arm, the bones of a bird's wing, and a dismembered nest of pine needles and fuzz. "I just wanted to be outside."

Charlie studied each treasure she held out, and I crouched down to Wynnie. "That might be what you want, but you must be with one of us."

Wynnie looked from my face to Charlie's, and tears filled her eyes. "I'm sorry."

I gathered her in my arms and held her close. "I just want you to be safe, darling."

"Only good things will happen here, Mama! I feel it."

I looked at Charlie as I hugged her, and there were tears in his eyes, for we both knew that this childhood belief was both beautiful and wrong.

CHAPTER 36

CHARLIE

Lake District, England

From the downstairs hallway, Charlie listened to Clara's warm voice flowing from the kitchen as she chatted on the telephone to her father in South Carolina. The golden glow of the sconces lit the hallway. Once meant for tallow candles, they had been converted to electric thirty years ago. Sometimes he caught a whiff of that old wax, which was still embedded in the stone walls. From where he stood, he saw the corner of the wooden kitchen table and the flicker of a flame under a kettle.

The kitchen was Charlie's favorite part of the house. Its brick walls and warm stoves, its low-beamed ceiling, along with the aroma of baked bread even when none was in the oven. A kettle was always at the ready.

Listening to Clara, he realized that the desire to protect her was taking hold. This emotion—a fierce impulse to take care of a woman he barely knew—was new to him. She hardly seemed to need protecting—perfectly at home with herself, her daughter, and her art. And yet.

Her voice rose and fell.

"Dad, I *am* fine; I promise. We won't be on the departing ship on the tenth. London was locked down with a hideous fog and we made it to the country, thanks to a nice family called the Jamesons. Yes, the man who found Mother's satchel. He doesn't know. No, he doesn't. I'm trying to find out. We had a scare with Wynnie. She's fine now. I've tried to call Nat and haven't gotten an answer. I love you, Dad. So much.

I promise to let you know anything I find out. We'll be home as soon as I can get a new passport from the embassy. I don't want to miss the Caldecott ceremony no matter what."

Then in a quieter voice said, "Dad, can you please tell Nat what has happened? I tried to call his apartment, but he didn't answer. I will find some way to send a telegram."

Without hearing her father's part of the conversation, it was as if Clara were reciting a poem in broken stanzas, lines to a song she hadn't finished, the puzzle pieces of a relationship between two people who had suffered the loss of the woman they loved.

It was astounding to Charlie that she spoke so lovingly of the mother who had left her. If his mum left him, he assumed his anger would erupt at the very mention of her.

"Eavesdropping, are we?" Clara's voice, and then she was standing in front of him with a grin on her face.

"Caught," he said. "But honestly, I was just waiting my turn for the telephone to ring the embassy about your passport."

"Oh, thank you, Charlie." She swept her hand into the kitchen. "All clear for you. And I will pay you back for that call. I would have sent a telegram, but Moira said there isn't a telegraph office in this village. That I'd have to take the ferry across Lake Windermere, and it all seemed quite complicated."

He laughed. "Not so complicated. The lake is right down the road, and the chain ferry goes back and forth, but it's quite all right, Clara. You needed to call your dad."

She moved past him, and he touched the wool throw she wore around her shoulders. She lifted her eyebrows in question.

"It's the family tartan."

"I was cold and . . ."

He kissed her cheek. "It's lovely on you."

Then he left her there in the hallway as he wondered why he'd done just what he'd done. It felt right and natural and he had just let the gesture flow out of him.

After he'd called his university pal at the embassy to hurry along Clara's and Wynnie's passports, he found Archie in the study, smoking a pipe and reading a financial report.

"Brother!" Archie looked up and grinned. "Tell me all about the beautiful Clara."

Charlie thumped his brother's shoulder and sat down. "Archie, I need to ask you something."

"First, tell me about Clara."

"As I told you on the phone, Father owned some of their family papers and she came to retrieve them and then got stuck in the fog with an ill child. Wynnie has asthma. Thank you again for bringing us her bags. It means a lot to her."

"You're welcome. And Adelaide wanted to get away as it was—the fog trapped us in the house for days. Tell me—what's your question?"

"It's the papers. You see, it is a language created by Clara's mother."

"Wow." He raised his eyebrows. "Like Tolkien?"

"Ah, didn't even think of that, but yes, an entirely new language." Charlie rubbed his forehead. "Would you have any idea how these papers found their way to Father's safe and office?"

"Did you call his curator?"

"Yes."

"Did you call the auction houses?"

"Yes."

"Then I can't help you, Brother. I wish I could." He grinned and tossed one leg over the other and leaned forward. "And I have a feeling you'd like to discover how you are connected to this woman and child."

"Wouldn't you?"

He laughed. "Indeed, I would. They are both so charming and you light up around them."

"Light up?"

"Indeed," he said. "Very different than when you were around Chelsea."

"Well, I sure hope so. I just want to help them figure this out. Help them get home."

Archie smiled that damn knowing brotherly smile that told Charlie

Archie didn't believe him. Then he looked back at his newspaper with the headline *London Fog Tie-Up Lasts for 3 Days—Robberies Break Out*.

"I need to be back in London." Archie spoke from behind the newspaper and then looked over it with a smile. "Adelaide has some luncheon she's giving for a friend getting married. I'd love to stay here with all of you and solve this mystery, but you'll just have to keep me updated."

"Thanks for bringing the luggage. Can you imagine being stranded in another country with nothing but one change of clothes?"

Archie laughed. "Brother, I believe you are smitten with this lady."

"Smitten?" Charlie stood with a laugh. "What are you, an old biddy at a tea party?"

"Enchanted, enamored, swept off your feet." Archie set down the paper and stood with a broad smile, clapped his brother on the shoulder. "Either way, be careful."

"She's something special, I will say."

"Or taken a fancy to."

Charlie shook his head and walked out of the room, enjoying the joviality of his brother's love and teasing, but lacking any answers.

He found Moira in the drawing room, cleaning a game of marbles while classical music played from the turntable in the corner, filling the space with orchestral tones.

Wynnie stood at the window with her nose pressed to the panes. Her breath met the cold glass and escaped in small wisps. Ice blooms lined the view's edges, and the snow continued to fall lazily, glittery. Wynnie saw him in a reflection and spoke without turning.

"The whole world changes when it snows," she said. "Even the shadows are different."

He came to her side.

"You notice quite a lot, don't you?" he asked.

"I do." She turned to him.

"Tell me about Emjie." Charlie had heard her speak of her invisible friend a few times now and had noticed how Clara didn't correct her, acting as if Emjie were always with them.

When he was a child, he'd fought the dragons and demons of an imaginary world with his brother. They'd made swords of fallen branches and shields of bark, and yet Charlie had known they were fighting something imaginary. He'd known that he wasn't truly a knight, and his brother wasn't a king, and still they'd played as if they were. This child believed her friend to be as real as he was, standing next to her.

"Emjie is my best friend." Wynnie now turned to him. "Except for my mama, who is really my best friend. But Emjie is the only one who will go on *all* my adventures. Mama can only go on some of them. And she tells me things that other people don't know. Not even Mama. And she takes me places."

"Like where?"

"Here."

He laughed.

"I've been here before." Wynnie placed her hand against the glass. "Right here."

"They call that déjà vu," he said.

Charlie felt Moira behind him, moving about the room. The music ended and the room turned quiet, with the scratch-scritch-scratch of the needle at the end of the record.

"What?" Wynnie asked.

"It's a French word that means 'already seen,' but it means a feeling that you've been somewhere or done something that you're doing right now."

"Whatever it is, it's not *just* a feeling."

"Where is Emjie now?"

Wynnie looked to her left. "I think she's playing in the snow. She loves it here very much."

"What does she look like, this friend of yours?"

"She's beautiful. She has long black curls that are never messy like mine. She has eyes so green you can nearly see through them to the world where she came from. Her nose is a tiny button and her ears are like little seashells."

"And her voice?"

"You know when you sang for us in London?"

"Yes."

"Her voice sounds like that, but like a girl. She's always singing a magical song."

"I don't sing magical songs. I just sing songs."

She shook her head vigorously, her glasses going crooked. She straightened them. "Oh no, that's not true. Emjie said your songs are bringing Grandma back to us."

He shivered. "Oh, Wynnie."

"You don't believe me." She smiled. "But you don't have to believe me for it to be true."

She withdrew her hand from the windowpane, but the foggy imprint of a little hand remained.

CHAPTER 37

CLARA

Lake District, England

"But you don't have to believe me for it to be true."

I entered the drawing room just as Wynnie said this to Charlie. They stood at the window watching the landscape being transformed by the falling snow. So many times, she'd said the same to me about Emjie. I watched Charlie's face as he reassured her that indeed he believed her.

"Hello!" I called out, and Charlie turned to me with a smile.

"How do we feel about going to the play tonight?" Charlie asked. "Mum is asking."

"We feel grand," Wynnie said, and clapped her hands together. "We must go!" She tried for a British accent and did a much better job than I had in my weak attempt.

The sound of the front door chimes interrupted us.

"Excuse me," Charlie said. "Probably more Christmas decorations arriving. Prepare to reside in a house of even more tinsel and lights and greenery and wreaths." He walked out of the room.

"Christmas," Wynnie said.

"Yes, and I think that means we need to find our way home."

"Not yet," she said, and turned back to the window. "Please."

I bit my lip and told her the truth. "Wynnie, I really don't want to miss the Caldecott Award ceremony. It means a lot to me."

"What if something here means even more?"

"Oh, darling," I said. "Only you mean more."

The snow stopped just as Archie and Adelaide bid everyone goodbye for London. I'd sent them off with a handwritten note and a plea for them to please send a telegram when they arrived in London. *We are in Northern England. Safe. Please call.* And I left the number for the Jamesons' house. Archie promised to send and shooed off any suggestion I might pay them back.

When their taillights faded in the dusky light, the rest of us left for the theater, the Vanguard bumping along the narrow winding road to the village of Hawkshead. First the lake was on our left and then it disappeared behind hedgerows that were so close that if I opened the car's window, I'd touch them. Charlie drove while Mrs. Jameson sat in the front seat, and Wynnie and I were in the back, where the car retained the smell of soot. Wynnie and I made faces at each other across the bench seat.

I was trying to get a sense of the villages and towns; we'd left Near Sawrey and made our way to Hawkshead. Charlie stopped at the corner, where a post wrapped in black and white stripes held three signs, one toward Hawkshead, one toward Tarn Hows, and one toward Windermere, the road curving and splitting. He took the bend on the left, and there we were in another village, one that looked ancient, timeworn, and solid.

We drove past limewashed homes, stone walls, pastures of sweet-faced sheep. Cobblestone streets and tight curves. We passed the ice cream shop and meat market, the flower shop, and the Queens Head hotel and pub, past the slate roofs and dark green doors, the bright blue doors and the yellow, and everywhere the greenery of Christmas, small lights twinkling from gas lanterns and entryways. Charlie drove down Flag Street and toward a whitewashed building with a peeling sign above it: *Burrough Theatre.*

"This town," I said. "Is it real?"

Mrs. Jameson laughed. "Isn't it marvelous? During the twelfth century it was a sheep walk managed by monks. Then it was a market village in the sixteen hundreds." She shook her head. "You surely don't want a history lesson. Just enjoy it."

"I'd love a history lesson," I told her. "I enjoy knowing how things started, what they were before they become what they are now."

"Did you know this is where William Wordsworth went to grammar school?" she asked.

"Really? Right here?"

"Right there," she said as we passed a whitewashed building. "Right off Leather, Rag and Putty Street."

"Odd name," I said even as I heard the great love Mrs. Jameson held for this place and land.

"It's what was sold on that street. And Christmas fair is next week," Mrs. Jameson said as she turned her head to look at us in the back seat.

It seemed nearly impossible to believe that only three days ago we'd been trapped in a sickly fog that could have killed Wynnie and now here we were in this place that seemed as if it existed out of another time, a land one could arrive at only through a portal.

Wynnie's wide eyes were taking it all in. She wore a green velvet dress with a lace collar that Mrs. Jameson had found in a trunk of old clothes. We both wore lamb's-wool full-length coats with rabbit-fur collars that smelled vaguely of mothballs, and I felt as elegant as if I were to be at a ball.

Charlie dropped us off as he went to park the car, and we stepped across the threshold of the wooden theater. The inside was as charming and rickety as an old sailing vessel, its hull shining and the cracks evident. The wooden seats wobbled as Mrs. Jameson, Wynnie, and I sat down in the front row and waited for Charlie. Players scrambled behind the red velvet curtain that billowed, pulsing in and out. Something dropped and someone laughed.

I remembered Finneas and how he was the first to tell us about this play. I surveyed the crowd to find him, but instead saw Charlie edging his way down the row to sit next to me, shedding his coat and settling in.

"Charlie," I asked, "do you know a Finneas Andrews?"

"I do!" he said, and smiled. "How do *you* know him?"

"We met him on the ship."

"He lives close to here. A farmer and shepherd and expert gardener, he's a dear friend of Mum's."

"How . . . what a coincidence."

"Indeed."

Then music began, a jaunty tune of flutes and piccolo, and Mrs. Jameson made a shushing noise at her son as if he were five years old. He rolled his eyes at me, and I smiled, facing the curtain.

I wondered how they would act out my mother's novel. I thought it nearly impossible to stage her story, with a magical world at its center. I'd seen *A Midsummer Night's Dream* onstage, and it worked, but this was a rustic small-town theater. Ten minutes before the curtain was to rise, the small room filled with patrons. Men, women, and children crowded in, filling nearly all the seats.

"How often does this play?" I whispered to Mrs. Jameson.

"This holiday season we've decided to have it every Monday through Friday night for two months. The first two years we played it only in the spring, but we have more people in the village during the holidays, so we moved it. We close January through March, for no one visits here but those of us who love the deep quiet of winter."

"Aren't I lucky that I'm here for this one, then."

"Aren't you." She smiled and touched my elbow, gave it a friendly squeeze.

I wondered if Mrs. Jameson would treat me differently if she knew my mother wrote the book for this play. Every hair on my neck and arms tingled with the approaching production, with the hints and clues that might be nestled inside.

If she was a patron of the theater, she must know more about who wrote the adaptation, who directed it, and how they were able to secure the rights. It was possible that Dad had granted rights and I'd never been told. I'd ask him next time we talked.

The lights dimmed and the curtain opened to reveal a fairy girl, a young woman with long dark hair that cascaded down her back in curls—obviously a wig, for only the true Emjie had such thick hair. A crown of red and white roses was perched on her head, and she floated about the stage on silk slippers, tossing flower petals.

Flute music floated from the side of the stage, and she twirled to its tune until it suddenly stopped. She turned on her tiptoes toward the audience. "Oh, you're here," she said. "How lovely! I'm Emjie and this is my land. I know you must wonder how I arrived here, for you most likely would love to do the very same."

The crowd clapped on cue, for who would not want to visit this land of rivers and hillocks of luminescent green trees and small animals hidden in the forest of fairies. This landscape was painted on wood and cardboard, a mirage at best, but the dream was as seductive as it was elusive. Wouldn't, she asked, any of *you* want the same?

"It all began . . ." the Emjie character said in a British accent. She paused while a tapestry of a city dropped behind her. It was, as near I could tell, an anonymous city of tall buildings and smokestacks, of cars and people and not a speck of green to be found. "In a city just like yours, in a house . . ." She walked to the side of the stage and stepped on a wooden platform. Two men slid the platform into plain sight, and on it was the interior of a house, with a mother and a father sitting at a linoleum kitchen table reading the *London Times* while Emjie watched them and they paid no attention to her.

"Mama," Wynnie whispered on the other side of me. "That's not Emjie."

I leaned over to speak into her ear. "I know, baby, that's an actress playing her."

"I know. But that's not how she sounds or looks."

"Shh . . . For now, let's just enjoy it."

"I can't." Wynnie covered her eyes and then peeked between her fingers. I squeezed her knee.

The story unfolded in a sixty-minute play that remained true to the book's plot. A young girl lives in the city with her parents. Her mother and father mostly ignore her for their work while Emjie makes a life outside in the tiny garden behind their home. It is there that she meets a flock of fairies, who sweep her away to their land. She has adventures and misadventures, from sea caves that flood to hailstorms that ruin her house of twigs and leaves, from meeting another child who wants to run away but ultimately doesn't, to a talking deer and bear who guide her from the mountains to the sea. One day she decides she will throw off the bonds of her earthbound life and join the realm of fairies.

I could have recited her last lines as the actress gently said them into the hushed audience. "I will be invisible to all but the few who believe." She lifted her arms and fairies of every hue from green to blue to yellow to pink descended from invisible strings in the ceiling and lit upon her arms and face and fluttered around her. Then in the growing dark, a rope descended, and Emjie reached behind her to fasten it to the waistband of ivy and leaves she'd worn for the last act.

I will be invisible to all but the few who believe.

Slowly she rose, high above the wooden stage scattered with paper leaves and flowers.

I knew the ending of the story, and still it took my breath away when she disappeared into the clouds above, the crowd rising to their feet.

If the audience read the rest of the book, they would know that Emjie left her family and her life to discover she was stuck in a dark fairy realm. It was lovely, in theory, for a children's story like Peter Pan, but in real life it would be both a nightmare and a horror to have your child choose a fantasy life over her life with you.

Or if your mother chose another world over a life with you.

I swallowed around the lump in my throat as the small cast of six came out to bow. Cheers rose with a standing ovation. The production hadn't varied from the book one bit, and yet a simple stage play could never show the depth and breadth of the novel.

An older woman with graying hair and a swirling patchwork dress seemed to glide onto the stage, waving her hands and then taking center stage to bow.

"Who is that?" I asked, squinting into the dim light, trying to find the woman's face with a spark of hope. Always hope.

"The director," Mrs. Jameson said.

"Her name?"

"Louisa Mayfair," Mrs. Jameson said as she, too, rose to her feet to clap.

Expectancy lifted like a balloon, deflated, and sank.

Louisa looked directly at Mrs. Jameson and held out her hand in acknowledgment, blew her a kiss.

The crowd slowly made their way into the cold night, wrapping coats and scarves, kissing each other goodbye. Charlie, Wynnie, and I waited while Mrs. Jameson went to chat with the cast. I realized even as I was doing it that I was searching every face in the room for something that sparked of my mother. It was useless, but that didn't stop me.

"Mama, I want to meet the girl who played Emjie," Wynnie said, and brought me back to myself.

"Don't you dare tell her she isn't Emjie," I teased Wynnie. "It will hurt her feelings."

"I won't say any such thing." Wynnie moved toward Mrs. Jameson, and I followed.

Mrs. Jameson looked down at Wynnie. "Oh, darling, did you love it?"

"Very much," Wynnie said in an unconvincing voice. Then she looked at Emjie. "What's your real name?"

"Irene," the girl said. "And yours?" She still wore Emjie's costume and flowers spilled from her crown.

"My name is Wynnie," she said. "This is my favorite story."

"Well, mine too." The young girl plucked a red rose from her crown and handed it to Wynnie. "You can keep this. It's from Emjie."

"Emjie doesn't much like roses. She prefers yellow jessamine, violets, and forget-me-nots."

"Indeed she does. But they aren't in season now, so she must do with red and white roses."

Wynnie laughed.

The girl looked up at Mrs. Jameson. "Was that better than last month? I changed the inflection in the middle part of the speech to try and find the emotion in the right place, as you said."

"It was lovely indeed!" Mrs. Jameson hugged the girl. "With every performance, you improve. I am quite disappointed that soon we'll have a hiatus."

"Mrs. Jameson," I said with a catch in my voice, "you help direct this play?"

"Oh," Mrs. Jameson said. "I never direct. That is Louisa's and Eliza's job. I am just a patron with great interest, and a producer as needed."

"Eliza?" I asked.

"Eliza Walker. She wrote the play."

"Mama!" Wynnie nearly exploded off her feet. "That's your author."

"Yours?" Mrs. Jameson asked.

But I was mute, stunned into silence. Eliza Walker, author of *Harriet the Hedgehog*, had adapted my mother's work into a play.

CHAPTER 38

CLARA

Lake District, England

Sweat trailed down my back beneath my wool sweater as I stood in the stuffy drawing room back at the Jameson house. The furnace and the fireplace chugged out heat against the chill of the night. But I was sure that the sweat had more to do with anger than warmth—anger at feeling left out, as if secrets were whispered behind my back.

Mother's word on a garden sign; Charlie's mother knowing Eliza Walker, who wrote the play for *The Middle Place*; my mother's language in this family's London library.

Wynnie, Charlie, his mother, and I sat in that drawing room. We stared at one another, and finally Mrs. Jameson said, "What *is* it? What is wrong with all of you?"

"Mum . . ."

Moira interrupted Charlie, carrying in a tray of whiskey in cut-glass highballs. Apple juice for Wynnie. I took my glass and a long, burning swallow, and then finally spoke. "Charlie, allow me?"

He nodded.

"Mrs. Jameson, that play is an adaptation of my mother's book."

"Excuse me? Which book are you talking about?" Mrs. Jameson glanced around the room.

"*The Middle Place*, Mum," Charlie said. "Clara's mother is Bronwyn Newcastle Fordham, the author of the book."

Mrs. Jameson cupped her whiskey with two hands and her mouth dropped open. "Pardon me?"

"Yes," I said. The room about me faded: the windows with dark-green damask curtains turned to smudge; the newly hung boughs of evergreen on the mantel transformed into a watercolor backdrop.

"Are you telling me that your mother is Bronwyn Newcastle Fordham? I need to be sure that is *exactly* what you are saying."

"Yes. Bronwyn is my mother. She left us, me, over twenty-five years ago."

She spun her head to her son. "How long have you known this?" she asked.

"Since I found Bronwyn's papers in Dad's office and called Clara in America."

She closed her eyes for a moment. "You are the author's daughter, and you came to retrieve your mother's papers. Am I following?"

I looked to Charlie and nodded at him, an acquiescence that he might tell her the truth. "Mum, the story is that Bronwyn disappeared with a leather satchel that contained a dictionary of sorts, a key to words she created that are needed to translate the sequel to *The Middle Place*. She disappeared when Clara was eight years old. It was believed that she took these papers with her to the bottom of the sea, but instead they were in Father's library with a letter for Clara. I summoned Clara here, or, more accurately, the letter inside the satchel summoned her here."

Mrs. Jameson's face went still as the lake outside the window. The only giveaway that she was alert were her fingertips rounding the carved edge of the armchair, around and around. "Excuse me? What was in your father's library? Fordham's language," she said, and it wasn't a question. "Why would your father have such a thing. It's been missing for . . ."

"Twenty-five years," I said.

Wynnie burrowed closer to me on the couch.

"That doesn't make any sense," Mrs. Jameson muttered. "Not one bit."

"Do you know anything about it? Anything at all? Do you know how those papers found their way into our home?"

Then the first sign of real emotion played across her face as if something moved under her skin, a wind blowing, a whisper told. "I know nothing of this," she said so quietly that we all leaned forward. She looked at Charlie and then stood. "Why did your father have these papers?"

"That's what we were trying to figure out when the fog descended."

"Did Callum buy it at one of his auctions?"

"I don't know." Charlie clasped his hands. "But now they are mostly gone." He told her what happened on the way here, the rough sleeper, the river, the papers lost.

Mrs. Jameson brushed her hand across her forehead as if a stray curl had fallen across her face but her hair was pinned back, lacquered in place.

"Ah yes." She smiled at Wynnie. "Wynnie is from Bronwyn. I see. Clara, can you tell me about the papers?" She took a long swallow of her whiskey and set down the empty glass. She walked to the rear of the chair and held to it with her hands clenched on the back.

"The papers," I said. "Well, as Charlie said, they are a dictionary of sorts, a list of imaginary words that my mother created. We came to retrieve them in order to translate the sequel."

"I see."

"And Mrs. Jameson," I said. "There's something else."

She looked to Charlie, but he was watching me; I felt his soft gaze. "What is it?" she asked.

"I am an illustrator."

"Yes, your darling daughter told me so."

"I am the illustrator for Eliza Walker's *Harriet the Hedgehog*."

Mrs. Jameson let out a cry and her hand flew to cover her mouth. "You are the lost author's daughter. You are an illustrator who paints pictures for the woman who wrote the play about your mother's book. You are . . ." She paused and her hands gripped the chair as if to hold herself steady.

Wynnie chimed in as her gaze moved back and forth between us. "And Mama won a huge award for Harriet. It comes with a big gold coin."

I smiled at my daughter's enthusiasm when Mrs. Jameson asked, "An award?"

"It's called a Caldecott. It's an American award for illustrators. But that's not the thing here." I held back tears. "Do you know anything about my mother or where she is or anything at all? Or how your theater gained permission to adapt the book?"

"We were granted permission from the estate. It's been playing in the theater for five years or more. We had the rights over ten years ago, but it took that long to get it going, for Eliza to write it and . . ." Her gaze darted to Charlie, to me, and then back at Charlie. "Eliza wanted it staged here, and she was right—it is beloved."

"The estate would be my father, and he has never mentioned this to me."

"I didn't even make the connection until just now. Yes, Harrington. Yes. I haven't thought of his name in years. Thomas, is it?"

"No, Timothy," I answered.

"Mum." Charlie placed his glass on the coffee table and dropped his hands to his knees to bend forward. "Do you know anything about Bronwyn Newcastle Fordham's whereabouts?"

"No." His mother seemed unflappable, calmly looking between us; the only sign of tension was in the way she held to the chair. "I know nothing of a language or why your father came to purchase her papers or how Eliza was connected to you." She took a deep breath. "I am incredibly confused, and your father isn't here to help."

"Mum, can you tell us why this book? This play?"

"Eliza. She was insistent. She gave it to me long ago, and I'd been fascinated with the novel. Back when you were a child. Do you remember?"

He shook his head.

She looked at me and patted her eyes with the lace doily from beneath her whiskey glass. "And Eliza." She shook her head. "You are Eliza's illustrator."

"I am." I stared at Mrs. Jameson and her stunned expression. "You know her well, it seems." My voice shook and there was nothing to hide it.

"Yes, I do. She will soon be here for holiday. Eliza, I mean."

"Eliza Walker is coming here?" I jumped up as if the couch had thrown me into the air.

"Have you met her?" Mrs. Jameson asked.

"No," I told her. "I'm as stunned and confused as you seem to be. I didn't know Eliza was British, but I've never spoken to her. We've only written to each other. I thought she was from Maine."

Mrs. Jameson laughed, but it was weak. "Yes, she is from America, from Maine. But she married a local man, Thomas, a mate of Callum's, nearly thirty years ago, I believe. Maybe twenty-five? They split their time between here and London. But, Clara, don't you know that Harriet the Hedgehog lives here?"

"No, I thought it was Maine . . . the mountains and lake and . . ."

Mrs. Jameson shook her head. "Here."

"Mama!" Wynnie jumped up and threw her hands in the air to face me, grinning. "You've been painting this place and land and lake all along. Oh, Mama, I knew it looked familiar."

My mind turned fuzzy, and I couldn't seem to find my grounding or the right things to say. "Mrs. Jameson, might you introduce me to Eliza Walker?"

"I can, but she's not here yet. I think she arrives next week."

"Can you . . . describe her?" I asked, my hands shaking as I clasped them together.

"Describe her? Goodness. She's tall, brown hair. She's . . . oh, I don't know the right word, rugged? Outdoorsy in her way, but also elegant. Quiet and sweet." She paused. "Do you think . . ."

"I don't think anything. I'd just like to meet her and ask her how she came upon my mother's book."

Mrs. Jameson sat now and patted the chair across from her. "Sit, dear."

I did, and she reached out and took my hands, held fast. "I am so sorry about your mother, Clara. I can't imagine leaving my children, but terrible things happen to people. I am not hiding anything from you. If Callum knew her, then there will be a way to find her." She looked to her son. "You shouldn't have kept this from me all these days."

"I'm sorry, I really am. Clara and I have been trying to figure it all out, and I didn't want to aggrieve you in your mourning."

She looked to me and smiled. "I am here to help." Then she spoke to Wynnie. "I so hope you enjoyed the theatrical production of the book written by your grandmother."

"It was lovely, Mrs. Jameson," Wynnie said. "Even if Emjie doesn't have that many freckles."

I held my breath, and Mrs. Jameson laughed. "You are a darling child. Now I am going to retire, and together we will figure out this mystery of our families. Good night, everyone."

She walked out of the room with her back straight, not a wobble in her gait atop patent leather pumps.

CHAPTER 39

CLARA

Lake District, England

Charlie played his drum, oblivious to my presence in the entry of the drawing room. The beater moved rapidly, the wooden bulbs blurring in the dim light. The fire burned to embers while he sang in a language I didn't know but sensed in my chest.

The song rose from the earth, a hum of soil and rock, of grass and tree, of flower and leaf. He faced away from me, and I knew that if I saw his face, it would be transformed. I felt like a voyeur, but I could not walk away from this sound and his voice.

I'd tucked Wynnie into bed, and she'd been asleep before I'd kissed her forehead. With the energy of the night buzzing through me, I couldn't sleep, so I'd made my way downstairs to sit by the fire, but instead found Charlie in the drawing room.

He finished and then turned to me as if he'd known I was there all along. He smiled and the leftover aura of the song saddened the edges of his eyes.

"That was incredible," I said softly.

"Well, thank you." He set the drum on a side table. "You all right?" he asked.

"I think so. You?"

"Maybe?" he said. "What an odd thing how our families are tangled, and we knew nothing at all." He shook his head. "Not an inkling."

"Yes," I said, walking into the room and settling down on the couch nearest to the burning fire. "There's obviously much we don't know about our parents. But tell me something you do know—tell me about that song." I nestled into the corner and pulled the wool throw around my shoulders.

"It's an old song, too ancient to give you the true origins. But it always settles me when I'm unsettled. It's about a woman who waits for her lover to return from sea. 'The Moorlough Shore,' it is called."

"Can you translate it for me?"

"It is probably maudlin and oversentimental in English. 'Seven long years I wait for him by the Moorlough Shore.'"

"Waiting," I said. "Waiting and waiting. I know this feeling." I meant to sound light and free, but instead my voice was tight.

"Oh, Clara, I don't know what exactly to say, because that's a horrible thing to endure."

I pushed aside the emotions. "Tell me about this language, about the Celtic language."

He honored the way I'd moved past the subject and sat on the other end of the couch, twisting to face me. "I'm no expert. I wish you could talk to my father." He pulled a face. "Of course, we all wish we could talk to my father. What I know is that he'd say Irish Gaelic is one of the oldest languages. Some think it is the Adamic language."

"Adamic?"

"First language. The language Adam spoke. The language he created to talk to God. The language all others came from, but there is scant proof of that. The idea has some advocates, and it's a lovely idea, although ultimately unprovable."

"An original language," I said. "I never gave that much thought. The first language—the one all others came from."

He moved closer so our knees touched. "Yes. And what Father would tell us is . . ." He closed his eyes for a moment and then opened them. "He'd tell us that every culture infuses its language with a sense of who they are as a people, as a person, as a community. It shows us what they value, what they love, what they think about, how they label the world."

"Then for my mother to make up her own words, she felt that none of the other languages could define her life for her. If it's true that we make a language from what we are made of, then I can say this—Mother was made of deep emotions, of land and of nature. She hated being inside unless all the windows were open, even in winter."

"Language carries our sense of self, and it's possible she felt that the language she knew wasn't enough. But every language, every story, every song, is built on the ones before it. Some words migrate across countries and centuries. I see the roots of other languages in your mother's words, and she has also made them her own."

"I don't know her well enough to say. It's terrible, but I don't know her well enough to agree or disagree with you. I wish I could, though. The mother I knew was my childhood mommy, not the woman I read about in that biography." I paused. "But maybe we all aren't so different. I make sense of the world through images, you through music, and my mother through language."

"Maybe it's all the same?"

"Yes, but no matter how alike we are, we are different in one essential way. I would never leave my daughter. Never."

"You must have some inkling of why she left."

"I do—but it's what I heard you call bollocks. I'm assuming that means—"

"Bullshit."

"Yes."

"What are your mother's bollocks?" He tried not to smile, but it was a futile effort.

"That I'm better off without her as a mother."

"It's not true?"

"No, it's not."

"But she thought it was."

"Or so I am told." I waved my hand through the air. "Enough of that. I don't know her, obviously."

"Clara," he said gently, "my mum has been in my life all along, and do I actually know her? Not fully. Can we ever really know our parents?"

"But you *have* her. You have her here, and you can ask what you want to know. You might not get to the deep truth of her, but she's here. Mine is not."

"I've never asked you, Clara. What do *you* think happened to her?"

"It depends on the day or season of my life. If I'm going to settle into this day, into this night, I would say she survived, continued writing, and somehow your father has her language. Why? I don't know."

"Do you think it could be . . . I mean . . . when Mum mentioned Eliza. Do you think it's her?"

"I don't know, Charlie. I've hoped for so many people to be my mother that what is one more? To think that I was illustrating Mother's books and that she might have been here and is coming here? I just can't wish anymore for those kinds of things." I paused and moved closer to him. "I watched your mother's face earlier, and she truly didn't know about the satchel."

"You're right," he said. "I believe she is hurt."

From the back of the house came laughter and Moira's voice.

"The kitchen," he said with a smile. "Where our family or anyone living here gathers in the mornings and evenings, where everyone gossips and has a chin-wag before they head to their cottages or rooms. Most kitchens are cut off from the house, but Mum knocked the wall open, so it feels more like a gathering place than a secluded kitchen. You'll find Mum rolling the dough for pie as readily as the cook preparing dinner."

"When was the last time your father was here?"

"A month before he passed, we threw a lavish party for his fifty-sixth birthday."

"Charlie?" I leaned closer. "Have you asked your brother?"

"I have. He knew nothing of your mother or the papers. Listen . . ." Charlie stared off. "My brother and I are thick as thieves, two knights fighting the dragon, two boys who knew they'd conquer the world together, and if he knew anything, he would tell me. We might be very different now, but he wouldn't lie."

"How so different?"

"Life. Growing up." He absently twirled the drumstick in his hand. "There have been articles written about our family in the society pages. They say that Archie and I split the personality of our father into two parts: logical and mystical. Logos and mythos. Maybe we believed that? Maybe it's true? I'm not sure. But Archie has always been interested in the financial and political world of power. I have always been fascinated by the world of music and literature. Even so, it's not that simple. I enjoy running the financial division of the company and I have a head for it, and there was a time when Archie played the piano and read the same adventure novels I did. But the separation grew over time. We chose different universities—I studied at Oxford and Archie at Cambridge. But that doesn't change the core of us."

"I've always wanted a sister. Or a brother."

He placed the drumstick on the table as if just remembering he held it.

"And maybe I do have a brother or sister and just don't know about it," I said. "My mother's history is a blank book and I've filled it with so many stories, but it's all written in disappearing ink. If she took her life, which most assumed she did, she was trying to cure her own pain and I am devastated for her. If she ran away, she was a cruel woman and left her daughter and husband. How am I to know whether to mourn her or be angry at her if I don't know which is true?"

"I believe you'll find out what happened to her. She left you those words for a reason, and I don't think it's just to carry it on and translate her sequel. It's *for* you, which means there is something in it for you."

"But most of it is gone, Charlie. It's a meager list now, that's all. It won't translate her sequel to discover if there are any secrets hidden in it for me." Sadness swooped through my chest like birds. "I don't think she left it for me so I could find her in the world. I think she just wants me to find her in the language. That needed to be enough."

"Oh, Clara." He took my hand in his, wound his fingers through mine.

The laughter and chatter from the kitchen faded now. A light flickered and swayed across the landscape as someone walked to their cottage.

"Will you play another song?" I asked.

He hesitated and then nodded. "Do you have any requests?"

"I don't even know enough to request something. You choose. One of your favorites."

He picked up the drum and stood in front of me, ran the stick across its hide.

I didn't look away as his lips moved around the foreign words that carried more inside them than I understood. He closed his eyes for much of the song, and his hands seemed to have a life of their own.

He finished and again sat facing me. He wiped a tear from my cheek. "It's a mournful one, for sure."

"What is it about?"

"A mother."

He placed the drum on the ground and set the beater on the table. Then he took my hand and leaned forward. I closed the last inch between us, for I wanted that kiss as much as I'd wanted any before. His lips came to life beneath mine, and for the first time in years, my body awoke to touch. His hands found their way into my hair.

I was lost in that kiss, forgetting all that brought me here. The anxiety of the past days fell away, a waterfall over a cliff.

It had been so long since I'd felt this need, this unrelenting desire. So long. I'd been waiting for this, I now understood. Waiting for this every day since he arrived at the flat with his drum case.

A door closed and I startled, returned to who I was and where I was—Wynnie's mama in a house that held the secrets about *my* mother. I pulled away from Charlie and dropped my face into my hands. "I'm sorry. That was . . . I'm sorry."

He placed his finger under my chin and lifted my face to his. "I've wanted to do that since the moment you walked through my front door."

A door slammed, the patter of feet, and then the call: "Mama."

I touched his cheek, and I was gone.

CHAPTER 40

CLARA

Lake District, England

Morning arrived, and sunlight filled the bedroom with a bright cheerfulness that belied the nervous flutter in my chest.

I sat and noticed Wynnie was gone from our bed. I rose and cracked open the door and heard her voice among the others in the hallway. I quickly bathed and brushed my hair into a high ponytail, found some mascara in the dregs of my valise, and swiped some on my lashes. I knew I was taking too much care for breakfast, but now I must face Charlie Jameson.

After that kiss, the feeling that he saw me and who I really was overwhelmed me—what adolescent silliness. I'd forgotten the tenderness of need, of desire. But now it was here again, in the wrong place and time.

Yes, I'd been waiting for that kiss, or maybe I was waiting for Mother or answers and the kiss took its place. Sometimes I confused the emotions. Mother's leaving created such a great thirst of loneliness in me that through the years I'd tried to quench it with things that would never fulfill me. Including the wrong man.

I placed my hand on my stomach, on the bees of desire zipping around inside.

I'd left Charlie sitting on the couch in a room with candles dripping beeswax on the brass dishes, having no idea how he felt about us.

I opened the bedroom door and made my way to the breakfast room, and there they were: Charlie, his mother, and Wynnie, seated around the table and laughing. Charlie held a *London Times* with the headlines reading *TV to Show Crowning* and *5 Killed in Riots in Casablanca* and then in smaller type, as if it weren't an event that had changed our life, *London Blacked Out by Fog.*

They all looked at me.

"Good morning," Charlie said first, and maybe I imagined it, but I heard a question in the greeting. *Is it a good morning?*

Mrs. Jameson sat with her hands folded on her lap. The places were set, but breakfast wasn't out. She cleared her throat. "Clara, I must begin your day with an apology. It was rude of me to leave so abruptly last night."

"No need for apology," I told her as I sat, picked up the linen napkin, folded it onto my lap, and motioned for Wynnie to do the same.

"Yes, there is. I can't imagine what you've been through. And thinking I might have something to do with keeping your mother from you set me quite off balance. But I can assure you that I know nothing about this language or her whereabouts. I promise I will help you in any way I can."

"Thank you, Mrs. Jameson," I said.

"Pippa. Please call me Pippa."

Wynnie let out a sigh. "It's such a pretty name," she said. "A happy name."

I smiled at Pippa, at the way she softened. "Pippa, thank you for this refuge and sanctuary. I promise we'll leave as soon as I can get to London for my passport."

"Please don't rush. It aways seems such a waste that a child isn't here to see all the magical lights and decorations. This place quite assuredly sparkles come the holidays. Just waiting on my Charlie or Archie to give me grands."

"Mum!" Charlie said.

"Be careful what you wish for," I told her with a smile. Wynnie took my hand under the table, and I squeezed her fingers.

"I'm enchanted by your mother's work," Pippa said. "I'd love to talk to you about her. If you'd allow it."

"I can talk about what I remember," I said. "It's not much." I told her of my childhood memories of Emjie's fantasy world, of late-night swims and magical mornings. "Other than my childhood, I don't know much more than you can read in the articles and biographies. She left when I was eight years old."

"Same age as me," Wynnie piped up.

Pippa smiled at Wynnie and then returned her focus to me. "Your memories must be vague."

"Yes and no. There are some that are as bright and clear as that landscape outside. And then large swaths of blankness. Sometimes I don't know if what I remember is real or made up or a photo."

She nodded. "Memory is odd like that, isn't it?"

"Yes, it is."

Moira entered the room then and set plates of steaming poached eggs and salmon in front of us. "Good day to you all," she said. "A bright and lovely one it is!"

"Good morning," we all chimed in together as she slipped out of the room.

Pippa stared out the window. The sky was wiped clean of clouds, the blue of the deep glacial lake, one mirroring the other while the moody fells rose above. Pippa turned back to me. "And sometimes memories fool you. Fool you into believing that things were different than they were. It's like we must make it all better by looking back. Nostalgia."

"There's a book about my grandma," Wynnie said. "A book that tells her whole life. The life before Mama."

"I know, dear," Pippa said. "But I haven't read it." Then she looked to me and set her lips straight as if she were sorry for the stories about Mother. "Clara, can you tell me about your art and illustrations?"

"I can," I said. "Now *there's* a subject I know something about." I laughed and her smile was my reward.

We ate and chatted. Charlie remained quiet, nibbling at his breakfast and listening with a small smile, as if he'd been waiting for me to talk about my art and life.

"So," Pippa said, "you love illustrating?"

"I do," I said. "It is when I feel most like myself."

"How so?" she asked, taking a bite of her poached egg off a silver fork.

"I think there is another world inside this world. Many worlds, to be accurate. Mother wrote about them, but the images I draw aren't cut from the fabric of the world we see every day. Instead they come from a hidden place, a realm more fantastical, a bit more elusive and I hope incandescent."

Pippa's eyes, to my total surprise, filled with tears. "Yes. That's how I feel about my gardens and friends. I once gathered a little painting club," she said with a smile. "It was just me and Nelle and Isolde, and once in a bit a friend would join. We set up in the third-floor room, a perch above the world, and painted. I was terrible at it, but they were wonderful. I have some of their art in the house. I don't know why we quit." She stared off as if she could see herself upstairs with an easel and brush.

"I'd love to see some of the paintings," I said, even as I felt the desire to paint washing over me.

She nodded. "And the maps Wynnie told us about?"

"I started painting on them when my mother left us. I was, to be honest, obsessed with where she might have gone, and I wanted maps of the whole world. Dad found them for me. Some he'd order; others he found in old flea markets or discarded. I'd paint what I imagined existed in that land—flowers, trees, birds, fish—anything I could find in the encyclopedia. And then, sadly, I would try to imagine Mother living there. But it turned into more than a hobby. Now I get paid for it." I laughed. "That sounds crass. Meaning, people hire me to paint on maps of the places they love the best."

"Where do you imagine she went?" Pippa leaned forward.

"It has changed through the years, and I've imagined her as so many people, including Beatrix Potter, who Charlie told me lived a few doors down."

"She's my very favorite illustrator," Wynnie added. "Except for Mama."

"Well," Pippa said, "her house is called Hill Top and is now open to tour. They have original drawings and all sorts of things, and you can walk through Peter Rabbit's garden." She winked at Wynnie, who grabbed my hand.

"Let's go today!" Wynnie said.

I smiled. "We have no other plans while we wait for our passports, and I think that's a grand idea."

Pippa clapped her hands and looked to Wynnie. "Did you know that the lake right outside"—she waved her hand toward the window—"Esthwaite Water, is the very lake that Jemima Puddle-Duck flew over when she was looking for a place to lay her eggs?"

"Right there?" Wynnie jumped up and pointed in the direction of the lake, her face aglow.

"Yes," Pippa said. "Right there."

CHAPTER 41

CLARA

Lake District, England

I imagined a long path and winding road to the cottage where Beatrix Potter had lived, an enchanted forest and shaded glen. I was wrong. A simple white fence on the road bordered her patch of garden and home. Wynnie and I walked out the front door of the Jamesons' home, down the lane, past the next-door farm and the Tower Bank Arms, and there it was—Hill Top. The land hay-colored and covered in frost.

The simple house, which was made of stone walls topped by a slate roof, sat at the end of a long flagstone pathway, gardens leading us forward on either side.

"She lived here?" Wynnie asked.

"Yes," I told her. "Moved here after her fiancé died. Just up and made her own life with her art and her stories."

We reached the front door, where a woman in a blue uniform stood with pamphlets to hand us. But first we turned to look at the brick-walled garden, the rows of wicker cages, the wheelbarrow and watering cans. Behind it, the fells rose and sank like waves, the house cupped in the trough.

A man stood by the garden gate. He held a branch and then broke it in half, held it out to a woman bundled in a thick brown coat. As Wynnie made her way to the green iron gate that led into the yard, I smiled with a realization.

"Finneas," I called out.

He turned with a surprised look, and then he spied Wynnie and burst out with a "Greetings, ladies! Very fancy meeting you here!"

"Indeed," I called in return as I rushed over to greet him.

He shook my hand vigorously. "How did you find me? I am so pleased."

"I didn't on purpose." I laughed as Wynnie came to us.

He greeted Wynnie and then looked inquiringly back at me. "You just happen to be here?"

"Yes," I said. "It's quite a story."

"I have time," he said when the woman beside him made a coughing noise in the back of her throat. "Oh, how rude of me. Clara, please meet Susan Ludbrook, director of the museum."

She smiled. "Lovely to meet you. Seems we didn't collar the rose-bushes correctly. He's here to put us to rights."

"Not sure anyone can do that," he said, and then smiled at me. "Wonderful to see you."

"I thought you were a farmer," I said to him.

"Oh, I am. But gardening is my passion. And although I'm no expert, I help when I can."

Mrs. Ludbrook laughed. "Oh, he's an expert all right. Don't be fooled by this man's utter humility. We couldn't keep these gardens as they are without his help."

I stared at the charming vine-covered cottage. "Did you know her? Beatrix, I mean?"

"Yes, I did," he said. "And no one can truly do her garden justice like she did, but I try."

Mrs. Ludbrook spoke. "You know she didn't live here in the end; she lived across the lane. When she was here in Hill Top working, she was Beatrix Potter, but when she walked across this path to the house over there"—she lifted her chin at the pasture and the house beyond—"there, she was Mrs. William Heelis, and when she died, she left over fourteen farms, all donated to the government, which is why you can visit today." She nodded at Finneas. "Now off to work I go. Lovely to meet you both," she said to us.

Finneas and I wandered the lanes of the garden, Wynnie next to us interjecting questions about everything from the real Peter Rabbit to Mrs. Tiggy-Winkle, until I finally asked what preoccupied me. "Charlie Jameson said you know his family?"

He laughed. "Know them? I love them dearly. Callum was my mate, God rest his soul, and Pippa loves her gardens nearly as much as I do my own. May I ask how you know them?"

"We are staying with them," Wynnie said. "And you should see our room. It's made for a princess."

"Oh?"

"Remember those papers I told you about?" I asked him.

"Yes." Curiosity had him leaning forward.

"It was Mr. Jameson's library where they were found."

Finneas slapped the edge of a fence line and laughed. "How did I not see this? Of course it would be my old mate. I should have known the minute you told me about it. This is the kind of thing that obsessed him—literary mysteries."

I squinted into the sun, which had burst from a low cloud. I lifted my palm to shield my eyes. "How is it that the man I meet on a ship is friends with the man who has my mother's papers?"

"Because England isn't so big a country?"

I looked at him and he said, "But more likely because when the alltar conspires to show you something, if you are paying attention, you will see it and your life will be revealed."

"Alltar?"

"The unseen world." He smiled. "Now you think I'm batty."

"On the contrary," I said. "Now I think we can have a real conversation. Sorry to pepper you with questions, but do you know Eliza Walker also?"

"I do."

"Well?"

"No, just casually in the town. But she's lovely. A writer, you see."

"Yes, I know. I illustrate her children's books."

"Pardon me? You illustrate Eliza Walker's children's books? You draw Harriet?"

"I do."

"Wow." He stared off for a minute. "You are awfully tied to this place without ever having been here."

"I know. It's . . . odd, and I am trying to piece it together."

"Did you know Eliza lives here part-time?"

"I didn't until yesterday. I thought she lived in Maine."

"My, my." He rubbed his hands together. "The mystery deepens."

"Best explanation I've heard yet," I said.

His smile went to a thin line. "I didn't mean to make light, Clara."

"You didn't. It's all a mystery and I don't know if there's any way to solve it, but I'm here."

He smiled and Wynnie stopped next to us. "I can see Peter." She pointed at the far corner of the garden against the brick wall. "Do you?"

I bowed down and pretended to search. "He must have scurried away," I told her, and wished I truly could view all she saw.

"Do you?" she asked Finneas.

"I don't see him right now, but I have at other times." He smiled at Wynnie, and I thought she might hug him.

"Let's get out of the cold?" he asked, and nodded toward Hill Top.

After a tour of the charming house, a view from the window seat of Beatrix's bedroom, a few stories of her talents from sheep farming to horticulture to conservation, we heard the story we already knew about how Peter Rabbit was born from a letter she'd written to a sick child, and how she once fell in love with her publisher, who died, and how the man she married was once her solicitor.

Mrs. Ludbrook noticed I was staring at a page of indecipherable words under glass. "That's a page from her journal," Mrs. Ludbrook said.

"Can't really read it," I said leaning closer. "It's—"

"Written in her secret language."

"Excuse me?"

"Yes, yes. It seems that our industrious Beatrix created her own coded language so she could write whatever she wanted in her journal without her parents being able to read it."

"That's utterly fascinating."

Mrs. Ludbrook smiled at my interest. "Indeed, and there is a man trying to decode it, but I'm of the opinion that if Beatrix didn't want us to read it, then, well, maybe we shouldn't read it."

"Exactly," I said, thinking of my mother's sequel, of how it was quite possible she never wanted anyone to read it . . . until now.

After we inspected every square inch of the cottage—the hidden corners and tiny cupboards, the places where she drew inspiration, the way she made art out of the pieces of her life—I told Finneas it was time for Wynnie and me to scurry home for lunch. "They'll be worrying about us. We've given them all quite the scare, and I don't need them traipsing off to find me."

"Have you found what you were looking for? What you need?"

"No," I said, "I haven't. Unless you're asking if I've found the most enchanting land I've ever seen."

"I meant answers about your mother."

"None. If you know anything . . ."

"I don't," he said. "Callum never said a word about any of this. Not once to me, anyway."

"That's what Charlie and Pippa say, too."

He laughed. "Oh, she's Pippa to you now? Looks like you are nearly family."

I smiled.

"Well, I guess we all have secrets." Then he grew slightly serious. "I'll stop by and visit in the next few days. I've promised Pippa. I was just giving her some time to settle."

Wynnie lifted her head from a drawing from *The Tale of Mr. Tod*. "I've heard her cry, but when we see her, she's perfectly all right."

"That's the private part," Finneas said gently. "I've had my own private grief." He stood before I could ask why.

With promises to see each other again, we parted. As Wynnie chattered like a squirrel about all the wonders she'd seen, we made our way back down the lane. Across the meadow sat the white house of Mrs. Heelis and paths leading up to the hills. I wanted to walk those paths, to be led toward something I couldn't name.

We reached the Jameson house, where Charlie waited for us in the warm drawing room. We plopped down on the couches, and he asked us how it all went.

Last night's kiss seemed to linger between us, and I wondered if he wanted another in the same way I did. I folded my hands so as not to reach for him. The embarrassment faded with his presence, and now I just wanted more of him.

"It was so interesting to see where she lived," I said about Hill Top. "I had imagined something grander. Isn't that silly? I mean, we make our art from whatever life we have. It doesn't need to be grand to make something beautiful."

He smiled. "I'm glad you think so. Now," he said, "Moira has prepared an American lunch for all of us, or so she says."

"What is an American lunch?" I asked.

"We shall see."

"Charlie, I'm glad Pippa suggested I go today. It was the first time in a long time that I wasn't thinking about the mysteries that have been plaguing me. It was glorious. Time stood still for a while, and I let it all in."

"When here and now cease to matter," he said.

A tingle of recognition. "Eliot," I said, "T. S. Eliot. The line is 'Love is most nearly itself / When here and now cease to matter.'"

"Yes!" His smile was full.

"A nearly perfect poem in my opinion," I said. "It starts with 'In my beginning is my end.'"

He raked his hand through his hair. "And ends with 'In my end is my beginning.'"

"Mother taught it to me," I said.

He nodded. "I don't remember where I learned it, probably university."

I smiled at him and felt our connection, these threads of our lives pulling and pulling until finally here we sat. My God, I wanted to kiss him again. Wynnie watched us with a smile.

We stood up to go into the dining room when I stopped to face him. "Oh," I said. "And we ran into Finneas Andrews, our friend from the ship."

"He's a good man. How strange all the ties you have here," Charlie said, and placed an arm over my shoulder in a sudden gesture of such tenderness that I hugged him and lingered in his arms long enough for Wynnie to wiggle her way into the embrace.

CHAPTER 42

CLARA

Lake District, England

"Since the moment you told me about your mother I have been restless," Pippa said. "I want to help."

By the lake's shore, in the early morning mist, Charlie and I were a mixture of both shy and familiar with each other. We laughed about yesterday's "American lunch" of soggy meatloaf and macaroni and cheese baked to burnt and woke the sleepy glacier waters by tossing pebbles across the smooth surface and watching the circles grow outward. A low mist sat on the water, clouds that fell to earth.

That was where Pippa found Charlie and me the day after Wynnie and I had visited Hill Top. She pulled her scarf tighter as she faced us. "In my sleepless night, I found a few things if you'd like to hear about them."

"Tell us," I said, no longer feeling the dreaminess of the morning, alert now.

"Charlie, darling, all of those pages and pages that your father typed in his room?"

"Yes." He stepped closer to his mother and dropped the pebble he held.

"I went through the piles in his cabinets."

"You'd never done that before?"

"No. Why would I?" She looked quizzically at him as if invading anyone's privacy wasn't even worth a thought. "Even now I feel guilty about doing it. One of the secrets to a loving and long marriage is that one must always have a place for oneself, within oneself. These were his private rooms. I trusted him. What I found has nothing to do with your mother, Clara. And I'm sorry for that."

"What did you find?" Charlie asked.

"All these years as your father refused to talk about his family, as he was quiet about his absence during the Easter Rising, about his history and losing everyone he loved except Isolde . . . he hasn't talked about it because he has been writing about it. We have his entire family history, Charlie." Her face trembled as a single tear fell down her right cheek. She brushed it away.

"Oh, Mum, that is brilliant. I don't know what to say!"

I grasped Charlie's arm. "You have them! You have your father's stories now. He didn't leave without telling you, just like he promised."

Pippa nodded. "These stories will break your heart. We have them now. We have them forever." Pippa looked to me. "Nothing of your mother, I am so very sorry to say. But I made some phone calls. Eliza is in the village. She arrived just last night in time for the Christmas festival and to visit her husband's family."

"May I—"

"Meet her?" Pippa asked. "Yes."

"We've met on the bridge between our work—illustrations and story—but never once in real life. Not even on the phone. Eliza Walker changed my life."

"How so?" Pippa asked.

"My work had been published a few times before, and editors were suggesting me for other work, but *Harriet the Hedgehog* brought me the Caldecott and everything that will come after. I would love to meet her and thank her." I wanted even more than that from her. I wanted answers.

"You won the Caldecott," Charlie said. "Not Eliza, but I understand you'd love to meet her. It seems astounding that you never have."

"Today at three o'clock for tea?" Pippa asked.

Eliza Walker was one more clue in a long line of them that made no sense and didn't connect. Maybe she was the one who could attract the random pieces of filament like a magnet and draw them all together.

Charlie and Pippa stared at me, and I realized I wasn't answering. "Yes," I said. "Please."

I would finally meet the woman whose books I illustrated, a woman

I had collaborated with yet never met anywhere but on the page and in my imagination.

—

Nestled in the middle of Hawkshead, Eliza Walker's home was only a block from the theater where my mother's play was performed. We stood in front of a whitewashed stone house with a gray slate roof and a bright yellow door. Charlie and Pippa walked briskly up the stone pathway. Wynnie and I held back. I wanted to take this all in, I wanted it to mean something, to remember the day I met the woman who changed my life by hiring me to illustrate her stories I once believed were set in Maine.

The door opened, and voices rang out from inside. "Charlie! Pippa! Come in, come in." A booming voice soaked with a British accent. He was a stout man, thick and short, with a ruddy face and a bulbous nose, charming as an elf.

Wynnie and I made our way to the front door, and he held out his hand. "Thomas Walker. And who do I have the pleasure of meeting?"

"I am Clara Harrington, and this is my daughter, Wynnie," I said.

He shook our hands with vigor and smiled as if we'd brought him a gift. Then he looked over his shoulder to the inside of the cottage and hollered out: "Your brilliant illustrator is here, Eliza! Come, come and meet her." He looked back to me as he stepped aside to let us all enter the warm home. "How astonishing that you are here in Cumbria."

Once inside, all I could do was look for Eliza. An unnamed hope fluttered inside, and I was afraid of it, afraid to nurture it.

Eliza entered the living room where we all stood by a blazing fire as it crackled and warmed the room. She smiled at me, and I looked so closely that I must have been rudely staring and squinting.

I hadn't voiced my hope, but it was alive all along—a wish and a longing that I'd been illustrating my mother's books, that she'd wanted me alongside in her creative endeavors, that I was with her even though she'd left me.

The hope fizzled as quickly as I recognized it, gone. This woman carried nothing of my mother in her. Sure, she was as Pippa described her, but she was older, not nearly as tall as Mother.

"Welcome," Eliza said, and first turned her attention to Charlie and

Pippa, hugging them and exclaiming how very happy she was to see them on her first full day in Hawkshead.

"Thank you for your kind letter about Callum," Pippa said as she held Eliza's hands. "It means more than I can say."

"It seems impossible that he is gone," Eliza said. "He was such a force of vibrancy, such a tender and wonderful man. They don't make men like that much anymore." Next to her, Thomas coughed and Eliza grasped her husband's hand. "But for you, darling, but for you."

Then she turned to me and to Wynnie, nearly holding our breath.

She walked to me and held out her hand. "And you must be the enchanting illustrator who has brought my Harriet to life. How wonderful that I can finally meet you. I thought it would never happen! I must say I could not have hoped for any better. You have enlivened my stories, and I will forever be grateful." Her mixed Boston and British accents were a jumble of sounds.

I shook her hand. "Lovely to meet you, too, and this is my daughter, Wynnie."

"I love Harriet," Wynnie said. "I'm happy she came to visit you. What will you do with her next?"

Eliza laughed, the warm sound of a grandmother who might pull a child on her knee and tell a story. "Now that's a mystery until I sit down with her to tell another story."

Wynnie bounced with excitement. "Can you hurry?"

I chimed in: "Thank you so much for having me be part of Harriet's world. It's been an honor." I pushed past the flash of disappointment and reminded myself of the gratitude I owed this woman.

"Come now, let's have tea, and I want to hear all about how you have found your way to Cumbria and then to me."

Settled in the living room, each with our cup of tea and plates balanced on our laps as we nibbled the most buttery scones I'd ever eaten, we chatted about Eliza and Thomas's journey back to Cumbria, how a squirrel had made a nest in their bedroom while they were gone, and how very happy they were to return.

The subject turned to my arrival. "It all has to do with my mother," I said. "And a large stack of old papers that were found in Mr. Jameson's library."

"What kind of papers?"

"Her writings," I said. "My mother was . . ."

In my pause, Eliza gently said, "Yes, Pippa told me that your mother was the author of *The Middle Place*. How astounding." She looked to her friend. "But, Pippa, you didn't tell me about the papers." She focused on me now. "Are they connected to the sequel the world was always hounding her for?"

"Close. They were words, a list of words she'd made up." I hesitated. "But that is exactly what brought us here. Well, that and the poisonous fog."

"Oh, wasn't it awful?" Eliza said. "Well then, it looks like we have Callum and his library to thank for this lovely meeting."

"Pardon?" Pippa asked.

"Callum was the one to suggest I ask my publisher about you, Clara."

Pippa took a sip of her tea as if nothing was amiss, as if they were talking of the beautiful day. "And how did that come about?" she asked.

Charlie sat next to me, and he pushed his knee against mine, a quiet reminder that he was there.

"Don't you remember? You were there, too," Eliza said. She closed her eyes for a moment and then opened them as if she'd been retrieving the memory. "The spring festival of 1947. It was storytime in the theater, and every child in town was there, as a rainstorm sprang up."

"We gave out Flakie bars," Pippa said. "That might have helped. It was packed—children on the floor and in every seat, mums in the aisles." Pippa's voice pitched higher with the memory. "I remember. And you read your first hedgehog story out loud to the children. But her name was different back then . . . is that it? Am I remembering correctly?"

"Exactly! Her name was Hermione, but the publisher in the end thought the name was too British, so we changed it to Harriet. Too difficult for children who were learning to read to pronounce, they said."

"Yes." Pippa smiled. "That spring day while a storm rattled the old theater, you mesmerized every child and mum under your spell when you read that first book."

"I'd just sold it to a small press in Boston," she said. "And I was trying it out for the first time. No pictures, then."

Eliza smiled and her eyes nearly closed with it. "You and Callum and the aunts were there, do you remember that?"

"Yes, we'd all come for the festival and wanted to hear you read."

"When it was over, Callum came to me and said he knew of an incredible illustrator. He'd seen her work in several Little Golden Books and thought I might suggest you, Clara, to my publisher."

"Is that so?" Pippa asked. "Callum always did know so much about children's books."

I couldn't keep quiet any longer; I fairly burst with the question. "That's what I was told—that you found my work in a Little Golden Book and thought we might pair well together. But I thought the publisher suggested me, not the other way around."

"No, I brought your name to them, from Callum. Everything I know about you came from him."

CHAPTER 43

CLARA

Lake District, England

Evening arrived with bright stripes of orange across the sky and above the lake. I realized that the day we were meant to sail home had passed. Wynnie and I quietly walked through the halls of this 1700s slate-and-stone house, with views across Grizedale Forest and the Coniston mountain ranges, as the weight of daily life receded and my breath eased. I understood this wasn't my life—or a real life at all, for that matter. But still, it was lovely.

Nat was probably losing his mind; I read his thoughts as if they flew across the sea to me. *I told you so. I told you it was dangerous.* But this truly felt like the least dangerous place on earth.

With each passing day, Nat's voice lessened in volume. I'd called him numerous times, both at work and at home, and the phone rang endlessly. Dad had tried to reach out, and I wasn't ready to call his parents in Georgia and worry them, not yet.

I did my daily count—two weeks and three days until the Caldecott. Soon our passports would be ready, and we'd rebook our journey home. But for now I settled into the fact that there was little I could do to change anything. I longed to get out on those hills outside our window, to discover what rustled above the lake.

Wynnie and I stood admiring the fir tree in the foyer, mercury balls of many shapes and hues hung from every branch, glittering in the chandelier light. "Now come along," I said to Wynnie in a bad Pippa imitation.

She laughed and we found our way to the bedroom.

I opened the door and Wynnie cried out. "Mama, look!"

At the window stood an easel with thick artist's paper clipped on its edge, and next to it sat a wooden table with a palette and tubes of paint, as well as a brown crockery jar full of sable brushes. I went immediately over and ran my fingers across the soft brushes.

Maybe, just maybe, there wasn't always a rotten spot in the middle of every one of my stories with men. Maybe Charlie was exactly who he seemed to be.

"Did you tell him you wanted this?" Wynnie asked.

"No." I hugged her close. "These must be left over from Pippa's art club of aunts and friends."

"What do you want to paint, Mama?" Wynnie pointed out the window. "The lake? The trees? The mountain with the little snow hat?"

"I want to paint one of Grandma's words." An opening appeared inside me that felt something like forgiveness or maybe something even larger, like acceptance. If the remaining words were all I had left of her, then so be it. "'When the sky breaks open; transformation that changes you into who you are meant to be; into your very essence.'" I recited the meaning of *talith* as if it were tattooed onto me.

"Then paint, Mama." Wynnie jumped on the bed with her book and lifted it high. "Did you know that this whole book is set right here? It's a big adventure, and the kids get to take a sailboat to the island in the middle of the lake all by themselves."

"Do they now?"

"Yes, they do. And it's all right here, one lake over." She curled into the plush pillows.

I outlined the painting with charcoal. I thought of the sketches in Beatrix Potter's house and the many threads that tied all of us together, and about how often women needed art and language to find their way in an inhospitable world.

I squeezed a drop of azure paint on the palette and dipped the brush. My hand moved across the page, and I mumbled *talith* as I swooped the brush upward with a long line. While I painted, Wynnie came to my side, and I thought she was watching me until she said, "Mama?"

I turned to my daughter. How I hoped the world could be different for her, that she might not need to make up a language or hide behind a veiled word, that she might be able to express herself fully. "Yes?" I asked.

She pointed at the top page of Mother's words. It was the sentence I'd translated on our first night in London: *This wild world holds more than you can see; believe in make-believe.* Then below, in one straight line, I'd listed each of Mother's made-up words from the sentence.

Wynnie tapped it. "Violet."

"Pardon?"

"That says violet." She ran her finger down the paper. "The first letter of each word in that sentence you translated, it spells violet."

I glanced down. "No, honey. 'This wild world—'"

"No!" she said. "Grandma's made-up words. Look."

Yes, Mother's words. My heartbeat thumped in my ears, warmth rose in my cheeks, and my arm tingled. "That can't be a coincidence," I said. "It's an acrostic."

"What is that? A-cros-tic?" She stumbled over the word.

"When the first letter of a list of words spells something. Violets were Mother's favorite flower. She planted them all over the garden. She brought them inside when they couldn't grow outside."

"Why violets?" Wynnie asked.

"Who knows? They are wild with heart-shaped leaves, and every March they would bloom again, and she was always looking for them. She swore you could eat them, and she'd pop one into her mouth to prove it." The memories were crisp. "She says . . . said they were symbols of inspiration, but she could have been making that up."

"It's what Emjie wears in her flower crown," Wynnie said.

The knowledge slammed into me as real and sure as a rock thrown at my chest—there was no doubt, not for me, not anymore. Mother redefined herself. She was leaving hints behind in her language.

"I need to call your papa."

CHAPTER 44

CHARLIE

Lake District, England

Charlie stood in the hallway and heard Wynnie's voice from behind the closed bedroom door. He didn't want to intrude on their privacy, but he was curious how Clara felt about the gift he'd placed in the room for her.

If he could give Clara anything, it would be the truth about how her mother's papers found their way into his father's library. But he couldn't give what he didn't have.

He'd ruffled through the gabled room on the third floor to gather the paints and easel from the makeshift studio where Mum and her friends once painted, drinking tea during the day and gin fizzes at night. It'd been years since Mum went up there, and when he'd asked her if she might allow Clara to use the supplies, she'd been thrilled.

He planned a second surprise. He wanted to bring his father's typewriter to Clara so she might type her mother's words. For now, it sat in a small room off his parents' bedroom on a wide pine table overlooking Esthwaite Water. Scarred and dented by decades of family use, the table was once at the center of the kitchen before the room had been modernized in 1932. Father had it carried to the alcove of the bedroom, where someone else might have put a plush lounge chair or couch with a reading lamp.

When Charlie was a child, there were nights when he would sneak from his bed to sit in the hallway and listen to the rhythm and dance of the typewriter keys, the click and clack, the song it made in the night hours when the rest of the house was asleep. One night Father left his room to make his way to the drawing room for a draft of whiskey and found Charlie asleep against the door, lulled by the lullaby of the clicking keys.

"Son." His father knelt and shook Charlie's shoulder.

Charlie awoke to investigate the face of the man he wanted to know more than he wanted anything in the world. He sat straight. "I'm . . . sorry."

"Were you out here spying on me?" His grin in the brass sconce's golden light told Charlie he was amused, not annoyed.

"I like the sounds the typewriter makes," he said.

Father carried Charlie into the room with the typewriter. He set him in the lounge chair, tucked a wool blanket around his son. "Then let's listen together." And he sat to type again.

Another night, years later, in a London pub, Father sat in the audience—the room clouded with cigarette smoke and full of men lifting toasts—during one of Charlie's performances. Father told all those around him: "That's my boy. He started playing the drums because I played the typewriter."

Charlie rolled his eyes. "Always back to you, right, Father?"

The men bellowed with laughter, and yet Charlie knew the truth of the offhand comment. Anything that Charlie loved was partially born from all that his father loved.

All those years his father was at the typewriter, Charlie hadn't known what Father was writing. When Charlie asked if he could read what was on the pages, the response was: "They aren't for reading. They're just for writing."

It had seemed such a ridiculous notion to a young boy. All those hours writing something that no one would ever see. What a colossal waste of time, he'd once thought. Now Charlie understood the need to express oneself without feeling that anyone could weigh in with their heavy opinions and half-cocked ideas.

It was a relief to know now that all that time his father was typing tales of the life he could not speak out loud. Bronwyn, Clara's mother, made up her own language, and Charlie's father hid his—both having untold stories that needed to find their way out.

Sometimes his father and Clara's mother seemed to say in unison the same thing in different ways: the internal landscape of the soul needs to belong to oneself before it can be shared with others. Some creations were for the creator and no one else. The creative act as discovery, a quest for oneself.

Clara's mother—she'd released her *one* book into the world for all to analyze and pick apart, to sift through and form their expectations about her. The world used her writings as a weapon against her, placed their own projections and shadows onto her. It was no wonder she kept her words hidden in a satchel.

Thoughts and questions jumped from tree to tree in his mind like a wild bird trying to decide where to land.

The reason his father owned that satchel itched at Charlie. Yes, it could be bothering him even more because Charlie seemed to be falling for the woman's daughter, for her voice and bright laughter, for her insight, for her bravery and her kindness, for the way she looked at her daughter and protected her without smothering her. Clara was quite extraordinary, and since the moment he'd seen her at the front door, he'd wanted to kiss her, as he'd finally done two nights ago.

Now he wanted more.

CHAPTER 45

CLARA

Lake District, England

"Dad, did you give anyone in England permission to turn Mother's book into a play?" I held the phone to my ear while I leaned against the oak table in the kitchen. The aroma of bread baking filled the air.

"Ah yes!" he said. "But to be honest, I'd forgotten about it. That was eight or nine years ago. A small play in a small town in another country by a woman who was enchanted with your mother's novel."

I stared at the brick wall where copper pots hung from iron hooks. A window with diamond patterns of iron mullions revealed that outside, afternoon sunlight slanted across the lake, creating shifting cloudlike shapes. "Did it cross your mind that she might be here? That Mother *wanted* the play made?"

"In England? Of course not."

"Dad, before you met her, she traveled all over the world on ships and schooners and . . ."

"I know, ladybug." His voice was soft, so I kept on.

"From Hawaii to the Pacific to California and Maine, to Newfoundland and Nova Scotia."

"Clara!" A sharp knife of my name. "I know the places your mother traveled. And I know how you've harbored hope for so long, but that can be a dangerous thing. A long time ago, a woman sought permission for a play, and I gave it. It's simple."

His voice was uncharacteristically cold, but I understood enough about this kind man to know that anger was his defense. His protection from grief and from hope.

He adroitly shifted topics. "Lilia is asking about you. She's been worried, but she's also thrilled you're having an adventure."

"You told her I was all right, didn't you? I sent her a letter, but who knows when it will arrive."

"I told her, ladybug."

"Dad, have you gotten ahold of Nat? I sent a telegram and can't get him to answer at home or work."

"No. Do you want me to go to his workplace?"

"No, I'll call again."

Wynnie paced the kitchen in circles listening to every word, and I held my hand up for her to stand still; she was making me nervous.

"Listen, Dad, I know Mother is gone," I said. "But this Jameson family must know something. Why would Charlie's father have the satchel and his mother be involved with the play?" I left out the garden sign. I wasn't sure why, but this didn't feel the right place for more information. "And, Dad . . ."

"Yes?"

"Something else."

"What is it?"

"Eliza Walker lives here part-time. She married someone from Hawkshead. I met her this afternoon."

"Your Eliza, Harriet's Eliza?" This time his voice held surprise.

"Yes."

"My God, what is happening?"

"Clues, that's what's happening."

"Or they're coincidences," he said.

"Yes, they are, but they are also something more. It's like I'm still in that London fog—nothing is coming clear to me."

"Come home, sweetie. Come home with Wynnie and we can slog through this language and decide what we must do with it."

"Don't you care why they have it? How they found it?"

"No. I can truly say I don't."

"Dad, do you know anyone named Violet?"

The distance stretched between us. I wanted to see his face, to watch his reaction. "No, I don't know anyone. Your mother—"

"Was enchanted by them. Yes."

"Why are you asking?"

"It's something in her words, some sort of code, I think."

"Code?" he asked.

"I'll try and figure it out. I will."

"Please hurry home, ladybug."

"I am, I promise. All I'm doing is waiting for our passports. I really don't want to miss the awards ceremony."

After we'd said our *I love you*s and Wynnie had talked to him for a moment and told him about the lake Jemima Puddle-Duck once flew over and how it was right outside the door, I hung up, and Wynnie looked straight at me. "You didn't tell him we lost some pages."

"Not yet."

That was when we noticed Moira in the doorway holding a tray of half-eaten scones. She didn't acknowledge that she had heard our conversation but instead told us: "The doctor has arrived to check on both of you."

"Oh, that's so kind. We are really all right," I told her. "Healed and rested."

But despite my protests, Moira motioned for us to follow her along the quiet hallway to a room in the back of the house where I'd never been.

Here, double doors opened to a sweeping view of the east side pasture. Bulky furniture and overstuffed couches gave the room a chubby, comfortable feel. Dr. Finlay stood by a large pine table. He smiled as we entered. He looked as if he'd been born in the wrong era, wearing a suit with a tweed vest straight out of a Jane Austen novel.

Pippa stood next to him, and they'd just finished laughing about something. She turned to us with a smile. Everything in that room was swathed in pastoral green, including Pippa, as if she'd dressed for the setting.

"Well," Dr. Finlay bellowed, and patted his stomach. "My patients seem to be doing just fine!"

"I hope so," I said.

He motioned for Wynnie to join him and then reached inside his large black bag to withdraw a stethoscope. After he listened to her chest and back, instructed her to take deep breaths, and checked her pulse, he declared her fit as a fiddle. I nearly asked him how a fiddle was fit. All this talk of language and where words and phrases came from was making me overanalyze nearly everything I said and heard.

"Do you think that sulfur and fog caused any lasting damage?" I asked him.

He pulled his lips back so they disappeared, a straight line across his full face. Then he exhaled. "There's no real way to know. It doesn't sound like it now, but you'll need to watch her, be careful."

"We've been walking outside," I said. "That's all right, isn't it?"

"Yes! The air here is very healing. Bundle up, protect her throat with a scarf. But it will do her good," he said, and packed his bag of doctor paraphernalia, full of items as familiar to me as every nook and cranny of my childhood home on the bay. These were the tools that Dad used to diagnosis and fix. These were the tools that saved, if saving was possible.

"Thank you so much!" I told him. "It's time for us to be on our way soon, to travel home."

He shook his head. "No. Not yet, at least. With the season of colds and sickness, you can't take that chance with her. You too. I'd say you leave in a week at best. Make sure her lungs are healed and assure there will be no medical emergency halfway across the ocean. It's best to be prudent in these matters, especially with a child."

He listened to my chest and took my temperature with the glass thermometer and declared me well. As he bustled out and Pippa walked with him into the large gallery hallway, I looked at Wynnie. "It appears we are here for longer. Your wishes are your command. Or . . . maybe we should return to London now that it's clear. We can see all the sights we planned. The museums and the galleries."

"No," she said. "I want to stay here. Something is here waiting for us."

"Darling, that isn't up to me. We can't just move into someone's home."

"Charlie wants us here," she said. "I can tell."

"Well, it isn't exactly Charlie's house. It belongs to Mrs. Jameson."

Wynnie slumped into a chair. Then her eyebrows rose, and she popped up, her hand extended toward the far wall. "Mama!" she whispered, and I turned to see where she pointed.

On the far wall of damask emerald wallpaper hung a gallery of oil paintings. They varied in size, all of them either pastoral or seascape: Black cows belted with white in a pasture with hedgerows as boundary. A schooner on a storm-battered sea. Silver sheep in a paddock with mountains in the background, one I knew from the window in our bedroom. A shingled home on the curve of a bay.

"Wynnie." I exhaled her name and walked toward the image. "What in the world . . ."

The painting, about two by three feet, wasn't an imaginary rendering of our home; it was a clear and precise reproduction of a cedar shake house painted a maritime blue, timeworn and shabby, but solid on a springtime land with a flowering garden of violets. The bay was as smooth as the lake outside the window, the oyster shell curve of beach flickered under an unseen sun, and next to a battered dock, a small silver boat was moored with a thick rope. The windows glowed from within. A low white picket fence surrounded a garden of flowering beds, and the gate yawned open to the dirt path that led down to the bay.

The painting hung at eye level beneath another of a pheasant drooping from the mouth of a brown-and-tan hunting dog. I touched the frame and felt a rush of love for the house that had sheltered me for nearly all my life. This was the view from a boat or from a seagull dropping down to snag a flounder in the bay.

"How?" I asked out loud to the room, to Wynnie, to the unseen forces that had brought us here.

I held out my hand for Wynnie and she took it.

"Look at the left corner," she said in a whisper.

There, on just an inch of the painting, there was a charred corner of the house, a scab of darkness, like the bark of a tree, peeling and fading into the corner of the garden. In real life, in the world of the house as it was now, there was no evidence of the fire I'd started that sent my mother away, and here was solid proof that the fire remained. The scars might be hidden from sight now, but they never disappeared.

On closer inspection, a vine grew up and across the scab, a vine flowering with brilliant violets.

"Violets," I said.

"Violets," she repeated.

CHAPTER 46

CLARA

Lake District, England

Wynnie and I bundled up, slipped on wellies we'd been borrowing, and made our way outside. We walked quietly as we crossed the lane toward the lake. She held tight to my hand with an unusual pressure of insecurity. She, too, felt the world shifting, unsure and unsteady.

A squirrel skittered along the frosted ground and then jumped to land on a chestnut tree's scarred river of white bark beneath the brown. Its auburn fur shivered as it ran upward to argue in chitters with another squirrel on a low branch.

We walked silently until we passed the three stone cottages below the house. Each one was the same, except with a different-colored door, varied gardens, and pathways to the entry. Smoke feathered from two of the chimneys.

"Mama, there are clues everywhere, and it's not fair that I can't figure it out. At least with puzzles, there is a picture on the top of the box. But this is a puzzle without a picture—just odd pieces scattered about: Eliza Walker, a play with Emjie, violets, and now an oil painting. I move the pieces around in my mind and I can't figure it out."

"Neither can I, darling. Neither can I."

To the left was another path leading around the lake. I turned and we made our way toward the woodlands, away from the stone cottages. A black-and-white duck with eyes so yellow they seemed from a daisy slid across the lake, his silver-gray beak pointed straight for shore. Wynnie gathered small remnants of nature in her pockets—a pinecone, a feather, a rock, and a twig. We made our way along the south end of the lake, where we hadn't yet ventured, a muddy path curving around its pebbled edges. The path was rippled by tree roots and littered with fallen copper leaves.

"Clara! Wynnie!" Charlie's voice echoed through the woods.

I took my daughter's hand. "Here!" I called out, as he appeared around the bend.

He rushed toward us, his coat unbuttoned and his scarf loose. His wool cap sat crooked on his head, and it was obvious he'd run out in a rush. "There you are. I was ... worried." His brown eyes squinted against the sun.

"Why?" While stomping through the woods with Wynnie, I'd convinced myself that Charlie Jameson and his family were harboring a secret. I wasn't in the best of moods to see him, to be accommodating.

"Why am I worried?"

I stared at him without an answer, gauging his looks, wondering if everything he'd told me was a lie—if he, like Nat, hid a darker rot I couldn't see at first.

"I'm worried because I don't want you to become lost. There are hundreds of acres out here, and . . . if you take a wrong path, there are old mines."

"You're here to save us?" I asked.

He backed up as if I'd hit him in the chest. "What happened?" he asked, reading between my cold words.

"Tell him, Mama." Wynnie pulled at my coat sleeve.

"Is this some kind of ridiculous game, Charlie?"

"Game?"

"The dictionary. The satchel. Your father's old library. The play your mother helped produce. The garden sign. Eliza Walker. The painting. Is this some kind of game where I finally learn the truth? Because if this is a game, I'm losing very badly."

"Clara." He said my name gently. "The painting?"

I slumped in on myself, the anger emptied out. I sat on a chair-height tree stump, set my hands on my knees, and took a couple of deep breaths before I looked up.

"There's a painting in your family study."

"There are a lot of paintings in my family study." His voice was as cautious as if he didn't want to startle a small animal.

"This one is of a cottage by a bay."

"Yes, that one. It's lovely. I think it's Cornwall, but I'm unsure."

"It's our house," I said.

"In Bluffton," Wynnie said.

"What?"

I stood now. "That painting in your family study is of our home in South Carolina, Charlie. It is not a rendering; it is exact, all the way down to the charred left side where I set our house on fire twenty-five years ago."

"What the bloody hell?" He began to pace, his leather boots melting the shaded snow as the ground below turned muddy and brown. "Why would my family have a painting of your family's home? That painting is one of the many that Mum and my aunt and cousin painted."

"Was Eliza Walker one of Pippa's friends who painted in the attic? Would she know?" I was grasping for something to hang this anxiety on, something less amorphous than the disconnected clues.

"Yes, she was."

"Can we go ask her right now?" My voice trembled, electric with desire.

"Follow me," he said.

Charlie didn't walk in front of me, but beside us on the well-worn dirt path around the lake, guiding us silently. We returned the way Wynnie and I had already walked, past the upside-down rowboat, the frosting of ice cracking along the reedy edges of the lake, and past the first stone cottage, where drafts of smoke rose like clouds from the stone chimney.

"Where are we going?" Wynnie asked.

Charlie didn't answer her in any way but to take my hand in his, wrapping his leather gloved fingers around my own. The sun was high now, having shed its cumbersome garments of cloud, and sunlight darted through the bare branches.

We emerged in a clearing, and Charlie stopped. To our right, a path led to a wrought-iron fence that surrounded a gathering of only a few gravestones. They were old and worn, carved out of white stone, the newer ones of shining marble.

What ridiculous hope I'd clung to when the letter was clear: *If you are receiving this.*

I set my steps to walk into the cemetery, when Charlie tugged at my hand. "She's not there," he said.

We walked a few yards until we reached the second stone cottage. Curled and frost-nipped ivy grew along its west-facing side, winding toward a flagstone roof and stone chimney. A goldenrod-hued light shone behind the windows, the flicker of it hinting at a burning fire. A brass knocker shaped like a bird hung on the deep blue door.

Charlie stopped and let go of my hand, set both of his on the low fence of an enclosed garden. It was then that I saw the woman bundled in a green wool coat. She knelt over a leafless bush. In her hands she wielded pruning scissors, and she clipped off each frost-bitten appendage.

We watched her, her back bent over her work, her long chestnut-and-gray hair flowing down her back beneath a knit cap. Her hands were nimble in their gloves.

The world was silent but for nature's creaking and squawking, and there we were above Esthwaite Water when the woman stood and stretched. "Oh, Charlie dear, hallo!"

"Hallo, Cousin Isolde!"

He opened the gate, and I stood by a peeling white picket fence. The woman took two steps toward us, smiling. Not until she dropped her pruning scissors, not until she let out a cry, not until she fell to her knees, did I know.

The world peeled away: the cold and the wondering, the fear and the irritation. I was a child, I was a woman, and I was myself. I was a daughter and a mother. Fire consumed the curtains, and I watched in awe until my mother's arms were around me, dragging me outside. Then the sirens and a hospital room with elephants on the wallpaper.

And then now, here, the woman cried out, "Clara." This woman was on her knees, her arms held out as if I could run into them as a child.

I walked through the open gate and along the flagstones, only ten feet at most, and yet twenty-five years long.

I knelt next to her, the cold, hard ground grinding my knees, and she took me in her arms. "There you are!"

There you are.

She kissed my cheeks, first one and then the other; she wiped the tears I didn't know were falling, kissed my forehead with chapped lips.

Here she was, whole and alive, on her knees and saying my name in the voice I heard in dreams.

Her face was softly lined, her hair silver-streaked, her blue eyes slightly faded but to a more beautiful aqua seen only in the deepest lakes.

She ripped off her gloves and held my face in both her bare hands as if checking to see if I was real. Then she lifted my right arm, slipped back the sleeve, and gazed upon my scars. She kissed them, first my wrist and then my forearm. At the feel of my mother's lips, my skin tickled and awoke. "How are you here, my beautiful child?"

CHAPTER 47

CLARA

Lake District, England

"Mother," I said in a voice young and tender, hopeful. I stood.

The woman, no, my mother, gingerly stood and faced me and then looked to see Wynnie, who stepped forward into a puddle of light, a nimbus of her innocence around her. "I'm Wynnie."

The woman, no, my mother, leaned down and kissed my child on her cheek. "I am your grandmother."

"Your book is my favorite thing in the big world, and Emjie is my best friend." My daughter's voice held such endearing expectation, and I pulled her toward me. I wanted to wrap her in my coat, protect her.

Love and anger, despair and longing, relief and rage battled inside me like a churned-up sea battering against my ribs. I felt nearly faint, unsteady. I reached for Charlie's hand.

The woman, no, my mother, smiled at Wynnie. "I'd wondered where Emjie went." Her voice now with a slight British accent.

There was so much I wanted to say. Didn't I have a million sentiments inside me? Didn't I have questions and childhood imaginings of what I would utter if I found her? But I came up empty of any language, even hers.

I couldn't access the anger, only the longing that I'd carried with me to this moment.

"I am lost," Charlie said as he held my hand. "You are my father's great cousin . . . You are Clara's mother. You are . . ." He looked at me. "We are related?"

Mother touched Charlie's arm. "No. We are not related. There is much to explain."

Then Mother searched my face with the look I knew as a child when she turned her attention to me, the full-hearted and overwhelming devotion I dreamed of in the nights I cried myself to sleep, the adoration that once made me believe that if she was alive, she would come back to me. "You named your daughter after me?" Mother asked.

"Yes, I always wanted you there." The truth I barely would acknowledge flowed out of me.

She let out a cry of pain.

"How could you have done it?" I cried out, dropping my face into my hands. "How could you have left us?"

———

Mother's cottage glowed warm, and the kettle sang its song while we sat around her hand-hewn oak kitchen table. We cradled teacups with violets painted along the porcelain rim. *Mother*—it was so odd to think *this* word and attach it to *this* woman in front of me instead of to an idea. She'd made a mug of hot chocolate for Wynnie, whose feet bounced up and down under her seat.

We'd been silent in the tea preparation, as if we each and one needed to settle into this new truth: Mother was alive in a cottage at the edge of a lake in the wilds of England.

It was a cramped, timeworn, cozy space. Visible behind a white-painted wooden door with an egg-shaped brass handle was her single bed covered in white and pale-blue quilts. The living area flowed into the dark wood kitchen. The blazing fireplace crackled when Charlie set a new log onto the stack. Shelves lined the wall on either side, where books were stacked sideways, up and down, in piles two and three deep. Our coats and hats and gloves were bundled together on a bench by the front door. The low, wood-beamed ceiling held us all in the palm of this cottage's hand.

I wondered how long Mother had lived here. On the table, Mother lit two creamy candles in brass holders and then sat and faced me. My body trembled, and Charlie set his hand on my leg. "Are you cold?" she asked.

"I am not," I said, and then said again, "I need to know what happened."

"Clara." Mother's voice choked with tears. "My heart is so full right now, and it is breaking for the pain I see in you. I wrote this in the letter, but the truth is both simple and complicated—I truly did sew myself into my secrets. And after arriving here, even more so."

"I don't understand," I said.

"I know you have so many questions, and I promise to answer them all. But I want to begin here." Her voice cracked, nearly broke over the next words. "I have loved you all my days. Every day. Everything I have painted or created or taught has been *for* you. It will be and is nearly impossible to understand why a woman who loves her daughter would leave her daughter, but I will do my best to explain. Everything I have done since the day I left has been for you, an amends, a restoration of my soul—the language and the art. This life here in Sawrey has been my exile and my salvation, but the rest, the creations, have been for you."

I swallowed tears; I needed to stay strong and alert, understand. "Did you mean for us to find you? Did you lead us here?"

"No. I didn't want you to have to endure the pain of seeing me. I knew you did *not* want . . . this." She turned away and wiped at her tears, then looked back at me.

"So those papers. I wasn't meant to have them, at least not yet?"

"Ah, so that's what happened." She looked to Charlie. "You found my dictionary in your father's belongings."

"Yes."

"Why did Callum have it?" I asked.

"We'll get there," she said. "The hurt I see in you right now, that is the pain I didn't want you to feel. All I have wanted for you was to be able to live a beautiful life. And you have. I know."

I'd imagined, as a child at least, a mother who was an angel, who orchestrated my life from heaven. But Sawrey, as delightful as it was, was not heaven. And if she had sent good toward me, it was a farce, and a poor proxy for having her. "I would have rather had you," I said.

She shook her head. She was only fifty-five years old, and her handsome beauty hadn't faded, but the lines on her face told of a life lived in the elements. Those tears now caught in the story of those days etched on her cheeks.

"No, you would *not* have rather had me. I need you to believe me."

Wynnie and Charlie stayed silent as Mother and I faced each other, each with our own pains and reasons and memories.

"Yes, I would have," I said. "I most assuredly would have rather had you with me. So would Dad."

"Listen to me, my most beloved and only child, listen to me. You were better off without me. I nearly killed you, and for this I can never forgive myself. A young man died because of my negligence and escape to imaginary worlds, but I still didn't want my words to die with me—I wanted you to have them when I was gone, to know that I loved you by staying away from you."

"Why do *you* get to decide my life is better without you?" Anger seethed below the surface; I felt its burn returning.

"Clara, the decisions I made were irreversible. I faked my own death. I left you. How was I to ever return?"

"And what of my consequences of living without you?"

"If anyone could have been both mother and father to you, it would be your beloved dad. I have never loved anyone else. I have never taken another husband."

"You could have stayed and faced the consequences as we did."

"I could not cause any more heartache. I could not and would not return to a world where you'd have a mother who most likely would find herself in jail or a psychiatric institute for a while, medicated, treated, undone. This would have been as good as dead."

"But not dead." My voice held all the anger, all the frustration and hurt and heartache.

She leaned forward, pleading now. "I needed to let you mourn me, let me go."

"I can't accept this. I am . . . lost. You think they would have thought you unbalanced?"

"I know this, Clara. They'd already done so. There was no going back. You must know—you are the love of my life, Clara, and there was no going back."

"I have blamed myself. I thought my fire sent you away. I thought . . ."

Mother's left hand covered her mouth; her teacup clattered to the table, pale, milky tea running into the cracks of the oak table. She didn't move to wipe it up, but her face became distorted with tears. "No!"

Wynnie leaned into me, whispered, "Mama, she's so sad."

The sludgy feeling of missing her, the hours and days and months and years that the hunger for her consumed me, now rose in a tidal wave inside my chest. For here she was, right here in front of me.

I stumbled from my chair and knelt before her. She leaned down and I took her in my arms, the hardwood floor pressing against my knees and her head on my shoulder.

"*Adorium*," she cried out as I held her.

I opened my voice and my heart cracked only the littlest bit, and I couldn't say the heartfelt word in return. I'd held the secret word inside for so long that it didn't yet rise.

"What does that mean?" Wynnie asked, her voice buoyant.

Mother leaned down and kissed me on either side of my lips. She spoke while staring into my eyes. "To love with forgiveness, to love without deserving, to love when the truth has been exposed, to love with a heart that gathers the other into itself."

Wynnie gasped. "That's so beautiful."

Charlie cleared his throat, and we looked up. "May I ask something?"

Mother let me go and held her hand across the table for Charlie's. "Of course!"

"You are my cousin, is that right? Great cousin? Dad's second cousin? This is what I have been told. You were in America, you'd emigrated as a young child, so you weren't there when the Easter Rising took the rest of the family."

"I know I have much to explain. I have loved you as though you are mine, but I am not your cousin, Charlie."

CHAPTER 48

CLARA

Lake District, England

Charlie paced the small cottage. "Let me understand," he said. "You are not my cousin, but I have called you such, and you've been here for over twenty-five years. You tutored me and were family to me." I sensed the anger simmering below the surface of Charlie's voice. "Were we only a place to hide?"

Mother stood and didn't answer for a moment. Then she walked to the cupboard and gathered a chunk of cheddar cheese so yellow it looked like butter, along with freshly made bread. She set it on the table and passed out small white plates.

We watched her in silence until she answered Charlie. Her hands shook just enough to notice. "No, you were not just a place to hide. This is my home," she said. "Your family and you are home. When I arrived here, I felt as if all the pieces of my life were scattered about the world and this place was a magnet, drawing everything that is me, that is of me, to one place. Even now it brings my beloved daughter and grand-daughter."

"Does Mum know?" he asked. "Does she know who you *truly* are and were?"

"No," Mother said with a pained certainty. "All my life I have been trying not to inflict any more damage, and here I am doing so again. She will be hurt, that is true. But I love her like a sister, Charlie. You know that."

"As she does you." Charlie deliberately made his way to the small black phone in the corner of the kitchen. He dialed and then spoke quietly into it, his back turned to us.

Wynnie raised her hand as if in class; Mother and I laughed together. "May I ask something now?"

"Anything, my dear," Mother said.

"Did you send Emjie to me?"

"You see," I told Mother, "Wynnie latched on to Emjie after we read your book."

Wynnie tapped my arm. "Mama, that's not true. I met Emjie before you read me the book."

"But you heard us talking about her."

"No." Wynnie was firm, and I allowed her this grace.

"How is my darling Emjie?" Mother asked Wynnie. "Does she still wear that ragged old dress of ferns?"

"She makes new ones," Wynnie said. "Sometimes she wears real clothes, but mostly she doesn't. No one really believes in her."

"The eternal mystery—how do we believe in the make-believe?"

I'd heard Mother say this before; the memory was visceral and exquisitely painful. It was part of the sentence we'd translated and parcel of the life she'd lived. A farce if it meant leaving me.

"Yes," Wynnie said with eight-year-old assurance. "Not everyone can do it."

"You seem to believe in the mystery," Mother said.

"I do," Wynnie told her. Charlie hung up the phone and we glanced at each other and raised our eyebrows.

It was as if I'd walked through a portal and found myself in a land I could only imagine, one where my mother stood before me holding my daughter's hand and talked about Emjie, as if the tangled lines of our lives had separated and been pulled back together by a tugging of time and space.

I could not stop the unfolding of it all now.

"Mother," I said. "I have to tell you something."

"Yes?"

"They're gone. Most of the pages are gone."

"Of the dictionary?"

"Yes. I've lost some."

Charlie came near. "They were stolen; Clara didn't lose them. In the journey out of London, we were robbed. Clara saved what she could."

Mother nodded. "I left those for you, Clara, thinking they would mean something to you after I was gone. But there is no need for them now. I am here. You are here."

With a burst of cold air, the cottage door flew open, and Pippa entered in a swath of tweed and wool and leather. "Well, well, who is having a gathering without me? Should I be hurt?" She laughed and slipped off her coat, added it to the bundle on the bench.

"Mum," Charlie said.

"Let me." Mother looked to Charlie. "Please."

He nodded and pulled me closer, as if this was the way we usually were—holding on to each other in a storm.

Mother walked toward Pippa, took her hands, and spoke. "Philippa, I am Clara's mother, Wynnie's grandmother."

Pippa's brow furrowed and her head cocked as if she had heard a far-off sound. She looked at her son, at me, at Wynnie. "Isolde. I don't understand."

"I am Bronwyn Newcastle Fordham."

"The author?" Pippa asked in a quiet voice.

"Yes."

"So, you are not Isolde, Callum's second cousin." Pippa released Mother's hands and stepped back, held out her palms as if forcing the truth away. "I remember the day you arrived," Pippa said. "I remember it exactly, the sunshine of the summer afternoon, the way you touched the garden as if you'd already fallen in love with the place, the way my sons ran to you as if they already knew you. I remember it all. But it was . . . you aren't the last of Callum's family?"

My mother didn't defend herself but bowed her head. Still, I could not take my eyes off her. I wanted to find all the women I'd imagined through the years.

Mother found the strength of her voice. "I love you. And the boys. You are my dearest friend and I'm sorry. Pippa, please hear me: nothing about our friendship or my love for Callum, Archie, Charlie, or you has ever been a lie."

"You gave me that book. But it's actually *your* book. You—"

"Yes, I found it in the local bookshop and brought it home to you. I wanted you to have some piece of me that I couldn't share, a truth I could never tell you."

Pippa reached for the wall to steady herself. "My God. Callum gone. You a stranger." She seemed to sway in an unseen wind, and her hand shook as she lifted it to wipe at a tear.

CHAPTER 49

BRONWYN

Bronwyn looked around the room at the people she loved, gathered in a miracle of time and space. She desired, more than she'd ever desired anything, to find the way to cross this divide, to make them understand, to have them know the truth of her love for them, the reasons she left, the secrets she had sewn around herself, the self-imposed exile.

She wished to be absolved, and quite possibly that was impossible; she understood she was a coward. She wasn't afraid of much except windowless rooms, locked doors, and medications, and now she must start to find a way to explain.

And all she must do was start.

Now, finally, her daughter was here as the very beat of Bronwyn's heart, sitting in her warm cottage kitchen, wanting to hear her story. And the little one, Wynnie, the granddaughter, by her side.

How was Bronwyn to tell all that had happened? How to explain twenty-five years of a story she thought her daughter would discover only when she was gone? They waited, all of them waited. Pippa and Charlie. Wynnie and Clara. They looked at her with expectation.

"Let me begin with Callum," she said.

"Please do," Pippa said softly.

⁓

Bronwyn met Callum in September of 1915, before Timothy, before Clara, just as the leaves were turning brushed gold, falling slowly in the crisp air that hinted of a colder autumn than usual. It was dark, after eight at night, and Bronwyn sat around a blazing campfire along Lake Sunapee, a tranquil spot where she'd once spent evenings with her dad until he left them for the mistress. Flames of the bonfire reached for the sky. Frogs chirped, and the moon climbed the eastern sky. Bronwyn's group of friends waited for the stars to appear, one by threes, always marveling how much brighter they were here than in Boston, where they all lived.

Bronwyn and her boyfriend were cross with each other, irritable, their teeth set on edge by whatever the other might say. It was as if they'd become allergic to each other. You see, he was set to move that month because he'd won a prestigious job in New York City as a journalist, and he was begging his Bronny to join him, but she had no desire to go to New York. In fact, she felt near panic when she considered it. Maybe her reaction had something to do with her dad, and how he'd run to New York with his new wife, leaving her mother and her behind. Or it could be that she'd had enough of her boyfriend. Either way, the bitterness between Bronwyn and her guy came to ruin that night. She was angry at him for pressuring her and she was drinking too much whiskey too quickly.

There were six of them, three couples who spent the last year escaping into the woodlands every weekend, all of them with jobs they hated. They'd talk of what else they might do with their lives, including vivid fantasies of living in the woodlands or moving to London or Paris.

At this time, Bronwyn lived with her mother in a dingy apartment while writing copy for the *Boston Herald*. She was desperately trying to write a second book. She'd been trying for years by then, and they all knew, her mother included, that Bronwyn had quite possibly written her first and last novel at twelve years old.

While they sat around the bonfire, a group of men appeared, lost and cold. They appeared out of the forest like from some fairy tale—four men, Callum included, walked to the campfire, embarrassed to admit their plight. They had misread their map and were miles off their trail, becoming hopelessly lost on a trek through Mount Kearsarge State Forest Park. Bronwyn's friends took them in, fed them their beans and wieners, and sat up most of the night talking and laughing, enjoying their British and Irish accents.

They'd come from New York, where they'd been at Columbia for a semester to study business. They'd decided to take a hike near Mount Monadnock and find the secret Pumpelly Cave deep in the New Hampshire woods. The whole enterprise had been a disaster.

Somewhere in the middle of the night, Bronwyn's boyfriend, Brian, accused her of flirting with one of Callum's mates, William. When everyone retired for the night, Brian threw Bronwyn out of the tent, insisting that she betrayed him and their love by "making eyes" at William. The irony of it being that Bronwyn didn't know how to make eyes even if she'd wanted to do such a thing. She wasn't even sure which one of the four was William, to be honest.

That's where Callum found her, under the stars in a sleeping bag by the dying fire. The next morning, Callum and Bronwyn left before sunrise, and Bronwyn led him out of the woodlands. She never saw Brian again.

Now, with that much of the story told, Bronwyn looked to Pippa and held out her hand. "He was already in love with you and saving for that ring on your hand. He talked of you with such deep tenderness that I realized the love I had with Brian was nothing more than a redo of my parents, that I was imitating patterns that weren't mine. I wanted what Callum had with you."

Clara's eyes widened with understanding. "Mother! Brian. Was it Brian Davis?"

"Yes."

"So that biography was nothing more than sour grapes!"

"Yes, but sadly, much of it is true. I was mortified that those stories of my past were in print, but maybe that was part of my penance."

"Oh," Clara said, "there are plenty of secrets remaining."

Bronwyn thought they might be tired of sitting still, of listening to her, but everyone sat where they were, leaning forward, wanting more.

"Now I must begin where my life ended," Bronwyn said.

———

After the fire trucks, after one ambulance carried away the fireman and another carried Clara to the hospital with burns on her right hand and arm, after Bronwyn sat by Clara's side and wept for the pain she had inflicted on her daughter, Bronwyn heard voices in the hospital hallway.

She clung to Clara's good hand after the bandages were wrapped and as the IVs dripped, and Bronwyn listened to the police and medical personnel uttering the needling and painful words that pricked at her: *Arrest. Negligence. Fugue state. Unsafe mother. Firefighter gravely injured.*

Clara came home the next day, and Bronwyn already knew the truth: she must make a plan to spare her husband and daughter all that was coming her way. Whether in jail or an institution, she would find herself in a room without windows.

When Bronwyn was seventeen years old, back in Boston living with her mother and working at the newspaper, she'd had a fierce fight with her mother. Bronwyn's imagination, once such a point of pride for her parents, was now troublesome. Her mother decided that Bronwyn's flights of fancy were a symptom of a dangerous disease that kept her from doing the daily activities that Martha saw fit to order. She accused Bronwyn of psychiatric breaks when she spent hours alone writing.

One late winter afternoon there came a knock on the door. The men in white jackets and an ambulance took Bronwyn away at her mother's behest. She placed Bronwyn, a minor, in the psychiatric ward at Massachusetts General and demanded they "fix her."

And fix her they tried, in windowless rooms with sedatives and hypnotics that seemed to shatter her brain. With forced bedrest and labeled with words like *schizophrenia*, Bronwyn was trapped in a living hell until she was released for good behavior.

She left the next day, and Bronwyn never spoke to her mother again, although her mother begged for years and years.

All of that was on record, all of it was something that any policeman in Bluffton might find, and then they could accuse Bronwyn of having had another break. When Bronwyn woke in fear, and often she did, it was about the days of isolation, windowless rooms, and medications that made her body and mind disconnect from reality in a much different way than her stories. Her bones and body remembered, and the fears were irrational but vivid.

So, on the second day after the fire, when the police arrived to question Bronwyn about the fire—*What had she been doing? Why wasn't she watching her daughter? Did she know that a firefighter was critical?*—Bronwyn knew what awaited her. None of it was good.

Three days after Clara's discharge from the hospital, Bronwyn left in the family's Chris-Craft in the middle of the night.

In the backyard shed she used kitchen shears to cut off her hair, and then her husband's razor to trim the stubble neatly over her scalp. She carried that long wand of hair and tossed it into the bay off their dock, imagining it becoming transformed as soft nesting material for the pelicans and terns. Wearing her husband's old dungarees and flannel shirt, she used his surgery gauze to bind her chest flat. Being a lover of mythology and the stories that shaped a life, she chose her new name before she reached the Savannah harbor—Tristan: an Irish hero who was banished because of his great love for a woman he could not have.

Names meant something, they weren't to be taken lightly, just as creating words wasn't to be taken lightly, for they conjured and could be transformed into incantations or wishes.

Bronwyn might make others believe that despair caused her to take her life, but it was love that urged her forward. She would kill the woman she'd been but keep her body and spirit. She steered their small boat away from home, the satchel by her side.

She knew *exactly* what she was doing. This was no escapist imaginary world, and this was no accident. She was freeing her daughter and husband. She was frantic to save herself and told herself she was also saving them.

A purr and a groan of the engine and her mind reached the greatest loss. Into the darkness, she cried out her daughter's name. Her voice pierced the night.

Clara.

Bronwyn slammed down the throttle and navigated the boat into the inky night.

Clara the heart of her heart, her very own object of wonder, the *miraculum* of her life, would now grow up with the love of her father at the tidal edge of a land as ancient as time, and the knowledge that her mother loved her enough to leave.

Bronwyn abandoned her daughter to save her daughter, and with each recitation of Clara's name, Bronwyn sent an intention of love to the only place she'd ever believed understood or heard her—the unseen places where imagination lived and beat a drum for her attention, and her character Emjie waited for a new story.

Fear drove her forward. If she could find her way to England, there was a friend who might help. A man she'd been close to in the years before he returned to England in 1917 to his promised fiancée and a family business. A man who shared her obsession with language and its evolution around the world. A man who'd once said, "If you ever need anything..."

His name and kindness never left her. He might turn her away, but she knew he would answer the door.

The Savannah harbor glowed like the fire that had nearly stolen her daughter, and again she was struck by the truth—she could not be a mother any more than she could be an eagle. Both were impossibilities for her.

Once at safe harbor, she abandoned the boat, thrust the throttle to full horsepower, and pushed it to the outgoing tide from the curl of the Savannah Harbor while the sun burst on the horizon.

She immediately found an iron ocean liner with its plank down, an open mouth waiting for the merchant marines to return from their night at the local pubs. She'd talked her way onto a ship before, and she'd do it again. It wasn't difficult when they needed free hands, and she knew how to run a galley and clean rooms better than any cabin boy.

Passing as a man named Tristan, she remembered little of those days crossing the Atlantic. Once she arrived at Southampton in the fog of an early morning in 1927, she exchanged and used the little money she carried for a third-class train ticket and made her way to London, where she walked toward the house of an old friend with the power to hand her over to the police, send a telegram to America, or else help her become someone new.

She passed men in their flat caps and three-piece suits and women in their flowered dresses and headscarves, giggling as if the world was not coming undone. She passed policemen in tall black hats guiding traffic, open-topped red buses, and trams. Flat boats were crammed against the edge of the River Thames, and tugboats with their red stacks chugged along. The tall and wide silver grilles of the cars that moved along the streets glinted in the sunlight and the passengers were oblivious to her, just as she wanted. The white stone and tawny brick buildings loomed over the streets, which had gas lanterns that flickered in the evening light.

She walked and walked through parks and side streets until she knocked on the door of the St. James's house.

In Callum Jameson's library, they sat facing each other in large leather chairs. Bronwyn shivered with fear and hunger.

He reached over and rubbed his hand across her bald head. "What have you done, Bronny?" Tears filled his eyes.

"Bronwyn is gone, Callum. She can't be in the world anymore."

"Whatever the reason, I am so sorry. I loved Bronwyn and will be sorry to see her go."

"Me too, Callum." She swallowed the tears, forced them down, for this was her undoing and she would not burden him with her emotions.

"What can I do?" he finally asked as he tapped his forehead with his fingertips.

"It might be too much to ask for your help, but here I am."

"It's not." He pointed at her satchel by her side. "What do you need?"

"This," she said, "is my life's work. The words I've been creating for a lifetime."

"You did it," he said. "You finally completed your language."

"I don't know if it's complete," she told him. "But I could not leave it behind."

"Oh, Bronny." His voice held so many emotions, none of which she could read. Then he looked up as if he really saw her. "We need to get you some food and tea before we continue this conversation."

Moments later, they were in the dining room at a large table, a crystal chandelier hung above them. He set a plate of cold beef and carrots in front of her, a slab of bread slathered with thick butter.

"My wife, Philippa," he told her, "is in the country with our nine-year-old boys for the spring holiday." He set his rimless glasses down and told her, "Your disappearance was in the *New York Times* two weeks ago. I read about it."

"That's why you didn't seem surprised," she told him.

They didn't talk of what made her leave—that was surely in the article, and more would come later. He sat quietly while she ate greedily and wondered if she might put a loaf of bread in her satchel when she left that night, because it was obvious now that she would need to leave.

Bronwyn ate to full and stood. "Callum, thank you for seeing me. But I'll have to leave now. It was unreasonable of me to expect you to help me."

"Don't leave," he said. "I won't turn you in. You must have your reasons to exile yourself from your family. If you are here, then I believe you can't return, just as in the New Hampshire woods that night."

"It's different, Callum. Last time you were saving me from a man, and this time I am saving him from me."

He stood and motioned for her to follow him. "We can talk more tomorrow after you've rested."

He showed her to the guest bedroom, a turret of comfort and ease where she fell into a dreamless sleep, a blessed absence of fear.

When she woke, she told him the full story and why she could never return—the fire, the death of the fireman, and leaving in *The Bronny*.

Sometimes, she told him, you must break your own heart. And that was what she'd decided to do.

"But wasn't this the first time?" he asked. "Surely you would be forgiven."

"Women like me are never forgiven," she told him. "And it did happen another time. I was writing, and Clara wandered away. A neighbor brought her home an hour later and said she saw Clara at the edge of their dock, about to fall in. She was five years old. There was already talk, Callum. A fireman died. Mother had me institutionalized when I was a teen. It would add up, Callum." She dropped her face and let the tears fall. "What they all say is true—I am not made to be a mother if I am putting my child in danger."

He allowed her to stay, and her grief followed her around the house for a week of recuperating—a dark and enveloping cloud that nearly devoured her. She walked the river of sidewalks in London, breathed the spring air. She found the parks and the pathways; she discovered the benches by ponds, and she stared at the bowl of sky, and again and again imagined being locked in a room where she would see nothing but concrete and tile, just as she had for those endless weeks in juvenile detention and the months in the facility where her mother had sent her. She thought of writing Timothy and Clara a letter, but they would never stop looking for her if they thought she was alive.

She should never have married, but how could she not marry the man who loved her, a man she loved with all her body and soul? And Clara—the gift of her life that she was abandoning.

She'd had them for a while, and she'd ruined it.

She ruined everything; that was also true.

On day five, Callum offered to call the doctor.

"Please don't. They will do to me what they have always done to me—lock me away, medicate me, offer to attach wires to my skull and send electric shockwaves through my brain to make me normal."

"But there is nothing wrong with you, Bronwyn. You know that."

"Timothy never expected me to be anything but who I am. Society is a different story. This time I made the final mistake—negligence that caused a death and injured my child. If you turn me in, I will understand."

"It wasn't negligence. It was an accident," Callum said.

"Not when you have my reputation. All I need," she told Callum, "is the opposite of what they will do if you call a doctor. I know how to heal from before, and it has everything to do with being outside."

In the night, she read endless books in his library, slept in a guest bedroom, talked to this kind man about writing stories, creating a language, regaining a strength she'd lost, until he set his hands on hers and with authority said, "Pippa can barely keep her head above water with twin boys. We need help."

CHAPTER 50

BRONWYN

Bronwyn watched as her daughter leaned forward into the story, and her friend Pippa clasped her hands on her lap with her jaw set tight, as if she held back tears. Bronwyn longed to take Clara in her arms and rock her as if she were a child. But Clara wasn't a child. She was a woman abandoned by her mother and might at any moment walk out of this room.

Bronwyn took a long, deep breath.

She'd offered them a summary that held within it a thousand other stories, but how was she to tell it all in one sitting? There would be years, she hoped, to narrate the intricacies, but for now she must try for the overall sweep of it without alienating those she loved with all her heart.

Bronwyn looked around the room with tears in her eyes. "When I planned to leave, and I did plan it, God help me, I thought of Callum, for we had a deep friendship. That year of 1915, all I'd wanted was a friend and to get away from Brian. After Callum returned to England, we kept in touch for about a year, and then I met Timothy. But the last time we communicated with holiday greeting cards in 1920, he was married to his great love. He was married to you, Pippa, and he was living at St. James's. I knew his address and he'd said, 'If you ever need anything or find yourself in London' . . . and I did need something. I needed protecting and he'd done it once before."

"He's a protector," Charlie said. "Yes, he is."

"I became his second cousin Isolde, who'd been educated in the United States and wasn't in Ireland during the bombing, and thusly had taken on an American accent," Bronwyn explained. "When my resolve melted and I wept into the night for you, Clara, and for Timothy, I reminded myself of a life of medications, a trial, institutions where they would lock me away. I imagined Clara with a mother damaged by drugs or shock therapy, and knew, as deep as my bones, that an absent mother was better than a damaged one, a locked-up one, a medicated one."

"The rest," she told Clara, Charlie, Wynnie, and Pippa as they sat around her table, "the rest was deceit, but my love and devotion was as real and true as the earth beneath our feet. I love the Jameson boys. I loved Callum and love you, Pippa. When the weight of pretending became too much and it was time to run again, Callum told me that it was time to quit running."

"Your love for Callum?" Pippa asked with a tight voice.

"And the love I feel for you, Pippa. The love anyone would feel for a friend who saved them, protected them, and understood them."

"Stop!" Clara stood now, as if she'd been jolted from the chair. Bronwyn watched her daughter's face change from anger to soft need to anger again, and yet her voice was young. "What did you do here?"

Pippa answered Clara while still staring at Bronwyn. "Everything from tutoring to watching the children to helping in the garden. We employed her as well as the truth that she became part of the family."

Clara shook her head and bit her lower lip. "I'm glad you knew her for all of that." Then she turned back to Bronwyn. "And I love that you've lived this great life full of love and understanding, Mother. Bronwyn. Isolde. I don't even know what to call you!"

Bronwyn sensed the hurt emanating from her beloved child, and it pained her, a cleaving in her chest. She could explain and explain her story, but the words were inadequate to heal the hurt of being abandoned. Bronwyn knew that as deeply as she knew her own heartbeat, for her father did the same to her. Even to her own ears her explanations sounded hollow.

She left to save her daughter. That was the truth.

"I know there is so much still to tell us. Tell me." Clara's voice was thick with unshed tears.

Bronwyn nodded. "I pray I have many more days and years to tell you the parts that matter."

"Can I hear about the wall?" Wynnie chimed in now. "You built it, didn't you?"

"I did, darling. I did. I built it one stone for every day I have been away from your mother and from you and Timothy. I started it the day I arrived here. I carried each one back from my long walks. Every single day, I add a stone and think of Clara and Timothy. I wanted to build something beautiful from the grief, a place where flowers and vines would grow."

"The stone wall around the garden is about us?" Clara stopped pacing and went to Charlie's side, absently placed her hand on his shoulder.

"Yes," Bronwyn said.

"What word could possibly describe how I feel right now?" Clara asked. "The anger. The relief. The childish dream come true, and yet . . . Even you, Mother, even you don't have a word for any of this. I know I don't."

"An important assignment for us all," Bronwyn said. "We can and we will."

"I am unsure I want one," Clara said. Then she shuddered and headed toward the door. "I need to leave. I need to . . . take a breath . . . and leave."

Bronwyn reached out her hand. "Please stay a bit longer. If you need or want to leave me after we talk, you may. Please don't go. Listen to me, my daughter. I always threw myself headlong into happiness, chasing it with a fervor and frenetic need that never satisfied. It was how I got myself into many of my troubles—that desperation for happiness, when I had no idea what it actually was. But it wasn't until you came along that I knew—you gave my life meaning."

Clara lingered at the door and then opened it, sunlight streaming into the room, along with a shiver of cold air.

Bronwyn stood and walked toward Clara, who was deciding whether to run.

"I know I ran," Bronwyn said, "and I have no right to ask, but can you stay? Please."

"Why?" Clara turned toward her mother.

"Have you ever been locked in a room without windows or light?"

"No." Clara placed her hand on her chest.

"I have been."

"I read about it. When you were a teenager, and you ran away from that family in California."

"Yes. And one more time when I was a teenager. I would rather die, and that is the awful truth, Clara. I would rather die than have that happen to me again. When the police came to the house after the fire, when the whispers started that I was accountable for a young fireman's mortal injuries with my negligence, that I was to blame for your injuries, I knew what was coming, Clara. I knew where I was headed, and where that would leave you and what it would do to me and to you and to the man I love."

"You aren't talking about the asylum or jail, are you?" Clara said. "You were afraid you would take your own life and leave us with that."

She bowed her head. "I am ashamed, possibly a coward, but yes. I was afraid I would remove myself from the world."

"Then why not come back later? You could have come back any time after things . . . settled down."

"No! It was too late by then. I couldn't leave here. Your life had moved on."

"That's an excuse and you know it."

"Maybe so. I was terrified to upset the balance I found within myself here."

Clara paused. Then she spoke what must have been an awful truth for her. "I always thought something was wrong with me."

"No!" Bronwyn cried out. "It was me. Something was wrong with me. Broken in me. Shattered in me. I could not let you see it!"

"Mama?" Wynnie called, and Clara reached for her daughter and returned to the room, leaving the door open.

Bronwyn closed the door and continued as best she could. She was growing tired, all the years unwinding in such a short time, but she could not give up.

She told them how she had met Beatrix Potter in 1930 while she was out walking in the woodlands, how they became friendly even as Bronwyn no longer wrote imaginative stories, for it broke her heart. Their conversations, during long walks, taught Bronwyn she could remake her own life.

Eventually Bronwyn gave Pippa her book, *The Middle Place*, and she opened her life to the children in the village, tutoring them in art and language. She focused on gardening and painting, on finding lost words that could touch her own heart.

"But what made you stay?" Pippa asked. "What made you finally stay put after all your years of running?"

"You. Your family. This land," she said. "I was done running."

"You sewed yourself into your secrets," Wynnie said, repeating the line Bronwyn had written in the note to Clara.

"Yes. Yes I did." Bronwyn felt the tears rising.

"I wish you would have stayed with us," Wynnie said. It was a simple wish.

Clara dropped her face into her hands, and Charlie set his hand on her shoulder. Bronwyn watched them. If Charlie and Clara didn't already know it, she could see they were falling in love.

"When did you give the language to Callum?" Pippa said, and Bronwyn looked at her dear friend. The distress in her eyes was nearly too much to bear, but Bronwyn would not look away.

"When I wrote the last word over ten years ago, I packed my papers and asked Callum to hold on to all of it, and then give it to Clara when I was gone. Then someone else could decide what to do with the words and the sequel of Emjie's fate."

"Emjie!" Wynnie exclaimed. "What happens to her in the sequel? We can't translate it now because Mama . . . because that lady stole the papers and—"

"Oh, darling," Bronwyn said with a break in her voice. "Our Emjie. We will unfold her story, don't you worry."

"M-mother." Clara stuttered over the word she hadn't used in twenty-five years. Bronwyn felt a pressure of pleasure in her chest. Clara leaned forward now. "Have you written anything since that day of the fire?"

"No." She paused and told her daughter the truth. "That was also my penance."

CHAPTER 51

CLARA

Lake District, England

Wynnie and I left the cottage where my mother had lived her life after me. We returned to the house, gathering trinkets of nature—acorns and feathers, seedpods and moss—in an effort to distract ourselves with beauty. This was all so huge.

I thought about Charlie and how he must have felt the moment he learned that the cousin he adored was my mother. I was very much a part of this family that I'd met just a week ago, and all along they'd been an integral but invisible piece of my life. It would take time to absorb and understand. For now, I needed to call Dad and Nat. I lived in another life, and this was not mine.

The phone rang at home and Dad answered. "Come now," I said to him. "Please. Mother is here."

He didn't ask for an explanation, but a sob escaped, and he hung up with promises to arrive on the first plane out. I called Nat at his house, and again there was no answer. I was tired of tracking him down, but again rang the body shop where he was working part-time until he found something full-time, only to hear: "He isn't working here anymore, Clara. I'm sorry to say."

Deep sadness and that bitter taste of disappointment returned to the back of my throat. Again. Again his life of chaos and unpredictability had gotten him fired from another job, even the one at the body shop that was meant to be temporary until he found another one in finance. I'd suspected that without me and Wynnie, he would slide back into the ways that destroyed his life. Maybe if we hadn't left, if I'd been a better wife . . . if if if.

"What happened?" I asked Tony.

"I'm really not at liberty to say. I'm sorry."

"Tony, I've known you since second grade. Tell me something. Anything. Is he okay?"

"He seems to be fine. Saw him at the Crab Claw last night."

"All right," I said, and hung up.

I downright knew that it wasn't my place to keep Nat on the straight and narrow; I'd done that for years and I felt sick with the scenarios of what might have happened: stealing money from his place of work to pay gambling debts or disappearing for a few days to hit a poker table. I could only guess.

That night, Wynnie and I took dinner to our room; I was overwhelmed by the knowledge and information. I was relieved and I was ebullient; I was sad, and I was floating with the thought: *My mother is here.* A hunger, a ravenous hunger for her, was sated, but only for the moment. I would want more and more. I couldn't face her right now. I needed to be alone with Wynnie, to avoid a false face or smile. There was nothing left in me for polite conversation.

As night descended and fingers of twilight scratched across the Cumbrian fells, I tucked Wynnie under the sheets and stroked her back until she fell asleep. My mind rattled through the unsteady truths:

Mother was alive; she'd come to England to hide. She believed she could never return without damaging Dad and me. She'd quit writing but painted, taught children, and gardened. She made a life by Esthwaite Water and paid penance by hauling a stone every day to build a garden wall. She'd been here all along in another life, in ways that I'd been afraid to imagine.

These sharp facts lined up inside me, swords of truth cutting a space between what I'd once believed and what I now knew.

I had found my mother, but I was unsure she'd ever wanted to be found.

Sleep would not visit me as it had Wynnie, so I listened to her even, clear breathing, grateful. After a while, when the room felt as if it floated above the frosty land, I made my way to the drawing room to find a glass of whiskey, something to help me sleep. The new moon offered no light; the night was dark as black velvet outside the windows.

I heard Charlie's music before I reached the drawing room. I leaned against the doorway and listened with my eyes closed. The music moved through my chest and opened something in me that had only begun to be pried apart with Mother's story.

His music ended, and I opened my eyes to see him looking at me. He set down the drum and his stick. "You found her." He came to me, and I fell into him, let him hold me. His wide chest felt like a place to land. We sat on the couch.

"I can't really believe it. But what does it mean now?" I looked at his kind face, at those warm eyes that never wavered from mine. "Why didn't she come back for me? Why did she stay with *you* instead?" I took a breath for the next truth. "You had my mother."

"Now I remember, she is the one who taught me the Eliot poem."

"Yes." I felt the ballooning of something too much, something that would take me from who I thought I was, toward someone I might be.

"The Irish," he said. "They have words like your mother's."

"How so?"

"One word meaning more than its simple definition."

"Like?"

"They have a word for ladybug, what I've heard you call Wynnie, and it is translated as 'God's little cow.'" He paused and drew closer, closer still.

"A little cow?" I laughed, and he continued.

"They have a word for a choppy sea that is translated as 'the fisherman's garden is under a white flower.'"

"That's so beautiful." My voice was a whisper now, and something in me knew what might come next. "Tell me more," I said.

"When they say thank you, they are saying, 'May you have a thousand good things.' The translations are more than the word. They are deeper. This is the kind of language your mother was creating—words that came from within her. It was all she had left to share with you."

I fell against him. He knit his fingers into my hair, and I wanted more of him. He stood and took my hand, and there was no doubt where we were headed. In fact, I very well might have led us there if I'd allowed myself to be clear-eyed.

Once in his room, he locked the door and looked at me as if he could see right to the knot of loneliness nestled inside, that he could undo this tangled piece of me with his touch. I reached to unbutton his shirt, and when I'd finished and placed my hands on his chest, I lifted my face for the kiss that consumed me. He unzipped my dress.

Desire broke loose from its underground world, and there was nothing else in the room but that, so long buried.

We didn't speak in anything but touch, and I wanted more than he could give, and yet without my understanding how, everything he gave was enough. I whispered it was okay, that I wanted him. I told him not to worry as he fumbled to try and explain his hesitancy. We made love as he filled the hollowed-out spaces of my questions, the ones that echoed in the night with a need I didn't understand. Everything that had ever happened to me seemed to bring me here, to the land where my mother lived, where Charlie Jameson waited for me.

The moon pressed itself against the windows, the long call of an owl far-off, and we made love as if this was the night that must last for all the other lonely ones to come, as if this was the first time and the last. As if we must experience what it meant to desire and to be desired, as if it would never happen again.

———

Pippa sat alone at the glass-top breakfast table. The newspaper was folded unread on the chair where Charlie usually sat.

Pippa smiled sadly at me, and I wondered how she was absorbing the news about Mother, and if she had any idea of how I'd spent part of that night.

"Good morning, Clara."

"Good morning, Pippa. How was your sleep?"

She laughed in a gentle co-conspirator manner, as if both of us knew there wouldn't be sleep with such news as we'd received yesterday. "There's been a call, and your father is on his way," she told me. "Moira received his message this morning. He's booked on the Pan Am flight that lands in London at six a.m. in two days' time, and then he'll travel here by train. The details are written down on a sheet of paper in the kitchen."

"I invited him without consulting you," I told her. "I'm so sorry. I just—"

"I am so pleased he's coming," she said. "I would have asked him myself if I could say the words."

"My dad," I said, "the man who swore he'd never sit in a metal tube that flies over the ocean, has made an exception, it seems."

"You found your mother," Pippa said, as if announcing something I didn't know. "Isn't this so strange? I don't quite know how to . . . I am . . . quite beside myself."

"And confused and upset, I would think. Just like me," I said as Moira appeared with a plate of eggs and hash, setting it down in front of me.

"How wonderful," Moira whispered to me as she bent down. It was possible that if she hadn't taken that satchel from the closet, if she hadn't broken the rules out of grief for Callum's loss, we'd never be here now. I wouldn't know my mother's arms around me for the first time in twenty-five years.

"Thank you, Moira," I said.

"For?" she asked, and stood with a smile.

"Everything. All of it. For getting us here, for . . . all of it." She nodded with a knowing smile. I asked, "Where's Wynnie?"

"Miss Isolde . . . your mother took her for a walk. We thought it best we let you sleep."

"Charlie?" I asked.

Pippa answered, "He is dragging down more Christmas decorations from the attic. I wanted the box of silver beads for a tree in the drawing room. Having you here, having Wynnie— Oh, Clara, it has just lifted my spirits."

"Pippa, I am so glad. And the house looks like a wonderland," I told her. "It's extraordinary, as if it's ready for a party any day."

"I usually do have a Christmas party, but this year it just felt like a step too far. With Callum gone, it's hard to make big decisions. I feel weighted down. Heavy. A party is . . ."

"Too much."

"Yes," she said, "it is. I've never done anything like that without him."

"I could help," I said. "If that's what you want to do."

She swished her hands through the air as if shooing the thought away, and then folded them in her lap.

"Clara, I need to say something to you about Charlie."

I nodded, and her gaze darted toward the doorway checking if anyone was within earshot. "Charlie?"

A hot blush made its way up my chest, and she continued. "His heart has already been broken once and terribly. You might not be able to make promises, but I will ask for one anyway."

"Yes?"

"Just be truthful with him. Always."

I raised my eyebrows and Pippa leaned forward. "I know what a man falling in love looks like, darling."

"I . . ." I set my hand on my chest, where it felt as if it would spill out its contents of desire right there on the table. "I won't make any promises to him or anyone else that I can't keep," I told her.

"Now, Clara, it appears," Pippa said, setting her monogrammed napkin on top of her finished breakfast, "that you and I are in the same boat, to use a timeworn metaphor. Six and two threes."

"Six and two threes?"

"Yes, meaning the same."

"Ha, yes," I said.

"Your mother."

I nodded. "It appears she has deceived us both."

"And that we have both loved her very, very much."

"Yes."

"Clara, I have been pacing nearly all night. Charlie gave me Isolde's . . . your mother's biography, and I read much of it in the wee hours."

"It's sad, I know," I told her, and ached with the knowledge that Pippa Jameson knew about Mother's past lives, the jumble and raw-edged horror of so many of her days.

"It is sad," Pippa said. "What strikes me the most, what clanged against the din of my selfish anger, is this." She paused as if finding her words. "My God, the shame and fear your mother has hidden from the world, from us, and from you is almost incomprehensible. It began in childhood and never stopped—this idea put upon her that there is something wrong with her, that she needs to be fixed, that she is different and no good for this world or for love or even for motherhood. I can't imagine the disgrace and shame she's carried."

"Oh, Pippa." I dropped my head and felt the warm tears fall with the exhale of sobs. My righteous anger was shifting into mercy.

Pippa sat quietly, allowing the tears, until I felt her hand on my shoulder. "I don't condone her deceit or the leaving, Clara, but I do understand. Can you imagine?"

"No," I said, and pushed my chair back to stand with Pippa. "I can't. And she's carried it alone," I said with the slow wave of compassionate understanding approaching like a rising sun. "Most of her life she was told there was something broken and wrong with her and she believed it. All that fear. All that shame."

"Yes, alone," Pippa said. "She wanted to save us, Clara, but instead she's hurt us. This must shame her also."

"I don't know what to do, Pippa. She's my mother. She left me."

"Forgiveness," she said, "is a mighty strong force against fear." Pippa came to me and did the most unexpected thing—she kissed each cheek and then hugged me, holding me the way I'd always wanted my mother to do.

CHAPTER 52

BRONWYN

Lake District, England

Wynnie walked next to Bronwyn.

"Grandma," Wynnie said. "Can I call you that, since I've been calling you Grandma all along?"

"Yes, I'd love that," Bronwyn said, and took her granddaughter's mittened hand.

"I need to know something."

Bronwyn looked down at this marvel of a girl named after her, the daughter of her daughter. Bronwyn's breath caught and held with the dishonor of leaving her. "Tell me what you need to know," Bronwyn said. She would tell the child anything she needed.

"Did you create Emjie, or did she come visit you like she visited me?"

"She visited me, and I told her story. Or that's how it felt."

"We share her, then," Wynnie said, then stopped to straighten her little glasses and look straight into Bronwyn's eyes. "Mama doesn't see her or know her."

"Your mama is most likely angry with me and therefore can't see Emjie. And that's okay. That's what she needs for now. But you, you needed a friend." Bronwyn stopped and pointed at the long, wide acreage near Hill Top. "That, my darling girl, is where Peter Rabbit lives."

"I know. I came here with Mama a few days ago." Wynnie stopped at the gate. "Mama really likes Beatrix Potter. We have all her books, and Mama has even framed some pictures of Jemima Puddle-Duck."

"I read those books to her when she was little."

"She told me," Wynnie said.

Bronwyn set both hands on the fence post, for she needed to settle herself, to find a way to keep from crumpling to the ground in regret and loss. She steadied herself. "Beatrix loved the country just as I do, and you know, Wynnie, she *also* created a language."

"We saw it when we visited."

"Beatrix's language was more of a code than a new language, but just like me, she needed to hide parts of herself from the world."

"Why do we need to hide parts of ourselves from the world?" Wynnie tilted her head, and Bronwyn nearly bent over with the grief of ever missing a day of Clara's and Wynnie's lives.

She took a breath and answered as best she could. "Sometimes the world isn't so kind to people who are different, especially women," Bronwyn said.

"Yes. At school, Billy makes fun of my glasses, and my desk mate Florrie teases me for my little stories, and some moms look funny at Mama when she arrives at school with paint in her hair and on her shirt. So maybe hiding is something . . . we need to do?"

"It shouldn't be, little one. And I'm sorry I hid from you," Bronwyn said, and the tears felt warm on her cheeks. "That is my loss, Wynnie."

"Don't cry," Wynnie said. "You sent me Emjie."

Bronwyn sat on a wooden bench and patted the seat for Wynnie.

"Mr. McGregor is scary," Wynnie said. "He cooked Peter Rabbit's father."

Bronwyn laughed. "Indeed he did. The scary bits are always there."

"Why the scary bits?" Wynnie asked, and scooted closer, rested her hand on Bronwyn's leg.

Bronwyn paused and twisted to face this wise granddaughter and her inquisitive eyes. "Because the world has scary bits. Where is a better place to see it first than with Peter Rabbit?"

Wynnie nodded and pressed her lips together. "I see. Yes. And then we can know that there are still good parts."

"Yes." Bronwyn reached over and hugged the child and desperately hoped that for the rest of her life she might be lucky enough to take this chatter and stretch it for years. There was so much more to say about banishing terror and conquering darkness. "Tell me how you met Emjie," Bronwyn said. "I want to hear everything."

"I met her when I was making an oyster shell castle on the beach in front of Papa's house. We live there now, but we didn't live there when I was tiny. I was sad that day. No one was around to build the castle with me, then Emjie showed up. She hasn't left me yet. I know she will someday."

"She doesn't have to leave. Unless you want her to."

"Mama thinks I met her after she read your book to me, but that's not true. When she read it to me, I already knew Emjie. She told Papa that I must have heard them talking about Emjie. I know Emjie isn't just mine. I know she's yours, too—mostly yours. But I do love her."

"She's not mine," Bronwyn said. "No more than Peter Rabbit belongs to Beatrix Potter."

They sat quietly with the chirp of an unseen bird. Wynnie broke the silence with a wish she must have kept so deep that it burst out. "I want to make up words with you."

Bronwyn laughed. "Let's do it!"

"I can?" Wynnie asked. "I'm allowed to do that?"

"No one needs permission to define what they think and feel, Wynnie. No one. What in your life do you feel like no one can understand? Only you? A feeling. A person. A thing."

Wynnie stared off at the fells. She watched the bulky cotton of clouds lazily cross the blue, blue sky. They listened to the calls of birds, each different.

"I can't see well." Wynnie touched her glasses. "People forget that sometimes I can't see everything, even with these clunky things."

"Make a word, Wynnie. Tell me what that feeling is." Bronwyn pulled her close, her arm around Wynnie's shoulders.

CHAPTER 53

CLARA

Lake District, England

I was aware of Charlie's presence as he entered the breakfast room before I turned to see him. Maybe it was the way Pippa's face lit up, or possibly it was the way my body sensed him, but I took a breath to steady myself and turned. "Good morning," I said.

"There you are," he said, as if he'd been looking for me.

There you are.

Warmth spread through me, and I believed, for a breath, that I'd come to England just for this, for him, for the way he was looking at me right now. This felt . . . authentic and solid, not frantic or needy as before. But I didn't have a record of smart choices in this arena, and I was careful, holding back the flood of feelings as best I could.

He walked to me, bent down, and kissed my cheek. He lingered long enough that Pippa smiled.

"Good morning, Son," she said. "Sit." She patted the chair next to her.

Pippa looked at Charlie with such love, the grief of Callum's loss nearly palpable, as if I could reach out and touch the spongy softness of it between them.

What was very clear was that this house, land, and everything it touched, from family to water to fell, belonged heart and body to Philippa Jameson. It might not be the grand manor and acreage of Graythwaithe Hall down the road or have acres dotted with the Herdwick sheep of the Heelises' lands, but make no mistake about it—she was the mistress of this landscape and all that rested within it.

It must pierce her heart to know that both her husband and my mother kept such a powerful secret from her.

"Mum, have you called Archie and told him . . . about everything?"

"Yes, luv, last night. He's as shocked as we are." She turned to me. "He's very happy you solved the mystery of your mother. He's a bit miffed Isolde deceived us, but I told him we'd give him more of the story later." She then looked at Charlie. "And to you he said only one word I don't understand, but I will pass it along: *besotted.*"

Charlie laughed. "Oh, Brother." Then he looked to me. "Where's Wynnie?"

"Out with my mother." I shook my head, shedding the cobweb tangles of the night and day before. I didn't know who I was, not yet, but I was someone other than the woman who only a day ago saw a painting of her South Carolina house in the parlor.

"Mama!"

Wynnie ran into the room and into my arms. She smelled of pine sap, of frost, and impossibly of roses. Mother drew up behind her and kissed my cheek, lingered as if to make sure I was real and there in the breakfast room.

"Guess what, Mama? Guess what?" Wynnie jiggled left and right on the tips of her toes.

"Yes?" I asked.

"I made up a word." She straightened her glasses. "Me! I made up a word."

Mother laughed, and I knew the sound of it—an echo of something lost—and my heart reached for it. "She did," Mother said. "Yes, she did, and it's beautiful."

"Can you tell it to us?" I asked. "Or is it a secret?"

"*Tilover,*" Wynnie said. "Do you want to know what it means?"

"I do," I said.

"Yes!" Charlie said.

"Please," Pippa chimed in.

Wynnie looked around the table and took a breath, lifted her chin, and declaimed: "To see only some of the world, but to feel all of it." Her voice was so assured and grown-up that for a moment I saw the woman she would become, an object of wonder, a *miraculum.*

The days passed as we waited for Dad. Shadows drowned the valleys and then retreated like the tides in our backyard in South Carolina.

The geography of this place settled into me, a complexity of colors and shapes, a world reflected in a mirror-lake outside the window, a stream-carved land. I stood near the water, the russet clumps of marsh grass surrounding me, as I yearned to be enveloped by the lake, to dive to its deepest ice-carved bottom.

Mother and I walked along the paths and through the woodlands. We sipped endless cups of tea, and we cried. We talked and talked about the dailiness of our lives.

Through the past days I'd asked Mother so many questions—while we walked on woodland paths and while we ate across from each other at the dining room table, and while we listened to Charlie play music in the drawing room. She was patient with me, answering everything that bubbled up, and repeating her answers and stories as if I were a child, which in many ways I was again.

Had there been another man? Had she loved again? No, she told me. Did she ever think about coming home? Every day. Did she miss us? Every second.

"Do you want to walk to Moss Ecles with me?" she asked that bright morning, the wind and rain taking a break from their appearances. The weather in this place changed so dramatically that one might wake up in the morning to believe one had slept through an entire season.

"Whatever Moss Ecles is, yes," I told her.

"A mile trek up the hill to a secluded and enchanting little tarn. I walk it almost daily."

"Take me," I said, with a deep need to see something, anything, my mother did nearly every day.

The pathway took us through trodden grasses and over muddy, pebbled trails. Over stiles and through gates, we continued upward, accompanied by the sound of our wellies splashing in the creek beds, the cry of unseen geese, and the creak of branches in the wind. The land swelled and sank as we walked. We reached a crest where a herd of sheep looked down on us, their placid faces watching in boredom from rocks beneath bare-limbed trees.

We didn't talk but instead allowed the silence to draw us forward and together at the same time, as if the unsaid words were as important as the spoken. The last two days, I'd exhausted us both with my questions.

The stone walls led us forward until we turned a corner and I gasped at the beauty. "Oh, Mother!"

"Yes, I know."

The tarn, the lake named after the Nordic teardrop, nestled in the pasture, a craggy outcropping of rocks on its shore. I climbed up the jagged rocks to look over the small lake with a little island in its middle. Geese flocked, and their honking was the only sound echoing across the fields and against the mountain range.

"This was Beatrix Potter's favorite tarn," Mother said as she joined me on the rocks. "She bought it with her husband."

"You read her books to me when I was little," I said. "I remember."

A small cry of grief fell from her lips, and she reached her hand for mine. "I remember, too. I remember everything. Every moment. Every single moment with you."

"I wish I did, too," I told her.

"I will tell you whatever you want. I promise."

The geese protested in loud honks, and Mother and I both laughed at their outburst, watched them skim the water as they flocked to the other side.

"You and Beatrix had a lot in common?"

She grew serious. "Yes, in some ways. Our secluded childhoods and creating languages, but she was more like you."

"Me?"

"Your illustrations. Your strength. Your belief in yourself."

"I don't think that's true, but I like that you see me that way."

Then she told me legends of the area, from the Crier of Claife to the ghost stories of Calgarth Hall. We walked down the hill toward the hamlet of Near Sawrey, where my mother had lived her life since she'd left me. I viewed the village as a bird above the town, where whitewashed houses and slate roofs winked in the sunlight.

"Tell me more. More about your days here," I said as we walked over a metal cattle guard.

And she did.

As we waited for Dad, I wrote snippets of the things she told me into a notebook, trying to make sense of her story, what sense there was of it to make. I found myself making a list of her years and where she'd spent them, doing what.

I deeply desired a narrative—this happened and this happened and then this happened and here is the reason. But that was a child's dream—to make sense of the lost years.

She gave me reasons, but they could never drive out my feelings of abandonment and grief. Only her stories and truths had a chance of filling those places.

Each morning when I woke, a part of me believed I would find her gone, that after we'd informed her that her husband was on his way, she would again leave, afraid to face him above all. But each day she was still there.

Pippa, too, needed to understand who her beloved friend was, and they'd spent hours alone. Pippa and I weren't battling for her attention; both of us needed answers that would *not* come in a few days' time.

The second afternoon, Pippa found me at the end of the main hall as I stood by the Christmas tree in the foyer. "It's beautiful," I said, and touched a sterling silver ball with Charlie's name and birth date etched on it.

"I had that made at his birth," she told me. "One for each boy."

"I cross-stitched one for Wynnie."

"Do you believe they ever notice the small things we do for them?" she asked.

"I do. I think. I hope." I turned to her. "I remember so many of the little things my mother did for me, but maybe that's because I had to live off those memories. But I do and did notice."

"I'm sorry for what happened. I really am. I can't imagine what you have been through, and still, here you are."

"I know it must be hard to understand that your husband kept this from you." I spoke, hoping I wasn't overstepping. Her tenderness made me feel I could confide in her, and I needed to acknowledge the misery she must feel. I wasn't in this alone, and I wanted her to know I understood this. "If your husband had sent her away or called the police, I would not be here now. I would never have found her. She would have run again."

"I've thought about that, too. I'm not happy he kept this from me, and somehow I also see the necessity of it. There are parts in all of us that we keep to ourselves; we need our private self, that's true. And I can't blame my husband for this. He was the love of my life, and I know I was the love of his. And what happened here does not take away from that."

"Did you ever want another life?" I asked. "I think about that, about how she just up and made a new life with a new name."

"I believe we've all wondered about living different lives, but that doesn't mean we don't love the one we have. We are given one finite life, and the alternates fade when we don't choose them. But"—she stared off into the distance—"that doesn't mean we don't wonder."

"Yes," I said.

She smiled. Then a call came from the back hall, and she was off.

I considered making my way to the kitchen to try Nat one more time. I didn't want to call his parents in Georgia and worry them, and I'd already called his place of work. The knot inside me that had started to form the first time I realized his gambling would destroy our lives grew tighter each day. Something wasn't right with him, and there was no way of finding out unless he answered his phone.

Despite my best promises to myself to be careful with my heart and with his, I found my way to Charlie's bed each night with a language that we hadn't defined. I worried this was a charged lovemaking fueled by emotions that could never settle into something real and solid. I swung madly from anger to relief, from hurt to love, from confusion to clarity, and still each night we found each other.

One late night as we stood in the wan light of the kitchen, sneaking a cut of sponge cake and smothering it with clotted cream, I told him: "I want to be careful. I know it doesn't seem like it, the way I come to you, but all my life I have been trying to fill this mother-shaped hole in my life."

"I am not leaving." He kissed me with the taste of sugar on his lips. "Do you regret this?"

"How can I? I have a tinge of guilt, that is true. I'm not being careful with our hearts or anything else. This is how I found myself married to Nat."

"You married Nat because you were pregnant with Wynnie?"

"No! But because he was . . . my first." I blushed. "And last, to be honest. Do you think less of me now?" I wanted to tease him, but I truly needed the answer.

He took me in his arms. "Less? Oh, it's not possible to think anything but lofty thoughts of you, Clara Harrington. I am right smitten with you, and if we are making you feel guilty, we shall stop right now." He lifted his hands in the air.

"Do not stop," I told him. And he kissed me again.

⸻

On Sunday, Mother and I took a quiet walk down to Windermere Lake through the two hamlets of Near and Far Sawrey, along the winding road to a ferry dock. This lake was the largest of all fifteen, and Mother pointed across to a bustling town. "It's a honeypot over there. We prefer the quiet of Sawrey."

"A honeypot?" I asked.

"Meaning busy. Busy as a bee."

"I love that," I told her. "Such a good word."

That evening, Mother, Pippa, Wynnie, and I sat around the drawing room. Charlie had gone into town to pick up the car from the repair shop, where the fender had finally been fixed after our collision with a cow during the awful day we'd driven here in the fog. I looked out the window at every sound, searching for his headlights. I yearned for him, and I tried to hide it.

Another Christmas tree had appeared in this room, and it glittered with tinsel and lights in the far corner. Dried fruit and bits and bobs of the outside world hung from its branches—nests and pinecones, bearded lichen and twigs and feathers. Two huge stuffed pheasants perched on the floor at its base. Pippa urged Wynnie to place all her treasures she'd found on the land onto the branches. She called it "Wynnie's tree."

"The sequel," Mother said into the quiet.

I leaned forward and felt the questions about it I'd held tight bubble up. "Yes," I said. "We still have it. The pages are safe in Bluffton, if that's what you're worried about."

"Oh, dearest, I'm not worried about it. I never want to see the sequel again."

"What?" Wynnie looked up from the book she was reading and exclaimed, "But I want to read it! I want to know what happens to Emjie."

CHAPTER 54

CLARA

Lake District, England

"The sequel," Mother repeated as if the words tasted bitter.

"Yes," I said. "Do you want to wait until Dad arrives to talk about this?"

"I will have much to say to your dad, but Emjie has come to Wynnie."

"You know," I told her. "We can't translate it now. I've lost most of your words and—"

"I can translate it if it's what you wish. And then you can read it in its entirety. But what happened to Emjie in that book is an old version of how I saw the world and everyone in it."

"Tell us anyway!" Wynnie begged.

"The version I wrote is not what I would write today. I'd prefer to let it be for now. I was in a much different time when I wrote that sequel; it was before I met Timothy. I was in a terrible state. I did not give Emjie what she needed in that version. That's why I kept it hidden until I might rewrite it." She pressed her lips together and her face twitched. She cleared her throat.

"You can change all of it, Mother."

"Is it all right if we leave that version alone? Let it stay where it lies, untranslated?"

"Yes," I said. "We can do that if you'd like." I imagined that pile of papers, all those untranslatable words, that entire story of Emjie on Dad's desk at home where I'd left it.

Mother looked to Wynnie. "Together we can give Emjie new adventures," she said.

"Yes." Wynnie slipped her hand into mine as if to tell me I was part of this. "And Mama can draw the illustrations. After all"—Wynnie sat up straight—"she's a Caldecott winner."

Mother spun her smile toward me. "You are? This is so wonderful, so grand. Why didn't you tell me right away?"

"We had some other things to talk about, I think."

She laughed. "Does Eliza know?"

"Of course," I told her.

"We must celebrate." She beamed, her smile wide and tears in her eyes. "Oh, Clara, I am so proud, even if I have no right to be, I am."

The room shimmered with light. If this was the land described in those *Harriet the Hedgehog* stories, maybe more would be revealed.

"Mother," I asked, a question that had been brewing and nearly forgotten, "did you tell Callum to suggest me for *Harriet the Hedgehog*?"

"I knew he did so, as I was there when he suggested it, but I didn't tell him to do it. I was stunned to silence when he did. I didn't know about your Golden Books or your illustrations until then."

"How did he know?"

"He kept up with you. He had someone check in on you occasionally, but he didn't tell me until then. I didn't know until that day, and from then on, I asked so many questions that he told me what little he knew—you'd married, you had a little girl, and your work was stunning. That your father was doing well." She closed her eyes. "But that's all. Even that was too painful, and he never mentioned it again. I didn't know you'd left your husband until you told me."

Silence pressed down until Pippa piped up. "Isolde . . . Should I still call you that?"

Mother nodded. "Yes."

"Did you know Callum was writing his family stories?"

"He was?"

"Yes."

"I didn't know. He never spoke of it. Not once. We weren't confidants like that, Pippa. I want you to know that. His respect and love for you was beyond reproach. You had each other for thirty-five years, and you have each other still. The only secret we kept was my origin, how I arrived, and who I was. From there, he never spoke of it again except the day I told him I would leave, that I could not ask him to keep this secret any longer. He told me that my running days were over. He was firm. But kind as always."

"But," I said, "you knew about me and about Harriet."

"I did. I keep those books on my bedside table, darling. You are always with me in this way."

Wynnie clapped with childlike glee. "I knew it. I saw it. Your stories are right here. All your drawings, Mama. They are here. The lake and mountains and trees and bunnies. All here." She stood and threw her arms around my waist. "We've been here with Grandma all along."

———

The rain arrived the same day as Dad's expected train. In a low-ceilinged pub in Windermere, Charlie and I seated ourselves across from each other at a scarred wooden table. We shook off damp rain slickers and folded our umbrellas by our side.

The thirty-minute drive on windy roads, sideways rain clouding our vision while being squeezed by stone walls, all conspired to make me slightly nauseous. Charlie pushed the basket of thick-crusted bread the server had provided across to me. "Slather it with butter and eat up. You'll be better in no time."

Two men hollered greetings, and one asked Charlie: "When ya gonna bring that band up here? Too big in the britches for us now?"

"Soon, Freddy, soon!" Charlie called out. He returned his attention to me. "You're being awful quiet and . . . you didn't come to me last night. I missed you."

"I missed you, too." I cast my eyes down. "But . . ."

"But you're angry at me?"

"No! Why would you think that?"

"You said it the first night we found her—I had the mother you lost."

"I'm not angry. I don't know exactly what I am." I lifted my eyes to his again. "You grew up with my mother. You and I have been living across an ocean from each other, and our lives were . . . are such a complicated labyrinth, each of us circling the other without knowing the other existed. It is already too much. I can't figure out how tangled we really are, and have we made it worse by—"

"These have been overwhelming days, to be sure, and I am going to ask you something."

"What is it?" My stomach was jittery, buzzing with all the unknowns and Dad on his way, when Charlie said only one word.

"Stay?"

A simple request, and I leaned over and kissed him, settled my lips on his lovely mouth, and lingered. Then I put my forehead to his. "Oh, Charlie, I just can't."

He took my face in his warm hands. "I don't know what I think about all this talk of the unseen world, or tangled lives or even meant-to-be, but I do know this: I want you to stay. Whatever brought you here—whether your mother's language or the fog of London or sins of the past—whatever it was, it matters little to me. I want you to stay. Wynnie loves it. You love it."

"But it's not where my life is. Wynnie has a father. How could I take her away from him when I know what it's like to live without one of my parents? Not to mention the legalities and a divorce agreement that says I won't take her from South Carolina."

"Those can be overcome. Whatever it is you want to do, you can do all those things here, in Sawrey, in London, wherever you want."

"You can't know you want me here. Not after knowing me for a week, Charlie." I hesitated before speaking the truth that might send him from me. "And I can never have children. You have no future with me."

"You think my future with you depends on children? I don't want you to stay so I can have children."

"But someday you will want them, Charlie. It's natural, and you have a close-knit family; it seems impossible for you to think about never having any of your own."

"There are other ways to have kids, Clara. You know that."

"It's such a huge decision for you to make in only a week's time."

"More than a week." He smiled. "Ten days that have been nearly the best in my life. No, not nearly, the best. I can know I want you here. Isn't that enough for now?"

"I don't know if that's enough for now, and I can't take Wynnie from her father, and . . . even if this sounds silly, I don't want to miss the Caldecott Awards ceremony in two weeks."

"It's important to you."

"More than that—it's something all my own. It's about me and my work, not about Mother or Nat or—"

"I don't mean for you to stay and miss your award! You must go to that, but come back and truly stay. With me." He lifted his eyebrows. "I am not above begging."

I laughed and kissed him again. "I'd like to see what begging looks like for you, but I think I'm meant to find my own destiny instead of obsessing about my mother's or believing it rests with someone else."

"But she's here, too. You could come to know her more. Or just stay through holiday and the new year. I'll take what you can give."

"I know I'll come back. I know I'll find my way to her; she's only fifty-five years old. If I'm lucky, we have decades. But now, right now, I have classes to teach. I've thought much of what I want to do when I get home, how I want to take everything lovely from here and bring it home. I want to show children that it's okay to be imaginative, to have invisible friends, to make up stories, to draw creatures and fairies and dragons, to . . . dwell in your imagination while also living here in the very real world."

"I had that . . ." He hesitated, and I held up my hand.

Jealousy flared in my chest, a flash that singed the moment. "I want to be what I wish I'd had—someone to show me that I am not alone. Even though Mother ran, she left that indelible knowing in me and I want to leave it in others. I have Wynnie and we have a home."

"And you, if you'd like to know, you also have me. You have me in the palm of your hand. You have me wrapped around your little finger. You have . . . me." He sat back in his chair. "Clara, I wake up wanting you. I go to sleep wanting you. Not just that way," he said, running his fingers along the inside of my wrist, sending the heat of desire through me. "But to have you nearby. To talk to you about every word and lyric and thought. To hear your curiosity and wonder. To know you're in the next room. But, Clara, if this is what you need to do, if this is your path, if you need to go home, I am not going anywhere. I am *here*."

His want for me sent such a great thrill through me, a song I'd wanted to hear and didn't even know I'd longed for. But I would not abandon myself or Wynnie again: not for a lost mother, not for a gambling husband, not for a satchel in a river, and not for a man I had met only ten days ago.

"Charlie," I said, "I didn't come here to find love."

He shook his head. "But yes, you did."

"No, I didn't."

"You did indeed. You came to find your mother's love and found even more than that. Much more."

He was telling a truth that needed some time to settle over me. I had come for love, and that was true.

"What about you coming with me?" I asked.

He hesitated and I felt the unsaid words that were the same as mine. He had a life here. A band. A family. A world. But that wasn't what he said.

"That's possible, Clara. It is. If you mean it, after I settle Father's affairs as I promised, it's possible." When I didn't answer, he took my hand. "There is an Irish saying that I feel is all I want to say right now to make you understand."

"What is that?"

"You're the place that I stand when my feet are sore."

"Oh, Charlie." I kissed him, and what I didn't say, what I didn't tell him, was that he, too, had me in all the same ways.

CHAPTER 55

CLARA

Lake District, England

The rain stopped, leaving puddles on the planks of the Windermere station platform. Charlie and I stood quietly, waiting for the world to shift with Dad's arrival. Then the earth trembled with an arriving train, and Charlie and I stepped back a few feet as the gray train screeched to a stop and the doors split open with a hiss. Men and women in traveling coats and hats, bowing their heads to the cold breeze, stepped off the train. Women held children by the hand and men jostled suitcases off the cars.

I scanned the faces for my dad.

"Ladybug!" His voice rang out and I spun around.

Charlie nudged me and softly said, "Little cow?" He was reminding me of the Gaelic definition.

I rolled my eyes at Charlie, and Dad rushed to me. He set his suitcase on the platform, and we hugged for a long while, quiet with the words that no one could create. I didn't know how to start a conversation with all that was between us now.

He stepped back and kissed my cheek. "You look so beautiful." He smiled at me and then turned to Charlie. "Isn't she just beautiful?"

"Yes, sir, she is."

"Oh, stop," I spoke. "Dad, please meet Charlie Jameson."

They shook hands like proper gentlemen, and we made our way to the car. "Welcome to Cumbria," Charlie said. "We are so pleased you've made your way here. Everyone is waiting."

"How was your flight, Dad?"

"Bumpy and awful, and I needed to stay awake all night to make sure I kept the contraption in the air by worrying."

Charlie laughed and I kissed my dad's cheek, rough with stubble. "Soon you can have yourself a long hot shower and something to eat," Charlie said.

"No. Take me to Bronwyn, please." Dad climbed into the back seat and patted the headrest where I sat up front. "First things first."

"You must have a million questions buzzing inside you," I told him, twisting around in my seat.

"I do. But questions come later. I just want to see her."

Charlie drove us along the twisting road, between hedgerows and past sweeping fields. Dad asked, "Where's Wynnie?"

"Mother took her to walk through the woodlands."

"Well, isn't that something."

"Yes," I said, "it is. Was the hospital okay with you leaving so abruptly?"

"It's about time I took a long-overdue sabbatical," he said.

"Sabbatical?" I asked as Charlie drove through the stone pillars that led to the house. "You're taking time off?" I felt something approaching that I didn't understand.

"Yes."

Charlie drove up the snaking driveway and parked. The stone and granite house loomed in front of us.

"Is this an inn?" Dad asked, rubbing his hand down the length of his stubbled cheeks. He appeared greatly weary, as if he hadn't slept since the moment when I'd called him and said, "Come now. Please. Mother is here."

"No, sir. It's our home."

"Bronwyn lives here?" He opened the car door and set his feet on the pebbled driveway.

"No," I told him, and stood next to him, pointing toward the lake. "She lives in one of those cottages. The one in the middle."

He placed his palm above his eyes and began to walk in that direction.

"Dad, wait. Don't you want to drop off your things and clean up? Get something to eat?"

He stopped and turned to me. "I haven't seen your mother in over twenty-five years. I'm not adding one more minute to that time."

I searched his face, sunken with exhaustion. Was he angry? Expectant? "Dad, are you all right?"

"I don't know, ladybug. I just don't know. Will you take me to her, please?"

Charlie shut the car door. "I'll take the bags inside. You two head on."

"This way," I told Dad, and we set off through the frostbitten grass and then on to her cottage.

We didn't speak as we walked. I knew Mother waited for him, as a feather of smoke rose from the chimney while pale flickering light sparked in the windowpanes. We approached the small gate, and I had just opened it when he set his hand on mine. "I know this has been shocking. I should have asked the minute I saw you. Are *you* all right?"

"Sometimes," I said, and walked toward the door. We heard Wynnie's laughter and a soft voice, and we both stopped to listen.

"My God," he said. "Here we are."

"Yes, here we are."

He exhaled before reaching into his coat pocket. "I have a letter from Nat. Before I forget." He held it out to me.

"Does he know I've been calling him over and over?"

Dad nodded. "Yes. He said he'd call you but sent this letter first. I told him everything that happened to both of you and that you were safe."

Then the blue door with the brass knocker opened, and Wynnie ran out and threw herself into Dad's arms. "Papa!" He bent to hug her. I stuffed the letter in my coat pocket.

Mother stood in the doorway. In her blue woolen dress with her hair pulled into a loose bun at her neck, she stood as firmly as the ash tree in her yard, as solid as the stones of the wall she'd built for us, day by day, stone by stone.

Wynnie came to me, and Dad walked toward his wife. They stood facing each other until Mother's sob broke his name in half. "Tim-othy."

Wynnie and I watched my mother and dad hold each other in the barren garden. My dad's shoulders shook with emotion, and Mother's face was buried in his shoulder as he stroked her hair.

"I'm so sorry," she said.

"Me too," he replied.

"I have so much to tell you." Her voice fell over us. "I am so sorry—"

He cut across her words and placed his finger under her chin, brought her gaze to his. She collapsed against him, and he drew her inside, shutting the door gently.

⁓

Later that day, the drawing room fireplace at the Jameson house blazed, and the room glowed as we gathered. We were all there—Mother, Dad, Wynnie, Charlie, Pippa, and me—in a room that had held so many conversations and heartbreaks and revelations in the past week.

Dad and Mother had been alone for a long time while the rest of us had waited. Now, observing my father across the coffee table, I saw no anger, only the quiet dignity and ease that he always carried.

Forgiveness sat curled and waiting like a sleeping lion, and I wondered who would wake it first.

Moira brought the tea and then lingered in the back of the room. I didn't blame her. Even I wanted to know what would happen next, who would speak and what they would say. For there were twenty-five years of unsaid words in that room of damask curtains, frosted windows, and a crackling fire. There were twenty-five years of mystery and anger and love and rage.

"Forgive me," Mother said. "All of you in this room, though I don't deserve even one of you to understand."

"None of us deserve anything," Dad said. "That's the damned truth of it."

"Papa!" Wynnie said. "No cursing."

Dad smiled sadly and tapped his fingers on his temples. "I haven't asked, Bronny." He used her old nickname, and my childhood felt nearby, close enough to touch. "Did you stop writing altogether?"

"Yes. After I left, I wouldn't allow myself that pleasure beyond creating words I'd never use again. Words I'd leave for Clara. I have painted, but not written."

"The painting in the study," I said. "Of our house."

"Yes, I painted it for Pippa." She looked at Pippa. "Although I could not tell her, I wanted her to have some part of me, here. I gave her *The Middle Place* also. Pieces of me. Some truth, but not enough, I know."

"Your language," I told her. "What's left of it is upstairs."

She closed her eyes for a moment. Her hands gripped the edge of the chair, her knuckles whitened, and then her palms turned up as if letting go. "I haven't seen those pages since I gave them to Callum all those years ago. I swore I was done."

"Would you like me to go and retrieve them?" I spoke so formally, hearing my voice as another's. I swung wildly from formality to familiarity, for she was both to me now—intimate and foreign.

"Not right now," she said. "You don't have that biography, do you?"

"We do," I acknowledged.

She cringed. "I hate that it exists. So much of it is true, but it is the ugly past, a part of me I never wanted you to know about."

"Brian Davis," I said with a roll of my eyes. "He still shows up occasionally, wanting to know what happened to you. Now we know why he wrote it. He was obsessed with you. Is obsessed."

"He is a vengeful one, to be sure. But without him, I wouldn't have met Callum and then been free to be with Timothy. I don't believe everything happens for a reason, but we can make meaning of the things that come to pass. And without that awful love story I wouldn't have found Timothy and then had you." She looked at Dad with such love that I knew my assumptions were right—that she'd never stop loving him or me, and that only her own demons had kept her from us. Pippa was right—fear and shame were mighty powerful forces that kept us from those we loved.

Mother believed that in creating Isolde, she'd protected us.

Pippa looked to Dad. "Did you know my Callum?"

"No, I never met him. I met Bronny after that infamous hike."

"You would have loved him," Pippa said. "A dear and fine man."

And the lion of forgiveness stretched and yawned in the far corner of the room.

CHAPTER 56

CLARA

Lake District, England

I flopped on the bed in the sanctuary that had been mine and Wynnie's for almost two weeks. But it wasn't mine at all, really. This was not my family or my life, and I would not and could not abandon myself again as I'd done with Nat, turning a blind eye to all that was wrong so that I could revel in what looked and felt so good. But isn't that what love was and is? Abandonment of self? Possibly. But not to the detriment of wisdom. Not to the detriment of my daughter.

That's when Nat's letter my dad gave me caught my eye on the desk. I'd nearly forgotten about it with my parents' reunion. I made my way slowly to the desk, as if the letter needed to be approached with care. I picked it up and ripped open the envelope, pulling out a letter in Nat's handwriting. There was once a time when I'd loved seeing his script, when it sent a thrill to my body—a note of love or even just an XO.

A sense of dread washed over me. He would have called me with good news. Nat had passed this to my dad, and it was taped shut. Wynnie's name was notably absent.

I pulled out the paper and walked to the window to read it. It was short and to the point, written in block letters as if to make sure I never doubted a word.

Clara,
I must leave Bluffton. I am sorry. I am a coward and refuse to tell you on the phone while you are in England with our daughter.

I took a job with a fishing fleet out of Nova Scotia. I will never be able to start over here, Clara. I fell back into my old habits while you were away. Now no one will give me a job. I have ruined myself and I know that.

I must leave. I am not running away but protecting you and Wynnie. I will return. I promise. When I am done with this and I have money to help the family, I will return.

There was more, but I didn't want to read it. There would be words of love and regret and promises he'd never keep.

I dropped the letter on the pale green carpet.

These people who claimed to love me but left me for my own good, who abandoned me to protect me—what a farce. The man who was meant to love and care for Wynnie was now leaving her for her own good?

Charlie. I wanted him with such desperate desire at that moment that I felt weak with it, my legs wobbly. I also doubted the desire because so very often it was attached to abandonment.

I walked to the window and leaned my forehead against the cold glass to ease the press of a headache. Outside, I spied Charlie at the lake's shore. I wanted to run from the room, to him, to his arms. But that I would not do. First, I must understand what Mother's return and Nat's leaving meant for our life.

A few minutes later and a knock echoed through the room. I opened the door expecting Wynnie and Moira, but instead Charlie stood there with something in his hands.

"Yes?" I asked, wanting him to come to me, to smooth over this rattling that had come between us when I hadn't agreed to stay.

"I have your passports," he said, and held out two dark squares.

My throat tightened with the telltale sign of tears I would not let him see. I had my way to get home, but did I even want it?

I took the passports and closed the door without a word.

"Clara?" he asked from outside. "Are you all right?"

I wasn't.

———

Eventually his footsteps retreated, and I slid down the door, sat on the carpet. Nat's letter echoed with familiar abandonment—another person leaving for my own protection, but also, I realized, it whispered of freedom. I didn't know if I wanted that freedom, for therein were choices. My choices. It was almost easier when I had none. Nat had been part of my excuse for returning to South Carolina, my anchor even when I'd cut him loose.

A moment returned to me clear as the crystalline lake outside, a day with Mother in the backyard as we pressed flowers between sheets of tissue paper to preserve the petals and stems, the leaves and pistils, the pollen, and the calyx before they faded to brown death.

"This," Mother said. "Art comes from the same place as this flower." She'd pressed the flower into my hand. "It is all mystery and beauty and all of this, including us, including that flower, comes from the same place."

All mystery and beauty.

I stood with that memory as clear as a cloudless sky and thought of T. S. Eliot's poem, the one that Charlie and I had recited together with laughter because we'd both memorized it and now, I knew: Mother had taught it to us both. My mother was the knot between us, the one who brought us together.

In my beginning is my end. / In my end is my beginning.

I stood before the easel and opened a tube of azure blue.

The sky was splitting open. Two paths before me opened, and I needed to decide which one to take.

CHAPTER 57

CLARA

Lake District, England

All night emotion and art moved through me. At sunrise I made my way downstairs, where Charlie stood in front of me in the grand hallway. With little sleep, I knew the crash would come, yet for now I wanted tea.

"There you are," Charlie said, rubbing at his face, the night still resting on him.

"Here I am," I said. "Looking for tea." I struggled between throwing my arms around him and wondering if it was all a mirage: me and him, love, and all that came in its wake.

"Clara." Just my name on his tongue, the turn of his chin and the softness of his gaze, and I wanted to weep with exhaustion and surrender.

He held out his hands and I set mine in his and he held fast. "I'm so lost," I said. "How could our parents have done this to us?"

"To us? Maybe we aren't the victims here, Clara. Maybe we are the ones who have the freedom to become what and who we are, as they struggled a generation before us to do the same."

"That's a generous summation," I said, softening.

"Come with me," he said. He motioned for me to follow him.

We entered the drawing room and there, in the dusty dawn light, my mother and dad were asleep together, curled on the couch, his arm around her as she rested against him.

Charlie spoke in a whisper. "They waited up all night, hoping you'd come down."

Charlie's voice stirred Dad, and he sat up. "Clara."

"Dad."

Mother sat up, too. She looked around as if trying to remember where she was, and then she stood and walked to me, and silently stood in front of me. "Clara, I am here."

"I don't know what to do now," I told her. "All night I've painted while struggling between leaving and staying."

Mother tucked her chin as if bowing her head for prayer. "I can't ask you to stay, but I would like it if you would." She lifted her head now.

"Ladybug," Dad said softly, walking over to join us, "your mother is right about what would have happened twenty-five years ago. I could have tried to prevent it, but with her history, I might not have been able to. We will never know. She was only trying to protect you. For that can you forgive her?"

I sought for an answer inside, searched but was interrupted by "Mama," Wynnie's voice from the doorway, and we all turned. "This is so . . . pretty."

She was holding a square canvas with the illustration I'd stayed up all night painting. It was the scene of a sunlit path on Esthwaite Water, a shadow on the moon, and a young girl standing near the lake with her face to the sky and light spilling upon her.

Mother walked toward Wynnie and took the illustration from her hands, tears spilling down her face. "This is the sky splitting open," she said, her voice wavering.

CHAPTER 58

CLARA

Lake District, England

The sky was as blue as the paint I'd used last night. I walked along the pavement of Hawkshead with Charlie. We were running Christmas errands for Pippa while she spent time with Isolde and Dad. So far we'd avoided talk of my leaving, of rebooking a ship, of Nat's letter, or of finding our way to Southampton.

"What is Bluffton like?" Charlie asked as we passed under the shadow of St. Michael and All Angels church, its four-pointed tower above us on a hill.

"It's a small town, much like this, but on the edge of a river. Technically it's a bay, but goes by the name of the May River. It's as rich in history and stories as this place, a land that once belonged to the Native Americans and then was gifted to Sir John Colleton by your king Charles II in the early 1700s. Savannah, Georgia, is right across the river on the back side of the town. I've never lived anywhere else except when I went to college in Atlanta, so I don't know how to compare it to big-city living. Mom . . ." I realized I used the more tender name for her and felt a wash of comfort. I cleared my throat. "Mom and Dad once lived in Boston, but I've never even visited."

"What does your hometown feel like to live in?"

"It is coastal, and it feels briny and rich with the beauty of a tidal coastline. Everything new is born in those marshes and estuaries that look like veins running through the body of our town. There are four churches—Baptist, Presbyterian, Catholic, and African Methodist. The first questions someone will ask are twofold: Who are your people? Where do you go to church?"

He laughed. "That defines an area, does it not?"

"Yes, but things are newer at home. This isn't better or worse, I don't believe. But compared to England, we are still finding our way as a country, and it almost tore in half during the 1800s. A lot of mending still to go. But the people? For the most part, the ones I know well and love are like all the people you have greeted while we run errands. My dearest friend, Lilia, lives there. We've known each other since kindergarten, and about once a day I think how I'd like her to be here, to see this."

"You think she'd like it?"

"I think she'd love it. She'd see signs everywhere—that cloud means this, and that feather means that, and that shadow is telling us that we are doing the right thing."

"Well, maybe we are." He stopped in front of a small cottage on Flag Street, an overhanging portion of wall covered in slate. "Shhh. Listen. Do you hear that?"

The soft sounds of moving water. I looked around for its source and lifted my eyebrows in question.

"A stream," he said. "A stream flowing beneath the slate." He took a couple more steps and pointed at a break in the stones where the water rushed beneath us.

"A hidden stream beneath our feet."

"Yes," he said.

"We could make quite a lot of that, couldn't we?" I asked. "All the hidden things that have been moving beneath our feet."

"Ah, yes." He smiled. "So, it was here they would come to wash the clothes. This was a wool town, and they'd wash here on Flag Street. Maybe we could make a clean wash of it?"

I nudged him with my hip. "Taking the metaphor one step too far."

He threw his arm over my shoulders and lifted his chin. "St. Michael," he said. "Up there on that swell of earth."

"Yes?"

"Whenever you see a church named St. Michael, you'll know they built it on top of a pagan structure."

"Doesn't seem quite fair."

"Everyone builds on top of everything else," he said. "Stories on top of myths, churches on top of pagan sites, tall towers on top of landfills."

"Well, this town seems to have been here forever."

"Oh no, it hasn't. There's an old Roman fort only a mile or so away. History marches on."

"Yes," I said. "And nothing stays the same."

"Look at us," he said. "Here we are, and less than two weeks ago, I had never laid eyes on you, and now our lives will never be the same."

"No, they won't." I wanted to say more, to take his words and move into them instead of away, but I stopped in front of Hawkshead Grammar School as we moved along a back alley, juggling the greens and making our way to the butcher. "Such a hauntingly beautiful town," I said.

"Everyone we pass," he said. "I have a story about each of them, and they've known me since I was in a perambulator."

"Yes, and the same at home, except it would have been a stroller." I laughed. "And this has its flip side—they also know that my mother left us. It's annoying to have pity fall on me sometimes, but they all mean well, and I know that."

"Is your ex-husband from Bluffton also?"

"No, he arrived just as I came home from college. He was working at a bank in Savannah and living in a little place in Bluffton. We met at one of Bluffton's finer establishments called the Crab Claw."

"Is that similar to a social club in London?"

"Very similar." I grinned in sarcasm. "Just add a jukebox, sawdust, and shrimp."

He laughed, and the free sound seemed to expand large enough to encompass all that had happened these past weeks.

"We are formed of these things in our towns and cities," I said. "The things that have made us into who we are. I have mine and you have yours. They aren't so different."

"Not so different as all that," he said.

We walked and chatted while we purchased lamb flank from the butcher. We then paused in front of the theater. The hand-painted sign for Mother's play hung a tad crookedly on the front of the wooden-slat building. The morning wireless had told us that the temperatures would hover around five degrees Celsius all day. I couldn't quite convert that into Fahrenheit, but I was comfortable inside my wool hat and coat, beneath Charlie's arm as he pulled me close.

"This was here," I said while pointing at the sign for Mother's play, "and I never knew. Think of all the things I don't know!"

He laughed and then grew serious. "Do you know that the Lake District has the highest mountain in England and the largest lake?"

"No, I didn't. How fascinating. Tell me more."

"Did you know that in Penrith, right up the road, there is an ancient stone circle that is said to be a coven of witches, led by a woman they called Long Meg, and they were all turned to stone?"

"Now I do. Can you take me there?"

"Anytime," he said. "I'll take you anywhere."

"More," I said.

"Did you know that some say that they've seen the ghost of Uther Pendragon, the father of King Arthur, and he rides a great steed through the region?"

"Now that is something I'd like to see."

"And did you know that I am falling in love with you?"

I held his gaze but found no words. I hadn't been prepared for this. I hadn't found a way to say the same myself. I didn't doubt the growing love, it was evident and clear, but the saying of it would change everything, and then I'd have to decide whether to break our hearts or find a way toward each other.

I didn't come to England to fall in love; I came to solve the mystery of my mother. I looked down. How could I utter words of love, how could I say yes to him when it would mean changing my life completely, upending it and for him, a life without children of his own.

Through the silence, he took me in his arms and uttered in my ear, "You don't have to answer in kind."

I leaned back. "What about never having a family of your own?"

"Clara, a life with you and Wynnie *is* a family. I don't need a child with my hair and eyes. I need you. And Wynnie. And your love."

"Charlie," I said. "I'm not the traditional sort of woman you know here, or in my hometown, for that matter. It's difficult to fit in and I doubt I would here, either. At least in Bluffton they are accustomed to my quirks and inability to be the exemplary housewife and PTA member."

"Do you think your mother fit in? Beatrix Potter? Is there some sort of contract that states you must be a certain way to stay with me? Do you truly believe I fit in in whatever ways you imagine?"

"I look at Adelaide and at your mother, and at the women in town and in London."

"And?"

"I'm not like them."

"They aren't like you."

I couldn't argue with him about this, make him see that although I didn't fit the mold in Bluffton, they knew me, loved me mostly as I was. "I want so much, Charlie."

"Well, I want a full and adventurous life, and I also want you, Clara, I want you and Wynnie and a life like no one else," he said, and kissed me and kept me from the struggle to find my own words, for I didn't know what to say.

———

After dinner that evening, we found ourselves again in the drawing room. This time, Finneas Andrews joined us for dinner, and much of the conversation was around the proper time to plant the dahlia tubers stored in the basement.

We talked about the headlines in the paper and the reports on the wireless that told of how the deaths since December 7 were greater than those in the worst week of the cholera epidemic in 1866, and the numbers were still rising. Dad looked at Charlie and again emotionally thanked him for saving us and bringing us here, when we surely would have been at great risk if we'd stayed in London.

Then Finneas told us all the story of a local farmer who believed he saw the beloved golden eagle they all thought might have gone extinct, and Wynnie begged to hike to find it.

"I'll take you if you're staying." Finneas looked to me. I felt trapped by the question and answered with the truth. "We have our passports now and need to rebook our ship as soon as we can." I looked to Dad. "You, Dad?"

"I've taken more than a sabbatical, ladybug. I've taken a leave."

"Dad..."

"Papa!" Wynnie cried out and ran to him, snuggled near. "Aren't you mad at Grandma?"

The room sat stunned with the outburst and question she must have held so close. Dad grinned at Wynnie and then grew serious. "I was, and maybe sometimes I will be again. But, my angel, we must forgive when we love. We forgive when we understand why." He reached for Mother's hand, and she took it. "For twenty-five years I have been waiting, and this is what I want. Clara, ladybug, what do *you* want?"

I wanted it all to *mean* something.

I wanted all of this to be about more than me, about more than awards for my drawings of a hedgehog. I wanted it to be about my mother, for God's sake, and about my dad, and about Wynnie. I wanted to find out what was between Charlie and me. I wanted my life to be about art and creativity and doing exactly what I told my little class of eight-year-old artists—*show me what's inside.*

What if Moira hadn't taken that satchel out of the safe and placed it in Callum Jameson's library? What if the fog hadn't descended on the day we arrived in Southampton? What if what if what if.

Fate wasn't so much in my control as I'd proudly once stated. But what I did with that fate—well, that was up to me.

My insides were a tangle of desires and needs, while one thing was clear: I would not do what Mother and Nat had done. Mother ran and left behind a language, pain, and a mystery. Nat ran to Nova Scotia for a job that would pay and a place where he could shed his mistakes, begin again, for us, he said, all for us. I didn't believe a word of that. He was running from his mistakes as surely as my mother had from hers.

If I left here, was I running away from something meant for me or merely going home?

"What do I want?" I stood. "I want some air."

The lake, the one I had first seen out the bedroom window when I believed I'd seen it before and forgotten it, something from another time and place, that forgotten lake now called to me.

I walked out the front door and made my way to the side of the house, where I stood on top of that hill, looking down at the glacial water.

I walked the now-familiar path down the flagstone pathway, across the land, and through the pasture to Esthwaite Water. Emotions whipped inside me like the winds of a South Carolina hurricane. The spine of the fells rose above me, the skin of moss and fern, of willow and ash running along its body. The cry of the geese echoed from the place I disturbed them.

I imagined the waters in summer, feeling the relief of plunging into its glacial depths, of allowing the waters to fold over my head. The clouds layered themselves in strata and the breeze animated the leaves.

I'd illustrated this landscape for years now without knowing exactly what I'd been painting. I'd believed that everything I created on paper was a made-up land that I yearned to enter, a place where I could find myself at peace, but an imaginary peace.

In the dusk, everything fell away. The sky didn't split open and spill its mysteries onto me instead of my mother, but I did for one brief and ineffable moment see the truth of it all: the searching, the wanting, the creating and illustrating, the buried desires and longings—all of it was life itself.

Longing means being alive.

I'd gone in search of answers to barely audible questions: *What did I do wrong? Why did she leave me?* I'd set out to find my mother and the truth, but the solved mystery of her disappearance answered only one question: the *why* of her leaving. And that why was hers alone. That wasn't my answer.

For me, longing itself was the answer, the movement toward creativity and meaning and, yes, love.

I'd thought it *all* imaginary, but this reality was here all along. Mother had carried me here long before I showed up with Charlie Jameson.

So quiet—I was so very quiet, everything in me hushed and still. Here was the mystery—the lake was an antique mirror, silver and gray, the water still, the bulk of a scrubby island beyond—all while truth lifted inside me: I didn't want to be anywhere else. I was not rushing toward the next thing.

I was ready for Charlie now. I was ready for Mother. I didn't know exactly what had shifted or how, but there I was at the edge of a lake, my heart open for both of them. Something had been unmade in me these past weeks and was ready to be remade.

This was the sheer beauty of stillness.

Trust that stillness, my body said to me.

The lost words of my mother and the translation of her sequel were never going to answer the questions at the heart of me. The answer was in me—who I was in the world, who I loved, and how I forgave and lived and created. A pile of pages had never been the answer.

The way this place and these people felt is what I yearned for when I yearned.

They were what I wanted when I wanted.

They were what I attempted to create when I created.

I was wrong about forgiveness. I'd thought it a lion that might roar to life from the far corners, but it was quieter than that, much quieter. Forgiveness is a whisper of possibility, of openness. It was an act of restoration, an act of healing, an act of empathy.

Forgiveness, I understood, was only the beginning of what might come next, not the end of what had already happened.

A whisper of grass, and I turned to see him coming toward me. He hesitated a few steps away and I nodded: yes, come to me.

"Clara," Charlie said when he reached my side, and I was in his arms. He held me and we gently swayed together, a willow tree. "'Love is most nearly itself / When here and now cease to matter.'" He quoted Eliot, the lines Mother had taught us both.

"'In my beginning is my end,'" I said.

"'In my end is my beginning,'" he said, and held my face. "Here you are."

"Yes," I said with a great rush of truth. "Here I am."

CHAPTER 59

WYNNIE

Esthwaite Water, England
1962

We've agreed to scatter the ashes in Esthwaite Water today, but first I must meet the journalist who wants an interview about the Emjie book releasing this month, April of 1962—exactly fifty-three years after the first.

A World of Wonder—Emjie's Odyssey.

The spring morning is clear as the cut-crystal goblets in Pippa's cabinet. Sunshine scatters and splits through the newborn leaves all around me. I round the bend on the Grizedale Forest path where I've been walking since dawn. The evergreen and spindly spruce, the long-haired willows, and the stately alder surround me. The gnarled hawthorn bushes are covered with white blooms, a proclamation of spring. A kestrel swoops down as if to greet me on my morning walk, and I lift my hand in greeting, his golden wing dipping in turn.

Lus an chromchinn.

A daffodil.

Coinneal oíche.

Evening primrose.

Gráinneog.

Hedgehog.

I practice the words Charlie has been patiently teaching me for ten years now, a language of his father. Even if Charlie isn't blood, he's my father now, and I want to know everything of our family.

Mama is in Hawkshead to teach the Saturday-morning art classes at her school, Inside Out. She teaches the young ones of Cumbria that they can express their internal world with outside creations, from invisible friends to stories. Every year there is a display of imaginary friends, large-scale models created by local artists collaborating with children who explain what their imaginary friends look like. It's the most popular after-school program in the district, and now people are clamoring for it from Manchester to London.

I know every step of this land, and I bend to identify a puffball mushroom and avoid the temptation to break it apart. I pause at the reflection of the fells on the lake's mirrored surface, and when I turn to the slate house, I think of South Carolina and our old home on the May River. I love this place, but also I love what we left behind. For there is no moving forward or change without loss—that's what Charlie helps me remember.

Lilia and her husband bought our house from Papa, and they live there with her family, keeping the house full and alive. We visit once a year—it was a promise that Charlie made to Mama a decade ago. A promise he's kept, as he keeps all promises.

As for Pippa, a friendship with Finneas that bloomed in the greenhouse changed into something more. It began with gardens and then blossomed. Over a field of newly planted narcissus, Finneas told her he'd loved her for decades.

Their love story always makes me feel hopeful—his patience and her ability to reach past her grief to something new.

I wonder how much of our story this journalist will want. Will I tell her how Charlie took us all on an airplane ten years ago to Mama's Caldecott Award? How they married at the edge of this very lake the next year? I decide these are memories I won't share, ones that belong to just us.

I reach the lake and shield my eyes with my palm to glance up to where I see a tall woman walking down the swell of pasture to greet me. The journalist, a woman named Dot Bellamy who once wrote a famous magazine series about lost children from World War II, now wants our story of lost words and the new Emjie sequel.

Two weeks ago, Mama sat me down and said, "This interview is yours."

"No," I told her. "Grandma and I wrote Emjie's sequel together, and you illustrated the dictionary. It's not mine alone to do."

"You wrote *World of Wonder* with Grandma, and you helped choose the words for the dictionary. I will come in at the end, but you must talk about the sequel. We trust you."

I take this with great but heavy pride; I've been carrying that word *trust* around with me since Mama said it.

Tá muinín agam ionat.

I trust you.

Macánta.

Trustworthy.

We decided years ago to never betray the truth of how Grandma survived and where she lived, here with us. She wanted her work to live in the world and yet never the attention it would bring to all of us.

I wave at Dot Bellamy and walk the pathway toward her. My family has confidence I will tell the truth while keeping silent what needs hiding.

In the warm spring afternoon, a breeze off the fells flutters Dot's straw hat, and she places her hand on top of her head to steady it. She smiles with her red-lipstick mouth, and her eyes are warm. She has no dark edges and I smile in return. After introductions, I invite her into the house for tea.

"If you please," she says to me in her lovely British accent, "I'd rather walk with you."

"I prefer it," I say.

From her pocket she pulls out a small silver recorder. "Do you mind?"

I shake my head, and she clicks a button. She carries the recorder in the palm of her hand. We walk right past Grandma's cottage, even as Dot asks me her first question. "How did it come to be that you decided to pick up Emjie's story where your grandmother ended it?"

I tell Dot the bony skeleton of the tale, of how ten years ago Charlie called our house in South Carolina about the pages he had found in his father's library in London, of our trip to England on the steamship, of London's poisonous fog and our escape and the arrival to this place. I tell her of Mama and Charlie falling in love, and now, I say, we are here.

"And your dad?"

"He travels all over the world for work; he's a longshore fisherman now. He visits every year, sometimes twice, depending on where he's based." I don't much want to talk about my dad. He's safe and he loves us, but the world didn't conspire to have us all together like other families. Mama and I are now *this* family. Not all families look exactly alike.

Dot looks down to check on her recorder and flips it over to make sure the microphone is unhindered. "You're like her, I've heard. You're very much like your grandmother." Dot stops at the edge of the lake and stares across the water.

I don't answer this, for what am I meant to say? The words I would tell Dot would come in laughter—I am so much like her and so much not. We have the same best friends, I'd say. Mama and Emjie. But instead, I only smile at Dot because this is the hiding part of the conversation, the sleight of hand, the ability to make her look away from the obvious.

Dot turns to me and away from the view. "A child prodigy, it is said."

"No, that's not really true," I tell her, and straighten my glasses. "My grandma was a child prodigy. Not me. She wrote the first Emjie book when she was eight years old and published it when she was twelve. I wrote *World of Wonder*, but not alone. It's not the same."

"It's still extraordinary," Dot says. "A lost grandmother and a lost story, and you took both and published a glorious novel set in America on a southern shore where Emjie finds her way home. It's beautiful."

"I had help." Below this statement was the other truth—Grandma and I did it together. The book was ours. Emjie was ours. But some things are meant to stay private. Not every secret needs to be told. Let her assume I mean my mother.

"Will your mom . . . will Clara be joining us?"

"In a bit," I say.

"Do you still believe in Emjie?" she asks so pointedly that I know she's been holding it like a cork in a bottle of champagne, ready to burst.

"Believe?" I pause and watch the red and white water lilies bob on the surface of the lake, the color intense and the waters serene, each holding the other.

"Yes, do you believe?" she asks without looking at me.

"Do I believe in make-believe, that's what you want to know, am I right?"

"Possibly," she says, and now looks to me. "I'm curious about lost things and lost people and what becomes of them, how they are transformed. So yes, the opening epigraph of your novel is 'Believe in Make-Believe.' Do you?"

"I know this," I say. "I know there are stories waiting to be told, and I know Emjie walked by my side when I needed her the most. Do I believe in her? Maybe in the same way I believe in the tales that sustain us and brought my family to the right moment and place. Stories are made of unseen things, of imagination, of old tales and edges of lakes. Maybe Emjie is made of the same."

She nods as if she understands. "Do you know how your grandmother's lost and made-up words found their way to the Jameson library?"

"It's hard to live with unknowing, with not knowing certain things in our life. But we must."

She cleared her throat and took a deep breath. "What do you think happened to your grandmother? Do you think she's alive?"

"She's alive in me and in my mother and in our creative work," I say with too much precision, as if it is exactly what it is—a rehearsed line. I hope she doesn't notice.

"What about in the world? She'd be sixty-five years old, if I am calculating correctly."

"Wouldn't that be lovely," I say. "And nearly magical."

"Yes, it would be. What about the original sequel?" she asks. "Do you know what it told of Emjie's future?"

"No. We never read it," I said. "So many words were lost in the journey through the terrible fog that we couldn't use the dictionary to translate it. So we started over. We began again."

"Begin again," she says. "We always must."

"Yes," I say.

She laughs. "You aren't like other eighteen-year-old girls, Wynnie. But I am sure you've been told that before."

"Wynnie!" Mama's voice falls down the long pathway as she walks toward us; Mopsy, the golden retriever Charlie gave us for Christmas last year, runs alongside her like a loping pony about to trip over itself.

"There's Mama," I say. "She can tell you all about the dictionary."

"Do you have anything else you'd like to say about the sequel? About Emjie?" she asks.

I watch Mama walk down the lane; I glance at Grandmother's cottage; I close my eyes to find what matters most about Emjie and her sequel and how she found her way home. "I'd like to say that so many people believe the novel is about the invisible world and fairies and fantasy, and in many ways it is. But also, it's about finding home. It's about knowing where you belong and then doing something about that truth. It's about that sometimes awful and sometimes wonderful journey that can take you in wrong directions, but then being willing to begin again and find your way." I open my eyes.

Dot stares at me and I see hurt in her, a search for something she is always looking for. "Yes" is all she says.

Mama reaches us and all the introductions start over. "Congratulations on your second Caldecott," Dot says.

"Thank you so much," Mama tells her. "It never ceases to be a great thrill."

"Would you mind," Dot asks, "telling me all about the dictionary, *A Word for Everything*, and your illustrations for it?"

"I don't mind at all," Mama says. "Let's walk."

When Mama has explained all about the lost words and how she first saw them when she was a little girl playing hide-and-seek, how Grandma said she "found" them, how Mama organized the best ones and illustrated them, how the dictionary was meant to help others find their own words for the things they could not express, Dot Bellamy nods a lot.

"*A Word for Everything*," Mama says. "That's what my mother was looking for and that's what we've called the dictionary."

Dot clicks off her recorder and glances at the little gold watch on her wrist. "I have a train to catch back to London," she says. "But this has been the most glorious morning I've spent in ages. Thank you for talking with me."

"Any time," Mama tells her.

"I have another question that I wasn't sure I was going to ask, but I'd really like to know—and if you don't want it in the article, I can say this is off the record."

"What is it?" Mama asks.

"Do you wish you'd found your mother and not just her words?"

"I always want to find my mother," Mama says. "Don't we all?"

"Indeed." Dot shakes our hands and walks up the flagstone pathway without turning around to say goodbye. Her back is straight, but I swear I can see the tears that fall from her eyes.

Twilight settles on the lake, easy resting on the still waters. We sit on a blanket we laid on the shore next to the large boulders held by the earth. We are barefoot and our pants are rolled up to the knees. The urn is on Mama's lap. Charlie is on the other side of Mama, his wet hair dripping with the lake's clear water after his long swim. This isn't his to do; he is only here for love.

It has been just shy of ten years since Grandma fell to her knees in the dormant garden and cried out, "Clara."

Now is the right time for this scattering. It feels necessary before the new Emjie book is released.

Mama sets the urn between us and lifts off the top. We both reach inside to grab a handful of the paper's ash, the burned ruins of the sequel, the book that no one will ever read.

Mama and I stand and walk until the ice-cold water licks our toes. We open our hands and the orange-flower- and rose-scented breeze catches the ash, and it flies like the snowy soot that once sent us here, to Near Sawrey and Lake Esthwaite, and to our new life. The burned remains fly over the waters and lilies, over the rushy edge of the lake, a dark snow.

Then everyone else stands to join us. Grandma is on my other side, and Papa next to her. Then Charlie and Pippa. We are a row of family at the edge of Esthwaite Water. Our reflections waver beneath us, a knot of people who love one another, hurt one another, and then found one another in a land that seems created of deep magic.

The only daughter of an only daughter of an only daughter together at the shore of a lake forged by fire and formed by ice long before we arrived. Mama turns to her own mother and says their secret word, the one she couldn't say the day they found each other. "*Adorium.*"

Then Mama turns the jar upside down and dumps the remainder

of the ash, and just as Grandma's boat did so long ago, the dark flakes float away.

"To new stories," Grandma says.

"To our stories," Charlie says.

Mama lifts her hands, palms open in surrender, and the last of the ash falls from between her fingers. "All mystery. All beauty."

Note from the Author

Dear Reader,

It all started with a literary mystery and a secret language.

When I find a subject that gives me a chill-bump interest, I know a story hides within. I begin walking down that trail until I find what I am searching for in the forest of imagination, or—as more often happens—it finds me. It is there that I discovered the literary mystery of Barbara Newhall Follett, and I was enthralled by her life and story.

Born in 1914, Barbara was a child-prodigy author who started writing when she was five years old, penned her first novel at eight years old, and created her own language called *Farksoola*. By twelve, she had published an acclaimed children's fantasy novel with Knopf, titled *The House Without Windows*, a story about a young girl who runs away to live in nature with fairies and nymphs. Following this landmark novel, she continued to write but not to the same success. Her family life fell apart, and she struggled in many ways.

Tragically, in December 1939, at just twenty-five years old, she had a disagreement with her husband, walked out of the apartment they shared in Boston, and vanished. She was never seen or heard from again.

Her disappearance remains one of the most intriguing literary puzzles of the twentieth century. Barbara's papers are archived at Columbia University, where I learned that despite extensive searches and investigations, her fate remains unsolved.

I began this novel with a fascination about female writers who created entire languages to protect their words, thoughts, and stories from the judgment of family and wider society. I discovered that like Barbara, Beatrix Potter was another such author. It is no accident my fictional characters are led to England's Lake District where Beatrix Potter lived and wrote. One author, Beatrix, found love and legacy while creating a literary bastion; the other, Barbara, turned self-destructive and vanished. The deep and wild imaginations of these real-life writers, as well as their profound connection to the natural world, held me in their grip during the writing of Bronwyn's and Clara Harrington's stories.

Two smaller notes about the historical aspects of this novel: The Great Smog that sends Clara and Wynnie to the Lake District (also known as the Great Smoke) occurred in London in December 1952. Caused by a devasting combination of coal smoke, cold weather, and an anticyclone air pattern, a thick, choking fog descended on the city. Over the course of four days, the smog caused the deaths of approximately four thousand people. Subsequent analysis revealed that the total death toll was much higher, with estimates indicating that around twelve thousand people ultimately died as a result of the smog. This catastrophic event gave rise to London's Clean Air Act in 1956.

The Caldecott Medal that Clara is awarded for her work was established in 1937 to honor a British illustrator named Randolph Caldecott (1846–1886). This is a revered award for children's picture books given by the American Library Association. I took liberties with the timing of the Caldecott's announcement and ceremony dates to mesh with my story's timeline. This award also has ties to Beatrix Potter, as she was inspired by Caldecott's work and her father collected his art.

Receiving the recognition was my character Clara Harrington's deep honor.

This novel is inspired by real events but is a work of fiction. I took liberties with dates and facts for the sake of the story. For the true details of Barbara's and Beatrix's lives, the Lake District, the Great Smog, and much more of my research for the many facets of *The Story She Left Behind,* please see the resource section that follows and visit my website's Book Club Kit https://www.patticallahanhenry.com/resource-center -the-story-she-left-behind for photos.

I hope you find the journey through this novel as captivating and enriching as the inspirations that shaped it.

Warmly,
Patti Callahan Henry

If you're interested, here are some resources for further reading.

BOOKS BY OR ABOUT BARBARA NEWHALL FOLLET

The House Without Windows by Barbara Newhall Follett
Note: This is the original story written by Barbara, first when she was eight years old and published when she was twelve.

Lost Island by Barbara Newhall Follett, edited by Stefan Cooke

Barbara Newhall Follett: A Life in Letters, edited by Stefan Cooke

Barbara: The Unconscious Autobiography of a Child Genius by Harold Grier McCurdy

The Art of Vanishing: A Memoir of Wanderlust by Laura Smith

Website devoted to Barbara Newhall Follett by Stefan Cooke: farksolia.org

BOOKS ABOUT BEATRIX POTTER AND THE LAKE DISTRICT

Beatrix Potter: Drawn to Nature by Annemarie Bilclough

Beatrix Potter's Lake District by Gilly Cameron Cooper

Beatrix Potter's Secret Code Breaker by Andrew P. Wiltshire

The Story of Beatrix Potter by Sarah Gristwood, National Trust, 2016

Ghosts and Legends of the Lake District by J. A. Brooks

Rural by Rebecca Smith

Swallows and Amazons by Arthur Ransome

The Folklore of the Lake District by Marjorie Rowling

Wild Fell: Fighting for Nature on a Lake District Hill Farm by Lee Schofield

OTHER BOOKS OF INTEREST

Death in the Air: The True Story of a Serial Killer, the Great London Smog, and the Strangling of a City by Kate Winkler Dawson

Mother Hunger by Kelly McDaniel

Tales of Old Town Bluffton by Andrew Peeples

Thirty-Two Words for Field by Manchán Magan

Acknowledgments

This story exists in your hands, and not merely in my imagination, because of the support, inspiration, and encouragement of so many dear and brilliant people. This litany of gratefulness isn't in any order; there is no hierarchy of absolute gratitude.

To Atria and Simon & Schuster: you are the dream team. Lindsay Sagnette, you "see" story in ways that astound me, always taking my work to the next interesting place. I was honored to work with you. To Libby McGuire, who helms this Atria ship with wisdom and grace. To Megan Rudloff, I hope you never tire of me because I don't know what I'd do without you and your enthusiasm, planning, and answers. The creativity and dedication of this group inspires me: Dana Trocker, who knows my love language is data and lists and has the most innovative ideas! To Laura Brown, Lisa Sciambra, Dayna Johnson, Morgan Pager, Karlyn Hixson, Paige Lytle, Natalie Argentina, and to Jade Hui, who keeps the wheels on the bus. Thank you for working with me as such a visionary team. To the art department and the exceptional Laywan Kwan for the gorgeous cover, for knowing what the story needed and finding it in visual form.

To the incredible sales team at Simon & Schuster—and in memory of Gary Urda—I honor all of you and what you do to put our books into the hands of readers. I see you; I know what you do for all of us! You are the unsung heroes behind the scenes, and I am here singing your song.

To bookstores, librarians, and book clubs, to book bloggers, podcasters, and the entire literary community—this book is for you! You have been the energy I needed on the road this past year with *The Secret Book of Flora Lea*, and I know that you keep the reading world alive with your enthusiasm.

To my literary agent, Meg Ruley, who is willing and more than able to say when it is working and when it absolutely is not, whose honesty and unwavering support for me and my work has enabled me to dig for the best story I can find. And even she doesn't act alone in this endeavor—surrounding her is the best agency in the publishing world (this is a fact, I am telling you): the Jane Rotrosen Agency, and with endless gratitude I want to acknowledge Jessica Errera, who has the enthusiasm and energy that encourages and sparks creativity. To Andrea Cirillo, whose eye for story is unparalleled, to Casey Conniff, Chris Prestia, Jane Berkey (the visionary founder of this enterprise), Allison Hufford, Rebecca Scherer, and Jack McIntyre. Thank you for reading, for urging me to do better and go deeper, and for having my back in all things business and creative.

To my dearest friends who don't abandon me even when I abandon them to the imaginary world that makes me hard to reach. I do love you so and you know this.

To my writing pals who brainstorm and listen and plot and use tough love to say things like, "Oh, you think you're the only one who has ever had to delete pages or a draft?" (looking at you, Paula McLain). Special gratitude to Kristin Hannah, Christina Baker Kline, Lanier Isom, Lisa Patton, Ariel Lawhon, JT Ellison, Adrienne Brodeur, Signe Pike, and to all of you who say, "Tell me how the writing is going," and then listen and shift things for me. We share podcasts and articles and essays and inspiration—we are all in these wild waters together. To Paula McLain, who changed this story for the better every single time (and there were many) we talked about it. Since the day we met you have been a force for good in my work and life.

To the community of *Friends and Fiction*—you have been a sustaining balance and encouragement. Mary Kay Andrews, you've been inspiring me and making me belly laugh for over twenty-five years, and I treasure you. Kristin Harmel, your bravery, light, and courage make all of us better. Kristy Woodson Harvey, you get me, and I am so inspired by your ability to find the best in our creative and personal life. Meg

Walker, you are not only the fearless leader of *Friends and Fiction*, but also my incredible marketing manager and friend. You (and your family) have huge hearts of compassion, and wisdom to match. Ron Block, our rockstar librarian, you swooped in when we needed you most and you are a pure delight with your love of story and prose. Shaun Hettinger—who would have ever believed that our "tech nerd" would become part of the *Friends and Fiction* family? You are a rock. To our Friends and Fiction Book Club with Brenda Gardner and Lisa Harrison—and all our ambassadors and members—you are the lifeblood of all we do, and you make releasing a book into the world more fun than we could have imagined.

To those in the Lake District of England who showed me the magic of this place, I am indebted! Thank you to Anna Gray, who took me all over the land in a freezing rain and told me the mythical and powerful stories that brought that world *"created by fire and forged by ice"* to life. To David Bulmer and the Sawrey House Hotel—walking into the house turned hotel, after an all-night flight, was like walking into a storybook coming to life. David, you are the ultimate host, a kind man with great stories (looking at you, Ed the Elf), and my trip there changed this novel for the better. And thank you my dearest Serena and Stella for walking alongside me while I traipsed through muddy fields and babbling creeks, while we sat in pubs, and while I asked one million questions of our guide, our host, and the locals.

Always to my family—thank you for being on my team and loving me well even when I don't deserve it (which is often). My love for you is endless, and I couldn't and wouldn't do this without you. Pat, Meagan, Evan, Bridgette, Beatrix, Thomas and Lizzie, Rusk, and my parents, Bonnie and George. To my sisters, Jeannie and Barbi, who always believe *this* book is the best book.

I love this life of stories, and I thank all of you for taking these journeys with me!

About the Author

Patti Callahan Henry is the *New York Times* and *USA TODAY* bestselling author of several novels, including *The Secret Book of Flora Lea, Surviving Savannah*, and *Becoming Mrs. Lewis*. She is a recipient of the Christy Award, the Harper Lee Award for Alabama's Distinguished Writer of the Year, and the Alabama Library Association Book of the Year. She is the cohost and cocreator of the popular weekly online live web show and podcast *Friends and Fiction*. A full-time author and mother of three, she lives in Alabama and South Carolina with her family. Find out more at PattiCallahanHenry.com.